The Bleeding Wound
SANGRA POR LA HERIDA

The Bleeding Wound
SANGRA POR LA HERIDA

By Mirta Yáñez

Translated by Sara E. Cooper

Cubanabooks

Copyright © Spanish version 2011 Mirta Yáñez

Copyright © English translation 2013 Mirta Yáñez, Sara E. Cooper, Cubanabooks

Copyright © Bilingual edition 2014 Cubanabooks

All rights reserved. Except for brief quotations in critical articles and reviews, no part of this book may be used or reproduced in any manner without written permission from the publisher.

Published in the United States of America by Cubanabooks.

400 W. 1st St., Dept. ILLC, California State University, Chico

Chico, California 95929-0825

Printed in the United States of America

Cover design: Kellen Livingston

Cover art: Emma Hoppough

Text design: Kellen Livingston

Cubanabooks logo art: Krista Yamashita

English language editor: Margaret Wallace

Spanish language editor: Nancy Alonso

Editor In-Chief: Sara E. Cooper

First Edition

10 9 8 7 6 5 4 3 2 1

Library of Congress Control Number: 2014947370

ISBN: 978-0-9827860-7-9

CONTENTS

Translator's Foreword/Nota de la traductora	11/215
Dedication/Dedicatoria	15/219
Epigraphs/Epígrafes	17/221

Gertrude/Gertrudis	19/223
	42/245
	72/273
	103/300
	124/320
	145/339
	162/355
	187/377
	206/395

Martin/Martín	20/224
	26/229
	44/246
	63/263
	90/289
	105/302
	120/317
	136/331
	149/343
	192/382
	202/391

Woman Who Talks to Herself in the Park/ Mujer que habla sola en el parque	22/225
	31/234
	37/239

	44/246
	53/254
	62/263
	70/270
	76/276
	84/283
	90/289
	100/298
	109/306
	116/313
	127/323
	135/330
	144/339
	157/350
	168/361
	177/369
	186/377
	196/386
	206/395
Micaela/Micaela	22/226
	46/248
	86/285
	128/323
	173/365
	195/385
Estela/Estela	23/227
	47/249
	66/266
	93/292

	117/313
	159/352
	171/363
	181/372
Daontaon/Daontaon	28/231
	74/274
	82/282
	99/296
	119/315
	132/327
	142/337
	184/375
Lola/Lola	31/234
	51/253
	61/261
	84/283
	106/304
	134/329
	166/359
	175/366
	198/388
Yuya/Yuya	33/236
	41/243
	53/254
	79/279
	97/295
	112/308
	122/318

	138/333
	164/357
	178/369
	200/390
Maria Esther/María Esther	35/237
	39/241
	49/251
	157/350
	168/361
	179/371
	189/380
Willie/Willie	37/239
	55/256
	70/270
	95/294
	154/348
Hermi/Hermi	56/258
	68/268
	88/287
	100/298
	114/311
	130/325
	140/335
	151/345
	204/394
The India/La India	59/260
	76/276

	109/306
	147/341
	197/387

About the Author/Sobre la autora	209/399
About the Translator/Sobre la traductora	211/401

TRANSLATOR'S FOREWORD

The first time that I read this book (in Spanish), it had not yet been published, and the author still would make several revisions before the manuscript was accepted by one of the leading publishing houses in Cuba. One sweltering evening in Cojímar, Mirta Yáñez walked into her guest room, where I was staying, and nonchalantly handed me a CD labeled with a sharpie: *Sangra por la herida*. "You can read it if you want to," she said. If I wanted to? Was she kidding? I had been waiting for this for years. My heart had almost stopped a year before when she let out a hint that she was working on a new novel. So late into the night, huddled under my mosquito netting, grateful for any breeze that snuck through the open shutters, I read. And laughed. And cried.

The next morning I promised to do the novel justice in English. It has been an incredibly long haul since then (*Sangra* came out in Cuba in 2011), and Mirta has been patient. Mostly. Except when she was worried.

In my defense, this is a complex book. And let me say that Mirta isn't a cinch to translate in her simplest moments—if that phrase can be applied to her at all. She has a wickedly dry sense of humor, possibly the largest vocabulary of anyone I know, and a knack for playing around with language. She constantly incorporates obscure cultural references and insider jokes. Now in this *opus magnus,* she has created twelve narrators, each with her/his unique voice, who narrate in three distinct eras—the last decade before the Revolution of 1959, the revolutionary hey-day of the 1960s, and the last decade of the 20th century.

Getting to know so many characters well enough to render their peculiarities takes time. So I immersed myself in Gertrudis' erudition, Daontaon's foul mouth, Willy's camp, and Martin's melancholia. In the fall of 2013 my Latin American Literature class studied the novel in Spanish, and in the following semester my Literary Masters in Translation students read the first full draft of the translation. The conversations generated in those rooms have made their mark on what you have in front of you. Do not make the mistake of underestimating the current generation of college students—the so-called millenniums are capable of far more concentration and compassion than we give them credit for.

I could write scores of pages about the challenges and delights of this labor of love. That, however, will wait for another venue. Suffice it to say that these years spent working on *The Bleeding Wound* have whetted my appetite for more… Do you hear me, Rico?

Now that the translation is complete, heartfelt thanks are in order to those who made it possible. Mirta Yáñez is always gracious, generous, incisive, funny, and brilliant (not necessarily in that order). My dear friend Nancy Alonso is a meticulous editor, and her eagle eyes caught many an error. Meg Wallace, whom I've known almost three decades, provided insightful interventions, without which this would have been a much poorer translation. My family has been by turns patient, supportive, and a fire under my posterior. I love you Sandy, Jenny, and Dorothy June. Cubanabooks interns Kyle Heise and Vianney Bernabe kept me immersed in the novel for the last year of the project, spurring me on with questions and insight. A much appreciated National Endowment for the Arts Translation Grant provided funds, encouragement, and an introduction to many readers and colleagues. I'm grateful for all the support from my home department—International Languages, Literatures, and Cultures—and from my chair Dr. Patricia Black. Sincere thanks to all of you for making this happen, but especially to Rico, Private, and Kowalski, my *pingüinos*.

Sara E. Cooper
August 2014
Chico, CA

To those friends who stopped painting, playing the piano, acting in the theater, writing poetry, dreaming their dreams, for whatever reasons there may have been.

The air that surrounds man is unfamiliar and strange, and within it we are exposed to our own destruction.

> Prologue to *La Celestina*
> Fernando de Rojas

I'm pretty sure he yelled "Good luck!" at me. I hope not. I hope to hell not. I'd never yell "Good luck!" at anybody. It sounds terrible, when you think about it.

> *Catcher in the Rye*
> J.D. Salinger

At the very end, one's answers to the questions the world has posed with such relentlessness are to be found in the facts of one's life. Questions such as: Who are you? ... What did you actually want? ... What could you actually achieve? ... At what points were you loyal or disloyal or brave or a coward? And one answers as best as one can, honestly or dishonestly; that's not so important. What's important is that finally one answers with one's life.[1]

> *Embers*
> Sándor Márai

---

[1] Originally *A gyertyák csonkig égnek* (1942), translated as *Embers* by Carol Brown Janeway. New York: Knopf, 2001. P. 120.

GERTRUDE

I Claudia, Fausta, The Leopardess, Doña Segunda Sombra, The Catcheress in the Rye, The Little Princess, Oeidipus Regina, Cida the Championess, Romea and Juliette, Mother Goriot, Steppen-she-wolf, Tartuffa, Buddenbrookettes, Doña Quixota of the Mancha, The Femme Stranger, The Mistress and Margarita: seeing everything inside out? From "another" point of view? The story as I know it? *The gospel according to Mary Magdalene?*

Once in a while the dead ask, what happened to us? Doesn't anybody remember? Who will write our story? It only takes a little bit of forgetting for the dead to start impatiently closing in to demand their due.

I came to Comala, because they told me that it was here that my mother lived, a woman named Petra Páramo... More or less I could begin like that, although I'm not driven by the illusion of keeping a promise, I just want the murmurs to buzz and the cats to jump right out of the bag and onto the roof.

Maybe it's impossible to keep our nose in our own business and let strangers' secrets lie. Do you remember that Bergman film, *Smiles of a Summer Night?* One of the characters insists that a bedridden old woman explain why she keeps silent about certain risqué recollections, and she responds, with a malicious gleam, that *this* palace where she lived had been given to her on the condition that *she never reveal them*. Looking at my own situation, I am able to evoke my own memories in good conscience without breaking a single promise. *Memoires of Hadriana.*

The Invisible Woman, The Satyricona, Candida, Cyrana de Bergerac, Lady Jim, The Great Gatsby Gal, Martina Fierro, Poetess in New York, The Three Musketeer Molls, The Woman in the Iron Mask, Nazarina, Polifema and Galatea, Lazarilla de Tormes, Huckleberria Finn, The Sisters Karamazov, Olivia Twist, The Ladies—Naked and Dead...

And should I tell once more the old tale of good versus evil, the obsessions and lessons of youth, insanity and death, the hunters and the harpooned, with the sea as the backdrop, the capture of the white whale, of *Mobietta Dick?* Count me in, but "call me Jane Doe," just one of the ones, one of *Las Miserables,* in five volumes.

MARTIN

The scent of *sofrito* inundated the house. Martin resisted the temptation to note down for his novel how one puts together a Cuban *sofrito*, that fucking trend of including cooking recipes.

He had never been one to let the term "fucking" pass his lips. Ever since things started to go to hell, everything seemed "fucking" to him. In addition to the public disputes, the general state of calamity, the difficulty of writing, he was damned with the fucking luck to live in Alamar, over the bay in the area they called East Havana.

Despite his intentions, Martin's spirit assembled on an imaginary wooden table the slices of onion, the fragments of bell peppers scraped clean of their seeds, the carefully peeled and crushed garlic cloves, all to be submerged in boiling olive oil, slowly turning golden and letting off that ineffable aroma.

Martin flared his nostrils and jotted down on one of his mental note cards that the resonances of the *sofrito's* scents reminded him of *madeleines*, Marcel Proust's cookies. The emanations took him back to his grandma Antonia's kitchen on Amistad Street, in search of times hopelessly lost. That overly sophisticated reference jarred the senses and would only be of any use to him later, to add density to some text or another.

Martin's mother, with her back to him, was taking care of necessary kitchen tasks and didn't share in the evocation, split between the Proustian *madeleines* and the irresistible fragrance of the *sofrito*. Neither could she see Martin's anguish or the shrug of his shoulders, or in one swift glance she would have guessed that something was going on. She continued fully self-absorbed with the wooden spatula in her hand, stirring the ingredients in the oil so that they wouldn't overcook and lose their exquisite golden caramelizing as they bubbled.

Martin had time to adjust his psyche, swallow the lump that wobbled up and down his throat, where everything jumbled together—his nostalgia for his grandma Antonia's kitchen, the *madeleine* from when Proust was probably a grubby little glutton, his longing to write at least one memorable page like that one, and the smell of *sofrito* prepared by his mother. He tried to prolong for as long as possible this scene of innocence in the kitchen of his house, infinitely vulnerable like all inexplicably happy instants.

Martin continued to say "his house," although it had been almost thirty years since he had moved out, in the middle of the sixties, those fucking sixties, like everybody else who in those days abandoned their homes, some to study and live in the dorms as he himself did; others to an impenitent exile; the ones way over there, lucky or not, who could say, to war and death. But they didn't have anything to do with right now, the travelers, the suicides, the banished, the mess that had been building up in his mind. Martin closed the file of his memories of a generation and came back to surround himself with the smell of *sofrito,* his mother's hands with the wooden spatula, turning the chunks of onion, garlic, and bell pepper in the oil, just as he had seen her do forever, a little hunched over the burners, without an apron, and lost in her own thoughts, with a trail of spoons, jars, and dishes beside her; one wavering hand, her left, holding the handle of the frying pan, while her right hand stirred with the spatula the hodgepodge that the Cubans called *sofrito.*

"No," she warned him. "Don't even think about dipping a piece of bread in the *sofrito*. Wait 'til I put lunch on the table."

Martin retreated through the hall and sat down at the dining room table. "Have the results of those tests come in yet?" asked Martin's mother, pretending that she didn't care one way or another. "No, maybe next week," answered Martin. Those days of waiting, just to hear a confirmation of their fears, did nothing to lessen the fucking fear.

Martin leaned his elbows on the white and somewhat threadbare tablecloth. The perfume from the kitchen still reached him there, now mixed with the familiar odor of the furniture, that tenuous combination of varnish and humidity that marked his mother's house in the neighborhood of Vedado.

WOMAN WHO TALKS TO HERSELF IN THE PARK

The sky turned blood orange, and a strong wind came out of the northeast. And then a black cloud ran into a red one, and suddenly, the two plummeted down onto Havana. And Havana is dying…

MICAELA

Micaela was woken up by the dog's cries. Over the last few days, that same lament, a sort of anguished howl, started a few hours before dawn to end just a little bit later. You could also hear it around noon, and on one or two occasions she had heard it at midnight.

Most times Micaela didn't realize when it started. At some moment, the dog's whining, a consistently sharp and helpless sound, infiltrated her dreams and woke her up. When she already had her eyes open and was wavering between feelings of compassion and annoyance, the moans would stop abruptly. The sudden cut-off made her think that the puppy, for without a doubt it was some little bitty animal, stopped whimpering when it was given whatever it had been begging for.

The first time she had thought the dog had been abandoned, and gritting her teeth she had gotten up to look out through the blinds. Despite the fact that she couldn't tell exactly which patio the sounds were coming from, she was sure that the cries were coming from the building behind hers. On that occasion, when silence broke out, she had imagined the dog dying, from some painful disease, and she had felt bad for it, a sort of far away sadness like the one you get when the dramatic part of a movie is really well done.

Over the next few mornings, whenever the yelps started up again, she started to be haunted by those absurd thoughts of death and loneliness. On the surface, these didn't have anything to do with the dog's complaints, and they made her feel reluctantly disgusted with herself for climbing out so far on that limb of self-pity.

Last night, however, the pup's crying interrupted the Russian novel she was reading that had been letting her forget everything for a little while.[2] Well, not exactly forget. The first chapters had seemed so close to her own predicament that, from time to time, she couldn't help but close the book, get out into the fresh air, take a few deep breaths. At dawn's first light she finally fell asleep and yet again the dog's yapping broke into an absurd dream she was having, where her Aunt Candita was about to reveal to her, in secret, a sacred plea. Aunt Candita! She had left the country and Micaela never heard from her again. You can't just make the past disappear, Micaela told herself.

ESTELA

Estela was profoundly shocked to see her father's image on the TV screen. The videocassette had arrived from Cuba only a few hours before. When they had delivered it to her, she had placed the tape in her purse, bursting with hidden euphoria, conscious of how much she would enjoy getting back to her apartment where she could take off her overcoat and heavy boots. She would ask the girl to make her a real coffee, turn the heat up to where she would be nice and warm, open up the curtain so she could see the drizzle of this chilly London summer's end, get comfortable in Oscar's house slippers, sit back in her rocking chair with a throw over her legs, sip at the thick and barely sweetened liquid poured into a demitasse, ask the girl to, *por favor,* very carefully slide the cassette into the player. Then when she was alone in the silence of her bedroom, click, she would press the button of the remote control and gaze at the images of Havana that would appear on her screen. Oscar had gone to the trouble of walking down the entire *Malecón,* the sea wall and boardwalk surrounding Havana, from the Tower of the Amendares River all the way to La Punta, that unique spectacle of the most beautiful city in the world, only pointing the camera lens out toward the sea, without showing the houses eaten away by salt spray.

[2] Mijaíl Bulgákov's *The Master and Margarita* (1966).

How marvelous! Orgasmic! For Estela, all of this was probably much better than an orgasm of the usual kind. Estela and Oscar were so used to each other's moves that their bedroom business had receded into the background. They had been married for thirty years without suffering or having to pretend, they had similar tastes, and they didn't cheat on each other. Working in London had woven them into a deftly constructed nest of well-being that could only be threatened by outside forces. On the television screen rolled past shot after shot of the city, each selected by Oscar for Estela with great care. They had met in the university in Havana in the sixties, and they had got along beautifully from the very beginning. Neither of them felt comfortable with those radicals in the College of Humanities, the girls in their scandalous miniskirts and the boys with their long hair, protesting everything, passing for a bunch of hippies. Neither Estela nor Oscar were interested in protests; they both studied a lot, poring over books in the library, without sticking their noses into anything; they didn't get involved, they didn't complain about boring lectures, and they didn't open their mouths during class. Oscar cut his hair so short that it looked like a helmet of bristly fur, which was kind of charming amidst so many unwashed manes. Estela wore a wardrobe made over from her aunts' old dresses and while the other girls went to any lengths to find a new piece of fabric, she made it through those difficult years with the clothes that had been left behind in the family armoire. Her mother would alter the dresses according to her own tastes, which is to say, styles popular in the fifties, with full skirts and hemlines below the knee. And although it never occurred to either of them to try to call attention to themselves, or much less to be seen as out of the ordinary, they couldn't have gone unnoticed in the College of Humanities of that time period. You could say that their "good behavior," more in tune with a past that was assumed to be long gone, seemed paradoxically eccentric. Among so many rabble-rousers that invited condemnation, Oscar was the student that never made trouble, and Estela was the example of how a well brought up young lady should behave. When the cleansing assemblies started, and energetic young men from the other academic areas started to make a name for themselves in the College, the two of them felt more in line with the outsiders than with their own classmates. Little by little, Estela lost her petite bourgeois complex and Oscar his tendency to be a goody-two-shoes, or at least enough so they fit in with a good part of the Engineering and Pre-Med students, who were cut from the same cloth as Estela and Oscar. None of that, if Estela wanted to be honest with herself, explained the meteoric advances they both made as leaders in the Communist Youth.[3] Estela didn't know a darn thing about politics and just studied Humanities because her mother thought it was a "nice major." Overnight they found themselves on the cutting edge and life got complicated for them, although some things became much easier. The image of the *Malecón* focused in on the lighthouse, and all of a sudden, her father's face popped into the picture. Estela's mother had died a year before. Back then Estela had so much going on in London that she wasn't able to travel to Havana for the burial, so her father's hopeless expression took her by surprise. He had always been such a cheerful guy, so sure of himself. Estela noticed that her father's hands trembled and that he avoided looking straight into the camera. Nonetheless, when he started speaking leaning his head forward, as if searching for an invisible microphone, his voice was still powerful. He began to talk about the home, about how well they treated him, about the rocking chairs he could sit in all day long, about the meals served at the same time every day. He paused thoughtfully and said that he missed his dog, but that his daughter shouldn't worry, that here, in the facility, they were allowed to have a little garden. Of course water was scarce, so they made do quite well with cactus. "Cactus," he repeated, stammering, as if he had lost track of his place in a script. At that point the tape suddenly stopped.

---

[3] The *Jóvenes Comunistas* quickly became the most influential social and political club for youths to young adults in Cuba. External evidence of one's revolutionary fervor and commitment, membership historically has guaranteed one certain advantages and options not afforded to outsiders.

MARTIN

Last night was a complete disaster. By the closing toast of yet another literary encounter, Martin had managed, by running his mouth and pushing the highballs, to make a move on that sweet young thing, Daontaon, a sort of Asian name as best as he could figure, and she worked putting out fires in some way or another at the Alamar Cultural Center. Luckily, she had no intentions of becoming a poet, didn't even write children's books. She talked incessantly but her principle defect was the proximity of her apartment, in a building bordering the one where Martin lived.

The reefs off the northern coast of the East Havana Municipality, despite their less than inviting look, seemed to be the only accessible destination to allow them to put into practice the intended erotic acts that went along with such happenings. The gusts of wind pierced their very bones, and the stench of dead fish in that godforsaken place didn't help establish much of a romantic atmosphere. Still, it was better than risking that young woman getting a toe-hold in Martin's household. For her part, Daontaon didn't seem to be a bit impressed at finding herself in such intimate circumstances with a poet laureate. Several starving mongrels wandered about the area and, to top things off, Martin's cock wasn't exactly performing in a way to distract them from the surroundings. Daontaon let him feel her up for a while, politely listened to the two or three verses from Neruda that had never failed before, and then interrupted him to ask, "Do you have a car, *papi*?"

No, Martin didn't have a fucking car. In that instant Martin's cock deflated like a birthday balloon, and Daontaon grabbed the chance to give him the slip.

The following morning, Martin woke up so depressed by the behavior of his virile member that he took his fury out on his ancient typewriter and laid down two mocking paragraphs. One was against those hotheaded feminists, Americans who never shaved, and the other was against middle-aged women who already were losing their pubic hairs. He scratched out "pubic hairs" for seeming too prim and fussy, substituting for it a more vulgar term. Daontaon didn't fit into either of those categories, but that didn't matter a whit for literary production, and Martin would rather write anything other than that his cock had betrayed him.

Two paragraphs of worthless filth...worse than that, fucking untrue on top of it, he confessed to himself with the slimy sensation of a criminal.

Martin was taking too long starting his new manuscript. Every time he found himself facing a blank page, a phrase attributed to Bulgakov would start to swirl round and round in his head, a phrase he had discovered in that miserable excuse for a newspaper, *Novedades de Moscú*,[4] a relic of the Soviet press. Before the last of them disappeared from the scene, and despite their usual plodding prose, one could manage to tease out the odd pearl of wisdom from their pages. The phrase that was stuck in his head, "the manuscripts aren't burning," buffeted him about every time he tried to get to work.

They may not be burning, thought Martin, but they are being eaten away by insects, they're rotting in the humidity, they're being misfiled, they're asleep somewhere in a drawer.

Martin, in spite of everything, jotted things down on scraps of paper, popped the cherries of little red books, and afterward stored it all in a folder as material for his manuscript. When he had felt up to it, he had begun various attempts at a filing system. One of his folders collected titles and only that, in a quantity that surpassed the number of stories that could be written throughout the lifetime of all the writers who hung out at literary workshops. He could have made a living at selling titles; that at least was something he was good at.

Martin filed the two paragraphs on feminine topics in one of his folders. He stared at the frightening ream of paper without daring to slide a page in the cylinder of the typewriter and instead opened, with no joy, a datebook from five years prior. One of his many neuroses impelled Martin to write down his ideas only with a black ink pen. Sometimes it seemed to him that his fingers acted on their own and

---

[4] Loosely translated, the title means "What's New in Moscow."

designed the words themselves. A muddled seagull, having lost its way, flew past his window. Martin's hand wrote that oft-repeated verse but on its own, cut out, taken out of its original context, it became full of portent and allegory: *"volverán las oscuras golondrinas."*[5] The dark swallows will return. As a title for his next manuscript it wasn't bad.

DAONTAON

Daontaon was having a bad day. Her morning had been rather hectic, without even taking into account that now, just as she left the house, she had had a hell of a fight with the lady who rented the bottom floor. On top of that, Micaela refused to let her in, much less share a cup of coffee. And to think that she had gone expressly to tell her that amazing dream she had had about the *Titanic* and its furry millionaires. What a building she lived in, for god's sake. She tried at any cost to be gentile, to keep herself apart, but seriously, the hoi polloi of that neighborhood would try the patience of the Virgin Mary herself. Drunks, lice-covered kids, mental retards, crazy old ladies, mangy dogs, sexual perverts, bad-mannered louts, ragamuffins, delinquents, scum—although not her, of course; she was the public face of Alamar "Culture" and deserved to be treated as such.

But don't think that working in the "Culture" sector was a piece of cake. As soon as she got to her office, without so much as a coffee or anything, she would have to make like ten million phone calls to organize a funeral service. The deceased, according to Daontaon's not too humble opinion, was one of those types of which there were way too many in the world (and a beardless wonder, moreover); he had considered himself an "author of geriatric verse," whatever that was, and had died very inconveniently in the middle of the night. Since the baby-faced poet came from the rural interior, there was nobody who could take care of all the details, so the mangy cur ended up in her lap. Of course, who would want to "take care of the dead guy," literally speaking, his colleagues in

---

[5] Gustavo Adolfo Bécquer's famous poem from 1868.

the Literary Workshops? Ha. Not one. In the unlikely case that there was a single one of them not sleeping off a hangover, Daontaon doubted very much that he would feel like taking on such a task. Oh yes, you couldn't get free of them if there was a bottle of rum, or if a new poetess still in diapers showed up. Then they'd all come running like a bunch of lunatics, but…to take care of this dead guy from the boondocks? Ha. Daontaon was completely opposed to people who came from "the countryside" to pile on top of one another in Havana; she herself had done the same years ago, so she knew very well how they thought; they started infiltrating little by little, they'd get married to some shameless hussy (or, even worse, hook up with some queen), and there they'd be, installed in their very own apartment in Alamar, just like hers. That's why Daontaon hated the very sight of them. This one, the deceased, had started out writing children's books back where he was born, and since the field was overly saturated, he had the *darling* idea of writing poetry for the elderly. Poetry for the "Third Generation," please! People started citing them in public, a pile of old decrepit men just like him. They even had published a few of his things in that new creation, the "chapbook." What you see and hear these days is beyond belief. Well, the guy weaseled his way in, an ode here; a minor prize from some godforsaken town in Spain; an appearance in a "poet's convention" for Latin Americans, where besides the usual suspects, the "Whisky Cooperative," there was one dude from Finland due to a clerical error and three Argentines (who of course would have followed protocol perfectly) and that's it, period. The dead guy had achieved what was referred to in the "Culture" sector as *a little name for himself.*

Daontaon often felt the need to speak with a good measure of quotation marks, italics, and punctuation marks.

The geriatric rhymester—for the life of her Daontaon couldn't recall his name right now—took poetic portrayal so much to heart that he up and died of cirrhosis. Well, we're done with him now, and luckily he "hadn't left any *epigone*," whatever that ugly as hell word meant, that she heard Martin say; Martin that guy who thought he was a writer and lived in the building next to hers.

Once she had made a clean sweep of the burial business, Daontaon had to run around in a thousand different directions in order to bring back from limbo a color TV and VCR, owned by one of the Symphonic Orchestra cellists, and decommissioned by the cops during a roundup in the Campo Florida district about two months back. The agents for law and order (Daontaon was tempted to use quotation marks, but was just able to resist) had burst into said cellist's hovel and carried off the TV and VCR after informing his aged mother, the only person occupying the residence at the time it all went down, that the "confiscated electronic effects" (and now the quotation marks were indispensible) constituted **evidence.** Evidence of what?, whined Daontaon hysterically over the telephone, is it possible, please tell me, *compañero*[6] Lieutenant, that somebody was murdered with said equipment? Of course not, Daontaon answered herself. Unless you were talking about slowly dying of boredom from watching television, in which case you could say the TV indeed was criminal… But then why in the world would you want to blame the cellist and his *compañera* mother? I mean, really, be serious.

No dice. Daontaon had no other choice but to show up personally, and in the August heat, all the way down at the police station, and of course nobody else would do, it had to be her, to recoup the problematic items. "Don't take them away," begged the guards, "we're watching the summer shows." The nerve of those guys! But Daontaon was implacable in her duties, and that very afternoon returned the kidnapped TV and VCR to the cellist's mother, who sobbed with gratitude.

"One of these days you can treat me to a coffee, granny. And when you say coffee, you might as well say lunch, right? Right."

---

[6] The word *compañero,* and its female form *compañera,* are words ubiquitous in Cuban conversation and carry such specific cultural weight that no translation is truly adequate. In different contexts it might be rendered as co-worker, colleague, classmate, or comrade—the last term being the most general, but conveying an unfortunate comic resonance of Cold War Soviet formality. In Cuba, the term is a form of direct or indirect address that since the 1959 revolution has replaced a host of words like "sir," "ma'am," "Mr./Mrs.," "lady," and "gentleman"; it implies all people are on the same social level.

And now, to top it all off, this other little "case" in which all three ingredients were mixed together: corpses, police, and "culture." Unfucking-believable!

WOMAN WHO TALKS TO HERSELF IN THE PARK

A sewage pipe under the street exploded, and a creamy black sludge came out and flooded everything. And then even the highest buildings ended up submerged in excrement. And Havana is dying…

LOLA

Micaela would show up from time to time over at Lola's place. She didn't explain why to anyone; it was one of those things you didn't talk about. A few weeks ago she had met Lola's just hatched chicks, restless scant fistfuls of yellow feathers. Lola was keeping them in the warmth of an improvised incubator. These were the future lunches of her precarious survival!

Micaela observed one of them, the runt of the litter, who limped and found it difficult to get enough to eat. She mentioned this to Lola in one of those futile conversations that would arise between them to conveniently fill up the silence or steer them away from certain topics. Lola, polite and distant, explained to her that it always was like that; one of the flock, the most defenseless, had to be sacrificed.

Lola's indifferent tone agonized Micaela, to an unusual extreme, possibly because she felt so helpless. There was nothing she could do; it wasn't her house, it wasn't her chicken coop, and, in this case, Lola—like the ancient feudal lords—held power over life and death, at least for these hallucinatory yellow creatures: little chicks given over to the hazards of being raised in some family's home, a trick through which somebody had attempted to solve the problem of the scarcity of chicken feed; thousands of chicks just out of their eggs were distributed among

Havana households so they could grow up to be roosters and hens.

Micaela contemplated, with an exaggerated sense of angst, the chicks that had succumbed to inappropriate temperatures or illness, or had been inadvertently strangled by loving children's hands, or ended in the mouths of cats as hungry as their owners. Micaela flat out refused to go get her own, the ones that were "her share." Lola's fledglings, however, by who knows what miracles or machinations, grew into lovely birds.

On her visits, Micaela had been watching them grow, cackle, get fat, and dirty up the previously pristine terrace with their greenish excrement and she got used to talking in the midst of the stench that, like an specter of feasts to come, had become part and parcel of Lola's house, the house that nestled in a part of Vedado that hadn't yet gone to the dogs.

Micaela and Lola talked about the chickens a lot. What else did they have to talk about? It had been so long since Sara wrote or called. Bit by bit they ran out of harmless stories from the past, from when Sara and Micaela had studied together at the university. And she didn't want to exhaust Lola by talking about her own problems.

Lola was awfully run down. It was hard for her to walk, and she couldn't see very well. Her television was broken. Those little chicks and Micaela's visits, more and more infrequent, seemed to be her only forms of entertainment.

On her last visit, Micaela sat down out on the terrace and looked with misgivings toward the chicken coop. Fearfully she inquired about that unfortunate chick with the limp who had been bullied without quarter by its brothers of circumstance. Among so much suffering and failure, she felt a happiness all out of proportion to hear that her chick (hers?) had survived, had grown up into a mature chicken with manners just as bad as the rest of them, was now impossible to distinguish among the flock of untended plumage, shoved together in a cell too tight to allow them to grow with dignity, even if was supposed to be only an egg-laying hen house.

Micaela got up out of the armchair under the pretext of going to the bathroom and on the way back avoided returning to the terrace.

The moment in which the chickens would lose their status as laying hens, still innocent of their destiny as stews and fricassee, was growing ever closer. She couldn't stop thinking about how Lola's hands, which had fed, warmed, and perhaps even petted them with some semblance of tenderness, would be the hands that... Micaela didn't even dare visualize the scene in her imagination.

Saying goodbye at the door, Lola asked with poorly disguised anxiety when Micaela would be coming back.

YUYA

Yuya says that she was born in the tenement known as Los Muertos of Animas Street. And even that didn't satisfy the saints. Her mother, Georgina, from whom she inherited her name and her dark skin, had died during childbirth. Her father, José, a bricklayer from Galicia, fell to his death from a scaffolding the day before she was baptized. Yuya says that her poor grandma had come to get her, raising her as well as she could, taking in washing from the neighbors. But Yuya says that the entire start to her life had always seemed like a good sign to her. After all, how could things get worse?

At the wake of her poor grandma, her neighbors from the housing project advised Yuya to go to school. It was around the year 1960 and, as Yuya tells it, there wasn't much of a decision to make between doing strangers' dirty laundry and picking up the books. So she finished high school and, a few months later, she signed up for the Literacy Brigades, the dream of her poor grandma who never learned to read or write.

Yuya says that after that she was sent to be a teacher in the outback of the Oriente province, in a tiny hamlet between Tunas and Holguín known as Dead Man's Stream. In just about any small rural town in Cuba, you hear tales of a headless horseman or even a headless horse that comes riding out in the wee hours, terrorizing the locals. Yuya says that one time, in the middle of the coffee fields, she saw a black man with the body of a wolf, eating a still struggling wild pig. Somebody explained to her that she had seen the spirit of a Haitian, who in order to not die of starvation, had hung himself from a *guásima* tree back in the forties, and from that day forward he was able to transform himself into different animals, whichever one he wanted, be it a wolf, a wildcat, a crab, or anything else.

There in Dead Man's Stream, Yuya fell in love with a redneck about her own age and ended up pregnant. By the time her belly started to show, the literacy campaign was just about over. She said goodbye to her students and without losing her good humor, she returned to her dump in the ghetto and gave birth to her daughter, Eulalia. Yuya says that during the first few weeks with her little girl, on her own and without a cent to her name, it was like the heavens fell. But thanks to her lucky stars, her next-door neighbor Etelvina helped her as if they were family. Then in the midst of preparations for Lalita's first birthday party, poor Etelvina's asthma gave her such a choking fit that she had a heart attack. Yuya says that very night the old lady's ghost appeared to her, naming Lalita as her sole heir and directing Yuya to carve a door-sized opening in the thin wall that separated their two apartments.

Along with the rooms and furniture formerly belonging to poor Etelvina, Yuya took possession of all her contacts and listings for the *Bolita and Charada*[7] games, as well as the altar to Saint Lazarus, who had been so venerated by her neighbor. She also discovered, saved in an oaken trunk among mothballs and twigs sprigs of rosemary, a wedding dress that was in perfect shape, apart from a bit of yellowing.

The next day she set into motion new games of *Bolita and Charada* and aired out the trousseau provided for Lalita's future. Ah, and Yuya says that she lit a candle and a bit of tobacco for Saint Lazarus, her patron saint and *Babalú*,[8] eternally grateful.

---

[7] *La Bola* (or *Bolita*) and *Charada*, literally ball and charade, refer to various popular yet quite complicated games and cultural practices with elements of Bingo, Tarot, and Lottery. Set interpretations of dreams and auguries are linked to future happenings and often are taken as clues or hints for winning games of chance.

[8] In the syncretic Afrocuban religion, Babalú is the patron saint and protector of animals and the sick, and is linked with Saint Lazarus.

MARIA ESTHER

Martin's first wife didn't like sentimental outbursts in the least, and as the years went by her tendency to reject anything she considered as "getting too emotional" only became worse. Maria Esther and Martin had gotten together as a fluke, so to speak, at a party celebrating the end of their second year at university. Out on the terrace, people had started to pair up as the night went on. By eleven thirty, they were the only two left that weren't out on the dance floor, each of them in their own corner like poorly trained boxers. Somebody dimmed the lights, making possible the transition from twist and rock and roll to saccharine songsters reminiscent of Doris Day, those songsters that allowed the closeness of slow dancing. From the record player emanated the scratchy sounds of the already passé "Secret Love."

Martin asked Maria Esther to dance and at midnight, after the ritual kiss to welcome in the new year of 1967, he asked her to be his girlfriend, and she said yes. What remained of the late night they spent discussing Antonioni and Godard, *Red Desert* and *Pierrot le Fou*, the latest debuts of French New Wave film at the Cinemateca. Martin didn't care much for those films; in his innermost secret self he didn't understand them, although they were part and parcel of the lifestyle of the students in Humanities. One had to be able to speak knowledgably of such things; it was sort of a code among the initiated. Martin preferred Hitchcock and when he said so, Maria Esther cut him off sharply: "I don't like police thrillers in the least. Having a taste for them shows a lack of spirituality. Faced with the transcendence of death, you tell me—what does it matter asking who is the murderer?" Martin had to agree, even though he was disillusioned by such crushing logic, by that level of rationality in such a young lady. He didn't let his feelings show, out of fear of being thought a troglodyte. Moreover, the idea of death never occurred to Martin anyway.

Over the years of their life together, during those neurotic and boring years of the seventies, Martin heard over and over about the grade school run by nuns where Maria Esther had spent her youth. For somebody who didn't know any better, those stories could be taken as critical, even mocking. However, underlying her ironic tone bloomed a mellowed longing, a sort of approval. To a certain extent Maria Esther's strict moral code reproduced those old religious prejudices, shamelessly translated into the context of the college where she taught classes in literature. Maria Esther told about how in her old parochial school, if the girls were restless, garrulous, or even expansive, their devout teachers would make them do penance for hours, arms crossed behind their backs and mouths tightly closed with lips pressed in between teeth. To Martin that always had seemed a horrific punishment, and Maria Esther would talk about it as if it were no big deal, as if she would have liked to see the practice implemented once again in the school disciplinary system.

By the time their relationship was in its death throes, Maria Esther's replies were mere silences, and the marriage ended up sinking in calm seas. After a while, she got remarried a couple of times, divorced twice more, had a son, and from then on would shack up with a married man intermittently. Martin also had heard rumors that she was an alcoholic, although he wasn't totally convinced, as the scruples Maria Esther inherited from the cloistered nuns prohibited her from enjoying tying one on, rather the contrary.

Despite the fact that Maria Esther had never moved out of her childhood home in Martin's mother's neighborhood, it had been a good number of years since they had seen each other, and now she had become seriously ill.

Maria Esther, wasted and weak in her hospital bed, was not surprised by Martin's visit and motioned for him to sit down, with a vestige of the authority she used to wield. Her pedantic nature hadn't changed a bit, and the first words she spoke included a reference to the classics.

"Don't tell me any silly lies, Martin, how much time do I have left? Just like Oedipus, one can't help but search for the very truth that will destroy one."

WOMAN WHO TALKS TO HERSELF IN THE PARK

They dug a tunnel and woke up the giant serpents that had been sleeping tranquilly beneath the streets of Vedado. And so the serpents escaped, opened their tremendous maws, and swallowed them whole in one giant mouthful. And Havana is dying…

WILLIE

They call me Willie, and I've got a curse hanging over me.

"Open the door, Micaela! Open up, I'm telling you!"

The woman banging on the door is called Daontaon. She's got a reputation as a troublemaker and a blabbermouth. Micaela, the person resisting the assault, is the only neighbor in this building with good manners, besides Big Mike and myself. And her front door is the only one in this whole neighborhood that is clean and has a fresh coat of paint.

"I wonder if anybody's there." Daontaon pressed her ear to the door. I'd like to know if she'd dare to stick her ear against her own door, covered with disgusting stains, from what it was impossible to say.

"I know somebody's there!" Daontaon answered herself. She is one of those types who ask themselves questions and then give themselves answers.

Daontaon struggled with the shutters until she was able to force a tiny gap open, through which she peered inside.

"I see a light on. Ha! You're there, I knew it. What's more, I smell coffee. You're making a pot of coffee!"

From inside, total silence.

"Alright, *okei*, don't let me in, I'll tell you about it from here. I had a dream about you. Both of us were taking a trip on a boat, one of those really big ones like the Titanic in the movie. I don't have any idea where we were going. I guess we were going north. Don't you think? I mean, where does anybody go except for up THERE!"

Her "there"—in all capital letters—echoed down the stairs. And speaking of stairs… One doesn't know if others are as fortunate as this staircase, which throughout its four flights has manifested the cultural inheritance of Versailles. During palace receptions in said city, and I know this on good authority, everyone let loose and had a pee wherever he wished; so down the royal steps descended the amber nectar of princes and princesses. Well, same thing here. Our neighbors, unable to contain their urgent needs, proceed to let flow wherever they please. However, let it be noted, here they are more democratic than in the French court, allowing their emissions to mingle with those of dogs and cats, not to mention the pigs and goats that go up and down the aforementioned stairs at will. "Never has such a thing been seen here in Havana," comments Big Mike, thoroughly aggrieved.

Big Mike is already eighty-two years old. As he tells it, he has seen it all, although he still is baffled by the sounds of the farm animals here in the midst of the city: the braying, neighing, baaing, and howling of the victims as they are sacrificed by local killers. But in case there's any doubt, know that the butchers are our own neighbors, occupied during the day as office workers or common layabouts, turned into executioners when they are pinched by Famine. And to round out the clamor, what could be better than a chorus of barnyard vocalists, at every hour of the night: roosters befuddled by the apartment lights that they confuse with the golden orb of their ancestral countryside.

Big Mike has his own private war with the tenants raising chickens, goats, and pigs in the building. Up to now, he's lost every battle and has had to resign himself to inhaling the stench of well-fed beasts coming from the patio of the apartment above his, not to mention watching Tilingo drive a herd of goats past his front door and out around to graze in front of his balcony.

"Did you watch that movie, *The Titanic,* on Saturday? I'm sure you did." As already established, Daontaon will just answer her own questions. "In my dream, the boat looked like one of those gigantic cruise ships that even have a swimming pool on them. Can you imagine that? A yacht with a swimming pool, my friend, and you and I were there on the top deck with a pair of real studs. Millionaires…young, handsome, hairy chested… Blessed Mary Mother of God! Micaela! Are you listening to me? Yes, you can hear me perfectly. And you're drinking that coffee all by yourself, you selfish thing… and here I am taking the time and trouble to come and tell you my dream."

At this juncture, Daontaon changed her tune. She peered once again through the blinds and decided that Micaela wasn't going to give in.

"You aren't gonna offer me a cup of coffee? No. Girl, I hope that after I go ashore in New York and you stay on that ship, your Titanic runs into a block of ice and you choke on your coffee."

MARIA ESTHER

A little bit before Martin got there, Maria Esther had been pretending to sleep. The doctors had just had a shift change and hadn't held back from loudly discussing her case, with no beating around the bush. For all her ignorance of technical or clinical terminology, their hateful words, unequivocal, drilled into Maria Esther's soul without leaving room for even a smidgen of denial. The moment had arrived for her to lament all the roads not taken, all the lives she hadn't been given to live. Like all the things you shouldn't put off until later, but you do… Her defeats, heartaches, failures, dreams, none of them had felt insurmountable, not until a silly little stomach ache sounded the alarm that now it was too late. "Everything, everything is dying," Maria Esther said to herself, with muted dramatics. "And there's never enough time."

An impatient motion of her head shifted her face from the comfortable shade of the room towards a bright light. Beneath her still-closed eyelids, she began seeing white dots that continued to dance about even after she opened her eyes to sunlight streaming through the window. When the spots calmed down, one was left moving about close to the white ceiling and Maria Esther realized that, in fact, it was an actual mosquito.

The mosquito zig-zagged restlessly, as if it was in a hurry to finish something. And then suddenly, with no forewarning, it fell dead onto the tile floor. Maria Esther didn't know that she herself would die before the year was out, how could she know so precisely, but the small death of the mosquito made her realize that starting right then, everything that happened to her would become enmeshed, in some way or another, in the gears spinning toward her own passing.

Just then Martin walked in—Martin who now, much as ever, had to poke his nose into everything. He wouldn't be able to live with the idea of letting her die without having closure. That was just like him. He also seemed unable to take seriously anything unpleasant; he blew off anything bad, anything that was obviously bad.

Martin smiled at her but stayed stiff as a board, without saying anything, silenced by the enormity of what he was seeing. Maria Esther, of the long blonde braids, slim, with the permanent air of a schoolgirl in uniform, had transformed into this woman, bloated, purple bags under her eyes, whose saggy yellowed skin peeked out from the folds of her pajamas. And the most shocking of all, she was without a hair on her head, completely bald.

Guessing his line of thinking, Maria Esther tried to shift the mood.

"If you're letting me see you now, after all this time, I know for sure I'm about to go. No, wipe that look off your face. I'm not dead yet," she said, speaking with an exaggerated sense of ease, with a cheerfulness that in truth was an appeal for Martin to take control of the situation. She ran her hand over her scalp and tittered with a shadow of her old laugh.

"You caught me when I haven't even had my hair done… it's because of the chemo, you know. At any rate, at least there's nothing left to fear. I've already gone through the worst that could happen to me. Hand me that scarf and find me a mirror from the cabinet."

Martin held the mirror up to her face, and Maria Esther smoothed down the kerchief with a hint of flirtatiousness, avoiding looking him in the eyes.

"How is your mother?" asked Maria Esther, in a neutral tone.

Martin turned and stared out the glass panes of the window. Out there, far away, beneath a resplendent and vibrant sun, you could see the seawall, the ocean, a few milky clouds.

"Fine," he answered, but it seemed to him that he had said, "Badly, she is dying and she doesn't even know it." "Fine," he repeated.

YUYA

Yuya says she doesn't have anything to complain about. That she has always had something or someone to help her move forward in life. From her foray into secondary school she was left with the obsessive habit of reading every scrap of paper that fell into her hands, from history books to fashion magazines. Thanks to her extensive readings she was able to make an informed analysis of the various games of chance. *La Bolita,* despite having become illegal almost immediately, was still played clandestinely using the Miami lottery. Thanks to poor Etelvina's short wave radio Yuya was able to keep up with the game.

When it came to *Charada,* her grandma had taught her all the ins and outs of the particular version played in Matanzas. It was in that province where she, poor thing, fresh off the boat from Spain, had worked like a dog at the Santa Rita factory, before moving to the tenement in Havana when the economy had gone to hell in a hand basket.

On her own initiative, and typical of her insatiable intellectual curiosity, Yuya says that she also taught herself all the numbers of the *Charada* version called the *Cubana,* as well as those for the *Charada India,* quite the creative adaptation, and finally the *Charada Americana,* which wasn't that big of a deal. Yuya said she did it to try her luck at the different games. In the Matanzas variety, "Cadaver" is number 3, while in the *India* game the closest match was "Burial"—number 9; however, in the *Americana* there was the "Colossal Cadaver" as 64, while in the *Cubana* there wasn't a corpse to be seen anywhere. Jesus Christ on the cross! Yuya says that she, at the end of the day, takes her cues from the *Charada China,* the most popular game played in Havana. For a Cuban, the number 8 is, and always will be, a "Dead Guy."

In one of her ephemeral visits, poor Etelvina showed her the secret cabinet where she kept an image of the old *Chinito of the Charada*. Yuya says that it was clear that Etelvina had held him in the highest esteem, because the piece of paper with the drawing was worn and full of holes, and Etelvina had carefully glued it onto a sheet of cardboard that she then topped with another sheet, the two sewn together with black thread along the left side, so that it served as a folder of sorts. In the shadowy box, Yuya also found a thick sheaf of bills that she says weren't at all unwelcome.

In order to better understand her new vocation, Yuya sat through many long nights analyzing the drawing, which was of an old bald Chinese man, or as they say in Cuba 'a *Chinito*', with a long mustache that drooped down over the corners of his mouth. He was wearing a kimono and a pair of slippers ornamented with the symbols of the game. From his right hand hung a fish, number 10, "Big Fish," and the fingers of his left hand held a smoking pipe, number 36, "Pipe;" his right calf boasted an illustration of the "Eel" and his left the "Rat." On his right ear you could discern the "Butterfly" and on the left on the "Sailor;" on his right shoulder sat the "Nun" with arms crossed and on the left the "Deer" poised for flight. Right above his bald dome, drawing attention to his head, the "Horse" in movement, number one, just as it should be.

The *Chinito's* kimono was covered with these figures. Yuya says that his left sleeve with the "Spider" scared her, made her nervous, sent her bad vibes. Yuya preferred to stay with his right arm: "Turtle," "Snail," "Elephant," and the "Dead Guy," that number 8 that, according to Yuya, always brought her good luck.

GERTRUDE

Call me Gertrude. Even though that's not my name.

There are various famous women by the name of Gertrude. Ours is Gómez de Avellaneda, the very cream of the crop, a woman who outshone all of those poet wannabes of her time, lived her life just as she damn well pleased, and let herself be led by the will of Fate and the

Furies. True, she had to pay the price. She was maligned, scorned by her own lovers, not a soul attended her funeral, and a herd of envious men blocked her from gaining entrance to the *Academia*. Because of what happened later, none of that matters anymore. She, the greatest of all, is up there in the Pantheon of Gods, among equals.

The other "Gertrude," Gertrude Stein, was the one who that big ingrate Hemingway tried to get to spill all of her secrets when they were both in Paris, and then he had the nerve to fill a novel with malicious gossip about her. There's a bad apple in every bunch.

Back to what we were talking about. Now people have started up with a line about "how wonderful the sixties were!" Please, say it to my face. As if those years had been all fun and games; we can all join in and sing "Imagine," and pay no attention to the man behind the curtain. Are they trying to pretend they are stupid, that they've lost their minds, or that they just didn't get what was going on back then?

Listen up, is it that nobody remembers, or that *nobody wants to remember?*

Resentments? You better believe it. The dead are the only ones who are past all that. And each of us is going to tell our story how we want to see it, like *Rashomon,* or rather, *Rashomona.*

I can recall quite well what it was like in the Department of Languages and Literature, what the Colina was like, or the bleak reality of the free student housing at F and Third Street. In short, I remember what it was like at the University in the aforementioned decade—the good, the bad, and the ugly. And if only you could have seen Havana back in the day! A hotbed, a whirlwind, a big racket at any time of the day or night. It didn't matter if we were in a trench waiting for a nuclear missile to fall on our heads or at happy hour buffet at the Flamingo, listening to Meme Solís play the piano. It got so we could barely tell night from day: classes, ice cream at Coppelia, films at the Cinemateca, the Cocktail Club, studying till dawn, exams, political rallies, concerts, *Chez Bola,* the *Varona* Film Club, dances, the library, eating peas for lunch at the university dining hall when we couldn't manage a pizza at Vita Nuova, the beaches at *Santa María del Mar,* meetings of the University Student Union…[9] Then there was the swimming pool at the Riviera Hotel, those poetry readings at the Parque de los Cabezones, volunteer shifts, the Tower Bar, assemblies in the Plaza, Phys Ed, plays at the tiny *Tepsis* salon, music at the *Talía,* Saturday night parties, taking our turn at guard duty, study groups, exhibits at the Museum of Fine Arts, shooting practice, department gatherings, conferences, jam sessions, *tertulias,* slumming it, the nice part of the *Rampa,* not to mention the seedy part, the never ending story, don't you remember?

At night, especially, time stood still. It was like we had all the time in the world.

WOMAN WHO TALKS TO HERSELF IN THE PARK

The bridge fell, and nobody raised it up again; the corner of the Fortress fell to pieces and just stayed that way. And by that time the sea was hurting so much from all the rubble that she sent an enormous wave, which hit at Cojímar Bay and covered the entire city. And Havana is dying…

MARTIN

Time after time, over the last few weeks, Martin would dream about the novel he had never been able to write. On the first few occasions, he woke with a feeling of unease that he interpreted as the result of his routine state of frustration. It was more than ten years since he had published anything that was worth a damn.

In his dreams, Martin would find himself in a Kafkaesque chamber, surrounded by shelves of books, books, and more books, all of them identical. Up to that point there was nothing out of the ordinary, just

---

[9] The *Federación Estudiantil Universitaria,* or *FEU,* was a student organization with social, cultural, and educational pillars.

a stupid, boring dream in black and white that could show up in the nighttime hours of any neurotic writer, even those at the beginning of their career. But after that Martin's subconscious would zero in a bit more, and he would see *his novel:* in the middle of one of those indistinguishable bookshelves, repeating themselves forever like images in facing mirrors, the presence of one volume stood out from the others—a thick tome with red hardback binding and black lettering. It wasn't necessary to have read Freud to guess, any idiot could predict it, that his own name—Martin's—was on the cover.

In the beginning, Martin tried to convince himself that his nocturnal hallucinations would go away sooner or later. But as the nightmares continued, he ended up having to accept that they came from the depths of that malignant well of guilt that haunted him throughout the hours he wasted in drunken madness, after the rum and the specimens like that Daontaon character that flitted around the celebrity circles of literature, through his periods of sloth, his slacking off, his reluctance to admit that several years back he had stopped showing promise. For fuck's sake, all that was left was for him to start wetting the bed.

"What's got you so upset?" Martin's mother watched him suspiciously. The wait in the doctor's sitting area was going on too long, and both of them had worn out the regular topics of conversation.

"Nothing." Martin's thoughts, however, had turned to the unfavorable results of the tests they had run on his mother, which he had camouflaged beneath the dust jacket of a book, numbers that he would need to hide from her no matter what, keep totally secret, or even falsify if need be. Then he thought of the falsely cheerful expression on Maria Esther's face, an expression that couldn't hide she was on her last legs. Then of the alarming rumors that were circulating in the neighborhood about a murderer who dismembered his victims. In that precise moment he hadn't even been thinking about that fucking nightmare about *his novel.*

"A nightmare I've been having," said Martin, to avoid any pitfalls.

"Tell me about it, my dear," requested Martin's mother, settling down in her seat. Martin looked at her. Maybe all mothers were like that. Martin didn't know anybody, outside of psychiatrists and one's own mother, who would be interested in hearing about somebody else's dreams.

After hearing him out, Martin's mother watched him with that expression of hers that marveled at the simplicity of the problem that was tormenting him. Her reasoned response, so straightforward and natural, left him speechless.

"And what is your novel about?"

It came to him that during all the instances of that nightmare, he had never dared to open up the blessed book.

The next night, Martin again dreamed that he was going into the room. This time he got his courage up, reached out a hand that stretched forward, of course in slow motion, and pulled out from the bookcase the thick volume with a red cover and black writing that spelled out his name. He opened it up and managed to read the first enigmatic line, "all that glitters is not gold," an old saying from his Uncle Felix.

MICAELA

Micaela waited a little while more without moving a muscle, until Daontaon had left the premises. She was not in the mood to talk about dreams of hairy millionaires. Nevertheless, she continued to think about shipwrecks and catastrophes. As she washed up from breakfast, she accidentally dropped the last surviving porcelain cup from the set of china she had inherited from her Aunt Candita.

That's the way things are, things ended up getting old all of a sudden, everything broke all at the same time, one morning the cat woke up with no appetite, the windows would shatter with no apparent reason, the begonias in the flower pot dried up even though they were being watered, and the colors of the towels had become faded, as faded as her own face in the mirror. How can you fight against entropy?

Up to this morning, Micaela had put up with being ostracized, with being surrounded by vulgarity, with all of the useless tasks she had to do. But, as she picked up the shards of ceramic, she realized that her memory of her old Aunt Candita was younger than she herself was now, and something fell apart inside. The moment had come. Her epiphany made her decide to get rid of all of the useless crap she had collected throughout the years. She had nobody to leave all of her belongings to, and her role in past doings would die along with her. Could there be any doubt? She needed to let go of the lucky charms that she had been dragging around all her life.

Micaela imagined herself dead and imagined Doutaon knocking down the door, scrabbling through her cabinets, snooping around everywhere. Intruders, strangers invading the haven of her bedroom, the bathroom where she kept as treasures a few splinters of soap to clean herself up as well as she could, the kitchen compulsively in order despite the scarcity of everything. And who knows what else. She was terrified just to think that somebody might find the yellowed envelope filled with letters from Pavel, and with partially smoked cigarette butts that had meant so much to her at one time, and now she didn't even feel sad about throwing them out. Despite that, she couldn't stop her hand from trembling a bit when she tossed them in the garbage can, together with a thousand shreds of carefully torn paper, the shells they had gathered one luminous afternoon in Guanabo, her father's rusted watch, the porcelain cup in a hundred pieces, and so many minutiae that had no value except in the solitary realm of her memory. Anybody else would say that they were trash. So, why should she keep them any longer? She, Micaela, wasn't on the Titanic, so nobody was going to take an interest in her ridiculous things.

Her Aunt Candita, when something wasn't going well, would make herself feel better by telling herself that "tomorrow was another day." Micaela was no longer so sure of that.

ESTELA

As usual, Estela walked to the office and arrived before anyone else. The girl who cleaned the floors, a Jamaican immigrant, opened the door for her smiling ear to ear; she always looked radiant, although Estela couldn't for the life of her imagine why, the poor thing. On her way, Estela had stopped by the French bakery to buy a pastry, a cream puff, her favorite, overflowing with Chantilly cream. She could afford to indulge herself; despite her years she had managed to keep her figure, as did Oscar. With a paper napkin she carefully dabbed the corners of her mouth and her fingertips, then turned to read the recent faxes, nothing interesting. One, quite brief, from Oscar, announcing his proposed return date. A loud voice and the slamming door told her that the secretary had made her entrance. Olguita had been in London for more than a year, and she was still getting in to the office late. She swore that she was getting lost in the serpentine twists of the metro system, but Estela didn't believe a word of it. Back in the beginning she had tried to find some explanation for the girl's tardiness, be it some sort of intentional negligence, secret morning assignations, or obligations that she couldn't tell anyone about, but after a few months Estela finally resigned herself to interpreting it as simple ineptitude. Today, Estela didn't even lift her eyes from her paperwork as she heard the girl talking about how the escalators in the metro were so crowded that she had had to run up the other stairs, the "ones that didn't move," as Olguita called them, "Ughhh," she sighed, still exhausted by the effort of making it up "a mountain of steps." Olguita tossed down her plastic coat of imitation tiger skin and shook out her long dyed-red hair as if she were in the middle of the jungle. From one of her many bags she took out a thermos of coffee and offered a cup to Estela. She did that every single morning without noticing the snub of her boss's refusal; she walked through life so sure of herself, so full of that vulgar joie de vivre. A little while later, Olguita started to warble a song in Spanish as she brushed her hair, not showing any hurry to get started on the day's tasks. Estela watched her out of the corner of her eye and thought that Olguita behaved as if she still were in Havana. She pronounced the word "metro" just like she would have said "bus"; she filed her nails as she attended to their clients; and she chatted away for hours and hours on the phone, Estela could never figure out with whom. The office already had gone through various secretaries. The one before Olguita couldn't stand it and decided to go back to Cuba after only a few months. She said that she missed the sun. She had been talking about the sun ever since she had arrived, the Cuban sun this and the Cuban sun that, and the summer sun in London disgusted her, that's exactly what she said. As winter began she was caught up in some odd melancholy that made her run at the mouth, so that the incautious English who stood still long enough were shocked by the demented soul who went on and on about the various permutations of the Cuban sun. Finally she packed her bags and left her husband behind, an old man, curator at the British Museum. Estela couldn't help getting some enjoyment out of such a brushoff; the old cradle robber, a mummy just like the ones he took care of, had it coming for chasing behind a piece of tropical tail. Another one of the many secretaries that had passed through the office didn't really speak English, so she would respond to any situation by quoting fragments of Beatles' songs. In talking to clients, she would say good bye with an absurd "Let it be." Saints in heaven. And then there was the one who spent all her time pilfering pens, envelopes, file folders, paste, and even paper clips to send them to Cuba. At Estela's office, the travel agency servicing the island and the rest of the Caribbean, they had seen it all.

MARIA ESTHER

Martin sat down and took a look around. It wasn't bad, especially compared to that circle of hell, the room in that hospital where his father had suffered through his last days without running water in the bathroom, with the window shutters locked shut, the nurses yelling their heads off, and the food that made you sick. In contrast, Maria Esther's room, a semi-private, enjoyed comfortable armchairs, a telephone, and clean side tables; it smelled nice; and the light streamed in through the wide windows looking out onto the Malecón.

"Are you here to inspect the premises?"

"Yes, exactly," responded Martin, and Maria Esther noticed that she felt relieved at the turn that their conversation was taking. "At least you're better off that when we were in the dorms."

"The dorm at F and Third Street. What a thing for you to remember. How the years have passed!" Her answers were necessarily overly dramatic.

"The problem with time is the way that it goes by. We were twenty years old and all of a sudden we're in our fifties. I had a nightmare last night…" Maria Esther didn't say a thing. "In the dream I was watching television," continued Martin, "and onscreen I saw my own face covered by a death mask."

Martin hesitated at his own tactlessness. Maria Esther encouraged him to go on with a wave of her hand.

"You never watch television, I know that. So I'll explain it to you: in a celebration of my centennial they offered the hint 'famous Cuban writer,' and there I was, in a portrait surrounded by a black wreath," Maria Esther smiled, and Martin went on. "A panel of three scholars had to guess who they were talking about and the mother fuckers couldn't remember my name. Can you imagine?"

Maria Esther let out a dry little laugh and afterward a cough. She doubled over in pain, making a face, then slid back flat onto her bed.

Martin kept on talking, trying to act as if he didn't notice what was going on. Just to chit chat about any old thing, he lied about having finally started writing his next book, and said that he was going to read her a few chapters when he came to visit her next time. Maria Esther nodded agreement, still trying to get herself back together. Then the silence stretched out, and Martin felt like they had run out of things to say to each other. He didn't want to sink to the level of making insipid comments about family or the country's current situation, much less subject her to any of that.

Maria Esther was grateful that he hadn't asked about her family. How could she tell him that her only son, the doctor, had gone back on his sworn oath and only thought about opening a private hospital in Buenos Aires to take people's money and live high on the hog? How can you talk about so many defeats, one after the other, so difficult to live with?

"Truthfully I would like to be dead."

"What?!"

"Don't get all het up, Martin, I'm quoting Sappho. Wasn't that the verse that we repeated in Latin class when we were dying of boredom?"

Memory is so capricious. You tap into it and out flows just what you would never expect. After Martin left, Maria Esther dreamed about the dented, greasy trays they used to serve the meals in the dormitory dining hall; precariously provisioned with a handful of gritty watercress and a yellow broth in which some hard beans floated. When she woke up for the hospital lunch, some kind of stew without flavor or texture, Maria Esther smiled at the memory, telling herself that it very well might have come up as a logical consequence of her tedious sickbed diet. Afterward, another detail of her dream came to mind: behind that tray, as if in the slow motion of some documentary, nightmarishly appeared the hands, the body, the distorted face of The Dead Girl, the last time she saw her.

LOLA

With her television out of order she was dying, putting it plain and simple, she couldn't go on living.

Lola decided to barter an old silver-plated bracelet that used to belong to her mother, on top of the three best chickens from her coop, to get her TV repaired.

Micaela hadn't shown up lately. Nor did she get any letters from Sara. And she didn't get a call, not from anybody, nobody, on the phone. Day after day, Lola busied herself with chores around the house and let the hours drag by under an aura of tedium and unease. When the television programming started, she would turn on her set and leave it on any old channel, it didn't matter which, just white noise to fill up her empty home. Later she would surrender her mind to the glowing screen so that she didn't have to think. Finally she would get drowsy, fall asleep, without ever finding out how the movies ended.

An unexpected power failure yanked Lola out of a film about murders and corrupt police. Another nuisance in her life. In her poor excuse for a life, better said.

She lit a candle and opened up the windows so the breeze would dissipate the heat and mosquitoes that plagued her. Lola sat there for a while watching the flickering of the flame on the candlewick, as she tried to play deaf to the obscenities coming from the little park across from her house. After an hour had gone by, the light failed and Lola was left in the dark with the dreaded avalanche of memories, all of them bad.

In the most vulgar way possible, like something out of the worst soap operas, she found out that her husband was cheating on her. This had happened many years ago and, there was no avoiding it, her long list of bad memories always started off with Evaristo's betrayal. Evaristo had been dead twenty years already and for her his face was forever frozen in that cowardly expression, looking like a slaughtered sheep, from the time that Lola had confronted him with her suspicions.

Although grief by no means is shared out equally or fairly among humankind, pondered Lola, the greatest sorrows do tend to happen to all of us: death, illness, old age, loss. There are others that touch some and leave others unscathed. Hunger, for example. Or insanity, betrayal, disillusionment, failure, abandonment. Or loneliness. At the beginning of her adult life she wasn't afraid of anyone or anything. She wasn't crazy. Old age and death were a long way off. She liked her job and was healthy as a horse. She hadn't even yet felt the pain of nostalgia, that little shadow she saw in her father's eyes whenever he talked about Asturias.

Among her own misfortunes, the first was Evaristo's betrayal.

Then came abandonment. When Sara ended up staying, on one of her trips to Spain, Lola admitted to herself that there were some separations that were as bad as deaths. That second recollection came over her in spite of herself: Sara's face through the window of the car that was taking her to the airport, revealing her secret plans in a look heavy with meaning that drilled straight into her mother's eyes. The car started and Lola knew that she was saying goodbye to Sara, maybe forever.

Luckily, as she made her way toward her third bad memory, the lights came back on, along with the opening credits of another movie just like all the others, idiotic and forgettable, and Lola fell asleep in front of the television.

WOMAN WHO TALKS TO HERSELF IN THE PARK

The cocks from the countryside advanced on the city. On the toll roads, the main highway, and from every which way. Then came the hens, who laid eggs, the chicks grew up and pecking away, they went along destroying everything. And Havana is dying…

YUYA

Yuya says her natural gift for getting along with ghosts also helped her get ahead in life. Whenever she went to the cemetery to place flowers on her poor grandmother's tomb, she would ask for some piece of advice that she would then follow to a T. Her grandmother always had the grace to not appear in the tenement, as if she were maintaining a respectful distance from Etelvina's territory. According to Yuya, Etelvina didn't come around very often, only in cases of emergency.

Yuya says that from its first appearance, the folder with the image of the *Chinito of the Charada* had never let her down. She was endlessly intrigued by the question of why one set of numbers would show up and another wouldn't. How could she decipher the code to determine their position on the *Chinito's* body? Some symbolic configurations were easy to interpret, like the "Horse" that cautions us to think things through, or the "Saintly Woman," number 12, right above his heart. On the other hand, signs such as the "Dove" just above his right knee or the "Toad" above his left one, continued to leave Yuya bewildered.

And so, thanks to her supplications and the indulgences of the

Chinito of the Charada, Yuya met a son of the Celestial Empire who lived on Rayo Street. She closed up her two rooms in the tenement for the meantime and moved Lalita, her altar to Saint Lazarus, and the trunk with the bride's trousseau to the slum where the compatriots of Shu Shuang lived squeezed in like sardines.

Shu, more on the ball than the others, had taken possession of the patio, where he put together a set of ramshackle rooms, including a kitchen and a bathroom of his own. To be able to breathe the fresh night air and have her own tub to bathe in, and a private toilet, was more good fortune than she had ever hoped for.

Yuya says that at first she tried to get Shu to explain to her the significance of where the signs were placed all over the *Chinito's* costume, but she couldn't get him to say a thing about it. Shu worked as a typesetter using Chinese characters in one of those foreign language newspapers that were sold to the neighborhood locals. Like almost all of the genuine Chinese folks that she knew, Shu was delicate, reserved, and untrusting. He had his own beliefs, by now somewhat tainted by the influence of so many years on this side of the planet. Next to his impenetrable tributes to Sanfacón, his sticks of incense, a set of elephants made of veiny green jade, and a carved wooden pot containing some grey powder, Yuya respectfully set out the folder with the drawing of the *Chinito of the Charada* and her altar to Saint Lazarus, her papa *Babalú*, protector of cripples, stray dogs and hopeless wretches.

Shu's refusal to talk made Yuya despair. However, Yuya says, there in the Chinese barrio she felt right at home.

But it's true, living there gave her a life-long aversion to Chinese food. Yuya says that from her terrace she could see the owners of the corner diner set out, uncovered on the tiles, the fish for salting and the vegetables for drying. There sat the future daily specials, left out in the open through the night and more than once Yuya saw cats and rats forging their paths right over the provisions.

Another consequence of her move to the street of thunder and lightning was that from then on she avoided swearing, the best that she could, and never invoked the curse "may lightning strike you dead." Jesus Christ on the cross!

WILLIE

Kill 'em! Kill 'em! Kill 'em!

I've just been jolted awake to the rhythm of that phrase of one verb conjugated in the imperative. Exactly what or whom do they propose to "kill?" I don't even get up to find out. It could be a chicken, a citizen, or a domino move. It doesn't matter.

Although I'd like to, I'm unable to close my ears or my nose with something akin to an eyelid, that might impede the entry of the noises and the stench that the residents of this building generate, without the least bit of effort, twenty-four hours a day. Ah, but if I were only able to temporarily close my olfactory and auditory senses, and I were to go and gaze at the sea, the Havana sea, distinct and different from any other, it would be worth living here in this neighborhood. Had I already mentioned what it is called? *"Alamar,"* or *"To the Sea,"* in quotes and italics, as Daontaon would say it. And its inhabitants… Alamarians? Alamarites? Alamarants? Alamartians?

Alamar is characterized fundamentally by its sonorous ambiance: at any moment of the night or day, the most persistent sound is the howling of the madams calling for their brats. And we are not speaking of tender entreaties; on the contrary, beside these mothers, the very gorillas in the jungle would seem quiet. The youngsters, for their part, lose a good part of their human attributes when they are playing out in front of the building. Although *playing* really isn't the most apt term…

Another acoustic component consists of a racket that the members of this horde refer to as "music" and which can be heard for ten miles around. The aborigines of the building enjoy the habit of turning the volume on their stereophonic equipment up to the maximum in order to share it with their fellow dwellers. In the majority of the cases, as with my neighbor Daontaon, this din is composed of a repetition of identical ringing, thrumming, and growling sounds over an indeterminate period of time, which can vary between one week and two months, until it switches to another set of a similar nature.

Next to the clamor of the beasts that live alongside my neighbors—whom, without meaning any offense, could be catalogued as wild animals themselves—other habitual clatter comes from the crashes of demolition and destruction, the slang used by the big boys, the "homies," who by preference use the nocturnal hours to bellow at one another. Then there are the matrimonial spats with accompanying broken glass; the fierce slapping down of the domino tiles; the inescapable vociferations of the drunks, the "businessmen," and the con artists; the chatter of the gossipmongers, both local and urban; the crack of the bat against the ball or the ball against the windows and walls of the building, added to the typical expressions of emotion of a baseball game, almost always boiled down to two words of the popular parlance, or—better said—that of the prison population, which I do not care to repeat.

The topic of smells would be, likewise, a motive for another digression. Nevertheless, I am unable to delve into that in this precise moment, because I can see Daontaon stumbling toward my door with an odd enough look on her face that I decide to invite her in for a cup of coffee.

"Hey there, sweetie, are you gonna open up for me? Sure you will. I've got a hell of a story to tell you."

In actuality, I didn't even have time to unlock the bolt before she started telling me, still standing outside, about the appearance of a "torso" in the Cultural Center's dumpster, that's how she described it: a "torso," without legs, arms, or even a head, a "female torso" apparently.

HERMI

Herminia and Tristan, neighbors since they were kids, were alike as two drops of water, two homonyms, twin gods. In some details they were identical but in others, tenuous, evanescent, they differed. Since childhood, without knowing that they were repeating the game twins played of exchanging identities, they would pretend that each one was the other, to get double doses of treats, skip out on school work, and share boyfriends and girlfriends.

Their physical similarities made it easy for them, once they entered adolescence, to continue their switching of roles. One of Tristan's sweethearts was also Herminia—Hermi's—girlfriend, at the same time and none the wiser. And a leader of the Communist Youths, quite the macho gay-basher, made out with Tristan in the back of the Payret Cinema, without ever suspecting that below the feminine clothing were a set of tools as full and exultant as his own.

They had the same gestures, the same sense of humor, and a secret mode of communication, without words. It was almost like being in love, if the two hadn't rejected that idea as too tacky.

They also agreed upon fundamental ideals. "I detest ambiguities, and I adore ambivalences," affirmed Hermi (or was it Tristan?) in their particular style of making proclamations that were both bombastic and cryptic, especially for the majority of their listeners who ended up feeling lost in limbo for a good while.

But when it came to externals, they tended to complement or even oppose each other. For example, Tristan had an inclination for all that was old; Hermi, for all that was new.

One of the first Philco television sets seen in Havana was the one that Hermi's father bought. From the instant in which the black box lit up in their living room, Hermi began her fascination with the televised image; it was the only thing she would give herself to completely, barely coming up for air to take care of her basic necessities or to deal with the crises of the era. As she matured, she became passionate about reports of happenings anywhere in the universe, and about the concrete reality of daily life, as if she were a newspaperman; and then about commercials, movies, soap operas, shows about cooking or the home, social debates, and even cartoons.

Tristan, on the other hand, felt drawn to black magic, the esoteric, and riddles. He considered the television to be common and preferred to immerse himself in reading about the occult sciences and studies of the great beyond.

Halfway through the sixties they chose different majors at the university. Tristan started in the Literature Department, from which he was expelled at the end of his third year. Hermi chose the School of Architecture, where they would have loved to take her on as a professor but, nonetheless, she decided to leave academic life and make it on her own. She refused to give up her own very refined aesthetic and get into the daily struggle with construction grunts, bricklayers, and cement workers passing themselves off as architects. Neither was she willing to dedicate herself to boxing up prefab housing, nor to providing on-site supervision of the construction of buildings that were ordinary and exactly alike, nor in any way deal with what Tristan called, not to put too fine a point on it, 'stupidity and mediocrity.'

Thanks to her father's connections with a former producer of CMQ, the television channel with the highest ratings in the fifties, Hermi was able to do some coursework in communications and publicity. While still very young she started working in the sanctum of *Radiocentro,* with the dream of doing something new, something life changing, as Rimbaud demanded.

Tristan had gone into his university career already determined to make waves. When one of his classmates asked for his help in the creation of a "Christmas tree" that would be something out of this world, Tristan remembered the melodramatic report of a woman who had been dismembered back in the thirties, published in an old issue of *Bohemia* that his mother had stashed away.

The Christmas tree was set up in the front lobby of the College of Humanities. From its branches, in addition to one rubber—an innocent and unused condom—hung a naked doll, cut into pieces. The scandal was unprecedented.

THE INDIA

Her name was María Antonieta and, after everything that happened, many people thought that it would have been difficult to find a name that better suited her. When she was baptized, looking at her bronzed skin, her almond-shaped eyes, her curly mahogany hair, her relatives criticized her mother for having chosen such an affected name for the girl. Be that as it may, in the community of Saint Leopold, where she was to spend her childhood and teenage years, they never called her by her full name. Maybe it was because the name seemed too pretentious, but whether because of her features or due to the deeply rooted linguistic tradition of identifying oneself by an epithet, nickname, moniker, pet name, alias, or pseudonym, the neighbors took to assigning her various terms of endearment. The girl responded to them much more readily than to her given name, the one that her own mother still insisted on using.

Her mother, Clara Luz, called "the Professor" behind her back because she was so uppity, didn't rub elbows with just anyone, except to practice her emerging profession as a retailer of products that she brought all the way from Caimito in hopes of making a buck. The poor martyred Clara Luz, how she had struggled to make a better life for her daughter. But, despite having studied languages and the technical aspects of the graphic arts, when the other (metaphorical) shoe dropped, she left it all to go door to door with chunks of white cheese, bars of guava paste, and packets of coffee mixed with ground peas (or whatever grain was at hand, to tell the truth) to give her daughter the better things in life. María Antonieta, for her part, born of an unknown or intentionally forgotten father, stood out even as a child, making herself heard as she stomped through the apartment grounds in her wooden sandals.

When the "foreigner" (as those from elsewhere tended to be identified) ran into her in the lobby of the President Hotel, María Antonieta was generally known as The India. Patrick Rivière was the second person to call her "María Antonieta." Poorly pronounced, with an "r" that he drew out somewhat like a growl and the final "a" lost in a strangled whisper, it could be interpreted, however, as the caroling of the archangels.

A dried up, clumsy, grim little man with an unctuous manner, "The Frenchman" (as he soon was called by Clara Luz's neighbors) tied up his greasy mane in a stringy pony tail, which made up for the lack of hair on top by its length. He was a dull sort, truth be known, ignorant of matters of personal hygiene. But—don't forget!—French, straight from Europe itself.

The day that María Antonieta showed off her trophy through the apartment building, her neighbors offered effusive greetings tinged with curiosity. As a matter of fact, Patrick was the first genuine foreigner, flesh and bone, that they had ever come across. A few days later, The Frenchman had installed himself in the room shared by María Antonieta and her mother. Over the following weeks, The India started looking more well-to-do, but without showing off too much.

But…what was that guy doing there in Cuba? Where did he go off to every morning with his little black bag? Why did he act so standoffish? Was he an antique arms collector? Why in the hell did he cook spaghetti with basil? Didn't he like loud music? Did the domino table in the hallway really bother him? Yes, he was a strange sort, very out of place, the way the neighbors saw it. And if that wasn't enough, the people living in the apartments didn't know what exactly had brought him there from so far away.

In consequence, rumors started circulating about duels, and about mysterious deaths that had spurred him to escape from his own country. Ah, France, with her musketeers and criminals, like that Alain Delon in *Purple Noon,* wearing white loafers without socks! You couldn't expect anything good from people like that. But the mild-mannered looks of the foreigner, and his occasional (albeit cheap, to tell the truth) gifts to the neighbors, made them forget their fantastical notions for the moment. María Antonieta's neighbors went so far as to start flattering Clara Luz.

LOLA

From the terrace Lola was able to watch the sun sinking into the west like a ball of fire. The surface of the sea was in flames, and the clouds on the horizon shimmered with shades of orange and violet. Although she wasn't that high up in the building, she still could view flat rooftops throughout Vedado, broken up in different colors like a jigsaw puzzle, with their water tanks, clotheslines, improvised dwellings, air vents and chimney pipes, various types of antennas, and plates of zinc that roofed animals' quarters. Some of the roofs were neat as a pin, and others looked like the aftermath of a bombing. Here and there she could contemplate blotches of green, miniature trees or the fronds of a palm tree that seemed to grow out of the asphalt. Over to her right, peering between the buildings, you could make out the winding path of the Malecón. At night, intermittent flashes of light indicated the site of the Morro lighthouse. During the day, no longer surprised by anything, Lola observed flocks of vultures circling the Focsa skyscraper.

On the low cement wall along the sidewalk in front of her building, she could see Dr. Carvajal setting up each day. Lola watched her surreptitiously. They knew each other enough to say, "Hi, how are you doing," and Lola knew she had taught Spanish grammar for many years at the University. Just as she herself had done, Dr. Carvajal had dedicated her life to her job. In the old days, she could be seen leaving early with a satchel of books and papers; returning late at night dragging her swollen legs, tired and bloated from the long walk between the College and her house. Retired now, an old maid, Dr. Carvajal would sit every morning at the corner, balancing an open box of cigarettes on her knees. She didn't say a word, didn't hawk her wares; she just stayed right there, not moving a muscle, paralyzed with shame, as passers-by bought single cigarettes that Dr. Carvajal sold for a peso each, to supplement the meager pension that didn't stretch to cover all her meals.

Lola was more fortunate. She had a regular buyer in the building who paid her a good price for her entire quota of cigarettes as soon as she bought them with her ration book. With that profit, Lola would beef up her supply of coffee and, once in a great while, she would allow herself the luxury of getting some powdered milk on the black market. Because of her constitutionally good health, she didn't get milk in her daily rations. Although she had become accustomed to not having even a snack in the evening any longer, when she had to go without breakfast it drained all her energy.

Sara had been one of Dr. Carvajal's students. If she saw her now, selling cigarettes on the corner... Lola shook her head to dislodge her negative thoughts. On one occasion, there at Lola's for a visit, Micaela had gone out onto the balcony and noticed her. "That lady over there, she couldn't be, my God, that's not Dr. Carvajal, is it?" Lola didn't know what to say. Micaela went on, furious and desperate. "How is that possible, what are we coming to, isn't there anybody who can do something; that woman gave her heart and soul to the University, and now just look at her..." Micaela, usually so cool and collected, was spewing forth like a volcano, and Lola didn't know what to say to her; she had always preferred to keep quiet, to keep her opinion to herself, to stay out of the middle of things, to not get involved. And that's what she did, one more time. Micaela, walking out onto the terrace, saw the chickens shut up in their coop, shot a glance at Dr. Carvajal in her improvised kiosk, turned her head and spied the flock of vultures. "The world is coming to an end," she said.

Lola preferred to act like she hadn't heard her.

WOMAN WHO TALKS TO HERSELF IN THE PARK

A tremendous hullabaloo, music turned all the way up, dancing frenzies, drums, fistfights, motors roaring, sirens, confusion, mayhem. And then all the buildings burst open as if they were eardrums. And Havana is dying...

MARTIN

He knew that writing about one's own life worked fairly well for some novelists; however, aside from his adventures with groupies like Daontaon, nothing really happened to him. Tossing a handful of honey-roasted peanuts in his mouth to stave off midnight hunger pangs, Martin opened up a book by Borges. The sentence that jumped out at him had an unusually sentimental tone: "I felt what we felt when someone dies, the anguish—now futile—that it would have cost us nothing to have been better people. Man forgets that he is dead, conversing with the dead."

"A dead man that converses with the dead." He chewed pensively on the phrase as he grudgingly nibbled on the overly sweet nuts. Martin felt half dead himself, and his uncle Felix was one of the few people with whom he would have liked to have a little conversation.

He remembered the time that Uncle Felix took him to see what a television was, as unimaginable as if it were a chunk of ice in the jungle. The formula, resuscitated from his memory and written down as such, grated rustily on his nerves and Martin erased it.

When the first television sets came to Havana, they were exhibited like circus acts in the storefront across the street from his grandmother Antonia's house, "Amistad Street, just around the corner from Barcelona" everybody said. Uncle Felix only had to cross to the opposite sidewalk, holding his nephew by the hand, to initiate him into a fascination with what seems to be one thing but really isn't.

"All that glitters is not gold…" It sounded good as a title, an allegory about reality, about fucking appearances.

Martin held on to a few other perturbing memories from the street where he grew up. On that same corner was a bicycle shop, a dive that sold drinks, the H. Upmann tobacco factory, and a "date house." What a euphemism: "date house," meaning that motel destined for illegal or fleeting romances; that was one of the truly classic Cuban metaphors, Martin said to himself, as if he were taking notes for his manuscript. Dates with whores, between adulterers, or even just young lovers without an inch of privacy to themselves; dates that eventually ended up in trouble, knifings, and alcoholic declarations. Sometimes the "persecutor" parked there, another euphemism, the squad car with four gendarmes in their dark blues. The hand-blown glass windows and shutters of the Amistad Hotel remained closed and, as hard as Martin might try to decipher the mysteries of the place at which his grandmother Antonia glared like it was hell itself, he never made out anything exciting behind the wooden slats. Rather, his passion was enflamed on the other side of the hotel walls, in the store window, by those boxes with screens like ice and little people caught inside.

Every morning, Martin went exploring with his Uncle Felix. As they passed by the restaurant 'The Vegetarian,' they made their first stop of the day in order to say hello to the usual neighborhood suspects. Then they would continue on their way toward the corner of San José, where they would make their visit to the pharmacy, always having been given the task of acquiring stomach salts or some other peculiar packet for Grandma Antonia. Across the way was a nightclub, of equally enigmatic nature, especially when its tightly battened hatches would open up, and Martin would make out a frigid darkness that emanated a whiff of some sweet yet troubling scent. On the other two corners of the intersection were the butcher, with his loyal clientele (including Grandma Antonia), and their favorite café, where they would get their daily coffee, served with foamy steamed milk and slices of bread slathered with butter. If they turned right, in the direction of the Capitolio, they would walk right by the Campoamor theater, and crossing Central Park, they would arrive at the building housing the Asturian Center. On the other hand, if they went straight down Amistad Street they would run into San Rafael, Martin's preferred route because of the movie houses, the shiny window displays of the local businesses, and the candy kiosks. Still, almost without fail, Uncle Felix would set them off toward the left, in the direction of Galiano Street, and they would make their way around midday to the Casa Granda bar on Aguila St., with its oyster bar and its fascinating wooden trenchers that butted up against a canal, into which the empty beer bottles rolled without even breaking.

Across from Grandma Antonia's house, two vendors would park their carts spilling over with little manzano bananas, green plantains, American lettuces, oranges, onions, mamey fruits, and those enormous mangos that Martin's mother loved so much. "Come and get'em!" they would call. At midafternoon the ice cream cart would roll up, ringing its little bells, and a bit later came the announcement of "peanuts, get your peanuts," in that anonymous voice that Martin would have recognized anywhere.

Grandma Antonia's home occupied the building's entire second floor. On the terrace, Grandpa Severino had his carpentry workshop; on the lower floor, their neighbor Dolores had rented the rear of the building to a tailor; while in the little space under the stairwell somebody had set up a tiny jewelry shop. Finally, on the left-hand side stood the editorial offices and printing presses of *The Evening News*. Every day, on a precise schedule, the paperboys who peddled the dailies on the streets would come by to pick up their wares, while several peons stacked up the bundles of just-printed papers to load them onto an enclosed truck.

It was an intense mixture of tasks, tools, sounds, and smells that Martin took in as he waited for his favorite time of day to arrive. At last, before even the most daring couples would appear to disappear behind the shutters of Amistad Hotel, Martin, safely hand-in-hand with his indulgent Uncle Felix, would stand and stare at the screens of ice showing Mighty Mouse cartoons, episodes of Boston Blackie, and the fascinating commercials: *Taca taca taca t-shirts from Taca; Jon Chi Rice, Chi's so fluffy, Chi's never sticky, You're gonna love Jon Chi; I get more from Texaco; A slice of Sunday with Hatuey, my friend; Camay beautifies from the first bar; This is Cuba, Chaguito.*

The quirks of his memory folded the tapping of the typesetters and the humming of the sewing machines into the scent of fresh ink on raw paper, the scrape of the saw in his grandpa's workshop, the singsong offers of vegetables and fresh fruits, the bang of cigars being bundled, the sight of the whores that went in and out of the "date house," all together with the discovery of television. Broad but not at all alien is the world, thought Martin, and he penciled it on a scrap of paper, although that too sounded familiar.

ESTELA

Estela watched through the window. It was barely five in the afternoon and night was already falling. The trees of the park had been lit up for a while now by the lampposts' yellow light. She observed the people winding around like lines of ants, then her eyes turned to two bundled up old men who had settled down, backs straight, against the benches of Cartwright Gardens. She tried in vain to work up some sort of emotion. In a way she was happy with her lack of reaction; anything approximating 'gushing' filled her with disgust and disapproval. Luckily, Lucia had already gone home. Estela and Lucia had known each other since they were girls. They had gone to grade school in Güines, and then they had been together in the dorms. Lucia had worked hard to become a scientist of some note, specializing in shells or something like that, although, as far as Estela was concerned, she still acted like a country bumpkin. When the faxes came in warning of Lucia's imminent arrival in London on her way to Manchester, and that she needed Estela's help, just for one night, just a place to sleep, Estela had grudgingly agreed. She already knew that bad things would come of it, but she couldn't say no. To begin with, when Lucia hugged her at the airport, Estela felt a shiver of embarrassment for the condition of Lucia's luggage. It looked worn and outdated. Lucia didn't look much better herself. Maybe she thought she looked the height of elegance, poor thing. You could see that her shoes were cheap from a mile away and that her suit had been poorly fitted by some seamstress working out of her home, maybe Lucia's own mother. What was her name, anyway? She couldn't remember anymore, despite the many weekends that Estela had spent at Lucia's family's house, after they had moved to Havana, while Estela's parents still insisted on living in that wretched little village. Estela felt somewhat resentful about the intruding memories. During the first few months she was in London, her past had seemed close by and then suddenly, abruptly, it had receded, like in a film cut when a scene fades to black, the image disappearing, only to flash back to the present, but without background music. Lucia had hung onto her neck with that sentimentalism that had always been her weak point. Lucia smelt of violet water, the same way she smelled as a girl, and that recollection burst into Estela's heart with a delight that instantly turned to annoyance. Estela surreptitiously looked around to see if anyone she knew was enjoying the scene at her expense but she only saw tourists, businessmen in a rush, and travelers who were not in the least interested in her. Lucia flitted about, looking both happy and nervous to find herself in London. Out of politeness, Estela offered to take her out for a coffee. Fortunately, Lucia preferred to go straight to the house and clean up. As Lucia showered, a curious Estela went through the suitcase left open on the bed in the guest room. She found a family photo framed in cardboard matting. "How many children do you have?" she asked. From the bathroom, Lucia replied that she had two and launched into a monologue about what great kids they had turned out to be, how one played basketball and the other was a genius with languages, and blah blah blah until Estela stopped listening and went to make herself a drink. When Lucia came out of the shower she looked like a new woman, snuggled up in a terrycloth robe as if it were a fur coat, her damp hair wrapped in a towel. "If you want, you can take that robe with you to Manchester," Estela offered. Lucia accepted so naturally that Estela was struck with another incomprehensible backlash of irritation. Then Lucia let out a yelp and ran out onto the balcony. "I can't believe it, I can't believe it!" She cried, pinching herself dramatically, "I can't believe that I'm right here in Bloomsbury, my god!" Estela smiled in spite of herself; Lucia was always such a child, so over the top. Estela stood next to her and looked out at the park alongside her. "Can you believe it, Estela, who would have ever said that we would be here together in Bloomsbury? Do you remember when you wanted to be a writer? We must have read *Mrs. Dalloway* over ten times. Have you written anything else after the…?" Estela noticed how Lucia tactfully left the sentence hanging, although she wasn't quite sure how to decipher the "after" or "the" to which she referred, which of all the "afters" throughout her life Lucia was talking about. That's when Estela knew that this wasn't going to be all peaches and cream. "Letters," she answered jokingly, "lots of letters, lots of documents, and lots of reports." But Lucia had already moved on, as was her wont, to another topic. "Back in those days in Havana nobody slept a wink. Do you remember, Estela?" Estela didn't want to remember anything. "No," she answered drily, "I don't recall, and I don't want to either." Lucia gave her a look, quickly repressing her aggravation, perhaps remembering that after all she was only a guest, and she made an effort to go on chatting, avoid at all costs an irreparable silence between them, though she couldn't stop her voice from taking on a melancholy tone. Estela thought she sounded distant. "Your neighborhood is very pretty," said Lucia, all the enthusiasm gone from her voice.

HERMI

When Hermi's parents decided to emigrate, she elected to stay, to try her luck with the "wretched of the earth," to arm herself with faith in something new. She was left alone in the big old house, full of antiques and family heirlooms left in her care, together with an appreciable bank account in her name. Tristan, fed up with parental misunderstandings, moved in with her and took possession of one of the unoccupied rooms, taking out the ostentatious furniture and stripping the walls, leaving just a single bed and a marble table with two chairs with the air of a convent. There, at peace, he took to collecting rare books, studying various languages on his own—including those no longer spoken—and bringing home an occasional lover. He got up late and went to bed at five in the morning, spending most of his time reading and studying.

Hermi, for her part, transformed her bedroom into a psychedelic study with movie posters plastered all over the walls. She painted her furniture magenta and moved her mattress to the floor. She switched out an oriental paper globe for the teardrop crystal lamp and covered the windows with bamboo shades. Finally, she took the television set and placed it right in front of her bed. Back then, she was painting abstract swaths on linen canvases, doodling sceno-graphic designs, writing screenplays, and watching television. She also got ahold of a newfangled cassette recorder.

Her neighbors didn't look kindly on the changes, the terribly odd music, the traffic of "long-hairs," or "sickies" as they were commonly called, the strange hours and incomprehensible activities that comprised the life led by Hermi and Tristan. They, however, wrapped up in their own worlds, didn't notice that they were turning into suspects.

To top it off, Hermi often showed up accompanied by an older man who wouldn't leave the house until late at night, driving off in a VW Beetle. When a neighborhood commission appeared at Hermi's workplace covertly and denounced her for immorality, they were hoist by their own petard. As it happened, the man was married but he was a party militant and a department head at the TV station where she worked—CMQ. The commission went home with their tails between their legs, albeit committed to clean up the block of undesirables and "blemishes" (another word being bandied around by the press).

A serious sign that things weren't going well was when a friend of Tristan's disappeared, a Math student. At the university nobody had any idea of what had happened to him, and his family knew nothing either. Desperate, his mother went from hospital to hospital, visited police stations, and even the morgue. Nothing, the earth had opened up and swallowed Tomás.

A few weeks later, Tomás called them from the Military Hospital. There he appeared, skinny, shaved bald, covered with mosquito bites, enigmatic, with a hacking cough and a long, deep wound on his leg. He refused to say anything, to give anybody a word of explanation. Except for Tristan, who managed to get out of him that they had taken him to a forced work camp on a farm in Ciego de Ávila, surrounded by barbed wire, where he worked sun up to sun down cutting sugar cane under the watchful eye of armed soldiers. Tomás's brigade had included about a hundred recruits, almost all long-haired young men, some of them Jehovah's Witnesses or members of Gideon's Band. Tomás only told Tristan because they had had plans for that evening, and he had been waiting for Tristan when the men picked him up at the corner of L and 23rd, throwing him in a truck covered in bars. What in the hell was wrong with the world?

"Be on guard!" Tristan had warned him (or was it Hermi?) with one of his archaic, pompous pronouncements, "the enterprise will have been in vain if, on account of weakness or carelessness, one ceased being oneself."

WOMAN WHO TALKS TO HERSELF IN THE PARK

The streets filled with cysts and pustules. And then the potholes became so deep that the city buses fell through them into the fires at the center of the earth. And Havana is dying…

WILLIE

Daontaon took one of the stools from the living room and dragged it to the balcony. She sat down and scanned the neighborhood as though a gang of assassins bent on disemboweling her were going to attack from one of the other balconies. And then she took her own sweet time. The light had faded, and silence enfolded us. The blackout had caused the natives and their audio equipment to fall silent, vanquished for a few hours. The Gothic ambiance was completed with a candle and a kerosene lamp.

"Do you have any idea what kind of day I've had? You couldn't possibly," affirms Daontaon, her face turned into a horrible mask by the flickering candlelight.

"Tell me all about the torso. **All** about it." When the situation requires, I also tend to speak in bold and italics.

"Good god, what a morbid kid you are. A *torso,* a woman's *torso* with its arms and legs cut off, stuck in a sack. I'm trying to remember if there are any movies with something like that."

Daontaon settled down to review her catalog of films. In my case, when it came to mutilations, I only could come up with the scene of the horse's head in the mafioso's bed, The Godfather, part one. It didn't really fit, I fear.

"Humph, I can't think of a single one," Daontaon, annoyed, picked up where she left off a few seconds later. "Like I was saying…a *torso* wrapped up in rags, stuffed into a sack tied up with wire, and left, like it was nothing, right next to the trash bins, at the Cultural Center. It's an *outrage!* Just think, now I am the **principal** suspect."

"Of couse you are…and so am I."

"What do you mean, YOU are too? Kid, don't fuck with me, this is serious." Daontaon seemed offended.

I shrugged my shoulders. I wasn't trying to steal her limelight. After all, like butlers in a mystery novel, whatever happens, I'm suspect. That's what I thought, but I changed the subject:

"And how did they figure out that there was a dead person inside?"

"A *dead woman*," she corrected primly. "Three good-for-nothings, drop-outs from the tech school, the kind that go all day without doing a damn thing, they opened up the package and found themselves face to face with that number. And right then and there the circus came to town! In less than five minutes a patrol car had arrived, and they cordoned off the area. My boy, I can tell you I almost had a heart attack. They put the *torso,* draped with a blanket, in the parking lot. Have you EVER heard of A THING LIKE THAT?"

This time I didn't give her the chance to answer her own question, because the memory stirred like a cat in heat and scratched some fold in my brain where it had been stored away for so long. It was probably thirty years ago that I was on my way to the university on the Number 27. It was noon, and the sun was shining as if nothing perverse could possibly happen. On Línea Street, as we came up to the intersection with E, the bus slowed to a stop because of a roadblock, then started to inch along up to where we could make out through the windows, in the middle of the avenue, a little body covered with a sheet. Everybody was in a tizzy wanting to know what happened. It does seem almost impossible to refrain from sticking one's nose into other people's tragedies; one feels some mystical connection, something along the lines of "if it happened to somebody else, then it won't happen to me." The bus kept picking its way along, and what was occurring down in the street played out in slow motion. I watched as well. What caught my eye was how stunted, how tiny, how helpless the little bundle seemed, at the mercy of the curious. What had happened there? An accident? A crime? A suicide?

"Yes, a long, long time ago."

"You don't say…" murmured Daontaon, surprised, and in truth what she wanted to say was: "tell me everything, tell me **all about it**."

"Do they know yet who the dismembered woman is?" I responded in turn, diverting her gossip-fueled gaze away from the competing corpse.

Daontaon sat thinking about that last question. It was obvious that such a thing had not yet occurred to her. Her shock at the appearance of the cadaver next to the bin where she herself threw out her own garbage, the very existence of the chopped up body, not to mention the police interrogation, had occupied her mind so fully that she hadn't even considered the essential question of the victim's identity.

This is the first time, at least in my presence, that Daontaon has been rendered speechless.

GERTRUDE

You should have seen Havana back then! At our feet, from the 23rd floor of the dorm at 3rd and F, or from the heights of the Tower Bar, lit up with a thousand lights, in all its splendor. It was to die for, do you remember? And the magnificent Malecón, an odyssey that started at the turret of Miramar and stretched to the entrance of the port, with the lighthouse at the Morro fortress shooting out lightning bursts of brightness, at regular intervals as if the city itself was alive and breathing.

If back then somebody had asked me what I wanted to do with

my life, I would have said without any hesitation that I wanted to be a lighthouse keeper. A desert island, its wild jungle surrounded by the sea, by silence; nobody in my sights; no telephone, or meetings, or overfilled buses, or standing in line, or blackouts, and my job would be just that— to light the lamp at night, put it out in the morning, all of my time free to contemplate the panorama in front of me, to read, to think, as the light turned round and round. Like *Robinsina Crusoe*. The idea had come to me when I read *To the Lighthouse* by Virginia Woolf, and without thinking, in the middle of the classroom, I said that I would like to live in a lighthouse. You better believe it. They didn't say a word then, but when the opportunity arose they called me on the carpet and told me "that wasn't a job for a woman." And on top of that, they accused me of being individualistic and put a disciplinary write-up in my file.

Well, they won that one, I never again dreamed about living in a lighthouse.

Coming back to the topic at hand, "don't get lost in the side story," as it was so well put in *The Dialogue of the Dogs*, "and let your intentions be pure, even if your wit is not." Way up there, on the top floor of the Focsa, in the Tower Bar, one could just about manage the illusion of being in a lighthouse, at peace in the dark, in the groove, gazing toward the sea and drinking your *"cubanito,"* rum and tomato juice—the Cuban version of a Bloody Mary. I suspect that lighthouse keepers aren't allowed to "ingest alcoholic beverages." Every place of employment has its own rules. You better believe it. Although some of them end up being rather absurd.

In the dorm at 3rd and F "the girls" were forbidden to enter or leave the building wearing pants, save by special exemption when one was going to do volunteer work in the countryside. Do you remember? Good god, I'm the one telling the story and even I can't believe it. In the face of such a stupid regulation, we were left with no other option than to pull the wool over the eyes of the authorities. To go to the beach, our usual trick was to put on a skirt on top of our pants, roll those up to our knees, or a bit further up like shorts to be more exact, until we got barely half a block away, where right out on Avenue G we would take off the disguise. And coming back from the beach, the same operation in reverse: the skirt again hiding our trousers so we could penetrate the hallowed halls of the dorms. Like in *The Strange Case of Madam Dr. Jekyll and Mrs. Hyde*. As silly as it seemed, it wasn't up for discussion, it was The Rule. And similar to that one, there were so many others, some worse, that forced us to dissemble, to live a double life, to learn how to survive on our wits. *The Cloven Viscountess*.

Doesn't anyone remember any of what happened? At the least, back in those days, we could see Havana from the bar at the Focsa.

DAONTAON

Midmorning, Daontaon got out of bed trying to calculate what all she would do if she only had a week to live. My god, she was going to have to start taking steps; so many dead people and so many depressing situations were about to give her a nervous breakdown. To start off with, she decided to take the day off from work. As she made coffee, she heard a HORRIFYING racket coming down the sewage pipes. Daontaon would not be in the least surprised if a human torso was coming through the plumbing. It was enough to drive you crazy. She knew one thing for sure: before she died, she was going to burn down the entire building.

She sat out on the balcony as she drank her brew and took in at a glance the parcel of weeds in which various circles of trampled earth clearly indicated the movements of the primitives as they played ball. From several of the apartments came early howls, hammer blows, and the din of arguments. During the wee hours, a few of the natives had accumulated a considerable quantity of empty rum bottles, some of them in shards, on the bench beneath the only street light that still had a bulb. Along the path that led to the stairs, some unknowns had forgotten on purpose a few packets of something that smelled like rotten fish. Among the overflowing garbage cans she could easily make out the silhouettes of jumping dogs, although other figures that scrabbled around the revolting contents could be her own neighbors as easily as creatures of any other species.

Right through "center field" she could see Tilingo taking his goats out to pasture. Daontaon couldn't care less one way or the other, but… Ha! More than likely Tilingo ate the grass right along with them.

According to Willie, the number of deviants, idiots, inbreds, crazies, mentally handicapped, deformed, wasters, layabouts, morons, retards, and imbeciles per square foot in their building could be accepted, without a doubt, as a *world record*. Foremost among the bunch, Tilingo, like the majority, had no job and walked around shirtless and in a tattered pair of pants that left his parts showing, his *asshole* that is, to be direct. Tilingo, with his ass out in the open air and his herd of animals, said he had been sent by God. I'm sure.

Truthfully, as long as the topic of religion didn't come up, Tilingo behaved like a peaceful lunatic, but if he caught a whiff of hellfire or heard the beating wings of an angel, he would start to yell warnings about how sinners were going to be punished, provoking both general hilarity and the terrified scattering of his goats.

Over to the right, the "Dog-Killer" came out onto her balcony, a woman known by a variety of nicknames that went along with her varying behavior. Daontaon took it for granted that her "fellow citizen" hadn't bathed since the birth of her youngest progeny, one of the many vandals that hung around the environs with nothing better to do. From her apartment oozed fluids, stagnating during weeks in the hall of the stairway until the laws of physics intervened, making them drip down to the bottom floor through pure gravity.

And did the parade stop there? Well, of course it didn't. Trotting down the stairs was Palacios's grandson. What could he be up to? Nothing good. Despite his youth, he had garnered enough talents to reach third place and head up the waster cadets. He tended to play second-in-command to the "Dog-Killer," although his favorite way to pass the time was to beat up his grandmother.

Completing the ranks, old "Skin and Bones" from the second

floor snuck into his house, a package tucked secretively under his shirt. Daontaon found it beyond her to memorize all their names, but she *knew* that it was that "Skin and Bones" who—by the skin of his teeth—had escaped a guilty verdict for taking bottles of 90% alcohol from the Polyclinic and who, at the moment, made a living doing odd jobs in the neighborhood and robbing any old thing—such as screwdrivers or mini handsaws—from the homes of those incautious enough to let him in. Although, if you wanted to talk about thieves... Un-fucking-believable! In this building they'd even steal a rock.

Daontown shivered. Somebody had just walked over her grave. She was utterly sure that some of her neighbors slept in coffins and went out to drink blood at night. It wouldn't surprise her in the least if a serial murderer was living in their midst, even the very DISMEMBERER. She agreed with herself that, even given the danger of overusing all caps, this time they were perfectly in order.

Daontaon finished up her coffee and closed the balcony door with a bang. Outside the other specimens were coming out of their test tubes, and she didn't want to lay an eye on them. She preferred idiots, thieves, and even killers, to **posers.** And you better believe there were tons of them in her building. Ha. Just ask her!

WOMAN WHO TALKS TO HERSELF IN THE PARK

From the tar in potholes and the grease of car engines, a creamy fluid emerged and gushed along the streets. Then it overflowed the sidewalks and rose up to cover the gardens of the houses. And Havana is dying...

THE INDIA

Before long, the engagement of the Frenchman and The India was announced. To be more exact, the marriage, because they weren't fiancées for very long at all. From the time the question was popped until the day of the ceremony, barely five weeks had gone by. In the face of such a rushed wedding, there were, of course, a few malicious comments about her being pregnant, looking for European citizenship, or in some other way having lost her virtue.

The civil ceremony having occurred without much to-do, they set themselves up in a rented apartment (illegally, if you want the truth) that was the best part of the deal for the new couple.

If nobody in the tenements knew Patrick Rivière's past, at least they knew plenty about María Antonieta's: prostitution, scams, and public scandals. Nevertheless, at twenty-something years old, she still maintained a few vestiges of innocence. She was amazed by the froufrous that the Frenchman gave her; she dreamed about rocking a blue-eyed baby; and she held out hopes of getting her mother Clara Luz out of the slums for good, placing her in a "little house of her own," the dream of every Cuban from the days of the Candado soap commercial: "It's your house, mommy, all yours."[10]

The Frenchman and The India, to all outward appearances, got along together in perfect harmony. Neither one raised their voice more than the other, nor were they disgustingly sweet. It looked like they were well on their way to becoming one of those couples that grow old together and end up surrounded by a passel of grandchildren, the embers of their past misadventures cooled into a routine life. Clara Luz, still nicknamed "the Professor," left off her black market trading in foodstuffs and opened up a center (a very tiny one, to be honest, given the tight quarters where she lived) for spiritual consultation.

However, without warning, their downfall already had begun its course.

A few days before the macabre discovery of the torso, a woman's forearm, carefully shaved, wrapped in brown paper and tied with wires joined together with some fairly strange knots, was dug up by a dog out of an abandoned lot in Guanabo and dragged to somebody's back patio.

---

[10] During the promotion, any Candado soap bar wrapper could be one of the "big winners" of a new house.

Once the police force was informed, they made the decision to keep it quiet, so as not to unduly frighten the population. As a matter of fact, the crime roster had been eradicated from the newspaper at least thirty years prior.

Around that same time, the Frenchman, his sparse hair in disarray and a wild look on his face, showed up in María Antonieta's mother's room to announce the disappearance of his wife. The only clue consisted of a hand-written note with spelling errors (to add insult to injury) in which she made known that she was taking off with a lover. An important bit to add—they were leaving in a boat, destination unspecified, presumably headed north. Hearing such a story, Clara Luz attempted to find the fugitives with a few pleading phone calls to her cousin Cusita, who lived in Hialeah.

Since her calls resulted in no information whatsoever, they were left with no other option than to surmise (if the Frenchman's testimony was to be trusted) that The India and her lover had been lunch for the sharks inhabiting the Gulf waters, predators well used to such gastronomic treats.

Back at headquarters, the investigation around the female forearm led the authorities to believe that they were dealing with a particularly tricky case. In the initial forensic analysis of the severed extremity they found signs of violence that allowed them to infer a fierce struggle between victim and murderer before he was able to consummate the crime. They were able to prove, moreover, that the fragment of the cadaver had been separated from the body by a wide flat object with a pointed tip, such as an antique sword.

Then they found the torso wrapped in brown paper and tied with the now familiar wires, inside a bag on a mountain of garbage (accumulated over the years, truth be known) next to the Alamar Cultural Center. Officers of the peace were called out on an emergency basis, even though the difficulties identifying the body made capturing the killer that much more challenging. As usual, the press was silent on the issue. *Blabbermouth Radio,* however, took over, the result being that within a few hours everybody in Havana was aware of the case of "the woman chopped into pieces."

As other bits continued to come to light, it was hard to accept that those bad-smelling hunks of flesh could ever have been the lovely India.

On the other hand, nobody had bought the story of The India running off with her supposed partner in crime. It wasn't that she was past having an affair, a fling, or any other sort of adulterous activity (to be blunt about it), but rather that she had seemed too thrilled with her European treasure chest to have abandoned it and tried her luck on the high seas. What's more, her mother insisted, María Antonieta was phobic of water, didn't know how to swim, and she had never even wanted, on account of her terror of the ocean, to go sunbathing in Varadero.

Many years before, Clara Luz had gone with a neighbor of hers to identify the body of the woman's daughter, found dead of unknown causes. On top of the cot and covered by a throw, the body of the young girl was laid out in a somber room of the Calixto García Hospital. Her neighbor recognized the girl's face and fainted. Clara Luz was there for hours sitting with her in the Emergency Room until the poor lady got herself together a little. Then, in an act of piety, she had helped the woman dress her dead girl. Clara Luz remembered, as if it had been only yesterday, the girl's sweet little feet, without a blemish on them, with her toenails nicely trimmed, as she pulled onto them a pair of white school uniform socks before they closed the coffin. Not since then had anything like this happened in their tenement.

When they heard the rumor of the appearance of a female torso, her neighbors took it for granted that it belonged to the disappeared India, and that the other story had just been a fiction created by the bloody foreigner, who at this point they were pretty sure was a CIA spy or an official Nazi, at the very least.

YUYA

Yuya says that the second time she encountered the wandering soul of the Haitian, it was far away from where he had first appeared, in no less than the tiny park on Dragones Street, across from the Police Station.

Every afternoon, Yuya liked to go out on a stroll with Lalita, starting at the dimestore on Galiano. In the cafeteria there they would have a sandwich and a malted milk for lunch, and afterwards they would browse among the counters and then end with their obligatory visit to the second floor, where lamps were sold. There she would be waiting for them, Luisa, Yuya's old neighbor from the tenement and her only friend, dressed impeccably in white and with a handkerchief, open like a multicolored flower, tucked into the breast pocket of her blouse, the accessory that distinguished top level employees. Luisa managed to perfection a way of receiving Yuya's daily visit while continuing to attend to her customers with a smile that showed her flawless teeth. When the three would end up on their own, Luisa would perform her pretend magic trick, pulling from her handkerchief a piece of candy for her goddaughter Lalita.

Lalita, enthralled by the luminaries, would drift among them, convinced that they came from a fairy castle, as Yuya and Luisa chattered for a while about life and its miracles.

Yuya says that then she would walk holding Lalita's hand, gazing for a while at the various displays, until they made it to Zanja Street, very close to Shu's terrace. Nevertheless, Yuya would draw out their walk, enjoying the act of strolling along the busy main artery of the barrio with its scents of Chinese unguents and bittersweet spices, with the kiosks selling fried pork rinds, fresh fruit ice cream cones, and oranges peeled by a machine that took off their rind in one serpentine roll. They would pass through the colonnades of the winding streets (where in olden times the afternoons were filled with working women waiting for their clients), enjoying the paper lanterns shining like little nocturnal suns on any holiday—especially for the celebration of Chinese New Year; always greeted respectfully by the Asian pedestrians who moved aside as they walked by.

When she would cross Manrique Street, says Yuya, she was never able to stare openly at the intriguing building of the Shanghai Theater from the sidewalk. She would have given anything to be able to go in, even one single time, to see the show that was "for men only." It even occurred to her to disguise herself in some of Shu's clothing. The main problem was her bountiful bust, as her long hair easily could be fashioned into a braid and since many of the men sported one equally as long, it wouldn't have called attention to her.

Despite everything, the Shanghai Theater, that inscrutable place, remained a forbidden cloister.

Sometimes on their treks Yuya would take them down Dragones Street, narrow and packed with everything under the sun. From time to time they would run across the neighborhood eccentrics, like "Fu Man Chu," the old man who talked to himself and looked just like her old *Chinito of the Charada,* or they would take a rest across from the entrance way where students went in and out of the San Alejandro School of the Arts. Yuya says that she would have liked to study there; she loved the smell of the oil paints, the varnishes, and the fresh new paper. And although they never bought anything, she and Lalita would visit The Arts, just as if they were experts in the tools and materials the shop sold.

Three or four times a week, Yuya would get ahold of a pound of prime ground beef for *picadillo,* Shu's favorite food, in the butcher shop at Campanario and Dragones. Yuya says that Lalita felt an incomprehensible fascination in seeing the raw meat coming out of the tiny holes of the grinder, turned into long red tubes like floppy fresh noodles. At the market on that corner, Yuya bought capers and twenty-five cents of olives in a paper cone, both destined for the *picadillo,* and a chocolate bar for Lalita. In the bar across the street, they had one of those old Victrolas, and this one in particular was always playing a song by Beny Moré, "mi son, Maracaibo, para que tú lo bailes."[11] In a corner of the bodega, an old man ground corn, cranking a handle that wouldn't stop squeaking. From one of the upstairs apartments came the strains of a piano, sometimes an

---

[11] "My song, Maracaibo, for you to dance to."

entire piece played beautifully; other times, the scales being butchered over and over by a beginner. Yuya says that the memory of this combination of musical sounds always ends up making her cry.

On that same route, they would cross in front of the High School where her progenitor had studied English at continuing education night school classes. Although she had never known her mother, Yuya says that sometimes she had the impression that she was standing in the doorway at home, just watching her and Lalita.

When they would arrive at the small neighborhood park, they bought a strawberry snow-cone and rested on a bench under the shade of the trees before starting on their way back home. According to Yuya, that time she saw the Haitian in the form of a dying dog whose head was that of the old black man.

Yuya interpreted it as a warning, and knew that the moment had arrived for her to stop her dealings with the *Bolita* and *Charada*. She decided to switch to an occupation that didn't entail so many risks, so she turned her talents to the interpretation of dreams and other cabalistic ephemera.

DAONTAON

"Is Daontaon a Chinese name?" her new boss Braulio asked her, playing at being cool, cultured, and interesting.

"Unh unh," she shook her head and didn't say anything, leaving it all up to him.

"Wow, how strange is that...how did your parents come up with it?" insisted Braulio.

"From a song," and Daontaon waited for her new supervisor to fall into the trap himself. Ha. And that's exactly what happened.

"You don't say. Look, why don't I take you out to eat, and you tell me all about it?" Braulio continued, moving closer to the chair where Daontaon had settled: "Listen, don't you think that we could do some really great work here? More cultural activities for the people... I want you to be my right hand man, do you get my drift? In finding musical talent, and such."

Daontaon looked at him with one eyebrow raised. Busted. Another **poser.** They always had the same inspiration at the beginning, and later everything would go to *shit,* pardon the French.

"This afternoon?" he asked.

"This afternoon I have a meeting at the municipal building."

"Let somebody else go in your place." The new boss went back and sat down behind his desk. "Take the rest of the day off, and around three I'll swing by your place to pick you up…just jot down your address right here for me."

Daontaon wavered. Out of the corner of her eye she looked at the new boss and in a flash she catalogued him as inoffensive, easy to manipulate. Inexperienced, no doubt, and *married,* that was the icing on the cake, he wouldn't make things difficult for her. Ha. Another idiot like that guy Martin, her neighbor. This one, Braulio, at least he'd treat her to an expensive meal in some restaurant. So, she took his agenda and wrote down the address of her building and her apartment number.

"It's called "Siberia;" everybody knows me there," explained Daontaon.

An uproar on the stairs of the Cultural Center interrupted their conversation. Three dudes, classic types from the unwashed masses, were having it out over a topic that made no sense at all, at least not to Daontaon.

"That's white faggot music!" shouted a tall black man with bleached nap, the tendons in his neck standing out like purple cords. "Racist!" furiously replied a redhead whose own possibly light skin hid underneath numerous layers of dust, grease, and grime. A third, his ethnic affiliation impossible to discern beneath his layers of clothing, yowled improprieties indecorous enough to bring a blush to the cheeks of a stevedore working the docks. A few of the baby-faced painters from the community workshop laughingly egged them on. The new boss didn't seem phased at all. He swaggered out of the office and, like magic, the row turned into an amiable chat among the four of them about the last night's baseball game.

Daontaon said goodbye with a smile which Braulio, pleased with himself, returned with one of his own..

Ugh, at least she could manage to take a little nap after lunch. She had been up all night because of a HORRIBLE nightmare about killer asteroids. A rain of meteorites, balls of rock, fell from the sky onto her building, and nobody was getting out of it alive, not even the kitchen cat.

Oh my god, if she didn't get out of Alamar and soon, she was going to end up crazy or *dismembered.* She had to "play her cards right" with this new boss. Milk him. Spin a fine web. You never know…right? Ha.

WOMAN WHO TALKS TO HERSELF IN THE PARK

Thunder and lightning. In the middle of the enormous blackout the entire firmament lit up, the north winds howled in fury, and three thousand rays of lightning struck at once. And with that the city exploded like fireworks. And Havana is dying…

LOLA

Lola was listening, to her dismay, to a repulsive radio program about female orgasms. It wasn't the topic that bothered her, rather the comic bent to the script and, more than anything, the comments made by the creature who hosted the program. She turned the dial and was hit by the rhythms inundating the sound spectrum of the city, somebody who was said to be "all the rage." Ridiculous and incomprehensible for Lola. She shut off the radio and closed the glass doors to the terrace to dull the jangling noise of the street. She was getting old.

She only had one chicken left, and Micaela still hadn't come by to visit. Last week, at least, she had received a letter from Sara. A very lovely Christmas card. When you opened it, out came a little metallic rendition of "Jingle Bells." Lola opened it over and over, even though the season was long past; the mail service being so slow that the card hadn't arrived until the beginning of September. It didn't say much about Sara, but there was her tiny handwriting, wishing her a happy new year. Lola would have preferred a real letter, a photo, but nevertheless she made do with the card.

Dr. Carvajal had died of a heart attack the week before. When Lola stopped seeing her, selling single cigarettes out at her usual spot, she speculated that something must have happened to her. Yesterday they had found her dead. She had been lying there dying, alone in her apartment, for over three days. The police had to break down the door to get in, after the neighbors had sounded the alarm on account of the stench.

Lola figured it was better that way, after all, as it would have been worse if she had lived but ended up handicapped, immobile. Who would have taken care of her? Lola wished for the same end, maybe a bolt of lightning that would split her in half all at once, because she never wanted to go through what her downstairs neighbor was suffering now. She had been bedridden for two years, and her family barely did anything for her. The reek of urine reached all the way up to the fourth floor and sometimes in the middle of the night you could hear them yelling and cursing.

What's more, she couldn't stand the thought, not that, please God, of somebody else going through hardships on her account. Inevitably, Lola's bad times were each inevitably associated with a face. The third one on the list had her mother's face from the morning of her death. She had been in a coma for so many days that her parting had felt like a relief; finally, their long-extended crusade was over. Lola just sat there by the bed, stunned, not knowing what to do. After thinking about it for what seemed like forever, she decided to go and ask her next-door neighbor for help. Lola doesn't know where she found the strength to pretend; she acted as if she believed her mother was still alive. She had heard so many horror stories about endless red tape, how it could take hours to officially declare someone dead when it happened in their own home, so she opted for a ruse, a fraud, a sinister pantomime. The guy from next door situated her mother's limp body, still warm, like a marionette with flopping limbs, next to Lola in the back seat of his car, and he sped the two of them to the hospital. Throughout the ride, Lola put her arm around her mother's shoulders, as she had so many times before, and as she held her up for the last time, she rested her mother's lifeless head gently against her chest.

The charge doctor, after taking her vital signs, pronounced her dead. Faced with the young man's sympathetic gaze, Lola felt her face flame with shame and dismay. Although it wasn't that old lie that continued to torture her today.

Her mother's face, pallid and uncovered, as she lay, waiting for autopsy, on a rusty gurney in the emergency room hallway, invaded Lola's mind whenever she thought about death. Lola had watched her mother on the gurney from her seat on the bench and not even once had it occurred to her to pull the sheet—or something—over her face. The nurses, doctors, janitors, emergency room patients, continuously walked by her body. And Lola, she reproached herself for it now, had never even thought to drape a simple handkerchief over her face, as her mother— who had always been so prim and proper—would have wished.

Yes, they were hard times. With each disaster it seemed like the world was going to come to an end, and that nothing worse could happen. But Lola was starting to learn that the world was not coming to an end, or at least not in the way she had envisioned, such a long way from this slow, torturous, flow of ending.

MICAELA

Last night, Micaela had had another terribly obvious dream about her Aunt Candita. Candita, dressed in her yellow silk robe, the one covered in purple lilies, had rooted around in the trash bins on the corner until she found the fragments of her broken china cup. With no transition, there she was in Lola's own room, in that absurd house coat, the shattered porcelain cupped in her hands, and she was demanding that Micaela put it back together, that she glue the pieces. "It is our past, Micaela," she was saying, "fix it, any way you can."

Micaela awoke feeling melancholy. Her life choices had ended up making her a failure. When she looked back, in hindsight all she could see was history razed to the ground. Everything, everything had been ground underfoot: her dreams, her hopes, her family, her beliefs. Her past already lay buried by a degrading and boring present.

Before leaving the country, Candita, her aunt, had left Micaela some of her family treasures: unrecognizable portraits of the family; a beautiful serving spoon; a set of Baccarat stemware, covered with dust in the dining room china hutch; some clothes that Micaela had remade over and over until by now they had been cleaning rags for a hundred years; a picture of *The Last Supper* with Jesus and the Apostles in silver bas relief, an ugly fright she had hidden away in some closet; a gold chain with a medallion of the *Virgen de Caridad del Cobre* and a pair of diamond earrings, pawned back in the day for some certificates you could use to shop in the foreign currency shops and which had barely stretched far enough for Micaela to buy an electric fan and a coffee pot; and then there was that porcelain china cup which, in shards, had ended up in the trash.

And Aunt Candita? She hadn't heard anything but, whatever the case, she still was among the living. Or dying little by little in the distance, Micaela told herself. She'd finally finish dying all the way when word came of "what's new," as people tended to phrase it, using that strange term to announce anything novel, including death. When the famous passed to the great beyond, Micaela thought to herself, word spread immediately. Ordinary people, like her, stayed alive a while longer. Her family had only found out about great-grandma's death in Galicia twenty years after the fact. In all that time, Micaela's grandfather had kept on writing her dutiful letters, carefully recounting everything about Cuba, his offspring, his day-to-day life. Micaela, who had been a little girl at the time, was happy that her grandpa had continued to have his mother for all those extra years, and that the anguish of having been orphaned had come to him on the QT; like reading an old newspaper whose headlines had been long replaced by others, fresher and more urgent. But Micaela was never really sure if that false extension of life constituted good luck or bad. Dr. Carvajal had stayed "alive" until three weeks after her burial. Micaela had continued to imagine her in her covert sales of cigarettes on the corner, humiliated and beaten. She had been killed by Lola's telephone call announcing what had happened.

Also thanks to Lola, Micaela found out that the people who lived next to Dr. Carvajal had thrown all of her papers into the dumpster—including her photo albums and even her library. Micaela wasn't able to get to sleep all night. In spite of herself, she couldn't shake the image of those savages violating the defenseless secrets of the dead woman, the destruction, the loss of valuable books. All in all, it would have been better if Dr. Carvajal had thrown all of her keepsakes into a ditch herself, rather than a bunch of strangers doing it. She felt a stabbing pain nestle into her chest, just next to the pain of her impotence and her solitude.

When she finally managed to fall asleep, almost at dawn, that's when Aunt Candita showed up with her flowered robe and broken cup, asking her to do the impossible.

HERMI

Mocking, unpredictable, tortured, and brilliant; Hermi went over like a lead balloon at Channel CMQ. She laughed at everything and never learned to recognize danger. She barely noticed the suspicions that she was raising and believed completely that her colleagues were on her side. She liked what she was doing and although she ran into a few obstacles here and there, she managed to slip out of the devil's grip time after time.

Sticking her nose in where she had no business being, Hermi proposed innovations in the stagecraft and rewrote a few scripts that, with her modifications, lent an air of renewal to the routine dramatic programming. She captured the fancy of the viewing audience with the production of a musical. She got to the office before anyone else and was the last to go home; she floated from office to office, proposing ideas, offering her opinion; and, according to office gossip, she did what she darn well pleased. "She's a rogue operator," someone said, with a somewhat critical tone that Hermi didn't catch. Her days were numbered, but there was no way she could have known. Nobody made it their job to warn her, not even the guy with the VW.

While she was subtly weaving her own downfall, Hermi took classes in English and French at the Language Institute; she signed up for circulation privileges at the National Library; and she became a member of the Cinemateca. Week after week she would accompany Tristan to the debates held by the University Cine-Club at the Varona Theater, as well as to the play rehearsals at the Tespis Room. Somehow she still had enough time to comply, to the letter and with a smile on her face, with all her political obligations, volunteer shifts, and the nocturnal guard rounds in the neighborhood.

Her parents sent her several sheets of drawing paper and a box full of brushes and oil paint in tubes. With a magnificent Russian camera, Hermi cultivated a hobby of making photographic portraits of daily life in Havana. Abusing her bank account, she filled her bookshelves with a complete set of Aguilar Press imprints from the Modern Poetry store and, for good measure, added a couple of volumes of an encyclopedia of world art.

Among the perks offered by library membership was the opportunity to take out on loan reproductions of well-known paintings. Hermi carted home a different work every month, sometimes classical and sometimes contemporary. One of her favorites, Manet's *Luncheon on the Grass*, especially intrigued her. The painting showed a country landscape with two nude women, their modesty preserved by the painter, and two men dressed in suits and ties who projected a Bohemian essence despite that. Hermi was bothered by the relaxed look of their bodies, the overturned basket of fruit, and, in particular, the intense gaze of one of the women, who stared right at the camera lens, or the artist, or whomever stopped to look at the scene. What did that gaze mean?

In a notebook of lined paper with an orange cover, Hermi would jot down her plans for the future: study Russian, have an exhibit of her own paintings, direct a film, visit the Louvre, learn to play guitar, write a book on Cuban art. Devour the world in all its diversity!

WOMAN WHO TALKS TO HERSELF IN THE PARK

Here, there, and everywhere popped up little fire sprites, who flamed, scorched, and burnt to a crisp everything in their paths. And then the whole city turned into a mountain of ash. And Havana is dying...

MARTIN

He was still in a devil of a mood. He had set aside the whole day for writing, and he couldn't escape feeling obtuse, stuck. Closed up in his room, windows shut despite the heat, he still could hear the continuous chirping of Tilingo's flock of chickens. The constant *peep peep peep* and occasional screeches that made him cringe, kept him from concentrating. As hard as Martin tried to trace the nostalgic atmosphere of a glorious childhood, he couldn't manage to think of anything but sickness, misfortune, and unexpected deaths.

Memory, his at least, was doing whatever it fucking well pleased. The characters manhandled him and pushed him toward worrisome paths, to say the least. Among so much rambling around with his great-uncle Felix, how was it possible that the only stroll that would come into his head was that one. Although to be perfectly honest, one couldn't really call it a "stroll."

It was dusk on Christmas Eve. Martin had suddenly been seized with the desire for a toy, a complete whim at that hour, the fire truck that they had for sale at the toyshop on Galiano. Among Martin's vague contemplations, this recollection popped up with insufferable precision, particularly given the effort that it normally cost him to go into detail about anything of undisputable importance; now he had the futile vision of a red plastic toy truck, with a tank for water and a hose that sprayed it out in imitation of the authentic fire-fighting contraptions. A key wound it up, and it would ramble a few feet forward, blaring its siren and flashing its revolving, blood-red light. It was put through its paces behind a glass showcase by a smiling Santa Claus, who talked over a telephone with the kids that hung out on the street along with Martin, watching the marvels and mentally putting together their list of wishes for the Three Wise Men. Martin feared that such an extraordinary piece of machinery would be given by the Wise Men to another little boy, better behaved than he was.

The family troupe had already started arriving at Grandma Antonia's house. The Christmas tree glittered with multi-colored balls and garlands of lights that flickered on and off, beneath a delicate white blanket of artificial snow that Martin's mother called "angel hair." At its base stretched out the miniscule Nativity with tiny figures that recreated the scene in Bethlehem, cardboard mountains where the sheep were grazing, the growing crops made of green paper mache, the lake a round piece of mirrored glass and the river suggested by a shiny sheath of blue satin cloth. Martin was fascinated by the bridge where a fisherman sat, every year in the same position, catching a fish that flopped motionless in the air. More than the camels or the manger, Martin loved that little fisherman statue leaning back on one foot, back arched in the act of bringing the little bitty fish to land, in miniature porcelain perfection.

The scent of roasted ham and black beans mingled with the murmur of the festivities. On a buffet in the living room, Martin's mother had set out plates of nougat from Alicante and Jijona; a dish of olives; various cheeses on a silver platter; and a basket of pecans, hazelnuts, figs, and dates. Grandma Antonia stood vigil over the stuffed turkey. The men of the family quietly drank their wine. His aunts were singing, along with a record album by Pedrito Rico, "my Pekinese puppy…"

Even though the long awaited moment of sitting down for dinner was rapidly approaching, Martin insisted on going out to buy the little fire truck, maybe because it was another perfect miniature, just as fascinating as the fisherman on the bridge. Uncle Felix ended up giving in, as always, and they set out walking from Grandma Antonia's house, going down Amistad Street before turning at the corner of San Miguel, which ran up to the side of the toy shop.

At that moment his mind jumped, leaving a blank spot in his memory, and Martin now saw himself on his way back with the boxed toy, holding Uncle Felix's hand, walking up Galiano, which was ostentatiously illuminated with shiny Christmas ornaments strung across the avenue. There on Galiano they would pass the office building of CitiBank, where Martin's father worked. When they crossed in front of its gates, Martin turned around to look back at them. There was a group of beggars sitting on the steps in front of the bank entrance; a mother, three children, and a baby in the arms of a little girl. They were always there, skinny as rails and covered in filth; the ragamuffin children squatting on their haunches, and their mother, her head down and her hand outstretched. Martin had gotten used to their presence, to giving them a few pennies and moving on. But this time they surprised him. Were there really beggars on Christmas Eve too? Didn't they have anywhere to go on that night, which for Martin was so special? Until that moment, Martin had been so happy with his fire truck in his arms; Uncle Felix's sure hand showing him the way; his family waiting for him to start their dinner; the Nativity with its little figurines, plagiarizing life.

When they got to the house, Martin threw the toy into a corner and ran to recount what he had seen. His Grandma Antonia hugged him without a word, and he stayed there in search of some consolation. "What is going to happen to them, Grandma, who are they?" insisted Martin. "Some of the *Señor's* poor children," responded Grandma Antonia evasively. "Which *Señor*?" asked Martin, almost yelling, "How can there be a *Señor* that abandons his children on Christmas Eve?" And that's where the memory brusquely ended.

Last week on Sunday, Martin had been invited by some German colleagues, a married couple, to go to Santa Maria beach. Finally they had been able to shrug off the accumulated problems of the week before. The sea was delicious, the company good, and, to top it all off, he was drinking a cold beer. Then the woman approached. She stood out from the other beach-goers by the odd way she was dressed; her face was contorted in a grimace; and she walked with one arm tucked close to her body. With a guttural sound she asked for a "*peso*" and added, sounding ashamed, that she suffered from an ailment that had left her "like that." And now she needed a *peso*. A *peso* or a dollar?, was the question that the Germans asked wordlessly, with a glance. Martin took out a five-peso note from his wallet, but the woman wouldn't take it. "A *peso*," she insisted, almost in tears, "one *peso*." Martin didn't have a fucking single *peso*, much less a dollar, in case he had wanted to give that larger donation. The woman walked off, her head bobbing, without accepting his five *pesos*, and the mystery stayed floating along the beach.

A little boy who was pretending to fish in the sand made the same movement of that little porcelain fisherman in his Grandma Antonia's Christmas Nativity, and Martin remembered the fucking fire truck and his question about what kind of *Señor* could it be that would abandon his own children. From that day on he hadn't been able to get it out of his head.

ESTELA

When Estela left Lucia at the station so she could take the train to Manchester, she knew they wouldn't see each other again. The day before she had given in to her friend's childish whims. Lucia had apologetically confessed that she had two secret desires. One was to cross Abbey Road just like on the record cover and take a photo in front of the Apple mural where the Beatles gave their last concert on the terrace. Lucia had smiled at the camera and raised two fingers spread in the "V" for victory. The same places all the idiotic tourists wanted their pictures taken, Estela said to herself, with resignation. Secondly, to go to Highgate Cemetery to visit Karl Marx's tomb. When it came to Estela and Oscar, it had never entered their mind to go there, despite their more than ten years in London. As they strolled through the cemetery, a squirrel ran up a tree. Lucia pointed her ancient Kodak camera and tried to capture the image of the squirrel with its brilliant eyes. From what she said, and to Estela's surprise, "this was the first squirrel of her life!" With the exception of a few such comments, they didn't talk at all during their jaunt. Almost any given topic seemed touchy, not to mention that anything could set off Lucia's verborrhea, her ingenuous passion for every detail. At least she didn't ask to go shopping, in which case Estela would have been forced to invent some excuse. When Lucia hugged her, before boarding her train, Estela mentioned dully that she must be sure to call when she got back from Manchester. Lucia responded, "sure," without much conviction. Estela waited until the train pulled away, and that was that. Mission accomplished. When she got back to her office she found a message from some guy named Emilio who had a message for her from her father. Estela felt herself grow weak at the thought: another Cuban, another set of whims, what would this one want, to visit the house of Sherlock Holmes on Baker Street? Do a Jack the Ripper walking tour through Whitechapel? Visit Madame Tussaud's Wax Museum? Shop at the Duty Free stores? No, no, no. It was too much. Estela was not about to keep on wasting her time with this kind of foolishness. By no means was she going to allow her own life to get screwed up if all the Cubans on the island decided to pass through London and give her a call. Rrrring, rrrring, went the telephone, and Estela herself took the call. There was the Cuban. "Yes, speaking," agreed Estela, "oh, thank you so much, but the truth is that I have very little time, I can only see you for a few minutes, I work close to the university, we could meet…yes, getting there is very simple, do you have a map of the subway system on you? Good. Where are you staying? You can take the Piccadilly line straight here, the blue line, that one, northward bound, yes, going up. But first you need to take the

Central line, yes, the red one, and transfer at Holborn. No, what do you mean you are going to get lost, not at all, it's really quite easy, even the first time you take the subway, you'll see, and your stop, after you make the transfer, is going to be Russell Square. That's where you are going to get off, and I'll be waiting for you, that's right, there in the subway station. Great. At twelve noon, and for sure you won't get lost. Ciao!" When Estela hung up, she realized that they hadn't made a plan for how to recognize each other but, no matter, she would be able to make out the Cuban without a single hint. By noon it was drizzling hard and she picked him out immediately: the only man without an umbrella or an overcoat, just one of those thin Russian jackets, soaked through with freezing cold rain. The guy Emilio was shivering and looked scared to death by his first trip on the subway. There were little cafés all around, with central heating, warm drinks, and pastries, but Estela figured that the Cuban would be short on cash, and she couldn't go on spending her own money on every Tom, Dick, or Harry that came through there; so she walked up to him and, without letting him get a word in edgewise, standing in the middle of the station, she made it clear that she was in a big hurry and was sorry that she couldn't really spend any time with him, perhaps some other time. "Don't worry, I don't want to be a bother," the Cuban apologized, shamefaced, "I'm only here for a few days for a conference and then I'm going back to Havana; I brought you this package from your father, I didn't know if you wanted to send him anything…" Estela blinked and didn't say a word, more than a little flustered. The Cuban placed an envelope in her hands and said goodbye. Estela watched him disappear, walking toward the subway cars, and she put away the little packet from Cuba into her purse.

WILLIE

Big Mike is the head recalcitrant of the neighborhood. At the least provocation, he lets loose talking about how things were under Machado, when even the cows were starving but, no matter how bellies growled, never, he declares without anyone asking, never ever had there been such a hillbilly mentality, such thievery, such bad manners in all of Havana, and that being poor was no excuse for taking things that didn't belong to you. His mother, may she rest in peace, Big Mike's, I mean, earned a living as the building manager of a tenement on Animas Street, where she didn't put up with a bit of this chicanery, or foul language, or turning the place into a pig sty. Everything shone, the place was so clean you could eat off the floor; if somebody forgot a tool or dropped a dollar bill on the shared patio, there it would stay until its rightful owner appeared.

Since Tilingo has nothing better to do when he isn't taking his goats out to pasture, he sits and listens to him, so Big Mike takes advantage of the opportunity to harangue everyone else around and to tell them how to run their lives. Although nobody pays him the least bit of attention. "Feeble-minded old man, why doesn't he just lie down and die already." "Who does he think he is?" "Who died and made him owner of this building, anyway?"

And when Big Mike left his house to go to the bakery, people would throw rocks at his windows and sprinkle gasoline on his plants. What a model community!

Daontaon opines that Big Mike talks too much, being the *only one* who protests about everything. But you have to admit, a lot of people think the same way as Big Mike and just bite their tongues for fear of the consequences.

"Am I right, or am I right? Of course I am. Kid, all of those posers have their roofs tiled in glass, and not a single one of them could stand all the stones being thrown."

My theory is a bit more complex and has to do with the shaping and establishment of what I call The Scum. The Scum is composed in its very nucleus by vagrants, crooks, and drunks, although one also may count the odd transient tagalong. The Scum has its own trajectory, independent of the individual parts that form it. Sometimes it travels without any fixed destination until it finds an area ripe for settling down. Upon taking possession of a territory, the enclave can last for hours, weeks, or months, according to environmental conditions and the internal logic of The Scum. If the site turns out to be less than optimal, The Scum will move on; however, if it is able to establish its roost without notable impediments, it settles in for the long haul. Several distinct types of Scum exist, according to function: general inebriation, baseball celebrations, depredation, elaboration and execution of robberies, domino matches, orgies, and other various incarnations, according to the wildest imagination of its factions. One Scum, interestingly enough, is able to absorb all of the rest of them, in any of the formulations already mentioned. The Scum acquires its own language, which is accompanied by an artificial din.

The Scum of my building has decided to make Big Mike's life a living hell.

And what tends to happen when one chicken falls out of favor in the hen house?

YUYA

Yuya says that the secret of making fried ripe plantains is taking them out at just the right time. The strips should be left frying in the boiling oil only until they have started to turn golden brown. Once they are laid out on the plate, they will darken further on their own. Yuya says that if you let them get a little dark while they are frying, then once they have been out in the air for a little while the ripe plantains get so black, ugly, and tough that they are impossible to eat.

According to Yuya, the same thing happens with life, you have to know how to get out in time.

Luisa, Lalita's godmother, left behind the lamps at the Woolworth's, the multicolored handkerchiefs in her breast pocket, and her smile for the clientele, in order to get married to a military man high up in the administration. She moved into a mansion in Miramar and they never saw hide nor hair of her again in the Los Muertos tenement on Animas Street. Not even Yuya heard from Luisa any more, nor Lalita from her godmother.

They also lost the San Alejandro School of the Arts from their area. It was moved over to Marianao and with it went the students that had brightened Dragones Street. The Chinese inhabitants were left without their Chinese paper to construct kites. Nor could you find the powders necessary for pyrotechnical feats, so they stopped making the red firecrackers that exploded one after another on a string. The old man who ground corn went to a retirement home. The paper lanterns vanished, along with the young ladies with their sad eyes. The bar closed, and the Victrola was silenced for good. You never heard the piano any more either. Chinatown was no longer even the shadow of what it had been, and Yuya says that she made up her mind to move out of there.

Shu was reluctant, but he could see things from the perspective of Lalita, who in just a few years would turn fifteen and become a woman. In no way could one celebrate the arrival of such an august occasion on the terrace on Rayo Street.

According to Yuya, the mystics of Shu's land wrote their spells with yellow ink. Yuya threw herself on the mercy of Babalú, of the *Chinito of the Charada,* and of the entire company of saints from the Christian pantheon. Afterward, just to be sure, she wrapped up her list of wishes in Lalita's yellow robe. A few days later the house exploded. Fortunately, they didn't have a single serious injury to mourn and, what's more, Yuya was able to rescue their furniture and other possessions in good order. Right away, they were granted a brand new apartment for the three of them in Alamar, which in those days was a well-kept suburb in East Havana, right in front of the ocean, all the buildings sporting a fresh coat of paint and all looking exactly the same.

Once more they moved the altar and the oaken chest with the trousseau—their inheritance from poor Etelvina.

Like an island of misfits, in a set of tiny single-family houses put up back in the old days, a colony of Soviets and Eastern Europeans had settled in. Within a few weeks Yuya had made friends with Ludmila the Bulgarian, a soothsayer like herself.

DAONTAON

Un-fucking-believable! Living where Daontaon lives, in "Siberia," is living in the back of beyond. The armpit of the devil, the **asshole of the universe,** Daontaon added "bold" as the correct emphasis, so as not to defame other areas of the municipality.

The end of the world was coming and if she kept going the way she was, it would catch her there in the company of the weirdos that lived in her building. No way, no how. She had to figure out some way to better her life. She'd had enough of delinquents, writers, rappers, and eccentrics. Braulio, the new boss, her only hope for moving up in the social order, not only looked like he had just fallen off the turnip truck, a baby-faced boy, but, to top it all off, at the moment of truth he begged her, weeping, to use a machete to spank his ass, and such a set of fat lily-white buttocks that they'd make the Virgin Mary blanch.

Now that's some kind of machete-wielding guerrilla tactics, I tell you.

Well, Daontaon was going to wage guerrilla warfare alright, without anyone asking her, on the **posers** in her building. Ha. You should see them. Such serious little faces in their workplaces, so formal, so full of protocol in the neighborhood meetings, but then behind each other's backs they were cuckolding each other left and right. The blond in the second floor apartment barely waited for her husband to leave before bringing in the mulatto from the third floor; the skinny guy who lived on the third floor was holing up in the garage with the mulatta from the fourth floor; the bald guy from the top floor had an understanding with his next-door neighbor—who in her spare time would let in the engineer on the side; the big black guy on the fourth floor had a procession coming through his place whenever his wife was gone, of as many high school girls as he could get his hands on. And then, what happens in Vegas stays in Vegas; what you don't know can't hurt you; never air dirty laundry; and dead men tell no tales.

Not to mention the gossip-mongering, the shady dealings, the black market for stolen goods, the trafficking in marijuana, the illegal betting, witchery, cons, bribery, and conspiracies.

Who were they to tell her, Daontaon, what to do? *Nobody!*

They'd deserve it, every bit, if they were caught in a shower of murderous meteorites, or if a chunk of Skylab fell on top of them, or if they were burnt up by the tail of a comet.

Daontaon wasn't about to end up that way. No way in hell. She'd been on the verge of a nervous breakdown for some time now. In her nightmare last night, she had to go tell Micaela about it, Daontaon had opened up the dining room cabinet and found a human arm, and that arm looked *really, really,* familiar. Then in another compartment was a leg and that foot, she just *knew* she had seen it before. Finally, in the last drawer, rested the naked *torso,* wrinkled and pale, and that *torso,* now she recognized it, only could belong to her neighbor, to the very same Micaela.

Son of a biscuit-eater! She had to come up with some way to get out of there and right away. The end of the millennium was coming, and nothing good could possibly come of it if she stayed in the middle of all these opportunists, dismemberers, and **posers.**

WOMAN WHO TALKS TO HERSELF IN THE PARK

Out of the ground gigantic ticks started arising and multiplying every which way, and then jumped from dog to dog, from cat to cat, from goat to goat. When there weren't any dogs, cats, or goats left, they started jumping on the people. They sucked up so much blood that they floated in the sky like balloons and exploded. And then a red viscous rain fell on the city. And Havana is dying…

HERMI

To keep up their childhood trick, Hermi had cut her hair to the same prescribed length that Tristan had to have in order to be allowed into the classroom, and in the style of that actor in Passolini's film

Accatone. Searching through the bureaus in her house, she found an old *pince nez* that had belonged to her great grandfather. Then she figured out how to set the graduated lenses that corrected her myopic vision into the antique gold frame that had so much *panache,* such "swing." She also discovered other treasures such as a cigarette holder and a Masonic ring.

It was a glorious time! Hermi lived her life convinced that she was part of the glory, and also of the sacrifice. The conflicts at the university that Tristan told her about felt far away, and she never would have guessed that her own cohort would toss her out of the nest where she was forging the grandiose future she had chosen for herself.

But it was happening: they already thought of her as tainted. Behind her back, they were heating the water to boil her alive and eat her up. Why didn't she ever wear makeup? Is she living with a married man? And who else is living there? Why is she studying English? And that shameless skirt she wears? And those strange little glasses and her hair so short? And smoking with that bourgeois cigarette holder? Americanized? Immoral?

Her first formal warning came after she wrote a mention of the sign of Aries into one of the scripts, and it went out on the air unchanged. Horoscopes—what in the hell was she thinking? They weren't about to put up with that relic of the past, that kind of superstitious nonsense, incredibly dangerous.

They called her in right away to see what she had to say for herself. Hermi couldn't get it through her head why they were making such a big deal over such a ridiculous trifle. Going from the frying pan into the fire, she cited a passage from the Bible in her justification. She didn't notice the meaningful looks and the complicity in the faces of her accusers, expressing without a doubt: "this is a hopeless case." The guy with the VW intervened and, in Hermi's defense, blamed her behavior on impulsiveness and ignorance. She stared at him, eyes wide, incapable of understanding that such descriptors were being used to excuse her conduct. When she tried to contradict him, the guy with the VW silenced her with a severe "Don't interrupt while I am speaking."

Offended, Hermi bit her tongue. In consideration for the guy with the VW, the administration showed tolerance and let it go "this time," only giving her a public reprimand—although they did tell her that she needed to improve her personal appearance.

Right about that time, in the last month of 1966, the Cinemateca at 23rd and 12th had programmed a series of ten classics from film history and, so that nobody had to miss a single feature, they scheduled two showings, one at six and the other at nine, for four weeks running. Tristan and Hermi got tickets for both. Between the two screenings they would eat a hot dog and an ice cream at the Tropicream on 21st.

The day that *Battleship Potemkin* was the first feature, they walked out debating the different images when the show was over, profoundly impressed. On the corner, as they killed time, they ran into Guillermo, that inseparable friend of Tomás, about to get pizza at Cinecittá. Guillermo had an odd smile plastered across his face, and his eyes were bright.

They said hello as they always did, and Guillermo invited them to stand in line with him and get a slice, and then they all could go see *The Gold Rush* together. It seemed like a perfect night, a lucky night...

As they ate, Guillermo slid in the occasional funny quip and his fair share of insightful comments about silent film. All of a sudden he stopped dead, staring at the pizza as if it was a black hole in the middle of the table. "Do y'all know where I just got back from?" No one answered the rhetorical question. Guillermo repeated himself without taking his eyes from that hole that seemed to open like a black chasm in the table. "Do y'all know where I just got back from?" He smiled. Then he added: "From the cemetery."

Hermi and Tristan smiled back at him, waiting for some funny story or a tale of adventure.

"Tomás shot himself." And the horrible smile came back to his face.

Then, the three of them went to watch *The Gold Rush*. It was a glorious time!

GERTRUDE

The group, including The Dead Girl, got together at the Tower Bar from time to time. Over a libation or two, we shared stories of how things were going. Each of us had gone our own way after finishing prep school: some to CUJAE[12] to study engineering; others to the dorms at 12th and Malecón or 3rd and F; and a very few to universities in other provinces, leaving only two or three who didn't go on to college.

From the building at 3rd and F (do you remember?), you could see the entire city if you were lucky enough to have a room on one of the upper floors: the gardens in the Vedado, the skyscrapers, and the entry to the Bay of Havana. We couldn't go to the Tower Bar every day of course, a student budget barely stretched to cover ice creams at Coppelia in the summer and hot chocolate in the winter. O Greek Goddesses of yore, inspire an ode dedicated to those mugs of hot chocolate with churros from Carmelo's! When the north wind would start to blow, we would settle in at a table on the terrace of Carmelo de Calzada, right across from the Theater Auditorium, with a cup of piping hot beverage that would last us until the café closed. There some of us would study for the "Doctora's" Literature Exam, figuring out why Paolo stayed silent, deciphering Aquilles' coat of arms, and asking ourselves the real meaning behind the spell of the three witches that appeared at the beginning of *Lady Macbeth:* "When shall we three meet again? In thunder, lighting, or in rain? When the hurlyburly's done, when the battle's lost and won."

My chocolate sundae at Coppelia and my hot chocolate with churros at Carmelo's, my two vices from the sixties, consecrated to the venerable heights of "My mojito at La Bodeguita and my daiquiri at El Floridita."

Almost all of the rest of the time we lived on croquette sandwiches, if that. As much as we tried to save up from our university "stipend," twelve pesos (which increased each year so that at the end we were

---

[12] The Polytechnic University José Antonio Echeverría (Havana), in Spanish the Instituto Superior Politécnico José Antonio Echeverría, CUJAE, is one of the most respected institutions in Cuba for the study of architecture and engineering.

getting twenty) didn't go far enough to pay for a meal at restaurants like The Polynesian, The Emperor, Monseigneur, El Conejito or La Roca, the gastronomical circuit of Vedado connoisseurs. What's more, you were more likely to meet an extraterrestrial than to make a phone call and actually get in to one of those places. But when the wheel of fortune turned in our favor, we would get an anonymous message in the middle of the night, as if from Zeus, God of Thunder himself, conceding us the favor of a reservation, a divine table for six diners. And there we would go, crazy happy, to sate our appetites that had built up over the weeks.

Do you remember? In the midst of the sixties, the "good old days," the headwaiters, the *maitres d'*, believed they had divinely granted powers, and when they caught the scent of raggedy, starving students they behaved with the scorn of gods before mere mortals attempting to dine on flat-grilled steak with *congri* and *tostones* on the very Mt. Olympus. They treated us like *The Underbitches*. Nevertheless, when some high up gentleman in his *guayabera* made an appearance, they would bow and scrape like the servants they were. There were a few exceptions, but in those days it didn't seem that a waiter or a headwaiter in the city had been told about the ideal of "equality," or anything of the sort. And speaking of equality, no restaurant would allow in a woman wearing trousers, no matter how elegant she might be.

Up in the dorms at 3rd and F we were equals, equals in facing The Rules, equals in climbing up the stairs when the elevator would break down, equals in skirting the curfew, equals in doing the late shift of guard duty, equals in eating the hard beans and the wormy watercress salad, equals in cleaning the common room, do you remember? Since the running water didn't really run there, and the majority of the time the elevator was out of order, water for our baths and for all the cleaning had to be shuttled along in buckets up and down the twenty-three floors. But none of that tired us out. We were young and ready to take on the world, in the heroic style of *Sandokana*, strong and pure. Even though back then there was so much confusion and fear about the parameters of what was pure or impure... "I'm dirty, Milena, infinitely dirty, which is why I make so much fuss about purity," do you remember?—our favorite quote from that austere and not half strange gal who invented a story about a cockroach called *Gregoria Samsa*. In spite of everything, we felt pure. You better believe it.

MARTIN

Martin leafed through one of his standard default novels, the ones he turned to for inspiration when he got mired down. He remembered a writers' trick, a strategy he availed himself of often and always with good results. He got up and went to the kitchen, opened the can of coffee grounds, calculating that there was enough to make a decent cup. He washed the coffee pot mechanically and set it on the burner, meditating on the way *The Leopard* ended, with the family dog on the final pages skinned and turned into a rug; the manifestation of the banal premonition laid out without any apparent justification in the book's beginning, which at first could only be interpreted as a digression, a filler, until much later—really until the denouement, when its meaning is untangled, its symbolism revealed as perhaps the very marrow of the issue. Or just exasperation vented in an irrational act, pure existentialism. For example, if he, Martin, a writer terrified of the blank page, were to hurl the boiling coffeepot at his neighbor Daontaon—who was swaying her ass back and forth like a threshing machine probably on her way to the Cultural Center—it could be interpreted as a gratuitous act. Only later, when his motives began to be uncovered and these fucking weeks of confusion came to light, could the episode be understood in context, its motivation clear.

Instead of launching the projectile, Martin called in to work and told them about the cold that would keep him in bed all day long; then he poured himself a cup of coffee, added a spoonful of sugar and a shot of rum, and as he sipped it slowly, traipsing through the apartment, he felt less tied up in knots. A meaningful detail, that's what he needed. Martin thought back to when his Uncle Felix used to come to get him from school, and they would play at not stepping over the lines marking each margin of the sidewalk; whoever crossed over was the loser.

Like every other afternoon, Uncle Felix came to pick him up after school let out, and they were returning home down San Rafael Street, walking from Central Park to Amistad Street, window shopping, checking out what was playing at the Cinecito. They would buy little paper cones of peanuts, strawberry snow-cones, La Cotorra sodas, vanilla ice cream cones, chocolate shakes, *malanga* fritters, churros, jaw-breaker gumballs, candy, lollipops, toffee, ("then he gets home and doesn't want to eat anything, because of the garbage you buy him on the street," Martin's mother would complain) on the way as the two explorers advanced along the sidewalk, along the parallel stones making a curb, black granite snakes that butted up against the coffee and cream colored granite; a crystal clear current, but a dangerous one, filled with thrashing sharks, piranhas, and crocodiles; one that would swallow whole little boys who didn't listen to their uncles. The two pioneers would make their way through this murky zone, without looking around or stepping off the path, until they arrived at the safety of the ticket counter of the Duplex and the Rex without once having stepped on the boundary marker past which monsters of the deep were lying in wait. If they went over the line, they were dead men.

The last Friday in June, at the end of the semester, Uncle Felix stepped over the line. In order to distract Martin, as if he could be fooled so easily, all of a sudden Felix announced that he was going to write the family history. "Everything that has happened," he said, "since we first arrived from Spain."

The line as a border between reality and the dream world? Obvious, fucking obvious.

LOLA

When Lola woke up that morning, she didn't recognize her own bedroom. The light barely filtered through the curtains. The pink damask hangings had covered the windows since the forties and, so much time having gone by, they had acquired an increasing grayish tint that further obscured the scant glow. The queen-sized cedar bed frame, an inheritance from her parents, wide and solid, which occupied almost all of the space in the room, was flanked by the matching three-door armoire and the dressing table whose mirror was streaked with mercurial scars. On the faded wall remained a few portraits that Lola had not been able to take down: her wedding picture with Evaristo, Sara's baptism, a hand-colored portrait from the days when Lola was still a beautiful and daring young woman. On top of the dressing table, set out in order, were a few ordinary objects: a flask of cologne, her hairbrush with the mother-of-pearl handle, an empty powder-bowl made of Venetian glass, some medicine bottles, scissors, a little box with her rings, a few coins, keys that she didn't use any more, and a couple knick-knacks: a small figurine of a faun with a tiny flute to his miniscule porcelain lips, tinted in pastels, and a miniature Eiffel Tower. Who had given her that little tower? And those medicines… who did they belong to? The hairbrush with the mother-of-pearl handle had been her mother's. "Mama?" called Lola, out loud.

Before getting out of bed, Lola stopped to listen to the various sounds inside the house: the tick-tock of the wall clock in the dining room, the dripping faucet in the kitchen, the low humming of the refrigerator, the rattle of the rusty hinges holding up the ancient window in the bathroom, and the whisper of air through the ventilation shaft.

Since it had been several days since the building had had running water, Lola saved what she used for her morning ablutions in a wash basin, and used the soapy liquid to water the chamomile plant that she carefully maintained in a flowerpot out on the terrace. Afterward she cut a few sprigs and made herself a cup of tea for breakfast.

She had yet to finish drinking this infusion when she thought she heard someone knocking at the door. When she looked through the peep-hole, it was an effort to recognize her cousin, Esperancita. That morning, everything felt strange and alien to Lola.

"Come in, Esperancita, it's been so long since I've seen you."

Esperancita settled down timidly on the sofa and peered out of the corners of her eyes at the cup of tea that Lola was holding.

"Would you like some tea?" offered Lola.

Esperancita accepted with a nod and as she drank with small, polite, sips, it felt like a slap in the face for Lola to be confronted with her cousin's abject poverty.

"And what brings you here so early?"

Esperancita raised her faded old-maid eyes and gazed submissively at Lola.

"I'm on my way back from the cemetery," she explained. "Today is All Souls' Day…"

Lola commiserated in silence, although to be honest, she hadn't remembered. Nevertheless, in her heart of hearts, she was surprised November already had arrived.

"I went to the family tomb. I didn't even have a flower to take with me, God forgive me," said Esperancita, asking pardon as if it were a crime, "so I cut a few branches off a *flamboyán* and put them there. Has it been a while since you were there?"

Lola shrugged her shoulders. How could she count the years she hadn't set foot in the cemetery? She couldn't help it, Uncle Sebastian's burial came to mind, he was Esperancita's father, an Asturian whose humble face was the saving grace of that bad memory, archived in the depths of her mind.

So now Uncle Sebastian had made it onto the list of her bad memories because of Esperancita's unexpected visit. For many years he had been the top guy, the guy in charge of the billiard tables at the Asturian Center, where decency reigned, thanks to his high moral standards, and wives would accompany their husbands as they enjoyed a game of pool or dominoes. At the beginning of the sixties, when the billiard clubs were closed down, Uncle Sebastian had only a few more months before he was up for retirement, so some cretin sent him to be a street sweeper in the Quinta Covadonga. Lola saw him at it once and preferred to scurry off without letting him see her, which, perhaps, would have added to the humiliation of the man who swept with trembling hands. Later, Uncle Sebastian had a stroke and ended up confined to his bed. Esperancita took care of him devotedly for ten years.

"Why don't you stay and have lunch with me?" Lola thought about the last chicken that she had left. "I'll make a chicken and rice casserole."

Esperancita's eyes lit up and she accepted the invitation with an air of embarrassment. In her cousin's lowered head, Lola recognized the same defeated gesture she had seen in her Uncle Sebastian as he plied his broom with humility and resignation through the alleyways around the hospital, clearing away dried leaves and trash.

WOMAN WHO TALKS TO HERSELF IN THE PARK

Royal palms, fan palms, and coconut palms sprang up and grew everywhere, from sidewalks to formal gardens. And then the city turned into such a dense forest of fronds that it always looked like night. And Havana is dying...

THE INDIA

The neighbors of the barrio never forgot that sticky dog day afternoon when three police cars arrived in full color to take into custody Patrick Rivière, better known as "The Frenchman" or "The India's Flaming Husband," accused of the homicide of his own wife.

In the tenement patio phrases were heard such as "what else would you expect from a foreigner," "The India brought it on herself" (including a group inclined more toward "she deserved it for being such a slut," truth be known). Clara Luz, "The Professor," as a precautionary measure closed her spiritual center and returned to her state job, at a printing press for the Institute of the Book.

Of the official police machinations, few bits of news trickled through.

Despite the many interrogations they subjected him to, they were never able to get anything out of the Frenchman beyond what they already knew. He insisted that he had come to Cuba as a language instructor thanks to an agreement with a French university; his little black briefcase contained only tourist pamphlets and innocuous copies of *Le Monde Diplomatique*. He repeated the same story time and time again, although, over the passage of the next few days, his attitude was disconcerting. He didn't try to defend himself and his glare, at first so full of arrogant scorn, little by little lost its fire until all that was left were grey embers, barely flaring from time to time, mostly when he would hear María Antonieta's name. The Frenchman couldn't be shaken from his state of apathy, as if he failed to capture the gravity of the accusations that were leveled against his person.

Meanwhile, like a jigsaw puzzle, throughout a wide swath of northern shore of the Havana province more severed members of a woman's body were discovered, as clean as their current state would allow, packed up in the same butcher's paper and tied up with the inevitable wires. However, with the exception of the pubic area, not a single hair nor foreign object was found in any of the packages.

Without new clues, the investigators in charge of the case were presented with yet another major obstacle when, in a rocky crevice of the coastal "Reparto de Pastorita," they came upon two carbonized hands, without a trace of fingerprints remaining, wrapped up in the now familiar packaging. They couldn't help but notice the criminal's perverse preference for the region of East Havana, in which tourist destinations like Bacuranao and historical sites such as the town of Cojímar rubbed up against shitty barrios like Alamar.

But neither the head nor the right thigh had appeared.

Due to the lack of concrete evidence, Patrick Rivière had bail set and was freed on his own recognizance, although the police kept his passport and limited his movements to the area of Central Havana bordered by the bakery, the bodega, the vegetable market, and the shopping mall catering to those few with CUC.[13]

Every little while a trembling child, terrified woman, or irate man would show up with one of those bundles wrapped in brown paper in their arms. By now everybody knew what that might mean, but nevertheless, the weeks went on without the appearance of the severed head of María Antonieta (whose name now made all the sense in the world).

Facing this unfortunate circumstance, the forensic investigators were left with no choice but to initiate an exhaustive study of the victim's body, piecing together the various parts, taking measurements, testing bodily fluids, until they arrived at the conclusion that, as a matter of fact, the body without a doubt belonged to a woman between twenty and thirty years of age, of mixed race, medium height, and dark complexion, as well as a few other particularities that matched in every regard to the known attributes of the missing India.

The right thigh finally appeared in the ruins of some abandoned vendor shacks on Boca Ciega beach. A furtive pair of teenage boys, in search of cover from a sudden downpour, or so they testified under oath at the Guanabo Police Station, got the fright of their lives when they literally tripped over the stinking haunch of the "Dismembered Lady of the East Havana Municipality," as she was known by now.

And although a few people refused to believe it and insisted on imagining The India all in one piece, sunning herself on other shores (they meant "Miami Beach"), they had to give up when her mother, between screams and moans, declared that she recognized the pale trace of the scar her daughter had gotten from a half-opened tin of Russian meat; a mark that the meticulous killer, so determined to suppress any telltale mark leading to a positive identification, seemed to have overlooked.

Now all that was left was to wait for her head.

---

[13] The Cuban Convertible Peso, or CUC, is the legal tender given in exchange for foreign currency. The purchase power of the CUC is much stronger than that of the regular peso that Cubans receive as salary and use for most consumption. Some stores, however, only accept CUC and offer "luxury" items that used to be reserved for the diplomatic corps, and now are sold at the higher level to anyone with CUC in order to infuse foreign capital into the system.

YUYA

Yuya says that at first she liked Alamar. Especially in the mid-afternoon. With a thermos of Polish tea and crackers that tasted like cardboard, which she got on the black market thanks to some Jewish neighbors in the building, she would go with Ludmila and Lalita to the coast, to swim in the sea at "Little Russian Beach." The water was still crystal clear and if they really tried, they could pretend that they lived on a deserted island.

As the sun set in the west, Lalita would look for shells, sea urchins, and fossilized sea creatures; Yuya would gaze at the horizon watching the colors change as twilight approached; and Ludmila would tell stories of her childhood after the war in her home town Sofia, and make predictions about the future of the island.

According to Yuya, Ludmila made clear that for her prophecies, she had no need of crystal balls, magic pyramids, nor tarot cards, given that she came from "out there," stretching out her pearly white arm away from the sun setting in the Gulf waters.

Ludmila came to Cuba, as did so many others, following a young mulatto she had met while he was studying hydraulic engineering. Within a few years he grew bored with her, but nevertheless Ludmila elected to remain in the warmth of the Caribbean sun. Moreover, as she confessed to Yuya, there were problems back home, so far away: a miniscule apartment, filled with too many siblings, in-laws, nieces and nephews, not to mention very strict codes of personal conduct. Here she lived how she wanted, in her own style and according to her own preferences, in a charming little house decorated with tourist posters of Havana, with a garden, and mere steps away from the ocean. She enjoyed the luxury of bonus coupons that allowed her to buy the now exotic products like red meat and cheese in the Focsa stores and, through a well-established bartering system of canned food as well as psychic readings with Spanish playing cards, she beefed up her salary as a translator. Bulgaria was a million miles away, and she was in love with all Cuban men. Over there she was just one of the ones within the multitudes, but here she had gained a name as "the Bulgarian psychic," "the foreigner," totally unique, or close enough.

Yuya says that she was delighted by Ludmila's tropical transformation, her barrio slang pronounced with a European accent, her love of the cha-cha-cha, her revolving door of boyfriends, and her obsession with collecting as much gold as possible, even old dental fillings.

A few years later, Lalita entered the university to study biology and her classmates started coming to study at Yuya and Shu's house.

Yuya says that the crisis came about in the second year of Lalita's course of studies. One of her friends sold her out, a formal accusation was made to the authorities, and during a chaotic meeting Lalita was threatened with expulsion from the university on account of her family's belief system, the occultist ways she had been taught growing up. And to clinch the matter, her parents, Yuya and Shu, were acting practitioners, instigators, and adoring followers of not one, but of every cult imaginable—and that was the accusation that drove Lalita right out of her mind.

Yuya had seen it coming from a long way off. Her vision of a fish gasping for breath, wearing the Haitian's head, had told her that something was coming down the pike.

When Lalita got home, she was in a state. Besides the imputations that charged her with "ideological deviation" and "wishy-washy ideals," what hurt her most of all was that they had branded her entire family as anti-socials! And they had demanded that as a first step to demonstrate her commitment to the formation of the *new student*[14] required by the times; as evidence of her incipient redemption, her regeneration; and as a way to reintegrate herself into the way of the virtuous, she should reject, destroy, and completely get rid of the altar—the focal point of the contamination and corruption of the revolution's pure ideals.

---

[14] This is one of many extensions of Ernesto "Che" Guevara's concept of the *New Man* that would be needed to form a radical and revolutionary new society.

Lalita refused to listen to any such thing. They could stick the university where the sun didn't shine.

Yuya says that the circumstances merited the gathering together of all possible powers. She begged help from Ludmila and her gypsy ancestors. She went to the cemetery to visit her old grandmother and ask the intervention of the ancient Celtic pantheon. She asked Etelvina's spirit to lend a hand in solidarity. She prayed to Sanfacón, Babalú, and Saint Lazarus, and she made a promise to the Virgin of Caridad to take Lalita on a pilgrimage to her shrine in Cobre. She invoked the wandering Haitian and beseeched him to pitch in. And finally, with Shu's blessing, she moved the altar once more, this time into the closet of the innermost bedroom, where it remains hidden to this day.

Lalita, clenching her teeth the whole time, obeyed Yuya and pretended that she had been converted. Three years later she graduated in marine biology. Thanks be to Jesus and all the saints!

HERMI

For a long time, Hermi had been fascinated with a strange painting that hung behind the circulation desk in the research consultation room of the National Library. She didn't know the name of the artist, nor did she have any idea of what church was painted on the canvas; that little red church that seemed to float in a cloud, surrounded by palm trees, bells, streetlights, grates, a few incongruent bottles, phantasmagorical crosses that were laid out over the façade, and an ascending dove. A church that was as volatile as a bird in its transparency and gracefulness. Who in the world would be able to capture such a sense of spirituality, and with that degree of subtlety? Hermi adored that painting and would not have been above stealing it in order to own it, to have it always there in front of her gaze.

Tristan warned her not to miss the show that was on exhibit at the Museum of Fine Arts. Hermi knew that certain tone of his voice, exultant and smug. As well as she knew the futility of trying to get him to tell her why. Tristan loved to surprise her. Nevertheless, he let drop a hint that it had to do with a painter who had mysteriously disappeared on a transatlantic voyage from Paris to Havana. Acosta León, barely over thirty years old, had abandoned the old continent and set out to sea in December of 1964, yet he had never made it to dry land. Tristan wasn't satisfied with theories of an accidental death or suicide and had elaborated a complicated story of jealousy, envy, and dark passions that culminated in a criminal shove into the oceanic depths. Wiped off of the map!

The VW guy insisted on going with Hermi to the museum; he had that particular "bit of time" free, as his wife didn't expect him home early that Saturday. Against her better judgment she agreed to go with him; she wasn't feeling like giving into him after his attitude in that meeting where they had dragged her name through the mud, and where he had been so arrogant toward her and so obsequious with his superiors, covering his own ass and sacrificing Hermi's on the altar of who knew what.

A February northern had come in, and an ice-cold drizzle was falling. The VW guy parked his car in a far-off alley so nobody would see him get out of the car with her and he made Hermi walk by herself to the museum, where they would "run into each other" in the lobby, as if by accident. So much subterfuge just so he wouldn't be caught had lost its charm for her, now seeming merely pathetic. She was starting to see him for who he really was: good in bed, but a bit stupid and a show-off.

Hermi had barely taken a few steps into the gallery when she ran across—the painting of the little church! There, at the Acosta León exhibit, hung her painting, so overwhelmingly close, so right in front of her eyes, that she felt like she was floating around the room as well. The Church of Paula! That was the chapel represented in the picture. Overcome with emotion and the presentiment of a wave of revelations, she walked forward among coaches, guarapo venders, zoomorphic boats, sad-eyed faces, swings, trams, carrousels, vultures, monstrous handcarts, traffic lights, toys, wheels, screwdrivers, propellers, palm trees; not to mention espresso pots and coffee presses, the only true *Cuban cathedrals*.

There it was in all its majesty, corralled in a corner of Havana, Hermi's concept of art with a capital 'A.' Life's drama exploding in an ironic, flamboyant, burst of laughter; the humble nature of common objects reconfigured in a dimension that was at once terrifying and comical; reflecting love and hate, creation and destruction, water and fire, pleasure and pain, solitude and humanity.

Clueless about what was happening, the VW guy hoped to get the museum visit over with in a hurry, to get out of his mouth the bad taste that came from looking at these incomprehensible artifacts that had no place in a rational universe, pure trash. From time to time he tried to hurry her along, to no avail. His irritation grew as their time there stretched on, and the possibility of their having any time alone shrank. He asked himself why he was wasting his time on that decadent snot-nosed brat anyway. He watched her from a distance and what he saw was a poorly dressed and fairly flustered girl, who filled him with shame but equally with a desire to dominate her. Just a few more "times" and he was going to get rid of that nutcase. He couldn't put his marriage at risk for this sort of piece of work.

When they left the museum, they walked separately toward the car, as if they didn't even know each other. He got in first and, from behind the steering wheel, gestured that she should get in. Hermi looked at him, shook her head 'no' and, without a word, she gave him the universal sign of a break-up, the palm of her right hand sliding brusquely along the back of her left hand, meaning "it's over," and then she turned her back on him and walked away. The VW guy, stunned, started the car in a sudden burst of rage. Who did she think she was, to leave him like that?

As she walked through the freezing raindrops, Hermi felt like she was sinking, disappearing in the waters of a hostile sea.

WOMAN WHO TALKS TO HERSELF IN THE PARK

A building got mad and pushed the one next to it, and that one pushed the one on the other side, which pushed the next one in line.

And then all hell broke loose until they all started falling down, one by one. And Havana is dying…

ESTELA

Stretches of Brompton Road were covered with sheets of icy, dirty, snow. Estela decided to treat herself to a Saturday of shopping. The snow that had fallen the day before had turned into annoying gray patches. Her boots sunk up to the ankles in the slush, which varied between grainy sleet and viscous sludge. Estela went into Harrods, as did most of the people walking by: some to shop, some to warm up and escape the wet for a little while, others to enjoy the Christmas decorations. Enclosed walkways within the enormous shopping center allowed one to get to any part of the stores without stepping a toe out into the cold. At various intervals, the garlands and artificial pine trees covered with pearl-colored balls made you feel as if you were in a magical castle. The crowds happily complied with their consumer obligations, on the pretext of the birth of the Christ Child, despite the fact that the prices were somewhere up in the stratosphere. Estela searched for a bottle of men's scented aftershave and then asked the clerk to gift wrap it, as Oscar would be getting back just in time for the holiday, and Estela wanted to leave him his little present beside the chimney. She also ought to buy something for her father, too, but, after going round and round about it, decided it would be like throwing money into the street—since after all, why would he need to dress up over there, Estela preferred not even to name that place, where he was living now. Much less consider a set of silk pajamas like the ones there in the men's department, which would be nothing more than a waste of a considerable amount of money. It would be better to wait until her next trip to Havana and take over some scraps of fabric, so that a neighborhood seamstress could put together something useful for him to wear. All of a sudden Estela felt an urgent need to get herself an extravagant present. She wandered around the bottom floor among the designer fragrances and watches, strolled over just to marvel at the new computer gadgets, then went up to browse the home appliances, but she had to admit that she already had more than she really needed in that area. So, finally she ended up in the winter apparel department, where she picked out a beige leather jacket. Just to touch it made her feel marvelous; it was so delicate, smooth, and creamy, with just a few subtle irregularities. To tell the truth, it cost an arm and a leg, but she wanted to own it. And now. After coming out of the fitting room and paying with a credit card, she put her old coat away in the bag and slipped on her new one. As she looked for one of the exits from Harrods, she felt elegant and sure of herself. From time to time she would lift up her arm to wave the sleeve past her nose so she could revel in the unmistakable smell of fresh leather, of a brand new object as of yet uncontaminated by sweat or any of the emanations of urban life. On her way back, it started to snow again. Estela quickly walked around the park and made her way into her heated building. She had planned to spend the weekend in Paris, she even had gone so far as to make her reservation for the Eurotunnel, but the bad weather made her change her mind. They were predicting rain showers and wind on the weather, and the fun thing about Paris was to stroll through the streets. She'd rather just stay in her warm apartment in Bloomsbury, instead of being trapped in a hotel room. Back in her room, she changed out of her new jacket into a thick robe and served herself a snifter of cognac to warm up. Outside the drifts of white powder were falling harder on the gated concrete tennis courts, secure from intruders. In a few minutes they were newly covered with a virginal layer that looked like a cotton field surrounded by denuded trees like a regiment of upthrust spears. Unexpectedly, and no doubt Lucia's visit was to blame, her mind was flooded with the ill-fated memory of the Dead Girl. The Dead Girl had always talked about wanting to see snow for the first time and of going to Paris, which were just a few of her ideological transgressions; the ones that had bothered Estela the most. That's the kind of thing that had led to her downfall.

DAONTAON

Daontaon woke up with a raging headache. As soon as she walked out her door, she caught sight of that idiot Martin's face, staring at her from his balcony. That's all she needed, for people to spy on her. Could he be a narc? Ha. Totally possible.

That dream she had had the night before…Daontaon killing snails in the terrace of the building. **Crash,** went their shells under the soles of Daontaon's shoes. **Crash** and **crash; crash,** and more **crash,** until dawn. Jesus Christ on the Cross!

Then she wasn't pacified in the least by the interpretations that she got from Yuya, the psychic. That so-called witchy woman showed her an old piece of cardboard with a drawing of an ugly, wizened, Chinese dude.

"The snail rests here on his right sleeve, do you see it?" she started to explain, licking her lips in a fervor of devotion.

Nothing. Daontaon didn't see a damn thing on that sheet that had been gnawed through by bookworms, but she said yes just to get out of *that*.

"Dreaming about snails warns you that the King of Clubs is on his way," said the psychic. "A blonde man, the perfect gentleman, connected to the arts."

Ha. Daontaon was all about "the arts." And the supposed "perfect gentleman"? Where was that Martian, she'd like to know! Not even on Mars. It was enough to die laughing, if she had been in the mood.

According to her own interpretation of dreams, if a King of Clubs showed up he would be some drunken artist. Without a doubt. And the shells, setbacks and lock downs.

And that's exactly how it went. Daontaon had ended up spending the entire last night at the Police Station because of a painter who specialized in blotches and scribbles (there was the "blonde man, the perfect gentleman"). They had him locked up with another guy who had helped him to transport his father's bones. Please. The skeleton of the *artist's* dead father, that had rested the last four years in a borrowed spot in a family tomb, had to be removed because the period of mortuary hospitality had come to an end. After the exhumation, and without anyplace to bury the paternal remains, the artist and his partner in crime had thrown down a few drinks to deal with their sorrow (and there was your Club!) and, drunk as skunks, they started a cross-city bicycle ride with the intention of getting all the way to Regla where the acolyte had a dirt patio; the friend doing the pedaling, the artist perched on the steering wheel, and his father in a backpack. Intercepted by the authorities, who demanded they explain what was in the backpack, the painter admitted that it was a dead person. "A DEAD PERSON!?" exclaimed the shocked patrolman. "Yes, look, it's the skeleton of my dear departed father, may he rest in peace," and, without having to be prompted, the artist pulled out a skull before the darkening eyes of the uniformed officer, who responded by requesting their authorization for transporting the bones. "Authorization?" Now it was the two friends who were flabbergasted. "Yes, authorization," continued the policeman, imperturbable, "the permission to transport an object of any nature from one place to another." No, they didn't have any sort of permit for his father. So, the whole lot of them, skeleton included, to the slammer.

Setbacks and lockdowns!

Daontaon was there at the station until midnight convincing the officer in charge to let them go, please understand, *compañero,* we're talking about a VIP here in the district. The "district VIP" was sleeping it off and snoring to beat the band, his arms wrapped around the backpack with his dead father's bones.

Just like she said, Havana is full of all kinds. And the worst of them in Alamar.

MARTIN

"A blood transfusion? For me? What for?" asked Martin's mother.

"The better to see you, my dear," replied Martin in a melodramatic tone, mimicking the famous phrase of Red Riding Hood's wolf. Although he was trying to keep it light, nonchalant, his voice rang false, as fake as the manuscript he was trying to write. "I'm going to make lunch" was her response and she walked out of the room, Martin's parents' bedroom, with the yellowed faces of his grandparents hanging on the walls; a painting of a nymph reclining on a Roman couch, surrounded by cherubs in their birthday suits; alongside a photo of him, Martin, disguised as a pirate. Buried somewhere in the dresser lay vestiges of the costume that his mother had pulled together: red and black satin, an eye patch, a handkerchief wrapped around his head, a cape decorated with skull and crossbones, a white silk blouse, and costume boots made out of black oilcloth.

He opened the wardrobe doors and started to rifle through the drawers, full of worthless papers; his grade school report cards from *Plantel Jovellanos*, his prizes in "Literature" and "Science," invitations to end of the school year galas, so carefully preserved by Martin's mother, and now so utterly out of date and useless. Among all the old papers, Martin found an ancient photograph, printed onto cardboard stock, with ghostly faces appearing out of the distant past. Who were they? What had become of them?

Martin's mother came back from the kitchen and sat down beside him. Martin had so many questions he wanted to ask her but didn't dare, blocked as he was by a new variety of panic: the spoken word turned into reality; uncovered the anguish of having so little time left together; accelerated her departure, her absence. At least that's how it seemed. But then how could he fill in all the blank spaces of his personal history? She, his dying mother, was the last one who could tell him about his past. He felt like a fucking vampire.

Grandmother Antonia and Uncle Felix had voyaged to the Americas in the first months of WWI. They came from a hamlet, San Juan de Parres, which was situated on the edge of a dusty dirt road that led off to the right just before coming to a medieval bridge that fronted the town of Cangas de Onís, dominated by Mount Auseva, a hermitage for the Virgin, and a tomb belonging to the royal family of Asturias. They returned to their tiny village, rich as could be, now referred to as the "Indianos," and had extravagant mansions built for themselves, surrounded by palm gardens and containing all sorts of tropical sensations, and they would sit around drinking coffee in the town plaza and telling fascinating stories of the Indies, where gold nuggets could be plucked like low-hanging fruit. And thus the "Pearl of the Caribbean" shone in the distance, the island that was called Juana when found by their ancestors, the conquistadors, arms merchants, sailors, laborers, second sons, missionaries, Don Juans, and fugitives from justice; that "Lovely Little Cuba" from whence came rumors of lighting-quick fortunes, musical mulattas, and a paradisiacal climate across the sea. It was a dreamland of golden breast plates that never appeared and a thousand things that did: bodegas, dry cleaners, tailors, the "Greatest of the Antilles" with its parrots and palm trees, the "Key to the Gulf," symbolized in the daguerreotypes of the jutting towers of the Morro, which the "Indianos" carried all the way to the skirts of the Covadonga Sanctuary, those great-grandparents of his, descendants of the proud King Pelayo, of those Asturians who never surrendered to the Moors. And in the midst of so much hunger and so much war, in the far-off land of Cuba it seemed gold was falling from the trees.

Pure past. Martin jotted down the idea as a possible title. Or maybe *Chimerical yesterday...*

YUYA

Yuya says that the neighborhood went downhill. Worse than in the tenement on the Los Muertos tenement, and that was saying a lot. Alamar lost its fresh, just bloomed, image and started filling up with trash dumps, con men, plagues, starving animals, and people whose lives had apparently stagnated.

Little by little, the Russians with their samovars and baby dill pickles said goodbye. Also the Chileans and the one Hebrew family in the building. Their next door neighbors took their door and built a raft that made it all the way to the Florida Keys, in the same way as many other people Yuya knew, including her dentist. Ludmila was deathly afraid of airplanes; nevertheless, as Yuya puts it, nobody can walk off an island, and Ludmila ended up taking her leave as well.

Yuya says that the din from the slaughter of pigs and goats, sounds not well suited to the urban environment, turned into a daily occurrence and so it became necessary to shut all the windows tight just to get away from those squeals that rent her heart. Jesus Christ on the Cross! With the impunity of the night, beer bottles would fly out of the upper floor windows and fall with a crash to the sidewalk. The buildings became dingy; the handrails of the staircases, rusty, started falling to pieces. The areas of greenery were tramped underfoot and turned into deserts of dirt and excrement. The trash, petty crime, fighting, and plain bad manners remade Alamar into gigantic and horrifying tenements. Into a residential shantytown, where it looked like squatters had built with whatever came to hand, according to Yuya. It wasn't even safe anymore at her old favorite little beach.

Yuya says that Lalita came back from one of her many scientific expeditions with a girlfriend who had been kicked out of her house. Lalita convinced Yuya and Shu that it would be perfectly fine for the two of them to stay in her little room together. Yuya wasn't all that happy with the arrangement but, once Lalita got an idea into her head, there wasn't any way to talk sense into her.

From what Yuya says, when she talked to Lalita about the cedar chest, her inheritance from poor Etelvina, with the bridal trousseau all ready for the day of her wedding, Lalita looked at her with a strange expression and told her that the trousseau would have to sit there and wait. Such a response surprised Yuya, mostly due to the brusque tone with its shadow of irony, which she had never heard from her daughter before. Shu merely raised an eyebrow and, as per usual, neither offered an opinion nor was shocked in the least.

One Sunday, Lalita and her friend went to the coast to bask in the sun. A while later they returned, a mess of cuts, scrapes, and bruises. A couple of guys they had never seen before had jumped them. Lalita's friend had a black eye and a bloody lip that continued to bleed profusely. Lalita had been scratched, kicked, and sported quite a cut on her forehead, but Yuya says that what scared her more than anything was the look in Lalita's eyes. Despite Yuya asking her over and over about what happened, she closed herself off in a hostile silence.

Yuya says that after having thought it through, turning it over in her mind, a few days later she took advantage of a northern, bundled up, and went out for a walk along the coast. Being winter, the shores were deserted, the waves battered against the reefs, and sea salt began to cover the exposed skin on her face, which stung beneath the strong rays of the sun. However, the freezing wind gave her thoughts a cold clarity. Yuya walked along the outcroppings, looking at the spiral and fan-shaped sea shells, the dried masses of algae, the empty cans, and endless scraps of wood. The sea mercilessly threw back all that it considered unacceptable.

Yuya says that she decided to shake off the sadness that had enveloped her, and then she made the decision to leave Alamar. But not by raft or airplane, but rather by means of a moving van. She traded houses with somebody in Vedado and got the hell out of there.

GERTRUDE

Pure and distinct, you better believe it. *I sing my woman self, Portrait of the Artist as a Young Woman, The Magnificent Meaulnes, The Idiotess, Tonia Kruger, Demiana, Promethea Unchained, Juana Cristobalina.*

Now to get down to business. A Carnival troupe, moving in synch, tends not to tolerate soloists, nor exceptions to the rule, *the star that shines and kills,*[15] nor anyone that throws their uniformity in their faces. So, first a few shining stars appeared, and then to pay the price of their innocence, A Season in Hell… *Damned souls, if I were to take vengeance!,*[16] like a charm, we would invoke those little verses of that young lady of France, *I*

---

[15] Cuban independentist writer and philosopher José Martí.
[16] French writer and philosopher Arthur Rimbaud.

am another, who would cover up her genius under the name of a pedantic and ne'er do well cousin. To be perfectly frank, that particular translation never convinced me, sounding too archaic, too burnished. *Evil bastards, if I...!* Or even better, clearer, *You sons of bitches, if I were to take my revenge!*

Has anyone ever heard the story about the Chinese sparrows? Well, it seemed that an overpopulation of sparrows was endangering the crops, so somebody came up with the solution of setting all the Chinese peasants to work, for hours and hours at a time, beating cans with sticks. In that way, they kept the swallows circling above, frightened, without touching down anywhere, until they fell to the ground faint from exhaustion, and thus thousands and millions of swallows died, beaten to death with those same sticks. Could that story have been based in fact? I don't know, but every time I remember the '70s, the tale springs to mind.

It was in that decade that the prohibitions came into bloom. Do you remember, or don't you? In those days, to give an example, no woman was allowed by herself, nor when accompanied by a female friend, to enter a bar. Not even with her own mother! Penelope and Telemaca were home penning the Odyssey while Ulysses was out tying one on with his buddies.

Back then a lot of social pressure was focused on young ladies who studied at the universities maintaining their intact hymens. Not only did we have endless discussions about the young men who wore their hair long in our assemblies and grassroots committees of the Communist Youth, but also about the virginity of the "females," do you remember? When one of us would lose it and, thanks to loose lips, the whole scandal was made public, at the very least she would lose her scholarship and depending on the circumstances, she could even be kicked out of the university. If the deeds were done overseas, the sinner would be sent home in punishment, a dishonorable discharge, so to speak. And the worst of the worst, you better believe it, was if the love affair implicated some exotic Slavic soul.

When it came to the guys, they were not allowed to show signs of "effeminacy," such as sporting sandals, earrings, or loafers without socks.

Neither were they allowed to wear tight pants, shave their heads or grow their hair long, nor much less grow a mustache or beard.

Remember, they wouldn't let us wear miniskirts or black rimmed glasses, practice yoga, have a crucifix around our necks, or wear baseball caps whether they were for Havana or Almendares, just like we weren't allowed to play cards, or read comic books like *Superman,* or novels by Corín Tellado.

Well, in that last case the prohibition didn't affect us in the least. I mean, really. We gals did NOT read Corín Tellado. No way. We wanted to be part of the vanguard, following the very latest things: free love, pop art, anti-poetry, free cinema, rock and roll. Although that world was kept at a distance, from time to time news would filter through. Thanks to Yuri Gagarin, we found out that the entire planet earth looked blue from space and in a newsreel from the Film Institute we could see with our own eyes, in a moving picture for the first time, a furtive image of The Beatles.

All of that, which seemed so provocative back then, sounds so ingenuous now.

Like a funhouse mirror, music can sweeten the cruel reflection of our memories. Those were the good days. Every day of the week, night after night, at a quarter to eleven, *Alone with You* in Radio Progreso, Elena would sing "a melody springs from the depths of my heart," and then Meme, "made with my music, somewhat sad, like me" and "but let me tell you, if you see me cry…" and then finally confessing in a duet, Meme and Elena—backed by a quartet—would end with "it's not that I'm unhappy, it's just that you really get to me."[17] And then it was time for *Nocturne.*

Every Saturday we broke out of our routine; with only four bucks in our pockets, we'd hit the Cinemateca, a pizza at Vita Nuova, and ice cream at Coppelia. With whatever was left, we would while away the hours listening to Teresita[18] sing at The Coctel, the nighttime dive

---

[17] Cuban singers Elena Burke and Meme Solís.
[18] Cuban singer Teresita Fernández.

frequented by the young and naïve bohemians. Teresita would be sitting on the corner of the sofa, "for you there is no loneliness as long as I exist," and every one of us would think the song was for us, and that someday we would find that special someone who would chase away our solitude. *A Love of Lady Swann.* Before we learned with *Segismunda* that life is a bad dream, and that bad dreams too are nightmares, we would touch and squeeze each other on the bar stools or on the cushions tossed about the floor, nursing our one highball, and singing in unison "you told me you loved me, and now I'm crying."

The Dead Girl knew all the songs by heart.

For all of us girls on scholarship, the night would end when the bells rang out midnight, just like Cinderella's middle of the night adventure when she met her princess. The Rule Books mandated that we got back to the dorms before one in the morning. After that, it would depend who had the night watch, if she would turn a blind eye or put you on report.

All around us the atmosphere was changing, and we didn't even know it. *A Confederacy of Dame Dunces.* We were so complacent, and suddenly the whistle started to blow.

So, one day out of the dictionary leapt the word "purge."

The year was 1967, and Giggiola Cinquetti was saying she wasn't old enough to know better, but we sure were. We were all twenty years old. Marta Strada wanted to be held close and then forgotten; Ela was saying goodbye to happiness.[19]

WOMAN WHO TALKS TO HERSELF IN THE PARK

The sky filled up with vultures. They flew in flocks and made their nests on the balconies of the skyscrapers. And then millions of baby vultures cracked open their shells and launched themselves out to search for carrion throughout the city. And Havana is dying...

---

[14] Marta Strada and Ela O'Farrill also are Cuban singer-songwriters.

MICAELA

Through the half-opened blinds Micaela saw the ball of flames blossom where the sea met the horizon. Her head hurt so bad she thought it would split in two, and she just didn't feel strong enough to face her daily routine. A strong odor of disinfectant came from the building's stairwell, and that same dog from who knows where had just had its early morning cry. On top of everything, her own cat was still refusing to eat, even when Micaela had served her the last of the milk in her special bowl. For herself, she had mixed a glass of water and brown sugar, then she took an aspirin and dabbed a little Chinese ointment on her temples. A night of insomnia had left her in a bad way, and hungry to boot. She searched through all the soup pots and managed to rescue a few spoons full of baked-on rice. She ate breakfast standing up, keeping her eye on the sun as it rose higher and higher in the blood red sky. Ever since Hurricane Flora had blown the roof off the thatch hut where Micaela's brigade was sleeping during the coffee harvest, she was suspicious of those fiery skies.

During the wee hours the morning before, in order to get rid of the mosquitoes that were buzzing all around her and to take her mind off her sleeplessness as the blackout stretched on, Micaela had crafted a homemade lamp. She used some rags as a wick, stuffed them in a little bottle filled with a bit of kerosene, just as she learned to do from the hillbillies when they needed some light during the long dark nights of the countryside. The slight scent of scorching cloth and the black smoke that coated the ceiling, her face, and even her nasal passages brought back other nights like that one, back in her youth, lit up by an oil lamp, in the middle of the Sierras, with her brigade of coffee pickers, with the Dead Girl, her friend since junior high.

She found out about her friend's death by accident, when she called Sara's house, three days after it had happened. Micaela remembered that the handset of the public telephone had dropped out of her hand and then she was running, running, down streets and more streets, until she ended up in the funky neighborhood where the Dead Girl had lived. She fled down to the end of the hallway of the old building, as she had done a thousand times before, slammed her knuckles on the door, again and again. A few moments later she heard the deadbolt slide back, the door creaked open up a sliver, and she could make out the profile of a man who looked beyond exhaustion. Micaela stammered a few words of condolence as the man listened, nodding his head without saying a word. From inside the apartment came the sound of continuous sobs. At last, the man murmured his thanks and closed the door. Micaela realized that she hadn't even told him who she was.

As Micaela looked for the exit, she discovered the Dead Girl's socks hanging out in the patio. She wouldn't normally have noticed them but under the given circumstances, she recognized them with a start. There they had been left, those pairs of socks that survived her. In their prime they had been red with two white stripes, a thick pair of socks that now gave testimony with their faded colors of a long time out under the sun and rain. And there they were still, hung out on the tenement clothesline, forgotten, shamelessly announcing their presence, shouting their "We are still here!" A dark silence thickened behind the closed doors of the other apartments of the complex. Micaela never went back there again.

A little before dawn, Micaela looked for something else to do to distract herself. She didn't want to pick up the Russian novel that had made her feel so heavy, and so she decided to transfer over information from her tattered old address book, plagued as it was with so many people who weren't around any more. When she got to the Dead Girl's name, she remembered those red socks on the line. She was there a while, paralyzed, staring at the name that nobody mentioned anymore, the address of a street that had been left behind, the little numbers that she had punched in so many times, traces, lost clues, remnants of the past… After turning it over in her mind a few times, she couldn't make herself leave it out and she copied down the Dead Girl's contact information, with the telephone number that had ceased to exist years ago, into her new little book. Not to do it would have seemed like she was giving her the *coup de grâce*.

Micaela turned again to look at the ball of fire hanging in the sky. The horizon was still red, and Micaela said to herself that bad weather was coming for sure.

HERMI

Like lightning storms in a drought that kill without warning, Hermi would never know what happened.

They started off accusing her of immaturity. Then they found out that she was writing back and forth with her parents, who had settled in New Jersey. Then, to put the icing on the cake, the guy with the VW, her discarded former lover, started a rumor that she was aiding and abetting Tristan and his unnatural love affairs in her house. Without ever knowing what she was doing, Hermi inspired a great deal of mistrust, and they put her under observation.

They were hard times, the bombing in Hanoi had taken over the news, and all sorts of conduct could end up being labeled as antisocial, or the product of "the poison of a decadent ideology." And the panorama was shrinking: no longer acceptable was scenography that looked "surrealist" or "psychedelic," or any mention of the Marquess or the Gentleman of Paris.[20] What did they think they were splashing on the screen, on our healthy TV programming, those crazy tramps? Much less could they talk about anything remotely close to publicity or doing surveys, Freudian analysis or the mass media's focus on violent crime; don't dare mention anything about existentialism or God, nor use Confucianist or religious words like "inclement" or "fanatic," much less spread stories about the supernatural or put forth those individualistic programs under one person's name, putting them on a pedestal. Even worse, and of course branded as Satan's spawn, were the characters of Pototo and Filomeno, and even Mamacusa Alambrito.

---

[20] The Gentleman of Paris is one of Havana's favorite legendary characters, a crazy man—supposedly of the aristocracy—walking the streets of the city.

It was then that Hermi put together a script on cinema verite and free cinema. She had just seen *Black Peter* by Milos Forman. Hermi wrote passionately about Czech film, intergenerational conflicts, the problems adolescents had in confronting adult spaces, opposition to traditional schemata. In those days another film was all the rage, *Starci na Chmelu,* which was pulled out of the theaters and blackballed.

Hermi's screenplay was censured too and they asked her, instead of reviewing the forbidden film, to comment on an idiotic Slavic cowboy flick called *Lemonade Joe.* In response, Hermi wrote an analysis of structuralism. And that was the last straw.

Although it was hard to pin down exactly when it started, all of Hermi's projects were being turned down without any justification, or put off with some absurd reasoning. They mutilated sections of her scripts without bothering to consult her; they stopped telling her when they were holding meetings and kept her from going on air with any feeble pretext; they gave her dry and boring work to do; they gave her the most punishing shifts and made her labor alongside the stupidest of her co-workers. A black cloud had descended on Hermi.

Once in a while they would let fall phrases like "bad apple" or "hard case." The guy with the VW stopped talking to her and, along with him, a goodly number of the bosses and their secretaries. Some of her peers avoided running into her, staring up at the ceiling or sneaking down another corridor if they saw her coming.

They transferred her to the section dealing with children's programming for the radio, where "she could be more useful." For Tristan, it became clear that they were, without scruples, shunting her off the "great possibilities" road; a passive-aggressive strategy of confining her to the most insignificant spaces, where one supposes that ideas are not in play. Hermi trusted that with her dedication to her work, she would be able to crawl out of the hole she had fallen into.

But she tied the last knot in her own noose when, interfering in a meeting about dramatic television programming to which she had not been invited, she proposed adapting the novel *In Cold Blood* for a soap opera, defending her idea with indisputable arguments and fervor. Hermi was fired from her position, tossed out on the street, and stuck with the label of "trouble-maker," which would probably stay with her until the day she died, and then show up in her eulogy.

DAONTAON

The night before was a full moon, and she, Daontaon, just to be on the safe side, locked herself inside early—deadbolt and all, heaven forbid a werewolf should come and attack her (or a she-werewolf, which would be the same or maybe **worse**) because here in her neighborhood ANYTHING could happen, am I right or am I right? Of course I am. On top of the dismembered headless woman (not to mention the fact that her neighbor Micaela had taken to talking to herself, god help me), at the gift exchange for work she ended up with a *shower curtain,* for god's sake! Ever since she saw that movie *Psycho*, she hadn't ever been able to take a shower behind a curtain again, not even if she had owned one, just to be perfectly clear. Jesus H.! In order to keep watch in case some crazy killer showed up, and so that she would be ready and able to take defensive measures, as she was completing her daily ablutions, Daontaon never stood with her back to the door, which of course she kept wide open, and she continued with her old habit of taking a sponge bath and rinsing with a jug of water like she had done when she lived in Banes; she wouldn't be caught dead in a shower, even if there had been running water in the bathroom plumbing. Not that there was, let's just be honest.

Until the day before yesterday, her boss Braulio had kept her on light duty for three weeks, on a real plush assignment, doing a census of deaf mute children for a chorus. But then all hell broke loose as they had to prepare for a full inspection coming "from above" that would check the status of every little task they had been assigned.

So first it was finding a dentist to repair the dentures of Francisquito the rocker; then it was a radiator—even a second hand one—for the Moskovich, the comrade translator for Hungarian and other such languages; then she had to come up with a back brace for the old widow of that professor of lyric poetry who had fractured a vertebra horsing around with the grandchildren; and after that go to rescue the video that customs had expropriated from the girlfriend of that rapper from Zone 7, Aguilucho Tusao. I'm telling you what! This job was one unlucky 13 after another. Un-fucking-believable!

The worst of it yesterday was when she had to go and pick up a donation from this ancient man who had custody of all the belongings of his niece. The whole thing was *sadder than sad,* given that his young relative had *taken her own life.* Of course that had been about a million years ago, long before Daontaon had even dreamed about moving to Havana, although the poor old guy "continued to suffer" (that's how he phrased it) "*that hell* day after day, hour after hour, minute after minute." "WHY did she do it?" "How was it that NOBODY reached out to her?" "And where was I, to not do ANYTHING for her?" Daontaon could feel the capital letters vibrating like cowbells in every one of his questions. Don't get all upset on me, grandpa, or you're gonna have a heart attack. Have a cup of chamomile. Or better yet, a valium, do you have any? Would you mind letting me have one too? God bless you for that.

When finally they dragged the wooden suitcase out of the closet, the one with all the goods the old man was gifting to the Cultural Center, it fell completely to pieces like a cookie drenched in milk. Inside, instead of the treasures that this guy thought he had been keeping safe all this time, there was a whole colony of termites. The entire contents of the box had turned into pulp; a dark sticky mass where the little insects jumped around fat, dumb, and happy. Daontaon wasn't sticking her hands into that mess if her life depended on it. The old man, crying and slinging snot every which way, started trying to rescue the remnants of a grade school medal, the ivory fan from her first communion, a metal piggy bank with coins inside, pieces of a miniature chess set, the head of a doll whose body was torn asunder. Everything else, whatever else had been in there (Daontaon never found out what), had been completely devoured, leaving nothing worth a dime. Look, grandpa, I'm in a little bit of a hurry, just put all that in a bag, and I'll take care of it myself. What's more, said Daontaon with all the solemnity due in the moment, in the name of the Cultural Center of the Municipality of East Havana, and in gratitude for your noble gesture, I offer you this lovely brand new shower curtain, is that something you could use? Of course it is, why wouldn't it be?

Before closing herself up in her apartment with all the shutters drawn and all the deadbolts turned to keep out the werewolves, Daontaon threw the bag (termites and all) in the corner dumpster; it was just a worthless bag of junk. Well, she kept the fan for herself, as a souvenir.

LOLA

Lola opened one of the drawers of the dresser. She sat down on the side of the bed and stopped to try to remember what she had been looking for, among the dozens of photos and myriad documents that she had been saving over all these years: manila envelopes in which, at least for a time, she had attempted to file and classify it all; recipes cut out of magazines that had gone out of print decades ago; owners' manuals for equipment that no longer existed, including the one for the television set her father had bought in the early fifties; ownership papers for Sara's bicycle; Evaristo's medical records; hundreds of letters in shoe boxes or tied together with faded ribbons; an enormous case containing all of Lola's own diplomas and report cards; patterns for baby clothes; old calendars, address books, theater programs, yellowed newspapers. She couldn't figure out what she had been searching for. Rummaging through the piles over and over, she found a folder with her daughter's name on it. Lola slowly leafed through the photocopied pages of the packet of poetry that Sara had left behind. She also found Sara's one and only work of theater, full of scribbled annotations and with lines scratched through, all red ink in Sara's old childish scrawl. Lola remembered that some of Sara's classmates had accused her of "ideological deviation" on account of that script and had thrown her out of the Communist Youth. Lola didn't know how to help her daughter back then, and Sara inevitably started to drift away from her little by little.

Lola told herself that she should ask Micaela to help her decide what to do with all of Sara's old papers. Ever since those incidents at the university, she had never written another line. And speaking of Micaela, how long had it been since she had called?

Lola stayed a while on the edge of the bed without moving, Sara's writings in her lap, her heart weighed down with feelings of sorrow and helplessness. The quiet knocking at her door interrupted her train of thought. Only a few days back somebody had come by to visit her, although Lola couldn't remember who. She recalled that she had cooked chicken with rice, and the visitor had appreciated that a lot, but as hard as she might try, she couldn't remember who it had been.

When she opened the door, without having unlatched the chain, she could make out that there on the landing of the staircase was a mulatta woman, with an abundance of flesh, about Sara's age, dressed in bizarre attire. Or at least that's how it seemed to Lola. She wore a multicolored handkerchief on her head, partially covering her neon-yellow dyed hair, a loose-fitting Hindu costume, and a multitude of necklaces, baubles, bracelets, rings, and earrings that encircled all visible areas of her skin. Her attempt at looking younger was a failure but not her exoticism, which could easily get her mistaken for a background character in some movie. Her long and voluminous sari was gathered at the waist and then flowed over the rolls at her hips. She was sporting black silk stockings, extravagantly out of place—mostly because on her feet she wore brown leather sandals, through which poked her toes, sheathed in their delicate fabric. Nevertheless, her friendly appearance made Lola decide to open her door.

The strange character introduced herself as Yuya, her new neighbor.

WOMAN WHO TALKS TO HERSELF IN THE PARK

Millions and millions of termites took off flying through the city, took their positions, established kingdoms and colonies. And then they turned to eating every piece of wood in their path. And Havana is dying…

MARTIN

His balcony faced the coastline and its extension along the gulf shores. That morning, without a hint of a breeze and beneath a sky the color of grenadine, free of clouds, the water shimmered underneath the sun like a silver platter. In the distance, a few fishermen floated on truck tires with their lines ready for their prey. A pair of black dogs scampered happily along the reefs, next to a stretch of wildly growing thickets tangled with sea grapes. With a set of blinders like plow horses used, and focusing his gaze on only a fragment of ocean, Martin would have been able to maintain the illusion that he was on a desert island. But if his head shifted a mere few centimeters to the right or left, his eyes would fall on an abandoned tenement building or the ruinous construction of who knows what never finished project. The debris was covered with excrement and revealed to the open air its rusty iron skeleton. A line of behemoths with peeling paint stood a few bare meters away, dozens of identical buildings with not an iota of style or grace, like stone hippopotami covered in clay.

The bubble of silence burst, and the daily clamor intruded. Martin jotted down on one of his mental note cards that the living room was not a living room, nor the sea a sea.

Why in the hell was it so hard for him to write one fucking decent paragraph? Just one, one little paragraph with "love and squalor," without hippopotami. A story where everything that glittered wasn't gold; there was really no need to gild the lily of his childhood, on the contrary, it was so perfect that he felt the need to somehow tone down the feeling of paradise lost.

Grandma Antonia longed for her old territory: the mountains of Asturius, the farmlands at the skirts of the sanctuary of the Virgin of Covadonga, the granaries. For Martin's other grandmother, on his maternal side, the terrain had been a little more to the west: along the

Camino to Santiago, the Galician domain at Saint Xil to which she had never returned. The past, after all, was unreachable territory. Simple and stopped in time.

But it was another matter entirely when the moment came to put it down on paper! One little page could eat up forty years in a gulp and, vice versa, in five hundred sheets not a single thing might happen.

Time and time again, Martin had come back to redo that first line, the most difficult one, so they say. "The blind hummingbird alighted for a fickle instant on the windowsill." And this fucking first line went down the path of all the ones before, crumpled up in the bottom of the waste paper basket.

"Right there is your problem, my boy," Martin's mother had said to him. "It's very complicated." And Martin wasn't sure what she was talking about, the novel? Life?

Moreover, where should he set the perspective, the fucking "point of view"? First person or third person? A child, an adult, or some mixture of the two? Or perhaps make her a girl, to confuse the feminist members of the prize committee? It was the tone that would make or break the piece; as he himself liked to repeat at the literary workshops with that gaggle of drunks, adolescent boys, and pretentious young ladies who thought they were writers. But the tone kept escaping him, closing itself off from him.

And what name should he use? Should he leave it as a generic "the boy"? No, forget that, anonymity infected bad literature like a plague.

His Uncle Felix was almost always called Uncle Felix. According to the setting where the adventures were taking place, air, sea, island, desert, the Appalachian mountains, the Amazon, another planet, the North Pole, he could be known as Davy Crockett, Captain Nemo, Blackhawk, Flash Gordon, or any other appellation from the pantheon. If Martin's mother was upset, she would call him "damned uncle," and Mr. Hemingway, who would chat with him from time to time at the *Floridita* bar, just called him *"amigo"* with his broad accent. Uncle Felix had spent forty years trying to write a novel, although he never got past the first line. He wrote a lot of "first lines," and it never went any further. Once, Uncle Felix had attempted to get the famous writer to listen to one of his "first lines" and for his trouble was interrupted with a brusque "go to hell with your shitty literature." Uncle Felix didn't take it the wrong way, because Hemingway used to say the same exact thing about his own books despite being a renowned writer. When you are in the middle of writing something, you don't dare say a word about it or you run the risk of screwing it all up, that was his theory. What's more, if Uncle Felix wanted to keep on drinking with him, they had to continue talking about the extravagant asses of the Cuban women, stray dogs, recipes for Biscayne style salt cod, the best times to fish in Cojímar; the only things worth talking about in this life.

YUYA

Yuya says that her good fortune helped her more than once to get out of a scrape. Lalita was acting cagey about the promised trip to Oriente to offer their thanks to the blessed Virgin of Caridad. She would make up the craziest excuses, and Yuya had trouble getting it through her head that to forswear an oath was just going to leave her open to all kinds of misfortunes and evil spells. Every time that they started coming up on a September 8th, Yuya would remind her daughter of what she owed the saint, and Lalita always would respond by asking just how she thought they were going to get all the way up to Cobre.

She had a point, in that transportation out to the provinces was almost nonexistent, in that Lalita's schedule and homework took up all of her time, in that they were short of funds, in that Shu was refusing to stay on his own even for a single weekend, and in that Yuya had started suffering from back pains.

Yuya says that even though you always think that there will be plenty of time to get something done in this life: to fix what is broken, to ask for forgiveness, to keep one's word once given, that's just not true, time is exactly what there is never enough of.

The solution to their problems showed up unexpectedly. Yuya found out that the Virgin from Cobre, the authentic one from the hermitage, was going to go on a sort of tour around all the Havana churches, with each one hosting a mass in her honor. Yuya saw the heavens open up, and with the utmost discretion asked Lalita if she would be willing to come along with her to fulfill her promise at one of the stops the Virgin would make during her circuit of Havana. Lalita answered that if this would serve to pay her debt then she was game.

According to Yuya, if you can't go to the hills of Cobre, sure enough the hills of Cobre will come to you.

After making a few inquiries about the trajectory of the sacred image of the patron saint of the city, she found out that the following Sunday, the Virgin of Caridad from Cobre, the very one and the same, would reign at the altar of a parochial church called The Savior of the World, at Santo Tomás and Peñón, in El Cerro, a goodly distance from where they lived.

Yuya says that they went to so much trouble and ran into so many difficulties it was just like they had made the actual pilgrimage to the sanctuary. To actually purchase a bouquet of flowers was out of the question, so the day before they did rounds of gardens still surviving despite neglect, collecting *marpacíficos* and *vicarias*, and then boiled a few eggs, toasted slices of old bread and filled a few water bottles to sustain them along their journey. They set off toward their destination long before the sun came up. After waiting hours for the bus, they had to change routes three times, and finally ended up paying a fortune to the driver of a broken down heap to take them along Agua Dulce Avenue to where it crossed Calzada de Palatino, from where it still was a walk of six long city blocks. Out of breath, Yuya sat down on one of the park benches in front of the ancient little church and gave thanks from the bottom of her heart to all of them, Etelvina, her poor grandmother, her father San Lázaro, and the *Chinito of the Charada,* for not having run into the wandering soul of the Haitian in penance even once and for having arrived before the mass started.

Lalita's girlfriend, a declared atheist and unbeliever, accompanied them on their pilgrimage and, as things turned out, was hard to persuade to actually leave the church, she had become so fascinated with its antiquity and its quiet aura.

When the ceremony was over, they sat down to wait for the bus that would take them back home. During the almost four hours that they were left waiting, and through a series of conversations with the faithful who were congregated there at the bus stop, Yuya negotiated the move from Alamar to Vedado.

And the timing couldn't have been better. The very day after they finally moved out of the old place, Yuya found out about the appearance in that district of a woman who had been cut to pieces. According to Yuya, she took this as a good sign.

HERMI

In the meanwhile, Tristan had talked himself into getting involved in a theater group, to do anything that they needed, even if it were simply to be the stooge who shifted around pieces of scenery.

After the apotheosis of *Night of the Assassins*, new versions of classic sagas came into vogue, and everywhere you looked were Medeas, Oedipuses, and Elektras tripping across the boards in their togas. It occurred to Tristan to put forward for consideration one of Sara's plays, in which a young and handsome Charon ferried, and with all gentility, any dead soul who asked him to the Other Side, without requiring the customary obolus or any other payment. "There is no reason to add stinginess to the afflictions of already suffering victims," commented Tristan in one of his cryptic phrases. "The dwelling of Hades doesn't discriminate," he added. (Or was it Hermi?)

The bare scenography consisted of an intentionally artificial sea passage on a backdrop, a tattered curtain, and an ambiguous effigy of an adolescent whose forehead was stained with blood that dripped down into the right eye, in a very free-styled homage of the recently deceased Magritte's *La mémoire*. Spread over the stage was sand on one side, dried leaves on the other, and in the center a grey carpet decorated with mirror shards in Op-Art style patterns. Everything else was left up to the imagination of the audience. When you counted the mixture of Bola de Nieve songs interspersed with music from a band called The Doors, and an interminable overlay of "Baby, you can light my fire," the soundtrack was unsettling.

As the play was in rehearsals, Hermi and Tristan had the chance to attend a unique staging of the "Happening" at *Teatro Estudio*. "Don't you dare be so crass as to look but sitting right behind you is Marguerite Duras," warned Tristan. When the disconcerting spectacle started, they listened to the translator attempting the impossible task of making the texts comprehensible: "What should the form of a cigarette be, round, square, pointed, or what? What should the form of an ID card take?" Still, they thought they heard a few dry snickers of agreement from the back row. In the final moments, the actors started to come down among the audience slinging paint, and the spectators found themselves having to escape by crawling down the aisles. In the chaos, Hermi lost sight of Marguerite Duras and thus was cheated out of her one great opportunity to recite for her various lines from the entire script she had memorized of *Hiroshima mon amour*.

Never again would such extremes of hilarity find their way onto the stage. Sara's play was rejected as well.

For her part, Hermi applied at the Film Institute for any job they would be willing to give her, starting from the bottom up. After waiting several months, the information was leaked to her that some high up muckity-muck had blackballed her, due to the rumors that had been flying. "Uncertain morality" was the label that distanced her forever from her dream of making movies. Nobody ever explained anything to her nor did they allow her to say anything in her own defense.

Hermi took an old backpack from Tristan's days in the Literacy Brigade and stuffed it full with a pair of jeans, two shirts, a can of condensed milk, a spoon, a metal plate, and a kitchen jar, together with a bag of personal hygiene items, and her copy of Marcuse covered in cardboard. She then left to harvest vegetables in the Havana Hills, without anyone telling her to, the favored rehabilitation work for young adults. Every weekend she would come home dead tired and covered with red dirt; wash her clothes; prepare another can of sweetened condensed milk in the double boiler for the following week; and, dressed only in a sweater, she would set to painting the walls with doughy clouds and skinny moons á la Miró.

Not long after, the head of the Hills brigade asked her to leave off her agricultural work, although she received no explanation for this decision either.

All this was taking place when the already old news came about the Age of Aquarius, "Flower Power," and the hippies in San Francisco. And almost at the same time, with no transition, the news of Che's death in the guerilla struggle, the massacre at Tlatelolco, the shootings at Kent State, and the tanks filling the streets in Prague. The euphoria from the era when they all had been twenty years old had come to an end, and the world changed.

DAONTAON

If there was anything that Daontaon hated more than writers, it was "child writers." On the television screen, hands around a microphone, was a perfect example of one, with a Harlequin hairdo petrified in two waves that hung down to her shoulders, howling poetry that rhymed lasagna with ganja and none-ya… Un-fucking-believable!

"She deserves to be cut up into pieces," commented Daontaon, nibbling furiously on yam-flavored cookies. "Ha. Her, her mother, and her grandmothers."

"Have you heard anything new about the dismembered woman?"

"Oh, Willie, don't talk to me about that anymore, I've got too much stress already," replied Daontaon, staring nervously at her hands. "Lend me an emery board. All the craziness at the Cultural Center is going to be the death of me. All I can think about are termites and fire ants. Last night I spent the whole night in the strangest dream. Should I tell you about it? Of course. The building... Which one do you think I mean, sweetie? *This building.* Now, don't you be interrupting me making those funny faces, I lose my train of thought. Our building had been left completely deserted and, when I say 'deserted,' I mean that from one minute to the next the entire pile of our idiot delinquent neighbors had disappeared, not a single one of those sons of bitches who live here was left. Only *me* and a *writer*."

The italics buzzed through the room like a hive of bees stirred with a stick.

"And to top it all off, this *writer* had the same face as the jerk that lives right over next to us, in the building beside ours, that guy Martin who thinks he is something special. Ha. So it turns out that when he realizes that he is a complete cretin, a poser, who couldn't write his fucking novel, the *writer* started hacking away at everything in his path. Why are you looking at me like that?"

"Don't stop, go on telling me your dream."

"Are you going to make coffee? OK then. But that's how it ends. Before that, I was trying to call for help on the phone, but none of them would work. I told you to stop making faces at me. In the middle of everything, ghosts started appearing everywhere... Little kids with their heads cut off playing baseball, the dismembered woman holding her head under her arm, the old man's niece demanding her fan back from me, that gimpy girl who set herself on fire—do you remember?—because her husband was cheating on her. Even the wandering soul of Micaela's aunt who took off for the North. Have you ever heard anything like it? And down a staircase..."

Daontaon pointed with the emery board, grabbing it in her fist as if she was brandishing a hatchet, toward the place behind the wall where one supposed the building's staircase was located.

"Down some stairs just like these... What do you think was dripping down from one step to the next? Waves of poop? A sea of pee? No sirree, my dear. It was blood! Cascades of blood. And that jerk Martin gone insane, machete in hand, slicing up everything and everyone in his way. Good grief… Whose fault is it anyway, that he can't get it up to write one shitty story? There's crazy people any which way you turn these days. But the one who's really responsible for all of this is my boss, Braulio, who ever since I've been avoiding him, he's been giving me every crappy little pain in the ass job that he can think of, if you'll pardon the expression. Do you know what he gave me on Monday? No, kid, you can't even start to imagine. The historian who lives in Bahia has this parrot, and it escaped from its cage, and the idiot bird didn't even think of flying away like it should have. Oh, no. Instead it had to go perch on a bald high tension electrical wire and fried to a crisp right there, with its tropical feathers smoking like nobody's business. The historian practically had a heart attack on the spot, and we had to rush him to the Naval Hospital so they could put him on a Valium drip. But the most irritating part was trying to convince the people from the Electrical Company to send someone to climb up and take down the freaking bird. Because the historian got it into his head to preserve his dried out, fried, parrot. Do you remember that movie where a whole ton of winged beasties was attacking and killing everybody in sight?"

"*The Birds.*"

"That's the one, so all I need now is for all the friends and family of the electrocuted parrot to come after me. Jesus H!"

WOMAN WHO TALKS TO HERSELF IN THE PARK

The lions on the Prado had gotten so hungry that they were tired of being still as statues and came on down off of their pedestals. And then they went on to eat everything in front of them. And Havana is dying…

GERTRUDE

Memories are so slippery that you have to search for them and then pull them out of their hidey-holes. By brute force if necessary. You better believe it. Listen, we would have to tattoo them all over our bodies, like *The Illustrated Woman,* in order not to lose them and rewrite our own version of *Herstory* as Herodota did. Or take three hundred pages to tell our own unique and minimal account, *The Life and Opinions of Trystrama Shandy, Funesita the Memorious, The Book of the Dead Women.*

Our boring nights at the dorm took a turn when the Dead Girl made two fundamental donations: a pair of theater glasses, and a radio set older than Methuselah.

Thanks to that gadget we were guaranteed to get to class on time, punctuated by *Radio Reloj* and, moreover, maintain our own continuous background music. The soundtrack of nostalgia can refresh your memory faster than any madeleine dipped in tea, no matter what anybody says.

Do you remember? From the sonorous Music Festival in Varadero we took Massiel as the hymn to our wild times, with that "Out of Service sign," her "Hallelujaaahhh" and her roses in the sea. From *La dolce vita,* the instrumental "Patricia" inevitably evoking that strip tease scene that raised such a ruckus among the more Puritan. From *Cléo de 5 à 7* that heartbreaking "Sans toi," which had been so much more low-key when Meme's quartet did it. And that unforgettable *Mrs. Robinson,* even though we only managed to see her face when we finally had the film in our theaters twenty years later.

We didn't get to go to Jean Ferrat's concert in the Amadeo Roldán, but we went over ten times to see *La vieille dame indigne* and learned by heart her song "On ne voit pas le temps passer."

Those were the days when The Mamas and the Papas sang "Monday, Monday," and a blond Englishwoman, Petula Clark, "Downtown"… And "María Caracoles baila Mozambique," and each and every one of the clandestine records by The Beatles, needless to say.

Every Sunday morning, out on the little beach on 16th Street, you could find us singing "Cuando calienta el sol," "Venecia sin ti," and "Blowing in the Wind." And naturally, "muchas veces te dije que para hacerlo había que pensarlo muy bien...," and "If I Had a Hammer." At night, our hangout was always the café that used to be a funeral parlor, on the corner of 23rd and M, transformed into a Cultural Center of psychedelic colors until they shut it down, before we'd go out and "do the rampa," walking up and down La Rampa Boulevard, to the rhythms of *La Caminadora*, "she goes walking along, she goes dancing along..."

Although what they wanted was to make us feel guilty, to wash clean our sins of studying the Humanities through physical effort, to dirty our hands with the sacred earth and earn our sweat through healthy manual labor, to strip us of the "soft white underbellies" we had as pseudo-intellectual pups through grunt work—do you remember, or don't you?—we loved going to the agricultural camps on those weekends that they called "three for one." Three weekends off, and one on. Or the months long stretches of our vacations: picking citrus fruit on the Isla de Pinos or strawberries in Banao, plowing furrows for vegetables, or cleaning the fields of cane any old where.

There we would sing ourselves hoarse with the words of some anonymous bard, "I hope to remember how I felt when she walked by... the ashes of my illusions...." And, too, the old songbook of the partisans and the Spanish Civil War, inspired by the off-tune voice of one of our professors, "And if I die on the battle field, take my rifle in your hands..."

The Dead Girl, for her part, would croon the lines of "I climbed to the top of a great green pine for her to see, but only made out the dust of the carriage taking her away from me... So giddy-up, giddy-up, the first scene's over and now comes the shoot-em-up..."

We'd sing along in the train wagons, in the open-backed trucks, in the broken-down buses, on the top of the ferries, in the carts pulled behind a tractor; we'd sing in Cadenas Plaza, on the stairs at the university, in our dorms, underneath the trees at the entrance to the College of the Humanities, in the pool, around bonfires, in the fields;, we sang and sang and sang. We never stopped singing.

Daily life doesn't have a soundtrack, but the past sure does.

THE INDIA

O, how the winds of fortune shift for those fallen from grace! How fickle are the masses! And more than any, those squashed in together in tenements, slums, and multiple-unit housing.

When the news started filtering into the neighborhood and people heard of the violent acts perpetrated by the murderer on the body, now sliced up, formerly envied, of The India, those who knew the Frenchman (even those who had benefited from his gifts of largesse, truth be known) came together in a vengeful band. Once the doomed couple's apartment had been razed to the ground, they made away with anything that could have any possible value, which explains, months down the road, the absurd appearance of blunderbusses, daggers, and foils in a few Havana homes.

That weekend, as a result of the ingestion of a few bottles of wine, spoils of the justice-seeking sortie, people's spirits came to such a boil in the tenement that they went so far as to plan a good beating for "that dirty white boy." Passions ran even higher after the transmission, on Saturday night, of a movie about good blacks and evil whites in Mississippi. Patrick Rivière stayed clueless, having no idea that he was the butt of their shouts of "Down with the Klu Klux Klan!" Neither did he manage to understand that the insults and roars of fury were coming together in such a rythym and cadence that they were drowning out the rumba that was monopolizing the airwaves, "don't cry for her, don't cry for her, she was the great bandit herself, grave-digger, don't cry for her." Nevertheless, just to be on the safe side, the Frenchman holed up in a two-star hotel that was within the perimeter of his house arrest.

In the meanwhile, The India's mother Clara Luz, "the Professor," kept herself from falling completely apart with a mixture of lime flower tea and Valium, in the hopes that the rest of the cadaver would appear so that it could be properly buried in accordance to God's laws, not to mention other pagan laws. What remained of María Antonieta, (a name presaging such a bad end) after her anxiety-filled life and disorderly death, after having passed through the hands of the Dismemberer, the street dogs, the police, and forensics, lay on ice in one of the drawers of the morgue, in wait of its still wandering head.

Just about then one started to hear certain horrifying stories about the incursions of foreigners among the feminine flock during the tragic Havana of the '90s. People gossiped about sadistic Germans who kept their wives as servants with medieval manacles around their ankles; of Italians who kidnapped mulattas for purposes of the Sicilian mafia; of ripe old Spaniards eager to reinstate the tradition of harems; of English sex traffickers looking for workers for the porn industry and, in particular, they talked wildly about an Arab millionaire who, under false pretenses, had his fiance's corneas removed.

At this stage of the game, the Frenchman refused to modify his testimony in the least. Up until that moment, he had continued to insist on his version of the lovers and their nautical escape. Outside of that story, they couldn't get a single word past his lips. The weeks continued to go by, and María Antonieta's head still hadn't made an appearance.

On the other hand, after the infuriated hordes had intruded upon you-know-who's apartment, any possible proof of charges was destroyed. The vengeful neighbors had gone in and made off with not only every object of good quality as well as all of the food from the refrigerator, but even took the clothespins—really, everything but the kitchen sink. And if there had been butcher paper, barbed wire, scalpels, X-acto knives, or other cutting implements that could have been used in the hacking apart of a human body, they were now dispersed throughout the entire barrio of San Leopoldo.

Other details kept the arm of justice from being sure. The experts had noted that the way the funereal packets had been tied only could have been accomplished by someone well-versed in the arts of nautical knots, which tended to reinforce, to some degree, the husband's claims and the existence of a lover who in some way was connected to the seafaring life. Patrick Rivière had no alibi, although neither did he have a motive, at least nothing more than implied jealousy, and so the possibility of other suspects and perhaps the alleged lover gained credence. Moreover, in reality, the beheaded body could belong to some other unidentified individual. If the head itself didn't turn up, it was impossible to bring formal charges based simply on a mother's interpretation of a marking on the deceased's skin, perhaps the aforementioned scar or perhaps just a birthmark.

Some questions remained unanswered: Where did the butcher paper come from? (Or from whose stash of butcher paper had some been purloined, to be more exact?) What sort of weapon had been used to cut the woman's throat and, later, to cut the body into pieces? And what was the deal with this wicked predilection for the eastern zone of the capital?

The head of "The Dismembered Lady of the East Havana Municipality" was the only thing that could close this case with such a complex set of circumstances.

In the meanwhile, rumors about the crime flew from mouth to mouth and inspired several writers in the literary workshops to write short stories, and even one poem.

MARTIN

Upon her arrival in the New World, Grandma Antonia went to live in the home of a relative, the owner of a bakery. Uncle Felix had gone to cut sugar cane in Matanzas. During the meanderings of their Atlantic voyage, Grandma Antonia had found more than enough time to teach him to read and write. Thanks to that, they were able to keep in touch through the mail.

"From a mania for letter writing he graduated to the vice of writing literature," lamented Grandma Antonia. Their baskets were always filled to the brim with papers; books piled up in every corner; he developed a habit of pecking away at the typewriter until the wee hours of the morning; his little poems, even some with an erotic flavor; the horrible reputation of having a writer in the family, which is the same as saying a lunatic, crazy as a bedbug, a delinquent, a pauper, a bum, with his head always in the clouds, "Damn him and the moment that I rescued him from ignorance and contaminated him with the alphabet," concluded Grandma Antonia.

Martin's mother lifted her eyes to the cloudless sky as she always did when her thoughts took a turn down some back alley. Then she stared at him, not a little perplexed by so many falsehoods mixed in with more accurate memories, "My dear boy," she said, "your uncle, may he rest in peace, never lived in Matanzas." Martin's mother continued to read carefully, but her unbelieving gaze frequently shifted up toward the heavens.

Uncle Felix, with baggage consisting mainly of fifty journals in which he had become accustomed to jotting down everything he saw happening around him, took up residence in the room at the end of the hallway; bought a single bed made of iron, an armoire, and a side table of wood and marble. There he placed a second-hand Remington, his only luxury, which he had packed in the middle of his clothing and shipped all the way from the sugar plantation.

At noon, the family was getting together for their main meal, Martin's father took a short break from his workday at the bank, Grandpa Severino came down from his workshop, and Uncle Felix emerged from his self-imposed literary prison. Martin liked to observe the goings-on of the household, hidden behind Grandma Antonia's screen, cross-legged like an Indian, peering through the opening between the partition and the wall. Martin's mother moved down the corridor toward the dining room, her hands around a serving bowl, an imposing tureen filled to the brim with pieces of chicken, golden potatoes, and noodles; a porcelain dish transported with as much majesty as a royal crown. Grandma Antonia, usually so intransigent in everything, was indulgent in the matter of the soup. "If the boy doesn't like it, give him something else." "Oh, Antonia," Martin's mother dared to respond, if a bit weakly.

"I don't know what is up with that boy, to keep himself hidden away behind that screen for so long. He's going to go crazy reading so much."

"Nobody goes crazy because of that," chimed in Uncle Felix.

"Don't you go sticking your nose into it," replied Grandma Antonia from the kitchen, "he's been back there three hours already, and it's time for dinner."

In the middle of the plains of the Wild West, nobody cares about what time dinner is served.

Martin's mother raised her voice to warn that the soup was getting cold. Uncle Felix, sitting at the table, raised his palm to his mouth, beating in a soft rhythm and letting out an intermittent noise, sounding like an Indian. Then from the kitchen came a cry. "It's not such a big deal…" Uncle Felix started to say. He was cut off by the sound of Grandma Antonia's body hitting the tile floor. Martin's mother ran out screaming, "ohmygod ohmygod ohmygod!"

Martin's mother scrutinized his manuscript with disapproval. "I never made you eat soup, my son. What a liar you are."

HERMI

"In order to petition the Palace Destroyer, lady of our thousand and one Havana nights," said Hermi (or was it Tristan?) as she bought a bouquet of lilies at the corner of Zapata and 12th, the entrance of the Colón Cemetery.

Guillermo needed company and had asked the two of them to meet him there. It was time to "get Tomás out," the exhumation of his provisional sepulcher, as was the custom in those collective mausoleums, and to move his bones to a definitive resting place.

Neither Hermi nor Tristan was in a very good mood. The conclusions of the purge committee, the so-called "setting of limits" in the theater sector, had been released the month before and, as they had feared, Tristan had been expelled from the group. In the final judgement, he was sentenced to work as a smithy in Cubana de Bronce, in order to avoid vagrancy charges and the certainty of jail time.

Tristan, after his eight plus hours in the shop, would return at dusk with his clothes reeking of smoke and grease; he would take a bath and then set himself to cleaning the grime out from under his fingernails, which he had always kept so pristine and which now were as torn up as his hands, covered with cuts and blisters. Then he would eat a bit of whatever there was, standing up, without saying a word, and then he would fall into bed and sleep like the dead, night after night. At the start of the new day, Hermi would hear him leave before dawn, moved and surprised by his determination not to give up, not to be beaten. An hour later, she herself would leave, without any breakfast, to catalog books in the warehouse of a library in Arroyo Naranjo. Hermi's job was, at least, cleaner, although the intense humidity and lack of light gave her a constant runny nose. As her only perk, at lunchtime she was allowed to read from the collection of rare manuscripts.

Guillermo finally arrived, with a packet of clean cloth and a bottle of perfume, as custom dictated, to properly dispose of Tomás's remains in their final destination. "We could have used some eggplants as well, to make a tribute to Oyá, the patron of fury and change."

As they walked along the central avenue, bordered by trees that mitigated the searing heat at three in the afternoon, a taxi crossed in front of them, braked to a sudden stop, and Tomás's mother got out, looking rushed. She was dressed with extravagant elegance and clutched to her breast a bag full of soft cloth. She motioned to Guillermo to come closer, and they spoke for a few moments. Afterward, Guillermo came back covered in a cold sweat. He moved his lips into a grimace that was an attempt at calm, and from his throat emerged a hoarse whisper. Tomás's mother had asked, almost demanded, that he go away, told him that this was strictly a family affair.

The taxi entered the labyrinth of silent side streets, and they followed at a distance, without exchanging a word between them. When the car stopped in front of four grave diggers who were chatting animatedly;

Hermi, Tristan, and Guillermo stayed back a bit, hidden behind a chapel like a band of criminals, and there they settled in to wait. After a while other people arrived, carrying their own bolts of linens and fragrances: some driving, others walking, coming down the dilapidated pathways, covered with weeds, that divided the graves. The sky was completely empty, without a cloud in sight. At that hour the sun's rays spilled out pure fire, and everyone's faces became covered in dust that mixed with their sweat. At last, the cemetery employees started their labor and without much ceremony began laying out the coffins in a row along the width of the avenue. Each loved one came up to the remains of their dearly departed, fished around in the human ruins, and placed them in the perfumed cloths they had brought. The mixture of the various distinct emanations floated as a fog over to where they waited. "My orange shirt," murmured Guillermo. From there, they saw how Tomás's mother guarded the remains of her son in the bag of linens, intermingled as they were with a few rotten shreds of the orange shirt that Tomás had liked so much and that had served as his funeral garb.

"She's taking Tomás's bones to Mexico, where his grandfather is from. She says she's getting out of here and that she isn't going to leave her son behind."

When everything was over, Guillermo still holding his package in his hands, and Hermi with her useless lilies, they sat down to rest beneath a flamboyant tree in full flower. Surrounded with such serenity, Guillermo told them about a book he was reading, *Top of the World,* that in one of its chapters it described how the Eskimos abandoned their elderly to the storms when they no longer fulfilled a function. "We're already in the storm," said Guillermo, resentfully, "at least, when it's our turn, I hope they bury us all together and under one headstone, with the epitaph "finally on all of the black lists.""

"Our generation will die before our parents," and with that Tristan (or was it Hermi?) closed the conversation and placed the lilies on an abandoned tomb.

It was Saturday and they had the afternoon free. They walked in silence, going down 12th Street, then taking the Malecón all the way to Paseo, having nothing better to do. They remembered that sometimes at the Riviera Hotel bar Marta Valdés would perform, so they walked into the delightful darkness to drink a cold beer.

In the months that followed, Hermi threw herself furiously into painting several surrealist scenes with cows grazing on La Rampa and empty balconies melting beneath the sun, balconies from whose bars hung strings of heads, all of a decapitated woman whose face couldn't be seen. The head was always the same one, a faithful copy from one of Dali's landscapes, the one of a fleshy-assed woman painted from behind, looking out a window. The Bay provided the background with a Christ of Havana kneeling before a crucified woman, the sinner redeemed through her own suffering.

WILLIE

"Ha. I'm not gonna let anyone have a wake for me **here;** *over my dead body,* I'm telling you," pronounced Daontaon, spewing her natural logic.

The *here* to which she refers with such dramatic italics is the Funeral Parlor of Alamar. At first glance it looks like a storage unit, a mechanic shop devoid of tools, an empty warehouse, an administrative office, anyplace other than the sacred site of the GREAT FAREWELL.

When one stops to look more carefully, the initial impression remains, a mere locality where one might complete some piece of business. One might say, along poetic lines, that it is missing the sheen of time, the accumulation of pain that sanctifies and ennobles.

I do not believe it is possible that the place lacks clients but if that should happen, the Funeral Parlor of Alamar could be turned into a gym or a nursery school.

Big Mike had died the week before. The Neighborhood Council took contributions to pay for the floral wreath, the one that is due all deceased. To sponsor that beleaguered bough as a "floral offering" sounds pretentious, but I imagine that it would be all the same to its recipient. On a sliver of purple material printed with gold-colored letters they had offered "Dear Big Mike, we will never forget you." I doubt that matters too much to him now either.

Within a sturdy grey box made of "pressed cardboard" Big Mike lay as frowning and recalcitrant as ever, dressed in his striped shirt, mended a thousand times at the collar, and his only pair of dress pants. His final vestment didn't include shoes or socks, so as not to waste articles in such high demand nor tempt a sacrilegious robbery. I'm not sure why, but the bare feet of the deceased always left me in waves of prudish embarrassment.

Around the time that it was getting dark, The Scum in its entirety came to sit in the burning chapel, or worse than "burning," hot and humid enough to suffocate you. With an innocence that would move the hardest of hearts, they exclaimed, "We're going to miss you so much!" And it was the pure and simple truth.

As prime time neared, when the soaps came on the TV, the attendees of the wake scurried off from the storage unit, first with discretion, and then, as nine o'clock neared, in full stampede.

After midnight, two or three drunkards showed up, as well as a couple who couldn't sleep, and about seven other strangers along with a bus driver who pulled the vehicle loaded with passengers up to the funeral parlor, to drink a cup of coffee to the memory of Big Mike, whom they had never seen before in all their life.

By three in the morning, the guard was fast asleep, and Daontaon was fanning herself under the light of the only functioning lamp. The mosquitoes buzzed, and a line of carpenter ants marched in formation toward the coffin.

"Listen, my dear, I'm going home to bed. For god's sake! This is too much for anybody!"

And there I ended up again, alone with a dead man. The last time was when Tomás shot himself. Sometime after midnight, his mother fainted, and they took her to the hospital. Given the circumstances, nobody, besides myself, the person who loved him most in the world, stayed by Tomás's side in the "great" farewell.

Nobody from the building was at Big Mike's burial either, because public transportation has gotten so bad. Before the box was lowered into a communal grave, at the last minute and in a hurry, the dead man's granddaughter appeared, a pale young thing who looked like death herself. It was a quick ceremony, without tears or panegyrics.

For a few days there was a respectful calm, silence reigned among the boom boxes, and even the birds of a feather limited their cheeping. I can't stop thinking how much Big Mike would have enjoyed such tranquility, but sometimes it takes dying...

It will be my turn to die soon. My time is becoming ever shorter. Nobody knows, not even Daontaon... Dot dot dot.

Without a doubt the neighbors will make another round of donations to cover a crown of flowers, the biggest one I will ever have, and the only one. They will whisper about my sins, "But didn't you know that Willie...?," with a bit of mischief, a little disgust, and a tidbit of compassion. And then they will take off, relieved, satisfied at having done their duty, and in a hurry not to miss another episode of their soap opera. Strangers will appreciate being able to drink a coffee above and beyond their own quota at my cost. No one will be at my burial, because who can you ask to get all the way there, with the heat, the lines, and how bad the buses are. Big Mike will save me a spot in the common grave, and finally he will have somebody who will listen to his endless harangues for all eternity.

The only thing that keeps haunting me is the idea of my bare feet.

For a few days, The Scum will behave with a degree of circumspection and Tilingo will do his best to keep his herd of goats under control.

But of course, by the weekend the party will be well on its way again; I'm not fooling myself.

"*Kid, you brought it on yourself,*" Daontaon will say as my only elegy, with italics and a period.

WOMAN WHO TALKS TO HERSELF IN THE PARK

Carpenter ants carved channels down the walls. The worker ants dug all through the ground, constructing silos, opening pits and caverns where they situated the nests of their reign. During the night, when the John Does were doing their best to procreate, warrior ants marched out in formation to build up food supplies and extend their territories. And that's how carpenter ants took over the city. And Havana is dying…

MARIA ESTHER

The Romans believed that men's souls stayed close to them, beneath the surface of the soil. And just where had she come up with that? Maria Esther, her eyes closed, tried to remember. Ah, from *The Aeneid*, nothing less. Virgil talked in detail about the process used to lock up "the soul within the tomb." During the ceremony, they would pray that the earth weigh lightly upon the spirit, accompanied as it was by all the things that it might need in the afterlife: horses, dogs, slaves, weapons, jewels, jars, clothing, wine for thirst and milk for hunger. With all that paraphernalia, one assumed that the sacred spirits would remain at rest to the end of time, satisfied in their subterranean dwellings. But if protocol wasn't followed to the letter, or if the ritual wasn't completed with the requisite solemnity, then the soul would be condemned to wander. She wondered if the Dead Girl's soul was drifting in eternal suffering.

Her encounter with Martin had incited Maria Esther to take apart the puzzle and put it back together again, but with the pieces stuck in different places, arms separated from bodies as if amputated, out of their traditional locations in search of a truer picture than the one she had before.

Puzzles. And why had she started to think about jigsaw puzzles just now? As a child, her technique had been to find the edge and corner pieces first, working from the outside inward, separating the pieces of cardboard by their colors. Once in a while a piece would get lost, and a segment of the picture would remain a mystery.

The Dead Girl was a missing piece in the mess of her life.

The voices of the interns going on their medical rounds roused Maria Esther from the mental meanderings Martin's visit had sent her on. The retinue buzzed like a hornet's nest around her new roommate, a young girl.

Over the weeks that Maria Esther had been in the hospital, a whole parade of heterogeneous sick women had passed through the bed alongside her own. Patients on their last legs, others suffering anemia, old ladies who had lost their marbles… All of them with an abundance of relatives who would congregate during visiting hours to share their opinions about other family members, illnesses, and the state of the nation. They came with thermoses of coffee, Tupperware filled with food they had rummaged: ham sandwiches, guava turnovers, fruit juice, according to the personal taste and economic circumstances of each one. Invariably they had pity for the solitary Maria Esther, without a single companion or visitor, and they would invite her to share in their feasts or their rounds of coffee. Maria Esther would speak a word or two just to comply with the formalities, although she gratefully accepted their good will and, more than anything else, the little sips of coffee, one of the things that she missed most from her former existence.

As Dr. Arguelles and the interns debated at length the patient's symptoms right in front of her, they squinted through the glare at the medical records and examined each detail of her clinical history, coming up with conclusions that left Maria Esther uneasy, and all the while the afflicted girl laid there without making a sound and with her eyes wide open. She had arrived the day before in the afternoon, and unlike the others who had filled the bed before her, she maintained an abstracted and almost hostile silence. At visiting hours nobody came to see her; she wouldn't take a bite of the food she was served; and, shockingly (to Maria Esther), she left her television turned off. The girl pulled the sheet up over her head, turned toward the wall, and apparently went to sleep. In the morning she managed a confused "good morning" as she listlessly ate her breakfast. Her skin had a yellow tinge, and her lips were pursed tightly in a gesture of either intense pain or disgust. Maria Esther observed her with curiosity and a bit of apprehension; either she was losing her mind or the new patient looked like the ghost of the Dead Girl.

Maria Esther found out, to her dismay, that the girl didn't know where her father was at the moment; that her mother lived in London; and that she had no other relatives.

"My dear," and the endearment didn't soften the blow of the news at all, "you need an emergency operation right away."

Dr. Arguelles' voice, which put an end to the girl's exam, made it to Maria Esther as if through a haze, wrapped up as she was in the cobwebs of her own anguish.

ESTELA

Another weekend without a word from Oscar. Estela started to shred outdated papers, including the old fax from Lucia announcing her arrival. Can you believe it, Lucia bringing up that old memory of when they had wanted to be writers? Futilities of adolescence. They already had too many years on them to be remembering that kind of silly stuff. Where had she stashed those poems? The next time she went to Havana she would have to do a major spring cleaning in her house or, that is, in the house that used to belong to her parents. At the bottom of the pile of papers on the desk, she found the package that her father had sent with the Cuban guy. Dang, she had forgotten all about it. Estela patted it and her fingers felt something like sand beneath the wrapping. She opened the small parcel and found a note written in pencil that introduced another wrapped packet. It was her father's handwriting, almost illegible: "Happy daughter," and with an arrow pointing to the forgotten word "Birthday." Ooops! Even Estela had forgotten her own birthday. Her gift from her dad was a little bag of coffee "from the bodega," that is to say, the monthly quota assigned to each Cuban through their ration books, a few ounces of coffee beans mixed with burnt chickpeas. Startled, Estela set the scarce amount of grounds on top of the bureau, as if it were a grenade without its pin. "Estela, I have a little matter to discuss with you," Olguita's irritated voice took her by surprise. Without waiting for a reply, Olguita came in and sat down on the corner of her desk, with her usual lack of courtesy. She gazed down at her orange-painted fingernails, she tossed her hair, and she adjusted one of the loops she had hanging from her earlobes. "I have to take some vacation time," she announced after that preamble. At first Estela stared at her, taken aback, and then she replied "Impossible" in a tone that brooked no reply, "we're in the middle of the high season, Christmas; what's gotten into you?" Olguita stuttered, and her mouth tightened into an expression that Estela had never seen on her before. "A neighbor let me know that they had to admit my little girl into the emergency room, like all of a sudden. I guess she's real sick." Estela didn't know whether to believe her or not. "You have a daughter? I had no idea. How old is she?" "Eighteen." Estela looked at her; Olguita didn't look old enough to have a daughter that age. "I left her with her grandfather, but then my father-in-law passed away, and now she's all by herself. Her father lives abroad, he started a whole other family there, he stopped writing us, and now we have no idea where he is." Resignedly, Olguita spit out the series of sentences as if repeating by rote a set of prayers learned by heart. Estela glanced at the package of coffee rations. "I'm sorry, Olga, but if you go right now, I'm going to have to replace you with somebody else; I can't get along without someone else here in the office with me; just imagine, I lost my mother and couldn't even…" Olguita interrupted her with a wave. "Well, go and start looking for somebody else, Estela, because I'm taking the first flight to Havana. Do whatever you want." Olga stood up from the desk corner and brushed off her skirt as if she had been sitting on ashes or volcanic rock. She set a card on top of the bureau. "Ah," she said opaquely, "this was left for you just a few moments ago." She shook out her long red hair, walked out of Estela's office and, badaboom, she slammed the door. Estela picked up the card and saw that it was an invitation to one of those "Latin American parties" as they liked to call them, unfortunately. Yet another chance to face the torture chamber: a ton of depressed Argentines who from the get go would be asking for freebies, any old thing, a book, a poster, a gratis trip to anywhere; all of them in "solidarity" with the cause, but leagues away from the island's backwardness and poverty, as if they were good for anything, drinking their whiskey and eating *paté de fois gras*. Then there'd be two or three nostalgic Colombians; a few Chileans who would stay up all night reciting Guillén poetry by heart; and, to round things out, a musical walk down memory lane with tangos, cumbias, rancheros, and boleros. Finally, and before the assembled party got so drunk they were reduced to crying about what they had left behind, of course, it never failed, black beans and rice, fried plantain, flank steak with piles of sautéed onions, the Cuban style feast prepared by Tussy, her compatriot who had been in London for at least a thousand years already. She had ended up a widow in the middle of the '80s and did her best to entice into her lair any stray Cuban who passed through the city. A few of them would stay with her for a short while, well fed, and then wham, bam, thank you ma'am. Others settled in and stayed longer like the mathematician, who at the end of his substantial repast dumped her for a woman from Holland with better looks. While the mathematician was in residence in London, though, all the parties had been regaled with Cuban music because, in order to scrape together a dollar here and there, this John Doe had cobbled together a sort of band, consisting of an electric piano, a cassette player as accompaniment, and a Scottish partner in crime who had learned to beat about on the drums, albeit not very well. Estela couldn't remember the name of the group, who these days were "appearing" in a dive bar in Amsterdam, cheating the poor tone deaf Europeans who confused the mathematician's gibberish with authentic Caribbean music. Jesus, Mary, and Joseph. The Cubans were quite a bunch of characters. Estela tore up the invitation into little pieces and, together with the packet of coffee, threw it all in the wastebasket.

GERTRUDE

With the Dead Girl's opera glasses we gazed out toward where the ocean met the sky, the horizon dotted with little fishing boats, barges, and oil tankers waiting for the guide boat to lead them into the bay; we held vigil with the cadence of the waves and, when the weather was bad, we watched the crash of the water that leapt over the sea wall at the Malecón and flooded the little plaza at G Street. We spied inside the houses all around us, not to mention their balconies and the line outside the El Recodo Café. More than anything, every Saturday we patrolled the entrance to the Turf Club at the corner of Calzada, a favorite for couples because of the dark interior, and from our window on the 23rd floor we dedicated ourselves to discovering who went in and came out of the Turf with whom: clandestine affairs, boyfriends who had escaped from their official girlfriends after dropping them off at the dorms at curfew, adulterous neighbors whose trusting wives slept soundly in their beds. But it was all very innocent on our part, no harm intended.

The truth was that the Turf was perfect for lovers, just as the Pico Blanco was the best place to listen to feeling; The Red Room or the Parisién for dancing between performances; Las Cañitas at the Havana Libre Hotel for studying before an exam; and El Ruedo for conversation.

Fifteen women on a dead man's chest! Ho, ho, ho and a bottle of rum!

When we got out of class, on especially hot days when we had nothing better to do, we would go pile into El Ruedo, the tavern at G and 23rd with a dusky Spanish ambience, do you remember? Walking in, out of the brilliance of the sun, we were momentarily blinded, running into the chairs as we found a place to perch. For the price of a single glass of sangria, the waiters would bring free little plates of fried chicken wings, with which we staved off our hunger pangs as we sat around the heavy wooden tables debating at the top of our lungs about politics, film, philosophy, or literature, to the tune of *paso doble* on the piano and with the terrifying visage of a bull mounted over our heads.

El Ruedo was a great place to spend time, until it all went to hell.

That afternoon, nobody had invited that guy, just another student in our year, to come with us but he stuck to us like glue and started being a pain in the ass from the get go, digging at his teeth with a fountain pen and asking loaded questions. Around 7 p.m., just like any other day, a guitarist climbed on stage and started to sing in the fashion of *cante jondo*, and then the flamenco dancer, in her white dress with huge red polkadots, full of folds, ruffles and trains, began her dance, accompanied by rhythmic clapping from the audience. Everything was fine until a rare shaft of light illuminated that the abundantly fleshy dancer had to have been about five hundred years old, with layers of makeup hiding her wrinkles, and the beauty spots that had been daubed on the top layer of the palette lay there like blow flies. If you really paid attention, despite the cheery stamping of her heels, she looked terribly unhappy, "just like clowns do," the Dead Girl had said. To tell the truth, she couldn't sing worth a damn, and her dancing was even worse, but that's what she had been doing her entire life, her life as an entertainer: living on the applause of the audience, the toasts that the drunks would make with their red wine, and the occasional boozy "olé," which our group supplied happily. Little enough to ask in exchange for the boatloads of crispy chicken wings...

On that afternoon that went down in our history, the guy with the fountain pen impetuously jumped up on the stage to give the old girl a little competition. At first, she put on a good face and tried to make the best of the situation; after all, that was her job, the reason she was paid, and this could be one of the times that she even got a tip. But when that jerk, laughing his head off, asked the audience to give a hand for "grandma," the chubby dancer broke into tears and fled the stage. Then the Dead Girl climbed up on the platform as well and, despite looking as skinny and frail as she did, she knocked the guy down with one swing. The scandal made the papers. As was to be expected, the Dead Girl got the worst of it, being a young lady who ended up involved in such a sordid situation. And that's how El Ruedo became off limits, and we lost any future good times we could have had there.

After that incident, I couldn't escape a particular sensation of insecurity. Our day to day occurrences seemed to continue in their same old routine but then, from one second to another, with a single misstep, they would enter into a strange and dangerous other dimension. Even though we didn't know it, in addition to the bull's visage that had been hanging over our heads, we had a sword just like the one suspended by a horsehair over the courtesan of Syracuse; that damsel named Damocles who laughed and sang, not knowing what was about to fall down upon her.

And, bam, from one moment to the next the conflagration was going to ignite. And we would have to answer for ourselves the same question asked at the end of *Galilea Galilei*. Do we save our own skin, or do we do the right thing, like Giordana Bruna?

Don't forget, they were going to try to take it all away from us, even our past.

YUYA

Yuya says that getting out of an apartment in Alamar and into some other place is almost impossible, but getting into El Vedado... A miracle! You couldn't deny that playing the card she had up her sleeve of that little apartment in the tenement in *Los Muertos* was a master move on her part.

Thanks to the inheritance of that little hole in the wall, which had been under lock and key all these years, forgotten by everyone, even Lalita, Yuya could make the most magical offer in real estate: the two for one. In other words, she could trade her two places, the one in Alamar and the other on Ánimas, for nothing less than a three bedroom apartment, complete with two bathrooms and a terrace with a sea view, prime property, in the most desired neighborhood in all of Havana.

True, the apartment needed a paint job, window repairs, and a certain amount of maintenance in the plumbing system, but Yuya felt triumphant! The master bedroom, with its own bathroom and a door out onto the deck, was occupied by Lalita and her friend, while Yuya and

Shu settled into the second bedroom, a room of larger proportions than their entire honeymoon residence back in the now nonexistent patio of the Barrio Chino. The third bedroom, much smaller and without an obvious occupant, was converted—thanks to the changing times around them—into their sacred altar room, with all of their saints and protectors on show, as they most definitely deserved.

Within a week of moving, Yuya considered herself a native of El Vedado. Lalita was finally smiling again after all those months, Shu was able to rest, and she herself felt like she had done what she was destined to do. Jesus, Mary, and Joseph! The work that it had taken her to decipher the innumerable labyrinths that had tied her up in knots all her life! According to Yuya, not even she knew the true beginning of her own story, much less how it would turn out, but her lucky star had helped her to untangle the mysteries that she ran into along the road.

After many years she ran into Luisa again, in the post office on Línea. She almost didn't recognize her. Yuya was quite familiar with the effects of aging within her own body but she was surprised at how much Luisa had deteriorated; she who had been so lovely and radiant selling lamps in the Ten Cent store on Galiano and now she was a mess, her mouth twisted into a permanent bitter curve, standing there in line to cash her retiree's pension, a few pesos that wouldn't last her until the end of the month.

They sat down together on one of the benches out on Paseo Avenue. It was threatening to rain at any moment, and the breeze off the ocean swirled the dry leaves around their feet. Luisa didn't seem to be in any hurry and, according to Yuya, without being asked she began to recount all of her losses: the big house in Miramar, the military gentleman, and the good life were long gone. The military officer had cheated on her for years with his assistant, a floozy the same age as her youngest daughter; Luisa had found out that, moreover, her husband had had a son out of wedlock before they had married; then her two daughters had it out with their father and even stopped talking to each other; they had been required to divide up the big old house into three separate living quarters, leaving her and her husband with the smallest, windowless, although still in El Vedado. They had sent the officer into forced retirement in the very bad year of 1989, at which point he had a nervous breakdown; then he became born again and was at church day and night. The illegitimate son, who had been disowned by his father, came to visit from Miami, and they reconciled. Now he "helped" them a little here and there. And if it weren't for that! One of her daughters decided to go live in Europe; she had "found some sort of scholarship to study there," or at least that's what Luisa had managed to make out, and they had heard nothing from her for some time now. The other doesn't speak to them, hasn't even let them meet their own grandchildren. To put the icing on the cake, the garage had flooded during the most recent hurricane, and now the Lada didn't run any more.

According to Yuya, the night before she had dreamed of the dreaded left arm of the *Chinito of the Charada,* as well as the two of spades. A double serving of misery. Falsehood, infidelity, and trickery. She had awoken upset, trying to interpret the message. As Luisa told her tale, Yuya sighed with relief: the allegory hadn't been meant for her directly, it was merely a warning of this encounter; in summary, a symbolic representation of the many years of Luisa's fate. Despite everything, Yuya felt an enormous wave of compassion toward her old friend.

Now it fell to Luisa to do everything: take care of her useless husband, do all of their errands on foot, clean the house, cobble together coconut "cakes" that she sold to try to make ends meet... By the way, did Yuya maybe want to order one? She'd give her a good deal because, after all, she still was Lalita's godmother.

Oh, how the world turns, says Yuya.

LOLA

Lola opened the patio door and exposed her body to the darkness of the blackout and the cold wind coming off of the sea. She groped through the shadows and sat down in the armchair, the wood so full of scents and scratches that it felt just like her own skin. A silence, that dreaded silence that opened the door to her memories, squeezed her heart like a claw. Which one? Which of all of her bad memories would come and torment her now?

To her surprise, a black hole, terrifying, worse than all of her bad memories combined, opened like a dry well in her head. And where had they all ended up?

"Lola! Are you up?" a strange voice spoke to her from the patio next to hers. "Lola, it's Yuya, your neighbor. I just made a pudding that has turned out delicious. Do you want to try some?"

Yuya? Lola didn't remember anybody by that name.

"Lola?" Now the voice was coming from the inside hallway. "Are you ok?"

Lola made out a faint light flickering between the slats of her shutters.

"Yes," she answered, "I'm..."

"Oh, you scared me half to death, Lola. I've been knocking for over an hour. Open up, I brought you a little dessert."

Lola walked carefully toward the glimmer and opened the door. There, with a smile from ear to ear, a candle in one hand and a bowl of creamy sweetness in the other, was her over the top neighbor. Lola let her in.

"The blackouts are different here in Vedado from the ones in Alamar," Yuya assured her, her logic incomprehensible to Lola, "they don't smell the same. Come on Lola, eat yourself a little of this pudding, it will do you good."

While Yuya nattered on and on, Lola sat down obediently and slowly, savoring each bite as if she were a child, she started to eat the white cream, redolent of lime and abundantly dusted with cinnamon. It had been such a long time since she had tasted anything like it!

"Ah!" exclaimed Yuya, almost yelling, "The lights came back on, just in time to watch my show! And what's this?"

Scattered over the dining room table were a handful of photos: Sara at twelve years old in her Literacy Brigade uniform, hugging an enormous pencil; a group posing for the camera, Lola with Sara in her arms the day she was baptized, all huddling in front of the door of the Church of Christ; Sara out on the patio, the day before she left, with her serious face on; Sara, all bundled up in the San Marcos Plaza, with a dove posed on her shoulder, her eyes full of irony; Lola and Evaristo with Sara, young and smiling, bending down to make sure they got into the shot; Sara, with her friends from her class at the University, out on the grand stone staircase, their arms spread wide, imitating the statue of their Alma Mater; Sara, laying face up in the sand on the beach in Varadero, clueless that the photographer was zooming in on her sleeping face; Sara, as a little girl, hugging a cat.

Yuya pointed at Sara and asked Lola who it was.

"My daughter's cat."

Yuya was going to ask again, but stopped at the sight of Lola's face, full of pain.

"He died a thousand years ago. I don't even remember what his name was."

Lola picked up the joyous photo of the Alma Mater and pointed out a girl wearing glasses, squatting at Sara's feet.

"And this is the Dead Girl. One of my worst memories," said Lola.

WOMAN WHO TALKS TO HERSELF IN THE PARK

From one of the potholes in the middle of the street erupted an immense column of smoke, and then another, and another, and they started spreading in all directions. And then out spouted jets of soot and thousands of poisonous gases. And Havana is dying...

MARIA ESTHER

Maria Esther had lost her faith. She had been an apostate since her adolescence. Her trajectory from being religious to atheist was accomplished with no friction or doubts troubling her conscience. Nobody forced her, nor did it cause any conflicts. One day God was still there and the next day he just wasn't, as calmly and naturally as a dry leaf that falls on account of its own weight.

When she was a little girl, she had complied conscientiously with her studies of catechism and sacred history. At the obligatory age she took her first communion with due solemnity. Fridays she abstained from meat and she spouted the doctrines professed by her teachers, the saintly little nuns who ran the Mary Help of the Sick Catholic School.

Throughout the sixties, she was aware that some of her classmates suffered and tormented themselves about losing their faith; others, on the contrary, were victims of the religious intolerance that muddied the waters in those days. She didn't feel a bit of doubt or remorse.

One time, at a literary conference in Rio de Janeiro, Maria Esther was invited by her colleagues to go and see the great sculpture of Christ Redeemer atop Mount Corcovado, a mandatory tourist stop. As they drove up through Tijuca Park, passing among a luxurious abundance of vegetation, the ambience stayed light-hearted and well within the habitual joking around between fellow academics. Upon arriving at the parking lot and embarking in the last ascending tram of the day, an unusual atmospheric phenomenon, according to her colleagues, covered the entire mountaintop with a volatile fog that didn't let you see a foot in front of you. Maria Esther stepped forward, lost in the haze, until she got to the circular platform that surrounded the base of the monument. All of a sudden, a gust of wind blew away the clouds and the effigy, a 125 foot-high concrete structure, was revealed before the startled eyes of Maria Esther, who immediately felt herself to be nothing more than one of the tiniest particles in the universe. Her faith returned like a sudden blow that took her breath away. She found that before her stood not a statue, but the Creator himself.

The sensation lasted only a few seconds. Her faith disappeared again, as quickly as it had come back, swept away by the breeze, But Maria Esther was unable to forget that moment of weakness, of vulnerability, of insignificance.

She never told anyone about it. The living tend to forget that they can talk to other living souls.

The second time she felt touched by evangelical mysteries happened when her own mother was on her death bed. According to what she remembered from her childhood, the only thing left for one to do under such circumstances was to pray, trust in some future encounter, wherever that may be, but Maria Esther felt incapable of believing. Nevertheless, deep within herself she sent out an unorthodox prayer: that even if she wasn't a believer her mother was so, please, could she die in peace as she deserved.

During the months of her mother's illness, everything had fallen apart on her. As it always seemed to happen in moments of crisis, everything went wrong at once, and no escaping it: her daughter had left the island for good, the old family dog had died, she found out about a conspiracy at her work to get her fired from her job, and then the refrigerator broke down.

Maria Esther would have liked to have had the consolation that faith brings. That was when she took up drinking. Now, laid back in that hospital bed, with her days numbered, she wished she was able to believe. With any sort of religion or certainty it all would have been easier, but she couldn't. She just couldn't.

The silent girl who had looked so much like the ghost of the Dead Girl didn't come back from the operating room. The nurse told her that she had been transferred to the intensive care unit. There she was debating whether to stay alive or not, or at least that was what Maria Esther wanted to think.

An abrupt breeze, like the one on Corcovado, swept into her mind the superfluous years of her life, together with all its abandonments, estrangements, culpabilities, and useless deaths.

ESTELA

Olguita left without saying goodbye. "It's better that way," thought Estela. Estela's office would operate in silence for the moment, until the arrival of another one of the many nutcases that tended to end up there. Estela went through the faxes and then made an unsuccessful attempt to communicate with Havana, in order to speak to Oscar. That the lines would be jammed due to the holiday explained in part the inability to get through, although at twelve noon on the dot, Havana time, when she finally got a call through, the operator said that the phone just kept ringing, no answer. "Is there another number you would like me to try?" "No," answered Estela, "there isn't another number." She locked up the filing cabinets and the glass-fronted door to her office, saying goodbye to her fellow workers with the customary "See you next year," or, in other words, see you next Wednesday, five days from then. The London fog, a thick cloak that obscured anything further than she could reach, made her feel like going for a little walk, moving along as if she were trapped in a ghostly breath that made her invisible. From time to time, the body of some stranger would appear out of the threaded white linen mists, walking past without meeting her eyes. Crossing Leicester Square, with all its theaters and the majestic Royal Opera House, she surprised herself thinking that Lucia would have loved to have taken a stroll there. She ought to be home by now, back to her banal preoccupations of "getting her hands on powdered milk" and "turning on the pump when the water went on," as she had recounted in her boring monologue. Fortunately, Lucia hadn't made a single comment about the Dead Girl. At least she knew enough to hold her tongue around that topic; after all, she was the only one among all of them who had any right to point the finger. Lucia "knew about it," and "she knew that Estela knew that she knew," in that obscure string of "knowing" that nobody was allowed to talk about. And at any rate, Estela didn't feel the least bit of compunction, despite all that had happened "afterward," in the Dead Girl's "afterward" before she had become the

Dead Girl. It was better not to stir up that whole episode, better to leave it be, untouched. Let bygones be bygones. She had never again run into that man who had asked them both to meet him so mysteriously in an empty room, in the basement of the Biology building, next to the Park of the Big Heads. Only Lucia and Estela. Not even Oscar could know about it. At that strange meeting, "talk about anything you'd like," he'd almost ordered, as he was rolling up one end of the recording tape onto a cassette before he pressed a button that started up the enormous machine, which had taken up almost the entirety of the table. Sitting in one corner, Lucia and Estela looked at each other, disconcerted by the situation. Chhh, chhh, chhh rasped the wheels going around, while the man watched them, waiting, a smile frozen on his perfectly shaven face. All of a sudden, Lucia, always so brash, let loose a laugh. The man authoritatively pushed the "stop" button and brought his chair around until he was facing them. With a fatherly air, he explained what was expected of the two of them. "It was necessary," he always used the impersonal form of the verb, that she and Lucia "get close to" the Dead Girl, who wasn't yet the Dead Girl. That they reach out to her, gain her trust, in so many words, and he made a forced gesture of displeasure, pretending that this was all repellent to him, that they "pump her for information." Find out everything that they could, how she thought, who she saw, what she wanted to do with her life, the man continued in oily tones, friendly-like, "it's for her own good," so that it almost sounded like once the wheels had been set into motion, that they were really going to be doing a favor for the Dead Girl, who wasn't yet the Dead Girl. "And without going into detail, of course," he added, "but her love life is of the utmost importance." Lucia refused, and her eyes opened wide as platters when Estela said yes. The man made clear that, given the circumstances, everything had to stay between the three of them, so as to "be of maximum help" to the Dead Girl, who still had a few more months before she would become the Dead Girl. Right when Estela crossed the street, close to Covent Garden, the mists dissipated completely and made way for a downpour. A pub on the banks of the

Tamesis, clean and well lit, beckoned her to enter and order a beer. It had been a long time since she had gone into a bar. And to go in on her own, to tell the truth, she hadn't done that once in her entire life.

MICAELA

That photo of Candita, her aunt. Micaela never looked at it, and now it was almost as if it was calling out to her, just like in her dreams. "Micaela, have pity on me." She had her hair up in a bun that gave her an air of authority, her chin jutted inexorably out, her pale face looked demanding. Micaela put the box of pictures away in the dresser, with caution, as if Aunt Candita was ready to jump out from beneath the cardboard lid and shake her by her shoulders.

Memory was as dangerous as going to sea with a hangover, Micaela muttered to herself. In the interludes of lethargy that permeated her wakefulness, she would once again see the Dead Girl's red and white striped socks hanging forgotten out on the patio of the tenement building. To top it off, the latest apparitions of Aunt Candita were making her dream in the wee hours of her insomnia, and in minute detail, of the house where she had lived as a teenager, in those days when nobody had died yet, nobody had left yet, and they were in and out all the time… In and out, went Micaela's horde of friends, neighbors, and relatives; an enormous family that didn't fit anywhere when it was time to celebrate some big event, and that always ended up congregating in their humble back patio on Animas Street, with her grandpa playing the harmonica and her Aunt Candita dancing the polka.

Also out on that patio, now merely rubble, her group of friends was in the habit of getting together to do homework and study for exams when they were taking classes at the university. Micaela saw in her dreams once again the discolored brocade tapestry that hung behind the wicker sofa where they would sit and drink lemonade; the snacks her mother would make for them, saltines with mayonnaise and Galician pastries from the bakery on the corner; the record player for their Saturday night parties; the runner that her grandmother had woven by hand decorating the top of the television set; her father beating on the radio to make it work; her uncle reading the newspaper in a rocking chair; the glasses kept upside down on a tray on top of the Westinghouse refrigerator; the one Thonet chair that sat next to the telephone table, in that hallway through which traipsed an endless file of grandparents, aunts and uncles, cousins, her mom and dad, Aunt Candita, the mulatto lady Etelvina who sewed her dresses when she was a little girl, her horde of friends, the Dead Girl, their dog Wolfie and her pups. Behind every blink of her eyes, in her dreams, her dear departed were haunting her. With Aunt Candita's reproaches she wasn't going to be able to go on much longer avoiding, as much as she wished she could, a thorough review of that past, a catalog of that wreckage, of the sunken ships.

Micaela bundled up in her ancient Russian parka and set out walking for the coastline, deserted at this hour. The sea looked calm, but was of a gun-metal grey that presaged a storm. As she walked through the sedums that poked up like dogs' teeth, a raging wind started, whipping grains of sand in her eyes and mouth with such force that it took her breath away. She felt like her head was going to explode.

Over the apparent calm, the gale beat against her sharply, cutting a swath through the layers of forgetfulness that Micaela had allowed, one after another, to settle over those old stories, stories pushed into corners so many years ago, when Sara, the others, the Dead Girl, she herself, were so young that each one of them still believed they were changing the world through their own actions.

She gazed at the ocean shoreline lashed by the wind's blows and to her it looked like a caricature of everything that was happening: a storm that would do away with any attempt she might make, one more time, to protect herself. Finally Micaela understood.

But…how was it possible that she ever had forgotten that Thonet chair? Where had it ended up?

LOLA

Lola painfully descended the stairs to go get her yeast roll, the one that was "hers," the mini-loaf listed on her ration book, just one a day per person, though sometimes smashed, rubbery, or covered in spots of mold. When she took her place in line, she found that they were running behind at the store today, and the people who had been in line since much earlier, all older and looking less than healthy, were talking in scandalized tones about a dismembered woman who had been found in Alamar. Alamar? That name seemed to mean something to her, vaguely. Who was it that lived in Alamar?

Lola tried not to listen to the disturbing details. While she waited, she began to feel an urge to run away, to escape, to walk a few blocks around the neighborhood. It had been so long since she had done that! Her old Sunday mornings in the Vedado shimmered far away, from another time, although Lola couldn't quite define what was different today. Perhaps the quiet air was full of an unusual luminosity, below the landscaped trees, maybe the surrounding tranquility emphasized the concert of strange sounds she heard, even the smells around her gave the impression as being somehow more noble.

Lola remembered a time when she still would go out each day to buy a crusty baguette of French bread, with its aroma of white flour and butter, from the bakery at Calzada and 18th. Her mother used to tell her that Calzada was one of the first streets in their barrio, maybe the oldest one of all. Back then, when Lola was just a girl, Calzada was narrow, bordered by swaths of uncultivated dirt that were slowly occupied by enormous manor houses with exuberant front gardens and somber entrance ways. To get from central Havana to that Vedado, still under construction, one would take a tram parallel with the coastline, intersecting with Linia Street, which got its name—pondered Lola, as she crossed Linia Street—from that very tram line. She was surprised to remember in such minute detail the clattering passenger cars, the bell that warned of its arrival, the handrails and seats made of wood, its tracks still visible underfoot only a few years ago.

Lola's parents used to bring her by tram to take the sea air at the well-known private beaches nestled along the reefs at the end of E Street; the beaches called Baths because they were natural spas among the rocks, little swimming holes cordoned off so that the bathers wouldn't run the risk of sharks out in the open sea. Lola's family rented an outdoor changing room there on El Progreso beach, with benches where they could don their swimming attire in privacy, as the modest mores of the age required, each family the owner of a tiny marine pool shielded from the eyes of other summer visitors by a simple partition.

Lola walked across a few more streets until she reached the corner of Calzada and 4th. On the next block was the Hotel Trotcha, where Lola and Evaristo had spent their honeymoon, three days in a room on the second floor of the annex, which had been built onto the side of the magnificent original building, and which the old Catalán owner Mr. Buenaventura, with his nose for marketing, had baptized "Eden."

The door to their old room, the last one on the left, opened up to the walkway that looked down upon the gardens, while the side window overlooked a wall of greenery, and the back offered a view of the ocean, origin of the coastal wind that circulated throughout. Lola remembered as if it were only yesterday the salt flavor on her lips and the look of the manicured patches of lawn between the paths, flowery mounds, and the central plaza with tables where one could sit and soak in the sun's rays or talk into the night under the hanging lanterns. The gardens at the Hotel Trotcha and the sea at dusk were the only happy memories that Lola permitted herself of those first days of her marriage with Evaristo, which had transitioned from their original "Eden" to a prolonged limbo, then finally to the pure hell of Evaristo's betrayal.

As Lola advanced slowly and painfully, practically dragging her throbbing legs, she recalled the Neoclassical elegance of the old hotel, with its four massive columns and red pitched roof covering the impressive second story, which was accessed via a majestic staircase flanked by mirrors and illuminated by fiery crystal light fixtures of a unique red, a carmine found only in Havana stained glass.

The last time she had seen the hotel, a few months before Sara had gone away, a small area of the gardens was still being maintained. Outside of that area, however, the grounds had deteriorated into the landscape of weeds and rubble all around the main structure. Outside of each room, all converted into barrack-style housing now, underwear hung to dry on the balustrade. In the principal edifice, the frontispiece sustained by the four pillars continued to stand tall, although the stained glass fixtures by then had been shattered. One surviving mirror, spotted black with rust, reflected a fragmented image of the trash accumulated in the corners of the old vestibule. On that day so long ago, Sara had scavenged from the ground a shard of the red crystal.

When Lola finally got to the corner of Calzada and 2nd and stopped in front of the ruins of what had once been the Hotel Trotcha, she thought she must have mistaken the address. In a deserted tenement one could barely make out a few meager vestiges of the once grand façade, the four columns that held up the portico eaten away by salt. Growing absurdly out of a corner of the damaged roof, a lone bush was the only remaining evidence of the orchards that had been there before.

Framed by one of the doorways that no longer led anywhere, Lola thought that she could make out, in the full light of day, the ghost of a woman without arms or legs, holding a small piece of red glass in her lap.

WOMAN WHO TALKS TO HERSELF IN THE PARK

All of the stew pots in all of the kitchens boiled over at the same time. So then the streets were flooded with a potage of chickpeas, some hard, some falling into mush, all yellow and reeking of rancid oil. And Havana is dying...

YUYA

Yuya says that on account of the heat, the mosquitoes, and her impatience at waiting what seemed like forever for the electricity to come back on, that Saturday found her still awake in the wee hours and with a bad feeling about what was going to happen. When the blackout finally ended, Yuya's eyelids had gotten stiff from straining open for so long, attempting to see in the dark. She climbed out of her sticky sheets, took a shower, and turned on the television. A car chase through the streets of Manhattan and an ambulance siren sounding through the streets of her neighborhood got mixed up in her head. Not even putting the fan on at its highest setting could dissipate the oppressive, humid, heat of the night. And something, something, something, was not right. Not right at all. Then she saw the Haitian, Yuya says she couldn't believe it was happening, the Haitian from *Arroyo El Muerto*, dressed up like a dandy and surrounded by Mafia characters, staring at her intently from a scene at some New York docks. His head was barely visible for a few moments before he was gunned down, one of the first to be hit, in the barrage of bullets that erupted.

The movie ended, the national anthem played, and still Yuya just couldn't get settled. The fatal omens had multiplied, increasingly shot through with gibberish, such as that spider who was shamelessly scampering around the handrail of the balcony. Disgust, pain, inescapable suffering. New York, on the other hand, in the Chinese game, signified the number 87, a warning of something that would happen all of a sudden. On top of all of that was the fact that just yesterday she had received in the mail an absolutely desolate letter from Ludmila the Bulgarian woman, sent from her native land, in which her friend recounted with bitterness, in her low-end Havana slang, that where she was "things had gone downhill in the worst way," and that Yuya should guard herself against the number 160 Darkened Sun as well as the Three of Spades, confusion, psychological alienation... Jesus, Mary, and Joseph!

From the interior of Lola's house the light of a naked bulb wavered, and Yuya noticed that the terrace doors stood wide open, a rare occurrence at this time of night. Maybe Lola was suffering from insomnia as well. Yuya didn't hesitate a moment before calling out to her and offering her a cup of tea. Now that she thought about it, she hadn't seen Lola for several days. According to Yuya, the last time that she had gone over for a visit, almost a full week before, Lola had been acting strangely, more than a little alarming—outright weird, to tell the truth. She, usually so reserved, a woman of so few words, had literally confessed to her a rather wandering story about some Dead Girl. Yuya says that as she listened, her heart filled with compassion, more than anything because there was absolutely nothing she could do to help.

Yuya says that once the rice is too salty, there isn't anything you can do to make it better; you might as well dump out the whole pot and start from scratch. But fate isn't the same thing as cooking rice; if you mess up, you can't start all over again. According to Yuya, you just have to eat the salty mess.

"All of her loved ones are dead by now, so the story can be told without hurting anyone," was the last thing Lola had said to her.

"Lola!" Yuya says that the first time she called over, she did it quietly. And the second time as well. But when she didn't get any response even when she was practically beating the door down with her knocking, she started yelling at the top of her lungs, waking up the entire building, not to mention the eleven thousand patron virgins of Vedado.

Yuya says that she barely even remembered Etelvina's face, but her insistent presence in the living room mirror told Yuya that she better get a move on, that she was dealing with a real live emergency.

MARIA ESTHER

Finally visiting hours at the hospital ended, and the rowdy family members of her present roommate piled out of their room. The TV set remained on, although Maria Esther didn't really care one way or the other. It didn't require any sort of action or decision on her part, but rather flashed and gurgled on like some kind of background decoration. She would have dearly loved to get her hands on the little flask of rum that she had carried around in her handbag for years, so she could check out and pass out, completely blank of any memories, of those presences that didn't allow her to avoid fulfilling the life roles that she had given herself. Her insomnia, characterized by a confused whirlwind of thoughts, had held her captive for many years before she had fallen ill. Now, the mental laxity provoked by her medications swayed her toward reminiscing, even though that revisiting of old scenes, the conjuring up of ghosts, was painful.

Oh, the specters that Martin had brought back to life! She didn't think that her "ex" would visit again. Ever since she had met him, back in that crazy decade of the sixties, he had a tendency to be frivolous, to undermine reality in an attempt to take away its control over him. And that's how he planned to become a great writer! Instead of getting irritated with him as she usually would, Maria Esther let herself feel some compassion. In each one of us reside many. She hadn't been able to recognize that when she should have and now it seemed too late, more than anything with her son.

Her roommate was talking aloud about the news stories. Maria Esther agreed without paying any attention; she had now been in the hospital four months, and whatever was happening outside the walls had no comparison with the destruction going on within her own body. She looked at her hands covered in liver spots and when she lifted her head to look one more time at the scar on her abdomen, she felt like she might faint. When she opened her eyes again, she still could hear the hmmmm of the television, the sick woman in the bed next to hers was still reciting her monologue, and the hospital room seemed as if it was stuck in a moment in time.

A little while later the nurse came in to give her an injection and Maria Esther asked her again about the girl, who perhaps was struggling to stay alive in some other freezing cold room in the building.

"Who are you talking about?" The nurse's confusion seemed genuine.

Maria Esther didn't make a big deal of it. The girl had been erased from existence, had disappeared like the dapples of light coming in the window. The ghosts from her past seemed more alive and tangible than anything she saw around her.

Martin, the Dead Girl...and the others, where had they all ended up?

What was the last thing that the Dead Girl had said to her, when they ran into each other on the street that damnable day? She couldn't remember. Oh, my god! How could she possibly have forgotten? "First we want to escape our memories, and then it is our memories that escape us." Who in the hell wrote that? Or had she just made it up? In her memory, the Dead Girl's mouth open and shut, without making a sound.

ESTELA

The noisy clientele at the pub, elbow to elbow at the bar, were watching a soccer game between Manchester United and their archenemy, Milan. It was only a recording; even though everybody knew the way it ended by heart, they celebrated each goal with enthusiasm and ferocity. Estela had sat down apart from everyone, in a Pullman booth with a view of the Tamesis River, grey and peppered with tree trunks that made their way down stream. She pushed the ashtray toward a corner of the table and, as she waited to give her order, she entertained herself by watching the candle flame that flickered every time the front door opened or shut. A young woman dressed in black, whose miniskirt was shorter than the little lace apron she wore, leaned over to ask Estela what she wanted to drink. Estela was shaken a bit by the voice so close to her ear and sputtered like the flame of the miniscule lantern when the woman's arousing perfume enveloped her. "I'll take a Guinness," she said, imitating what Oscar would order on the rare occasions they went out on the town together. The young lady walked away in the direction of the bar, but her scent stayed behind as a permanent fixture in the

Pullman. Estela stared through the window: the river at that particular spot wasn't all that wide and, since the fog had dissipated completely, she could make out a white skiff with a red keel that dropped as it moved away from the posts of the embarcadero. *Tling, tling,* sounded its bells, a horn's toot vibrated through the air, and the paddleboat wheel lazily started to turn. The boat pulled away from the dock and started to navigate upstream, keeping well off from the rapid current in the river center, away from which also fled a brace of ducks. "Ah, the enchantment of the fluvial path," the Dead Girl had said that one time, when she was almost the Dead Girl, as she climbed into a boat that they had rented on the piers at the Almendares River. It hadn't been hard at all for Estela to gain her trust. Over the span of a few months, Estela had stuck to the group like a leech, went to all of their boring twist and rock n' roll parties, the symphony concerts each Sunday. At the weekends of volunteer work she made sure that her own hammock hung as closely as possible to the other girl's, they worked the same furrow in the fields, she tagged along for the interminable film debates as well as for the decadent Bohemian Saturdays, including eating ice cream at Coppelia and singing children's songs by Teresita. When the Dead Girl had invited Estela to play mini-golf at the amusement park, she said yes, despite the fact that she considered it a huge sacrifice to waste a Sunday morning trying to knock little balls down a trench with a fake golf club. Estela didn't see the charm of it all, but everybody in the group laughed themselves silly. They were there for a couple of hours, until the Dead Girl proposed a boat ride. Estela refused to go along, but she was witness to the Dead Girl's traversing of the river with a flock of effeminate boys with long hair. One of them, who not that long before had been expelled from the university, tightly clutched a girl who looked just like him, his high pitched squeals feigning fright. It was the first time Estela had laid eyes on him. Another one of the gang had with him the four volume set of *Juan Cristóbal*. "Come on, Estela, come and have some fun with us," they shouted from the boat. That very night, Estela wrote a detailed report about the "enchantment of the fluvial path," the presence of bad apples within the university student population, and the evil influence of readings that promoted homosexuality. A few days before, Estela had snuck a few pages out of the Dead Girl's diary, which she attached to the report. The woman in the pub set a frosty mug in front of Estela, on top of a coaster decorated with the ubiquitous Guinness harp, then with a practiced move opened the bottle and placed it next to the mug. "Thanks," murmured Estela, who couldn't tear her eyes away from the girl's firmly muscled legs and the satiny skin of her thighs. She blinked several times as she tried to clear her head of the torturous thoughts that had crossed her mind. She made herself think about Oscar. The day before a fax had arrived explaining the reason for his delay: they had given him a promotion on the island; he would need to stay there for at least two years. Estela should come back immediately. She recalled the last time they had been there on vacation; everything in Havana had seemed foreign to her, faded, grimy, dark. Every little task, even the most trivial, took an immeasurable amount of time. But worse than anything else was her own irritability. When the fax had come, Estela decided to take a while to consider how to respond to it. Although right there, sitting in the pub, with her cold mug and the candle that contributed to the pleasant atmosphere, she told herself that no, she wasn't going back. She was sick and tired of hearing people talk about problems. Cuba was behind her now, forever. What's more, there in Havana she never would be able to wear her beautiful new leather jacket. She signaled to the girl and ordered another beer; it was only a day and a half before the new year, so she didn't hesitate to smile at the girl, wish her a Happy New Year, look her right in the eyes like everybody did in Cuba, looked at each other in the eyes, a custom that she knew seemed audacious in other locales. The girl came back, and Estela thought she brushed her hand when she sat down the other beer. But maybe it was just her imagination. From the open topside of the boat, a few of the passengers looked toward the shore without any real interest, huddled around the lifesavers. Estela felt a driving need to wave to them, so she raised her hand, fluttering it from right to left. Clearly nobody had seen her, because she didn't see a single wave back. As if it had just happened for real, the crowd in the pub noisily celebrated the old victory.

DAONTAON

No way. The world was falling apart! Is this any way to live, my friends? No way in hell. If it's not one thing, it's another. But not for her. Enough was enough. Daontaon had to get rid of that Braulio character for once and for all. Ha. ***A son of a bitch***, just like that, said with every letter bolded and in italics.

Hey Micaela, you're sitting there with your mouth wide open, don't tell me that your Aunt Candita is listening to us. Do you think I'm exaggerating? I'm barely telling you the half of it. Do you want me to keep going? Of course you do.

That Braulio, baby faced wonder that he is, the one with the guerilla tactics, yes, that one, was really putting the screws to her, piling on the work. No doubt he was getting Daontaon back for blowing him off. Who did that hothead think he was? Did he think he was god's gift to women? Ha.

The week before he had given Daontaon a **classified** mission, a secret, "on the hush hush," you know what I mean.

"I need to get this so and so off my back, she's making my life miserable," he had said to Daontaon, hiding his expression behind a pair of dark glasses that he didn't even take off when he went to the bathroom (to put it elegantly), using the tone of voice of one of those "Corrupt Agents" of the FBI, from the *Saturday night movies*. "And I need you to give me a little help, Daontaon. Do me a favor, and show up at this office building today," jotting down an address on a note card. "I'm gonna make this lady's life a living hell until she gets the message and gets the fuck off my back…"

Daontaon let the multiplying dot dot dots swirl around her, while the "Corrupt Agent" also jotted down the so and so's name. "I want you to accuse her of everything in the book." The "Corrupt Agent" thumped on the card with his finger, as if he were banging the head of a lawbreaker against the hood of a patrol car in a darkened alley in Brooklyn. "Make shit up, you've got plenty of that in you, I have no doubt. You don't have to actually make any concrete accusations, just a few insinuations, that will do to start off with. All I need right now is for you to start stirring up some suspicion…"

The poisonous ellipses started swirling around again in a pattern that to Daontaon seemed practically evil. The "Corrupt Agent" lifted his head, and even though she couldn't see his eyes behind the mirrored lenses, she *knew* that he was staring at her lustfully.

"And don't forget to come to the inauguration tonight," he ordered pompously.

To finish off the apocalypse, to top it all off, he had assigned her to the inauguration of an exhibit titled "Raw Vegetables and Raw Bodies," by that sculptress that makes such shockingly ridiculous spectacles. Daontaon had to cart around a bunch of weeds and smelly cabbages, and to place the horrors *artistically*. By the time the reception was to start, the plants and vegetables had started to stink to high heaven. The *body in the raw* came from the sculptress herself, who appeared from behind some crated radishes completely in the buff, as naked as the day she was born. Now you tell me! And right there, in the front row, next to a bunch of basil popping straight up out of an Aurika washing machine like some "alien," was the Minister of Culture with all of his buddies! What can I tell you, Micaela? It was a disaster. Braulio, his new secretary, that guy Martin, all of them were pretending like NOTHING strange was going on. The Minister's face was a work of art. Ha.

Then, when it was all over with, the "Corrupt Agent" came to put all the blame on Daontaon, saying he couldn't depend on anybody, that we were all a big bunch of incompetents, did he have to do absolutely everything himself, that it had been her job to review everything about the event beforehand. Oh, please. As if anybody, much less Daontaon, could stop those *artists* from getting naked in public. She retorted that the croquettes from the opening banquet must have been made out of ground *mad cow*, because otherwise who could ever have imagined, that such a monstrosity covered in cellulitis would decide to show "her parts" to the Minister? Without a doubt every artist in this country has gone on a mad cow diet!

Braulio, the big boss, with his worst "Corrupt Agent" scowl, told Daontaon that he was going to write her up for the incident. Somebody had to pay the piper and who better than she, the scapegoat. Well, Daontaon, for your information, has requested a transfer out of the Cultural Center.

The good news was that on her way back from the **secret mission** that was supposed to put Miss So and So out of the game, riding a bus filled to the gills with smelly, disgusting, good-for-nothings and delinquents, she had met a very elegant foreigner named Patrick, who had mentioned how much he liked Alamar. Daontaon had invited him to come by and visit her one of these days. "You haven't eaten any mad cow hamburgers, have you, darling?"

"Although he must have, because you have to be completely off your rocker, Micaela, with bats in the belfry, to want to come and live in Alamar. You get what I'm saying to you? Of course you do. But everybody's crazy about something. Patrick may be a baby-faced boy, but like that philosopher, can't remember who, said, 'nobody's perfect.' *Nobody*."

WOMAN WHO TALKS TO HERSELF IN THE PARK

The sun stopped stock still overhead at twelve noon and didn't move from its place. And so the pavement melted away, water everywhere came to a boil and started to evaporate, the bridges liquefied, and the buildings burned to ash. And Havana is dying…

GERTRUDE

If I lost my sense of sight, with only an iota of my memory I could still retrace that path that we traveled together thousands of times. You better believe it. But some of those recollections can get so you can't stand them any more.

Leaving the College of the Humanities, along the side of the Calixto García Hospital and going up the hill, the first thing was the coffee routine. Every afternoon, rain or shine, during the longest afternoon class break we all would stand in line for a coffee at one of the University Food Service kiosks. A demitasse of the strong brew for five cents and we'd continue the conversations that had started either in the classroom or on one of the blessed benches in the college lobby.

Along that same route you skirted the steps of the University Stadium to get to the entrance to the hospital and the bus stop for the number 20, then you would cross the short distance of Labra Street and enter the campus proper of the University of Havana. The military barracks were in the basement of the Physics Department, the Varona Auditorium was on the right, and the Great Hall was next to the Main Library on the left hand side. After that you would funnel out into the Cadenas Plaza, with its marble banks, palm trees, the small armored tank, and the stone steps that led to the so-called "Cave" of Political Sciences, with its eternal bust of Alexander Von Humboldt surrounded by lush vegetation and its cool shadow-covered benches where the café had been situated, as long as time had existed, faithful supplier of croquettes, spaghetti, or "bread with nothing on top." At the end of this backwards ordered pilgrimage, you arrived at the Administration building, the statue of the Alma Mater, and, finally, the grand staircase leading to the University from the city streets.

In those days the staircase always was populated by a flock of doves who had made their nests in the decorative niches along the concrete wall of the entranceway. Day after day, at any hour, the decrepit old lady would appear. From quite a way off, coming down Neptuno

Street, she would emerge—be it early or late—her little figure perfectly recognizable, walking quickly, a bit stooped over, as if she were weighed down. Her long gray hair was tied back into two braids, she didn't wear shoes, and she always had on the same faded but clean dress. We didn't know her name, but we would see her arrive, always barefoot, dragging her bags bursting with old bread, anxious to fulfill her daily mission of feeding the doves. As soon as they saw her coming, hundreds of birds would encircle her, so accustomed they were to her presence. The Dove Lady, as we were wont to call her, would greet them with a chirping that imitated to perfection their cooing sounds, and they all would come to eat directly from her hands.

The route is almost exactly the same today as it was then, although the doves on the staircase only fly about in our memories. Somebody once said that the jagüey trees around the College of the Humanities were growing out of sacred ground, the long forgotten Molinos Cemetery on the skirts of Príncipe Hill, planted there to isolate the bodies contaminated with cholera, during that epidemic that had lashed the Havana population so mercilessly in the eighteen hundreds. Nobody remembered that detail until we ourselves had also become diseased.

The Lady of the Flies; The Night of the Femme Assassins; Les Femme-Enfants; The Marquesa de Sade; Emily, or a Treatise on Education; The Sorrows of Young Miss Werther; The Prophetess; The Broken She-Spears?

Has anyone ever seen when a chick is cornered by his own clutch, inside his own henhouse?

Back to what we were talking about.

One event has stayed in the forefront of my mind, clearer than any of the others. In one of the huge assemblies of the Communist Youth at the Chaplin Theater, the entire coliseum resounded with furious demands that the "Humanities people" be punished. Do you remember, or don't you? Terrified, we tried to figure out what was happening, when all of a sudden, I made out the Dead Girl on the other side of the aisle. A mere ten feet separated us, but nevertheless I was completely unable to help her. When she had sat down, she had ended up isolated in a mass of irate pre-med students, stigmatized and jeered at for the simple fact of studying in the Humanities. For long minutes that seemed an eternity she was forced to just sit there, defenseless, listening to all of the accusations imaginable shouted in chorus by a circle of implacable lions. For the first time I saw in her a strange sort of fragility and impotence.

After that came the fateful year of 1968, and with it (and for a long time afterward) denunciations, false testimonies, interrogations, and verbal abuse… nothing would ever be the same.

In the last monologue of *An Enemy of the People*, the lady Dr. Stockholm, repudiated by the masses, came to an awful conclusion: "Listen, all of you. The most powerful woman in the world is also the most alone." Thirty years after the fact, I continue to ask myself what was the sense in all of that mess. To be perfectly honest, I'm still waiting for answers.

MARIA ESTHER

Maria Esther identified the clicking sounds made by syringes carried on metal trays. Somebody moved her right arm around, then rubbed her skin with a cotton ball, filling the frigid air with a nauseating smell. Then she felt a prick. Whoever it had been, they had forgotten to stick her arm back underneath the cover, and Maria Esther felt cold, very cold. Nevertheless, a feverish blaze was burning her lips. She tried to ask for water and for them to bundle her up well with the covers, but the words wouldn't come out, and she couldn't even open her eyes. She was as cold and thirsty as she had been that stormy morning of wind and rain when she had been scouring the Montparnasse cemetery in order to fulfill her old pledge to visit César Vallejo's tomb.

Her layover of a few short hours and the scarce bills she had in her pocket were just barely enough to get her tickets for the subway and entrance into the necropolis. Maria Esther couldn't afford the luxury of buying herself a beverage, although she longed like never before for a hot cup of any sort of brew. Out of the corner of her eye, she spied on the Parisians through the café windows, protected from the squall, sipping ritually and parsimoniously their steaming beverages as she raced down the street, her head uncovered and protected only by a useless autumn jacket. January's icy drizzle soaked into her bones, all of them, her arms and legs included; despite it all, she wanted to fulfill the oath that she had made in her youth; that romantic oath made with her circle of friends, foremost with the Dead Girl, that the first of them who was fortunate enough to make it to Paris would go and place a bouquet of flowers on the poet's tomb, laid out in that far off city as so many of her friends would end, scattered across the planet.

A watchman sheltered from the elements in a modest guard hut limped over to the ticket window, his expression dark and suspicious. What crazy tourist would get it in her head to walk around a bunch of graves in weather like this? Dispassionately and gesturing with a filthy fingernail, he pointed out a quadrant along Nord Avenue to Maria Esther.

The completely solitary cemetery was frightening. Maria Esther proceeded along the walkways, surrounded by bronze busts with the green sheen of tarnish, forgotten niches, shining mausoleums, crosses covered in dried ivy leaves, potted plants charred by the latest frost, dried up bushes waving about in puddles of slush under bare branches making hostile noises reminiscent of the caws of crows or some other monstrous bird. Halfway sorry for having undertaken the adventure, cold through and through, mouth dry, nose running, María Ester tried to make out the route to her destination. But, incredibly, each time that she thought she was drawing near to the corridor in which rested the sepulcher of the great Vallejo, the storm would worsen; as she would stray further away, a few ridiculous rays of sun would peek through as if to tell her she was going the wrong way. A yellow cat jumped down from a tree branch and landed in her path, staring at her with disapproval. Maria Esther told herself that this wasn't funny anymore.

"No!" she exclaimed out loud, as if speaking to the cat that listened unmoved, "I'm not dying here in this downpour, nothing of the sort."

Entirely disoriented, at the mouth of the *Via Ouest,* Maria Esther found herself in front of a modest pantheon, featuring no flashy design work but deluged with live flowers, paper roses, and even a few kitschy plastic gladiolas, as well as humbler offerings of all sorts: a worn down pencil, a cup of oxidized copper, sea shells, dried branches, stones of all colors and different shapes, a pen and ink sketch of the well-known visage of the tomb's occupant on a cloth napkin, drenched, its ink running in rivulets of rainwater, and a handwritten sign that said simply, "Thank you, Charles." That intimate, familiar, tone surprised her. As if between the artist and the writer that he honored there was an ongoing dialogue, which had just been interrupted by the minor detail of death. All of a sudden, she realized that she had arrived with her hands completely empty; what she had in her pockets hadn't stretched far enough to buy even a single flower for Vallejo—thus she decided to borrow from Baudelaire a humble bouquet. Among so many he surely wouldn't notice they were missing, a few of his flowers of evil, never so aptly named. The most repudiated, censored, and kicked around poet in the world, the devil condemned, and the gardener of all the imaginable bad fruits, wasn't going to take it to heart.

"I heard that you had been asking about me." The sentence shook Maria Esther out of her daze somewhat. She couldn't make out, at first, whose voice it was nor whose hand was patting her own softly. "You have no idea how much that meant to me, when I was down there scared to death."

"Down there," "scared to death," Maria Esther repeated to herself. Cold, pain, solitude, the words came to her sporadically, in a sort of an echo. Maria Esther wasn't sure if she was hearing them in reality or if they were coming from one of her own abysses. It also could be one of the spirits that prowled around her.

"At any rate, I survived," insisted the voice. "I'm the patient who was on the verge of death, your old hospital roommate... Do you remember me?"

Of course she did! Maria Esther wanted to nod yes, but she was never sure if she had managed to do so or not.

"You seem upset, do you think she needs something?" The voice had drifted away and seemed to be speaking to somebody else. Maria Esther felt somebody covering her with a blanket and gently wetting her lips with water.

"I came to say goodbye and to thank you," insisted the voice.

"Thanks to you, Baudelaire," Maria Esther managed to articulate, with supreme effort.

"What?" The voice sounded startled.

As the old Baudelaire might have said himself, death had not been able to plant his flowers in that young girl, thought Maria Esther, smiling to herself, to her own inner cypress.

From further and further away, disconnected fragments would reach Maria Esther: "It sounds like she's asking for some relative," "she's delirious," "she doesn't have much longer…"

Later silence reigned once more.

Oh Death, My Lady Captain, it's time now! Anchors away!

MARTIN

Martin's mother was running a wet rag over the stovetop, as she did every day after she made breakfast. The kitchen smelled like toast and fresh-brewed coffee. Martin took a sip from his cup, glanced up only to see that familiar look, a mixture of suffering and reproach.

"And did her son manage to make it to the burial?" asked Martin's mother.

"No…no. And nobody from the university. I didn't find out until it was too late. I didn't make it either."

Martin's mother opened her eyes even wider and beat at the air with her rag, as if she was chasing away some bug. That's what she did whenever a bad thought entered her head.

Their house had ended up half empty, after they had taken Grandma Antonia away in an ambulance to the Quinta Covadonga Hospital, permeated by a doughy silence that you could almost knead with your fingers. Their downstairs neighbors had closed their tailor shop early as if they were the ones operating on grandma in their own kitchen. Grandpa Severino had closed himself up in his workshop. If

Martin promised not to touch anything, he could sit there in the corner, nice and quiet. He would never be able to forget the sounds and smells of that carpentry shop: the electric saw slicing through two by fours like wedges of cheese; the jars holding nails of all sizes; the wood glue boiling away in a can; the containers of varnish; the magical double-sided magnet; the carpenter's square; and, best of all, the unsettling level, a wooden ruler with its glass tube, a green bubble floating to the left or the right depending on how you held it. That morning Martin lay back on the bench and watched his grandfather stripping off wood shavings in a thousand different ways, stroke after stroke, and on top of the shavings fell drop after drop of the sweat running down his grandfather's face. He looked very tired, but he kept working away at the wood. In the house the phone rang, and Grandpa Severino froze in place, holding the shaping plane in one hand and his forehead in the other, as if his head was about to fall off. When Martin's mother walked in, grandpa stared at her, his eyes red as tomatoes.

"Don't hold back, tell me everything," he said to her.

Martin's mother didn't say a word, but walked over and hugged her father, the two of them weeping. Then Grandpa Severino ran out of the workshop.

That's when Martin's mother noticed that he was sitting in the corner there and responded with one of her famous lines, "My sweet boy, you haven't had a bite to eat since this morning." Just a bit later she returned with a blue bottle of Phillip's Milk of Magnesia and a spoon. Coffee grounds spread on the soles of the feet to bring down a fever, a glass of orange juice every morning to stave off infections, milk with Quaker powder to increase calcium in growing bones, yoghurt culture to cure the flu, a swipe of blue methylene for a sore throat, gastrointestinal cleanses for just about anything, oregano poultice to get rid of phlegm, chamomile tea to get to sleep, and a spoonful of Milk of Magnesia in the face of important events, good or bad.

In book illustrations, when somebody dies you always see a little semi-transparent mist floating up out of the body. But when Uncle

Felix's cat Raskolnikov died, you couldn't see any mist coming out of him. At any rate, he must have gone to live in kitty heaven. The bad thing was that they never got to see him again, and to Martin that seemed the worst part about somebody dying.

Martin's mother started shaking her head. There had never been a cat in his grandparents' house, much less one with such a strange name. For Martin's mother, Death was always dressed in black and carrying a scythe, sometimes she had the face of a woman, and other times merely a skull, but for the most part you couldn't see much of the face hiding beneath that hood, and you never could see her hair. Would that be why they called her The Bald One?

When she first arrived in Cuba, Grandma Antonia had written long letters recounting their various jobs, every time they would move to a new place, when a new baby was born, the surprising customs of the Cuban people, every little illness that the kids had, without waiting for a letter back. Way over there, the family patriarch didn't know how to read or write. She also sent Christmas cards, obituaries, telegrams wishing happy birthday, postcards, baptismal announcements; sheet after sheet crossed the ocean to their mute addressee, until one fine day when the parish priest—flustered with all that mail being sent to nobody—decided to send an official notice of the far-away death that by that time wasn't very upsetting to anyone. Except, that is, for Grandma Antonia and Uncle Felix, who from one day to the next lost the reprieve from their pain for so many years, all those years that their father had been dead. Their grief was no less intense for the amount of time that had passed. It was a pale consolation, the fact that for all those years that they believed the family patriarch to be alive, that to all intents and purposes he had stayed living beyond his allotted time.

"The bad thing isn't the dying," Martin's mother concluded, "but rather dying for once and for all, when nobody remembers you anymore. What's that look for? Why don't you take a little spoonful of Milk of Magnesia?"

MICAELA

On that last night, Micaela woke up exhausted, eyes wide open, thanks to another one of those ridiculous dreams. The hands of the clock showed that it was four o'clock in the morning, that period before dawn when the entire universe seems to be standing still. Her chest still hurt like it had the day before, despite having taken a couple of pain killers after Daontaon had finally left her alone, taking away with her all those stories of beheaded women, informants, termites, meteorites, dying ants, ministers, dismemberers, and children infected by the literary arts.

But she was right about one thing:

"Micaela, your cat isn't even eating anymore. What kind of life is that? A *shit* life, pardon the expression. Put him out of his misery for once and for all…"

Micaela understood that she couldn't avoid it any longer, in fact. She was keeping him alive by force, and she was beyond being able to tell with any certainty if she was doing it for the cat or for herself. She had to make the hard decision to put him to sleep. "Put him to sleep," what a horrible euphemism, Micaela said to herself. Speaking of which… How were those little chicks doing at Lola's? And Lola herself? Micaela had not felt up to visiting her again since that last time.

She got up and, knocking into things along the way, got two more pills to take. She had hours of sleeplessness ahead of her. Micaela decided to get started on a few tasks that she had been putting off and that she wanted to take care of by the end of that wakeful night: with a shaving blade she cut her hair very short; then she plucked her eyebrows and filed her nails; after that, she wrote a long detailed letter, telling her friend Sara how she was surviving in turn of the century Havana, her friend who probably was living an existence that was a more luxurious and well-fed image of her own; later still she finished the blessed Russian novel she had been reading; and finally, she sat down to sort through the rice.

Micaela spread out over the table a piece of clean cloth and poured out on it two cups of rice. Well aware that she was mimicking the gestures of her mother, she went about patiently separating the good grains from the bad, taking out the little stones and bits of straw that made it into rice from the state. All of a sudden, Micaela recognized the fabric; it was the woven runner that used to cover the top of the television set, a moment of chance or destiny that reminded her that life's little jokes can be as eloquent as our dreams.

Micaela finished that chore and went back to lie down again. The sun was just about to rise, and she knew that she had a hard day ahead of her. Another one. As if he guessed what was to happen, her cat leapt on top of the bed and, sure of himself, curled up in her lap. Micaela stroked his fur and knew that there wouldn't be other occasions to do so.

In a little bit she would fall back to sleep. Oh, to sleep and not to wake, to forget about all the catastrophes around her... But as soon as she shut her eyes and began to drift off, she just knew it, they would be there, waiting for her, those red and white socks of the Dead Girl. And her Aunt Candita would show back up, begging her to have compassion, to not abandon her so far away, and to help bring her ashes back to Cuba.

Once again, in the silent night, she heard that dog start crying.

Micaela felt once more the sharp stabbing in the middle of her chest, and she opened and closed her mouth several times as if she were a dying fish. Then she squeezed her eyes shut tightly until the tears built up behind her lids. Before long her own moans were making a chorus with the dog's.

WOMAN WHO TALKS TO HERSELF IN THE PARK

The big old houses started groaning and complaining, weeping and wailing their abandonment until they were worn out. And then they started to creak and to break apart, and they ended up turned into dust and ashes. And Havana is dying...

THE INDIA

The strange matter of "The Dismembered Lady of East Havana" would have to be shelved as an unsolved case.

After searches, excavations, dredging, cutting back of brush, and an exceptional clean-up (extraordinary efforts for it not being hurricane season) in the entire aforementioned municipality, not a single object was found, among all the tons of garbage accumulated over the years, that could be taken for a human head.

They went over the interrogations of The India's old acquaintances and tenement neighbors yet again. They verified certain facts by tapping Cusita's phone in Hialeah. They applied pressure on the favorite suspect, the so-called "Frenchman," to reveal the hiding place of the missing piece of the criminal jigsaw puzzle. They looked around for a possible accomplice, perhaps a brothel keeper, who might have socked away the material still unaccounted for. And nothing. Not a thing.

Patrick Rivière kept to himself, almost a recluse, in his hotel room, where—reports said—he did little else besides frantically scribble in the wide-lined notebooks they used in grade schools.

As it was improper to continue stalling over the burial of the mortal remains of The India (or whomever they belonged to), all the pieces were turned over to Clara Luz, nicknamed "The Professor," so that she could make arrangements for a funeral. Thus was it made possible to inter the trunk and extremities in a burial vault made available by a neighbor (a benificiary of such a privilage because of his membership in the Galician society Natives of Ortigueira), under the promise of the relevant authorities to proceed with an exhumation of the mortal remains in order to complete the set, should the time come that the missing head were to be found.

The investigation ground to a halt due to the lack of incriminating evidence, and its only suspect, the citizen of the French Republic named Patrick Rivière, more well known either as "The Frenchman" or "The Dismemberer of East Havana," was exonerated without any formal charges having been brought. Nonetheless, just as a precaution, he was placed under permanent watch.

The India's mother, Clara Luz, once she had been put back into touch with her cousin Cusita in Hialeah (thanks only to the horrifying circumstances, truth be told), got her nerve up, entered into the lottery for a visa to the United States, hit the jackpot, made it through the requisite interview without any *contretemps,* put together all the necessary documentation, said goodbye forever to her rooms in the San Leopoldo tenement, and took the next plane (not a ship, for the life of her!) to search for the Cuban dream of owning her own little house.

Once his own painful process had wound down, Patrick Rivière decided to settle in as a French language translator for a publishing house that found itself in need of an expert in his native tongue. A rumor has started circulating that he has begun to write a mystery-suspense novel, plagued with obcenities and spilling over with prostitutes, refugees, and delinquents, all of its action taking place in East Havana.

In its own stead, the head of María Antonieta, The India, "The Dismembered Lady of the East Havana Municipality," continues to struggle on somewhere or another. Possibly it still nests inside a package of butcher paper, within the luggage of some woman of doubtful morality, or perhaps it rests underneath the floor tiles in some Alamar apartment.

LOLA

As if a hurricane had blown away her entire past life, Lola stumbled across Paseo Avenue. "Watch where you're walking, you stupid old lady!" howled a bicycle rider that barely missed running her over. It seemed that she didn't even hear him as she continued to limp along Calzada Street; after so many times she had traveled the same path, her feet operated on automatic pilot, following that magical route of the Sunday matinees of the Symphonic Orchestra and breakfasts at the Carmelo, from so very long ago. What year was that?

Lola stopped to try and remember…but what?

To her left, a pile of trash gave the impression of floating along the stagnant puddles of water that had pooled along the footpath. To her right, behind a fence of improvised posts, hovering above the once-tended gardens, the lush grounds of her childhood now weeds burnt to a crisp, were clouds of flies and gnats. A beat-up cardboard sign hung on the front entrance of a beauty parlor, in the olden days a favorite among the celebrity circles, declaring it *'closed for repairs.'* A block further on, under the marquee of the Teatro Estudio, a gang of teenagers, passing a bottle of rum hand-to-hand, grunted vulgar phrases, showing off, in front of a girl. As Lola walked by, one of the boys stood and punched the young lady, who froze stock still for a few seconds then cackled a weak laugh.

Finally, Lola made it to the corner where the Teatro Auditórium had once stood, now razed to the ground by fire. What was going on?

Lola let herself fall, flustered, onto one of the gray stone benches that made up the rear portion of an outdoor amphitheater, where the bands used to play in the good old days, in the park at Calzada and D, like it always had been back even to when her own grandmother used to take her on Sundays to hear the marching band play. She had never bothered to find out whose bust it was that stood with its back to the podium at the center of the semicircle.

Beginning in front of the Carmelo, Lola always had liked to stroll along the corridor of tall columns topped by a wooden trellis covered in an abundant climbing vine affording protection in the worst of the dog days and walk around the tank of clear water, to end up sitting at the roundabout in the front. Hidden by greenery and lamp posts, its own semicircle silhouette reflecting the other, as if it were a mirror made of marble, echoing the open air stage.

Lola looked around her. She would have sworn that right in that spot there had always been, from time immemorial, a statue of Neptune with his trident and his long petrified locks. Where had it gone?

Underneath one of the banks two starving street dogs were sleeping, curled up next to one another. A few feet away, a woman was talking to herself. The woman looked over at her, and in her eyes, Lola saw the reflection of her own stare.

All of a sudden Lola felt a sense of urgency, a need to hurry up. She had to get back. Where? The hours had flown by, and they must be waiting for her. Who, who would be waiting for her? It had gotten too late... Too late for what?

The deteriorated houses, the rotting vegetation, the rancid glares of the passers-by, seemed to her to be part of some act of expiation for who knows which one of her many sins. The Dead Girl. Could it be that the Dead Girl was imposing, with that whole debacle, some hidden significance on her old memories? Forgive me, forgive me, forgive me, she begged from the bottom of her heart.

As if guessing her own thoughts, the woman who was talking to herself then said to her, "And Havana is dying..."

YUYA

According to Yuya, Lola told her that from trying so hard to escape from her memories, she lost all control over them.

With the help of a few of their neighbors, Yuya broke the lock on the door and walked into Lola's house, with butterflies in her stomach from the fear of what she might find. The deserted apartment filled her with even more anxiety. It didn't look like anything was missing, and she didn't see any signs of violence. On top of the dining room table, a coffee cup covered in ants and a shallow bowl with the stinking remains of the pudding indicated that Lola had been gone for several days.

Next to the dirty dishes, the photo of the Dead Girl lay in the same place, just where it had been when Lola pointed it out in their last conversation. Yuya says that she had started to tell her that her entire adult life she, Lola, had worked in one of those important offices that had something to do with culture. Yuya didn't remember which one, at this stage of the game it really didn't matter. Lola had seen more than one member of middle management come and go, but her Boss, the great man and lord of his territory, both feared and adored, was assumed to be there for all eternity. Despite his whims and his flights of hysteria that were the norm, Lola obeyed him to the letter, she knew her place and what was expected of her. She knew every single municipal code by heart, she filtered his calls, saving him from the irritating and passing along the more pleasant duties, serving as his guard wall and keeping away any burdensome visitors. That was her job, and she did it with efficiency and perfect discretion.

According to Yuya, the Dead Girl had shown up without any warning right at Lola's office one day, to ask for her help, and showing how upset she was in the tone of her voice, she complained of a great injustice that was being done to her. Somebody was accusing her of Yuya wasn't sure exactly what, and truth be known she didn't even care to know. Lola knew the Dead Girl well, she was a young lady much like her own daughter, well-mannered and studious, but she couldn't do what the Dead Girl was begging of her, so sweetly, let her have a few minutes with the Boss. To put her on the day's agenda, without an appointment no less, and with this kind of a problem. There was absolutely no way she could do it, this kind of problem was always the most disagreeable sort of issue that could possibly be raised, and, to top it off, he didn't even know the girl, she was a nobody. She didn't belong there, and her petition would not be answered. Lola stayed steadfast in spite of the girl's tears; her own job was on the line, she couldn't put herself at risk like that, times were hard.

When aren't they? Yuya said that she asked herself, when haven't times been hard?

Yuya said that Lola hadn't been able to forget the state of desperation that the Dead Girl had been in as she left the office, I'm innocent, she had repeated, I didn't do anything.

A few hours later, Lola had found out that the Dead Girl had thrown herself from the eighteenth floor of a building on Línea Street. According to Yuya, what horrified her most about hearing that story was to realize that the executioners hadn't even been from the opposing side, they were our own.

Yuya says that then she noticed that the ration book was gone, it wasn't in its usual place. Lola must have gone out to get her bread and something had happened to her. Until dawn Shu and Yuya were wandering around from hospitals to police stations, without seeing a trace of her.

Yuya says that finally they found her in the park at Calzada and D, out of her mind and completely dehydrated. They would need to let somebody know about this, Yuya says, but who? Jesus, Mary, and Joseph!

MARTIN

Nobody went to the Dead Girl's funeral either. On that occasion, Martin waited at the entrance of the cemetery, beneath the pompous portico of the Colón necropolis, sacred ground of Havana with its sacramental waves of stone and its lying, tricky Latin inscription, *ianua sum pacis*. Peace? In the Dead Girl's battered heart there hadn't been nor would there ever be a chance for any peace.

The funerary hearse, with its primer paint and dented hood, without wreathes or any ornamentation, followed by a taxi in as bad shape as was the mortuary vehicle and with only two passengers inside, stopped only a few seconds. Martin saw the driver get out and walk over to the administration building, sign a paper and then return to his post in a hurry. Inside the taxi, seated in the other front seat, a middle-aged man, his face in a grimace of pain and wearing greasy overalls, gave the impression of having rushed out of his shop, without even the time to change his clothing for the burial. In the back seat, like a raft, floated the Dead Girl's mother staring fixedly forward. Martin didn't dare get any closer. The driver got the car going with difficulty, the motor firing off an annoying sound, falling silent, and finally starting up. The puny procession, without any flowers or mourners, did without the religious ceremony in the chapel, picked up speed, and didn't stop until arriving at the zone of the shared graves.

Martin hurried, cutting between the cemetery plots, to no avail.

The funerary convoy had gone ahead too quickly, and as Martin trotted along, his tongue hanging out from being too hot and too anxious, he watched two gravediggers lower the cheap pine box into the hole, with the help of two grimy cords. The chauffeur stayed behind his steering wheel with the motor running, and the mechanical racket could be heard from a mile away. When Martin was at last growing close, the Dead Girl's mother and the man in overalls holding her up, his hands on her shoulders, without noticing his arrival turned back to the taxi and made their way out of the cemetery. The burial had lasted less than five minutes. The Dead Girl had curled up for the last time in a communal hole in the ground, next to the others who had fallen from grace. But none of them more disgraced than she was.

For his part, Martin hadn't been able to get his hands on even one measly handful of wildflowers. Times were tough.

Martin convinced himself for a long time that perhaps words could change reality. Change the world, no; but our perception of life, maybe. Narrating something well, did that make it better? There was no way to make that funeral good. So words served, at least, to make people suffer.

The last person who had spoken with the Dead Girl before what happened had been Maria Esther. It occurred to Martin that he had never been interested in what she had told her, what her last words had been, but by now it was far too late to ask Maria Esther about it. Although he still wasn't sure that he wanted to find out. And in the case that he had wanted to go looking for them, those final pieces that would complete the puzzle never would have turned up anyway. Back in those years, Martin had had to keep his mouth shut in order to stay out of trouble. The seas had been rocking in a storm, and those were the waters he had to navigate, or succumb like the Dead Girl. Cowards like him, the fucking cowards like him, just kept navigating.

His childhood memories and all his fatuous pretentions of "love and squalor" seemed trite, even indecent.

Martin's mother folded his socks, sticking the end of one into its mate and rolling them into a ball, white balls of cotton that piled up on top of the bed by her side. By now she could barely walk and she had moved into her son's apartment. Martin cared for her day and night, although he let her do little tasks here and there so she wouldn't be bored. He also felt the need to see her as she always had been, the illusion that she was only there to keep his socks in order.

Just looking at her hands, Martin knew that *she knew*. A month? A week? A few days? They both knew she didn't have very long, but that didn't matter any more. In spite of everything, life had let them have at least this little time together.

"I'll be right back," Martin said.

He walked out to the shore, to the reef-lined coast of Alamar, and he sat down next to a stray dog. With one hand, Martin stroked the dog's head while with his other hand he tossed page after typewritten page into the waves beating against the rocks. Manuscripts don't burn, it's better to drown them, for them to sink down in the water. The sea isn't the sea, the sea is our backyard. Maybe a good first line. A fucking first line.

HERMI

All stories could be reduced to one, to an anecdote that could be uttered in a few short seconds, which was repeated over and over, ever changing, but never ceasing to be the same.

Did you cross the line, or didn't you…

That morning now so far away, Hermi and Tristan had seen the body tumble, its arms flailing like broken wings. They saw the Dead Girl fall.

At the time of the Mariel boatlift, they had come in a truck looking for Tristan and Hermi. They guys were carrying a list, and their names were on it. Hermi and Tristan had aged still looking just like the Celestial Twins, homonymous, so you still had to ask which one was which. It didn't matter one way or the other; they both were too much.

For a few days, a small horde of neighbors spattered the front of their house with eggs, rotten potatoes, rocks, and insults. "Go away go away go away go away go away!"

Hermi, since then, shrunk her infinity to within the confines of those walls. How horrible it would be, if over time, she found herself back on speaking terms with those who had brought the precipice so close. No, that, never. The street, the neighborhood where they had been born, ended up on the other side of a barricade, a wall of bricks and an invisible line. Those permitted to enter included the light, stray cats, sparrows, lizards, the sounds of the city and the particular Havana smells, but not people. Hermi withdrew like a turtle in her shell, she barred the windows, filled the living room with wheelbarrows full of dirt, where she then planted flowers, sowed seeds, grew vegetables, and watered them all every day. Through the upper stained glass windows the sun covered the room, and the plants she was growing flourished, shot up, bloomed, fruited. The living room isn't the living room, the living room is an orchard, a garden in miniature, but fiercely free.

Tristan settled in Puerto Rico. It was a three-hour flight away. But in this case they might as well have lived in different galaxies, light years from one another. "Only as time goes by will we be able to make sense out of our own stubbornness in being ourselves," said Tristan in one of his sententious pronouncements (or had it been Hermi?).

An act of repudiation. What else was left to try?

Years later, in a package that Tristan sent, Hermi received the reproduction of one of Bosch's painted slabs, his apocalyptic *Fall of the Damned*, an obvious satire given the distinct fates of the good versus that of the reprobates. In the darkness and confusion of the ochre colors, as fragmented torsos rained down and sibylline fires seemed to burn above, a pair of arms were trying to hold a body from drowning, or were they trying to hurry its demise? In the ominous silence of the painting, where one could only imagine the noise and the whirlwind of the souls that had been thrown down from heaven, a silvery light added horror and beauty to the scene.

When the Dead Girl had been falling for good, they had been falling too. They all had been falling.

WOMAN WHO TALKS TO HERSELF IN THE PARK

And then the bleach spilled over and all the documents, manuscripts, legal papers, contracts, letters, reports, papal bulls, diplomas, papyrus scrolls, plaques, certificates, inventories, permits, announcements, proceedings, memorials, testimonies, registers, programs, magazines, newspapers, brochures, and books, ever written or to be written, were erased until all the pages were blank. And Havana is dying…

GERTRUDE

Call me Gertrude. That hunt has come to an end.

From time to time men need to give birth to playful heroes and transform misery into great feats. All of it is false and banal. As an old victim of humiliations and mistreatment, the ancient fisherwoman of Cojímar knew all too well what the real truth was: *a woman can be destroyed, and moreover she can be defeated.*

One day before what happened happened, the Dead Girl sent me a letter written in her own hand that I have never, never, dared to read. I keep it sealed, just as it arrived, in a stack of inoffensive papers, and once in a while it comes to light, like a stick of dynamite hidden within words waiting for its time to explode. She also had called me a few times, and I hadn't answered, and after everything turned out as it did, when I asked myself why, I found only silence and blame. At first I wanted to believe that my distance had merely been what was called for at the time, my life had taken some rocky paths, and I didn't want to further disturb the Dead Girl's fragile hold on life with my own dilemmas, nor to put her into harm's way nor stain her innocence. At the end they had made us feel so dirty!

One tends to dream about re-encounters, but the victims of suicide are people who never want to encounter anybody ever again.

Somebody told me that she had taken off her shoes, and her watch too, which she stashed away in the purse that she left down below the window. Evidently there was no mystery at all. She didn't ask for forgiveness, she didn't throw her suffering in anybody's face, she just decided she wasn't going to do it anymore. As if she had been able to say I'm not going to write anymore, I'm not going to paint anymore, I'm not going to play the piano anymore... At the root of it, that's what it was all about.

Do you remember, or don't you?

Who killed the Lady Commander? The town of Fuenteovejuna, ma'am. All of us together.

We could keep on complaining about how we all felt half dead, but the Dead Girl continued to be the deadest of all of us.

Someday maybe I'll get the courage to read that letter.

The women lovers of the heathen Omar Khayyam, hidden behind the mask of their husband, wrote blasphemous quartets full of doubt and pain that they didn't have any right to express, under pain of stoning:

You say that wine is the only balm?
Bring me all the wine in the universe!
My heart has so many wounds... All the wine in the universe
And my heart is still wounded!

ABOUT THE AUTHOR

After graduating from a prep school for gifted and talented adolescents, the Raúl Cepero Bonilla Special Pre-University Institute, Yáñez entered the University of Havana in 1965. Five years later she finished her B.A. in Humanities. She continued post-graduate study at the same institution and received her Doctorate in Philology in 1992. Her area of specialization is Latin American, especially Cuban, literature, with a secondary focus on feminine discourse. A university professor and researcher for many years, more recently she has concentrated fully on her literary writing, journalistic essays, and the promotion of Cuban women writers.

The grand prize for poetry at the Concurso 13 de Marzo, awarded in 1970 for her earliest collection *Las visitas* [The Visitors], was the first of many accolades that Mirta Yáñez has received throughout her trajectory as a multifaceted writer. Considered one of the most relevant intellectuals of her generation, she has excelled in practically every genre she has tried: poetry, short fiction, novel, and essay. A screenwriter for film and television, she also has to her credit an extensive bibliography as a journalist and literary critic.

In 2004 Yáñez was selected for the MEET Writers in Residence program, hosted by the Maison des Ecrivans et des Traducteurs in Saint-Nazaire, France, where she finished a brief collection of stories, subsequently published in Spanish as *Falsos documentos* (as well as in French and German). Several of these stories are included in the anthology *Havana Is a Very Big City,* published in English by Cubanabooks in 2010. Increasingly the subject for academic and critical attention in the United States, her work as been featured in sessions at such major conferences as the Modern Language Association Convention and the Latin American Studies Association Congress.

Mirta Yáñez has presented lectures and taught courses all over the globe, including in Venezuela, Dominican Republic, Puerto Rico, Mexico, Chile, Spain, United States, Great Britain, Poland, Germany, and France.

In 2011 Yáñez's most recent novel, *Sangra por la herida/The Bleeding Wound* won the Critics' Choice prize for literature in Cuba—her fourth time winning this prestigious award. In 2012, the novel was awarded the coveted Premio de la Academia Cubana de la Lengua.

She currently resides in the coastal town of Cojímar, famed as Hemingway's favorite fishing spot, which is located just across the bay from Havana.

ABOUT THE TRANSLATOR

A Texas native, Dr. Sara E. Cooper (PhD University of Texas, 1999) is a Professor of Spanish at California State University, Chico. She teaches Spanish, Contemporary Latin American, Latina/o and Chicana/o cultural production and Gender/Queer Studies. She is the editor of *The Ties That Bind: Questioning Family Dynamics and Family Discourse in Hispanic Literature and Film* as well as *Lesbian Images in International Popular Culture* (also a special issue of the Journal of Lesbian Studies). Cooper is the translator of *Burnt Honey/Miel quemada*, a novel by Chicano Antonio Arreguín Bermúdez, and *Havana is a Really Big City*, by Cuban Mirta Yáñez. Her articles and translations appear in several journals and anthologies, including: *Letras femeninas, Chasqui, Confluencia, Cuban Studies, Kunapipi, A Changing Cuba in a Changing World, Cultura y letras cubanas en el siglo XXI, Tortilleras: Hispanic and Latina Lesbian Expression, Journal of Lesbian Studies, Interdisciplinary Literary Studies,* and *Challenging Lesbian Norms*.

Having turned her intellect and passion toward Cuba in 1998, Cooper is the founder of the Cuban and Cuban Diaspora Cultural Expression Discussion Group of the Modern Language Association and a member of the Cuba Section of the Latin American Studies Association. Through a long and gratifying association with Mirta Yáñez, Cooper has come into contact with some of the most brilliant and creative minds of Cuba's literary circles. Most of these talented and prolific women are practically unknown in the United States or to English readers in general. In 2010 she established Cubanabooks Press, dedicated to publishing Cuban women writers in translation.

SANGRA POR LA HERIDA

Por Mirta Yáñez

NOTA DE LA TRADUCTORA

La primera vez que leí este libro (en español), todavía no se había publicado, y la autora aún haría varias revisiones antes de que el manuscrito fuera aceptado para publicarse en una de las editoriales más importantes de Cuba. Una noche de calor sofocante en Cojímar, Mirta Yáñez entró en la habitación que reservaba para las visitas, donde yo me hospedaba, y con un aire despreocupado me tendió un CD en el que había escrito en la cubierta *"Sangra por la herida"*. "Lo puedes leer si quieres", me dijo. ¿Que si quería leerlo? ¿Qué tipo de broma era esa? Yo estuve esperando por esa lectura durante años. Casi había sufrido un ataque cardíaco un año antes, cuando ella había dejado caer una leve sugerencia de que trabajaba en una nueva novela. Así que hasta la madrugada, acurrucada bajo el mosquitero, agradecida cada vez que un soplo de aire entraba por las ventanas, leía. Y me reía. Y lloraba.

A la mañana siguiente juré hacerle justicia a la novela, traduciéndola al inglés. Ha pasado mucho tiempo (la novela salió en Cuba en 2011), y Mirta ha tenido paciencia conmigo. La mayor parte del tiempo. Salvo los ratos en que se preocupaba.

En defensa propia, este es un libro inmensamente complejo. Y permítanme decirles que a Mirta no es fácil traducirla aun en sus momentos más "simples," si es que se puede usar tal palabra con ella. Tiene un sentido del humor mordaz, tal vez el vocabulario más nutrido que he encontrado en mi vida, y talento para jugar con el lenguaje. Constantemente incorpora referencias culturales profundas y chistes privados. Ahora, en este *opus magnus,* ha creado doce narradores, cada cual con su propia voz, que narran desde el punto de vista de tres distintas épocas—la última década antes de la Revolución, momentos emotivosde los años 60, y los años finales del siglo veinte.

Llegar a conocer a tantos personajes lo suficiente para retratar sus peculiaridades requiere tiempo. Así que me metí completamente en la erudición de Gertrudis, la vulgaridad de Daontaon, lo picaresco de Willie y la melancolía de Martín. En otoño de 2013 los estudiantes de mi clase de Literatura Latinoamericana estudiaron la novela en español, y en el siguiente semestre los alumnos de mi clase de Maestros Literarios Traducidos al Inglés leyeron una primera versión de la traducción. Las conversaciones que emergieron en esos salones de clase han tenido su impacto en el libro que ahora está en sus manos. Y no se debe caer en el error de subestimar a la actual generación de estudiantes universitarios: los llamados jóvenes "del milenio" son capaces de mucho más de lo que pensamos.

Pudiera escribir docenas de páginas sobre los retos y las delicias de esta labor de amor. Sin embargo, eso será en otro momento. Basta decir que estos años trabajando con *Sangra por la herida* han provocado en mí deseos de más... ¿me oyes, Rico?

Ahora que la traducción se ha completado, hay que agradecer a la gente que la hizo posible. Mirta Yáñez siempre es gentil, generosa, incisiva, humorística, y brillante (y no necesariamente en ese orden). Mi querida amiga Nancy Alonso es una editora meticulosa, y su ojo de águila encontró muchos errores. Meg Wallace, a quien conocí hace casi tres décadas, ha contribuido con intervenciones penetrantes, sin las cuales esta hubiera sido una traducción más pobre. Mi familia ha sido ahora paciente, ahora un apoyo, y a veces el estímulo para seguir adelante. Sandy, Jenny, y Dorothy June: las quiero. Los estudiantes que colaboran con Cubanabooks, especialmente Kyle Heise y Vianney Bernabe, me mantuvieron plenamente involucrada en la novela durante el último año del proyecto, dándome energía con sus preguntas y observaciones. La muy apreciada beca para traducción del National Endowment for the Arts me dio fondos, ánimo y una introducción a nuevos lectores y colegas. Agradezco, por todo su apoyo, al colectivo del Departamento de Lenguas, Literaturas y Culturas Internacionales de la Universidad Estatal de California en Chico, y en particular a mi Directora, la Dra. Patricia Black. Una sincera gratitud a todos por haber contribuido con este proyecto, pero especialmente a Rico, Private y Kowalski, mis pingüinos.

Sara E. Cooper
Agosto del 2014
Chico, CA

A los amigos que dejaron de pintar, de tocar el piano, de hacer teatro, de escribir un poema, de soñar sus sueños, por las razones que fuesen.

El aire que rodea al hombre es ajeno y extraño y en él estamos expuestos a la destrucción.

Prólogo a La Celestina
Fernando de Rojas

Estoy casi seguro que me chilló "¡Buena suerte!". Ojalá no me haya gritado eso, ojalá que no. Yo nunca le gritaría a nadie "¡Buena suerte!". Suena espantoso cuando se piensa un poco en ello.

El guardián en el trigal
J. D. Salinger

Al final, al final de todo, uno responde a todas las preguntas con los hechos de su vida: a las preguntas que el mundo le ha hecho una y otra vez. Las preguntas son éstas: ¿Quién eres?... ¿Qué has querido de verdad?... ¿Qué has sabido de verdad?... ¿Con qué y con quién te has comportado con valentía o con cobardía?... Estas son las preguntas.

El último encuentro [21]
Sándor Márai

---

[21] Originalmente *A gyertyák csonkig égnek* (1942).

GERTRUDIS

Yo Claudia, Fausta, La Gataparda, Doña Segunda Sombra, La guardiana en el trigal, La Principita, Edipa Reina, La Cida Campeadora, Romea y Julieta, Mamá Goriot, La loba esteparia, Tartufa, Las Buddenbrook, Doña Quijota de la Mancha, La extranjera, La Maestra y Margarita, ¿verlo todo al revés?, ¿desde "otro" punto de vista? ¿El cuento como yo me lo sé?, *¿El evangelio según María Magdalena?*

A veces los muertos preguntan ¿qué fue de nosotros?, ¿nadie se acuerda?, ¿quién va a hacer la historia? Basta apenas un poco de olvido para que los muertos y las muertas acudan impacientes a pasar la cuenta.

Vine a Comala, porque me dijeron que acá vivía mi madre, una tal Petra Páramo... Más o menos podría empezar así, aunque no me trae la ilusión de cumplir una promesa, tan solo que rezuman los murmullos y salten al techo las gatas encerradas.

Quizás resulte imposible ceñirse a confidencias propias y repunten algunos disimulos ajenos. ¿Se acuerdan de aquella película de Bergman, *Sonrisas de una noche de verano?* Uno de los personajes requiere a una anciana apoltronada en la cama por sus razones de mantener silencio sobre ciertos picarescos recuerdos y ella responde, maliciosa, que aquel palacio donde residía le había sido entregado a cambio de que *no las revelara*. Visto el caso, puedo evocar mis memorias con toda tranquilidad sin romper compromiso alguno. *Memorias de Adriana.*

La mujer invisible, La satiricona, Cándida, Cyrana de Bergerac, Lady Jim, La gran Gatsby, Martina Fierro, Poetisa en New York, Las tres mosqueteras, La prisionera de la máscara de hierro, Nazarina, Polifema y Galatea, Lazarilla de Tormes, Huckleberria Finn, Las hermanas Karamasova, Oliveria Twist, Las desnudas y las muertas...

¿Y contar otra vez la vieja patraña de buenos contra malos, obsesiones y aprendizajes de juventud, locura y muerte, cazadores y arponazos, con el mar de decorado de fondo, la captura de una ballena blanca, de *Mobysa Dick?* De acuerdo, pero "llámenme Fulana", una del montón, de *Las miserables,* en cinco tomos.

MARTÍN

El olor a sofrito inundaba toda la casa. Martín resistió la tentación de anotar para el manuscrito cómo se confeccionaba un sofrito cubano, puñetera práctica en boga de incluir recetas de cocina.

De un tiempo a esta parte no se le iba de la boca el vocablo *puñetería*. Desde que las cosas empezaron a salir mal, todo le parecía "puñetero". Además de los conflictos públicos, de las situaciones calamitosas, de la trabajosa escritura, le cayó encima la puñetería de vivir en Alamar, el puñetero barrio de Alamar, en el este de La Habana.

Pese a sus intenciones, el espíritu de Martín acumulaba sobre una imaginaria tabla de madera las rodajas de cebolla, los fragmentos de ají espulgados de semillas, los ajos bien pelados y machucados, todo sumergido después en el aceite hirviendo, dorándose con lentitud y despidiendo aquel aroma inefable.

Martín abrió las aletas de la nariz y anotó en una de sus tarjetas mentales que las resonancias de los olores del sofrito lo asemejaban a *la magdalena,* el panqué de Marcel Proust. Sus efluvios lo remitían a la cocina de la abuela Antonia en la calle Amistad, en pos del tiempo perdido sin remedio. Esa asociación demasiado culta desentonaba y solo podría servirle más adelante para insuflar densidad a algún texto.

La mamá de Martín, de espaldas, atendía las exigencias de la cocina, y no asistió a esa evocación, escindida entre las magdalenas proustianas y la irresistible fragancia del sofrito. Tampoco pudo presenciar la angustia de Martín ni el movimiento de sus hombros, o de un único vistazo hubiera adivinado que algo pasaba. Ella seguía ensimismada con la paleta de madera, revolviendo las especias en el aceite para que no se pasaran en el hervor y mantuvieran el punto dorado de la exquisitez.

Martín tuvo tiempo de recomponer su ánimo, atragantarse la bola que subía y bajaba por los conductos del pecho, en donde se juntaban la nostalgia por la cocina de la abuela Antonia, la magdalena de cuando Proust era probablemente un guajirito glotón, las ganas de escribir al menos una página memorable como aquella y el olor del sofrito preparado por su mamá.

Trató de prolongar todo lo posible la escena de inocencia en la cocina de su casa, tan vulnerable como todos los instantes inexplicablemente dichosos.

Martín le seguía diciendo "su casa", aunque hacía casi treinta años que se había marchado, a mediados de los sesenta, los puñeteros *sesenta,* como todos los que, por aquella época, abandonaron sus hogares, unos para los estudios en la beca como él mismo, otros para el impenitente destierro, los de más allá, con poca o mucha suerte, quién podría decirlo, a la guerra y a la muerte. Pero no venían a cuento ahora los viajeros, los suicidas, los expulsados, ni los desbarajustes que se habían ido acumulando en la memoria. Martín cerró el archivo de los recuerdos generacionales y volvió a inmiscuirse en el olor del sofrito y en las manos de su mamá con la paleta de madera, dando vueltas a las cebollitas, los ajos y los ajíes en el aceite, tal como le había visto hacer desde siempre, algo inclinada sobre las hornillas, sin delantal y pensando en las musarañas, con un reguero de cucharones, pomos y platos al lado; una mano titubeante, la izquierda, agarrando el mango de la sartén, mientras su mano derecha revolvía con la espátula el mejunje que los cubanos llaman sofrito.

—No —advirtió ella—. Ni se te ocurra mojar pan en el sofrito. Espera a que sirva la comida.

Martín retrocedió por el pasillo y se sentó ante la mesa del comedor. "¿Ya están los resultados del análisis?", preguntó la mamá de Martín, aparentando dejadez. "No, quizás la semana que viene", contestó Martín. Esos días de espera, solo para la confirmación de los temores, no atenuaban el puñetero miedo.

Martín se acodó sobre el blanco y algo raído mantel. Hasta allí seguía llegando el perfume de la cocina, mezclado ahora con el familiar vaho de los muebles, esa tenue combinación de barniz y humedad de la casa de su mamá en el Vedado.

MUJER QUE HABLA SOLA EN EL PARQUE

El cielo se puso rojo naranja y llegó un fuerte viento del noreste. Y entonces una nube negra chocó con una nube colorada y, del golpe, las dos se precipitaron sobre La Habana. Y La Habana se muere...

MICAELA

A Micaela la despertó el llanto del perro. Durante los últimos días, ese mismo lamento, una especie de aullido angustioso, comenzaba unas horas antes del amanecer para terminar un rato después. También se dejaba oír al mediodía y, en una o dos ocasiones, lo había escuchado a medianoche.

La mayoría de las veces, Micaela no se daba cuenta de cuándo empezaba. En algún momento, el lloriqueo del perro, sostenido en un tono agudo y desamparado, se introducía en su sueño y la despertaba. Cuando ya tenía los ojos abiertos y dudaba entre un sentimiento de lástima o molestia, los vagidos se cortaban de manera abrupta. La brusquedad con que terminaban la llevaron a presumir que el cachorro, sin duda se trataba de un animalito pequeño, truncaba su queja al concedérsele algo que reclamaba.

La primera vez creyó que el perro había sido abandonado y, a regañadientes, se levantó a mirar por las persianas. Aunque no pudo precisar de cuál patio provenía el ruido, supo que el perro lloraba desde el edificio trasero. En esa oportunidad, con la irrupción del silencio, también se imaginó su muerte, de alguna enfermedad dolorosa, y sintió pena, una distanciada tristeza parecida a aquella ante una situación dramática en una película bien narrada.

Las madrugadas siguientes, cuando se repetía el llanto, le empezaron a acometer aquellos pensamientos absurdos sobre la muerte y la soledad. En apariencia, no tenían relación con el quejido del perro y le causaban un desganado disgusto consigo misma, por ese deslizarse en una pendiente de autocompasión.

La noche pasada, el llanto del perro suspendió la lectura de una novela rusa que por breve tiempo la había mantenida olvidada de todo. Olvidada era un decir. Los primeros capítulos le habían parecido tan cercanos a su propia experiencia que, de tanto en tanto, se veía obligada a cerrar el libro, tomar aire, respirar hondo. Con las primas luces del alba logró dormirse y de nuevo los chillidos interrumpieron por la mitad un absurdo sueño donde su tía Candita estaba a punto de revelarle, en secreto, una sagrada petición. ¡La tía Candita! Se fue del país y nunca más supo de ella. Nada puede desaparecer el pasado, se dijo Micaela.

ESTELA

Estela sufrió una chocante impresión al ver la imagen de su padre en la pantalla del televisor. La película de video le había llegado de Cuba hacía apenas unas horas. Cuando se la entregaron, depositó el casete en el bolso, llena de una euforia contenida, con conciencia del placer que representaría llegar al apartamento, quitarse el sobretodo y las pesadas botas, pedirle a la muchacha que preparase un *cafécafé*, graduar la climatización hasta un punto confortable, abrir la cortina para presenciar la llovizna de este frío fin de verano londinense, ponerse cómoda con las pantuflas de Oscar, sentarse en la mecedora y tirarse una colcha sobre las piernas, beber a sorbos el líquido espeso y poco azucarado dispuesto en un tazón, pedirle a la muchacha que, *please,* colocase con mucho cuidado el casete dentro del equipo, quedarse sola en el silencio de la habitación y después, *click,* apretar el botón del control remoto y ver aparecer en su pantalla las imágenes de La Habana. Oscar se había tomado el trabajo de recorrer todo el Malecón, desde el torreón del río Almendares hasta La Punta, ese espectáculo único de la ciudad más bella del mundo, apuntando con el lente solo hacia el mar, sin enfocar las casas mordidas por el salitre. ¡Una maravilla! ¡Un orgasmo! Para Estela, todo lo anterior resultaba casi mucho mejor que un orgasmo de los ortodoxos. Estela y Oscar se conocían tanto las mañas que el trámite de la cama había pasado a segundo plano. Llevaban treinta años de casados, sin tormentos ni hacerse de la vista gorda, compartían los gustos y no se traicionaban. Trabajar en Londres los había acorralado en un bienestar construido con habilidad donde solo lo externo podría resultar agresivo. En la pantalla del televisor seguían desfilando las tomas de la ciudad, elegidas con esmero por Oscar para Estela. Se conocieron en la universidad habanera de los años sesenta y congeniaron desde el principio. Ninguno de los dos se sentía a gusto con los revoltosos de la Escuela de Letras, ellas con las minifaldas escandalosas, ellos con los pelos largos, protestando por todo, haciéndose los "hippies". Ni a Estela ni a Oscar les interesaba protestar, estudiaban mucho, se pegaban a leer en la biblioteca, no se metían en nada, no participaban, no criticaban las malas clases, ni abrían sus bocas en las reuniones de aula. Oscar se rebajaba la cabellera hasta dejarla en un casquete de pelambre puntiagudo que tenía algo de encanto en medio de tanto crespo mal lavado. Estela usaba la indumentaria readaptada de las tías y mientras las demás muchachas del aula pasaban las mil y una para conseguir un corte de tela, ella siguió atravesando esos años difíciles con la ropa guardada en el armario familiar. La madre le cosía los vestidos a su propio gusto, es decir, al gusto de los años cincuenta, con mucho vuelo en la saya y el dobladillo por debajo de la rodilla. Y aunque nunca les cruzó por la mente la idea de llamar la atención, ni mucho menos ser tomados por distintos, no pasaban inadvertidos en la Escuela de Letras de aquellos años. Pudiera decirse que ese "portarse bien", más cercano al pasado que se suponía desechado para siempre, caía en gracia, paradojas de la vida. Entre tantos alborotadores mal mirados, Oscar era el alumno que no buscaba problemas y Estela daba el ejemplo de cómo debe comportarse una joven de buena crianza. Cuando empezaron las asambleas de depuración y enérgicos muchachos de otras carreras empezaron a dejarse sentir en la Escuela, ellos se sintieron más en comunión con los de afuera que con sus propios colegas de estudio. Poco a poco, Estela perdió el complejo de burguesita y Oscar el de niño bitongo, o en todo caso lo sería buena parte de los estudiantes de Ingeniería y Medicina, cortados por la misma tijera que Estela y Oscar. Nada de esto, se decía Estela a veces a fuer de sincera, justificaba la meteórica carrera de ambos como dirigentes de los *Jóvenes Comunistas*.[22]

---

[22] En pocos años los *Jóvenes Comunistas* se convirtieron en el club social y político más prestigioso para jóvenes de Cuba. Ya que era evidencia externa de un supuesto fervor y compromiso revolucionario, a la membresía históricamente se le ha otorgado ciertas ventajas y opciones fuera del alcance de los no afiliados.

Estela no entendía de política y estudiaba Letras porque la madre pensaba que se trataba de "una carrera bonita". De la noche a la mañana estuvieron en la cúspide y la vida se les complicó, aunque también se les hizo más fácil en otros sentidos. La imagen del Malecón se detuvo en el faro y, de repente, entró el rostro de su padre en la pantalla. La madre de Estela había muerto un año atrás. En aquellos días, Estela tenía muchos compromisos en Londres y le resultó imposible viajar a La Habana para el entierro, así que la expresión desamparada del padre la tomó por sorpresa. Siempre había sido un tipo jovial y seguro de sí mismo. Estela notó que las manos de su padre temblaban y evitaba mirar de frente a la cámara. Sin embargo, cuando comenzó a hablar, inclinando la cabeza hacia delante, como buscando un micrófono invisible, la voz seguía siendo potente. Empezó contando del lugar, de lo bien que lo trataban, de los sillones para mecerse todo el día, de la comida a horas fijas. Se detuvo pensativo y dijo que extrañaba al perro, pero que no se preocupara su hija, aquí, en el asilo, les permitían tener un jardincito, no había mucha agua y se daban con facilidad los cactus. "Los cactus", repitió, y se quedó titubeante como si hubiera perdido la letra del guión. Luego bruscamente se acababa la cinta.

MARTÍN

Qué desastre la noche anterior. Martín había logrado, después de mucha labia y varios jaiboles por medio, levantar a aquella chiquita en el brindis de clausura de uno de los tantos encuentros literarios. La muchacha se llamaba Daontaon, nombre asiático según todo parecía indicar, y trabajaba como una especie de apagafuegos en la Casa de Cultura de Alamar. Por fortuna, no tenía intenciones de ser poetisa, ni tan siquiera escribía para niños. Hablaba sin parar, mas su principal defecto consistía en la proximidad del apartamento donde vivía, en un edificio aledaño al de Martín.

Los arrecifes de la costa norte del Municipio Habana del Este, aunque inhóspitos, se presentaban como el único paraje asequible para las intenciones de poner en práctica los actos eróticos consustanciales a estos eventos. La ventolera pelaba hasta los huesos y los olores a pescado muerto en aquellos andurriales no contribuían a establecer un ambiente romántico, pero Martín ni jugando podía permitir que la susodicha se colara en su casa. Por su parte, Daontaon no mostraba ningún deslumbramiento ante la circunstancia de encontrarse junto a un escritor laureado. Rondaban por las cercanías varios perros hambrientos y, para colmo, el pito de Martín tampoco se manifestaba de manera que fuese posible olvidar el entorno. Daontaon se dejó manosear un rato, escuchó con cortesía dos o tres citas de Neruda de las que nunca solían fallar y luego lo interrumpió para preguntar: "¿tú tienes carro, papi?".

No, Martín no tenía un puñetero carro. En ese instante, el pito de Martín se desinfló como un globo de cumpleaños y Daontaon aprovechó para escabullirse.

A la mañana siguiente, Martín se despertó tan deprimido por el comportamiento de su artefacto viril que la emprendió furioso con su vieja máquina de escribir y redactó dos párrafos burlones: uno contra las feministas exaltadas, esas gringas que nunca se afeitaban, y otro contra las mujeres cincuentonas que ya estaban perdiendo sus vellos púbicos. Tachó "vellos" por parecerle demasiado remilgado y lo sustituyó por un término más grosero. Daontaon no caía en ninguna de esas dos categorías, mas a los efectos de la literatura daba igual y Martín escribiría cualquier cosa menos que su pito lo había traicionado.

Dos párrafos de porquería... peor que eso, puñeteramente falsos, se confesó a sí mismo con una sibilina sensación de birlador.

Martín llevaba demasiado tiempo tratando de iniciar un manuscrito. Cada vez que se enfrentaba a la página en blanco, le daba vueltas en la cabeza una frase atribuida a Bulgakov y que había descubierto en aquel periodicucho, *Novedades de Moscú*, una reliquia de la prensa soviética. Antes de que desaparecieran del panorama y aunque habían seguido siendo ladrillosos, se alcanzaba a rastrear en ellos una que otra perla de sabiduría. La frase empecinada, *los manuscritos no arden,* abofeteaba a

Martín cada vez que pretendía comenzar su tarea.

No arderán, pensaba Martín, pero se los comen los bichos, se pudren por la humedad, se traspapelan, se duermen en una gaveta.

Martín, a pesar de los pesares, anotaba en papeles, rompía la virginidad de coloridas agendas y después almacenaba en un archivo el material para su manuscrito. Cuando disponía de ánimo, había iniciado varios intentos de clasificación. Una de sus carpetas acumulaba títulos, solo eso, en mayor cantidad que todos los cuentos que pudieran escribir en su vida el conjunto completo de los escritores aficionados de los talleres literarios. Hubiera podido dedicarse a vender títulos, le salían bien.

Martín guardó los dos párrafos sobre temas femeninos en una de las carpetas. Miró el pavoroso haz de hojas sin atreverse a colocar otra en el rodillo de la máquina de escribir y abrió, con inapetencia, una agenda de cinco años atrás. Por una de sus muchas manías, Martín escribía siempre sus ideas con una pluma de tinta negra. A veces le parecía que los dedos actuaban solos y diseñaban una frase. Una gaviota aturdida, extraviado el rumbo, cruzó frente a la ventana. La mano de Martín escribió aquel verso tan dicho, solo que así, cortado, aislado de su original contexto, se llenó de significación y alegoría, *volverán las oscuras golondrinas*. Como título para su próximo manuscrito no estaba mal.

DAONTAON

Daontaon tenía el día malo. La mañana había sido bastante agitada, sin contar que ya, apenas salir de la casa, tuvo un conato de bronca con la inquilina de la última planta. Encima, Micaela no quiso abrir la puerta y brindarle café. Y eso que ella había ido expresamente a contarle aquel espléndido sueño con el *Titanic* y los millonarios peludos. Qué edificio ese, compañeros. Ella intentaba a toda costa ser fina, vivir aparte, pero, ay, la plebe del vecindario sacaba del paso a mariasantísima. Borrachos, niños piojosos, retrasados mentales, viejas locas, perros sarnosos, pervertidos sexuales, mal educados, zarrapastrosos, delincuentes, escoria, aunque ella sí que no, ella representaba a la "Cultura" y tenía que darse su lugar.

Tampoco trabajar en "Cultura" era jamón. A primera hora, sin merendar ni nada, se vio obligada a hacer como diez millones de llamadas telefónicas para organizar un servicio fúnebre. El muerto, uno de esos tipos que sobran en el mundo según la opinión especializada de Daontaon (y lampiño, por cierto), se consideraba a sí mismo "autor de décimas geriátricas", dígame usted, y había fallecido impropiamente de madrugada. Como el decimista lampiño provenía de provincia, no tenía a nadie que se ocupara de los trámites y la tiñosa le tocó a ella. Claro, quién iba a querer "cargar con el muerto" literalmente hablando, ¿sus colegas del Taller Literario? Ja. Ninguno. En caso de que hubiese alguno a esa hora que no estuviera durmiendo la mona, Daontaon dudaba mucho que quisiera ocuparse de semejante tarea. Eso sí, búscalos si había ron o aparecía alguna nueva poetisa en pañales. Ahí sí venían todos corriendo como unos locos, pero... ¿a ocuparse del muerto de provincia? Ja. Daontaon tenía todo en contra de la gente que venía "del campo" a colarse en La Habana, ella misma lo había hecho años atrás, así que sabía muy bien cómo pensaban, se iban metiendo poquito a poquito, se casaban con una berraca (o un berraco, faltaba más), y luego se quedaban ya situados en un apartamento de Alamar como el de ella. Por eso Daontaon no los podía ver ni en pintura. Ese mismo, el fallecido, empezó escribiendo libros infantiles en su territorio natal y como el terreno estaba muy copado, tuvo la *genial* idea de escribir décimas para la "Tercera Edad", ¡dígame usted! La gente se las hacía repetir en público, un montón de viejos decrépitos como él. Y hasta le habían publicado varios de esos engendros que llaman "plaquetes". Las cosas que hay que oír y ver. Pues el tipo se fue instalando, una décima por aquí, un premiecito de un pueblucho perdido de España, una intervención en un "congreso de poetas" latinoamericanos, donde aparte de los de siempre, la "Cooperativa del Aguardiente", había un turista finlandés por error y tres argentinos (estos sí inscritos con todas las de la ley), y ya, punto. El difunto tenía lo que en la jerga de "Cultura" se catalogaba como *un nombrecito*.

A Daontaon le privaba hablar con comillas, cursivas y muchos signos de puntuación.

El decimista geriátrico, no había forma de que Daontaon se acordase ahora de su nombre, se tomó tan a pecho la representación poética que murió de una cirrosis hepática. Ya salimos de él, y por suerte "no ha dejado epígonos", lo que sea que signifique esa palabra tan fea que Daontaon oyó de la boca de Martín, el tipo que se creía escritor y vivía en el edificio de al lado.

Liquidado el asunto del entierro, Daontaon tuvo que emprender mil carreras para dar por cumplido el salvataje del televisor en colores y el equipo de video de un cellista de la Orquesta Sinfónica, decomisados por la policía durante una redada en la localidad de Campo Florido, dos meses atrás. Los agentes del orden (Daontaon se vio tentada a usar unas comillas, no obstante declinó el efecto) habían irrumpido en el habitáculo del dicho cellista y cargado con el televisor y el video informando a la madre anciana, única persona ocupante del inmueble en el momento de los hechos, que los "efectos electrónicos confiscados" (ahora sí iban las comillas) constituían una *prueba*. Prueba de qué, reclamaba histérica Daontaon por teléfono, acaso, dígame usted, compañero teniente, ¿mataron a alguien con el aparato electrodoméstico? Claro que no, se respondió la propia Daontaon. Si se trata de la muerte lenta de aburrimiento por mirar la televisión, en ese caso sí, el aparato es criminal, pero... ¿qué culpa tendrían entonces el cellista y la compañera madre? Hágame usted el favor.

Nada. Daontaon no tuvo más remedio que personarse, con el calor que hacía ese mes de agosto, en la mismísima Estación de Policía, eso nadie más que ella, a la verdad, para recuperar los objetos de la discordia. "No se lo lleven", clamaban los agentes de guardia, "estamos viendo la programación de verano". ¡Le zumba el mango! Daontaon se comportó implacable en el cumplimiento del deber y devolvió esa misma tarde el video y el televisor secuestrados a la madre del cellista que sollozaba agradecida.

—Un día de estos le vengo a tumbar un café, abuela. Y quien dice un café, dice un almuerzo, ¿no? Sí.

Y ahora, para cerrar el día, este otro "casito" en que se mezclaban los tres ingredientes, muertos, policías y "cultura". ¡Apaga y vámonos!

MUJER QUE HABLA SOLA EN EL PARQUE

Una alcantarilla de la calle explotó y salió una nata negra que lo inundó todo. Y entonces hasta los edificios más altos quedaron sumergidos bajo los excrementos. Y La Habana se muere...

LOLA

A casa de Lola, Micaela iba de vez en cuando. No le decía a nadie por qué, eran asuntos de los que no se hablaba. Hace unas semanas conoció a sus pollitos recién nacidos, apenas un puñado inquieto de plumones amarillos. Lola los tenía al calor de una incubadora improvisada. ¡Allí estaban los futuros almuerzos de su precaria subsistencia!

Micaela observó a uno de ellos, el más débil, cojeaba y le costaba bastante esfuerzo alimentarse. Se lo comentó a Lola en una de aquellas fútiles conversaciones convenidas entre ambas para ahuyentar el silencio o evitar ciertos temas. Lola, cortés y distanciada, le explicó que siempre ocurría así, uno de la camada, el más indefenso, debía sucumbir.

El tono indiferente de Lola atribuló a Micaela hasta un extremo descomedido, tal vez por culpa de la impotencia. Nada podía hacer, no era su casa, no era su pollero, y, en este caso, Lola, como los antiguos señores feudales, poseía la potestad de la vida y la muerte, al menos sobre esas alucinantes criaturas amarillas, aquellos pollitos entregados al albur de la crianza familiar, subterfugio con que algún ocurrente había pretendido solucionar el problema de escasez de pienso, miles de recién salidos del huevo distribuidos por los hogares habaneros para que se convirtieran en gallos y gallinas.

Micaela pensaba, con exagerado desconsuelo, en los pollitos que habían capitulado por inapropiadas temperaturas, enfermedades, asfixiados entre las manos de los niños o en bocas de gatos tan hambrientos como sus dueños. Micaela se negó de plano a adquirir los suyos, los que "le tocaban". Los polluelos de Lola, sin embargo, no se sabe por cuáles misterios o mañas, se convirtieron en hermosas aves.

Micaela, en sus visitas, los había ido viendo crecer, cacarear, engordar, ensuciar de excrementos verdosos la hasta entonces pulcra terraza, y se fue acostumbrando a conversar entre la pestecilla que, como aura de venideros banquetes, formaba parte ya de la casa de Lola, enclavada en una zona del Vedado todavía no venida a menos.

Micaela y Lola hablaban a menudo de los pollos. ¿De qué otro tema podían hablar? Sara hacía mucho que no escribía ni llamaba. Se habían ido agotando las anécdotas inocuas del pasado cuando Sara y Micaela estudiaban en la universidad. Y ella no quería agobiar a Lola con sus propios problemas.

Lola estaba muy acabada. Caminaba con dificultad y veía mal. El televisor se había roto. Aquellos pollitos y las vueltas que le daba Micaela, cada vez más espaciadas, parecían ser su único entretenimiento.

En su última visita, Micaela se sentó en la terraza y miró con desazón hacia la jaula de las aves. Con temor, inquirió por aquel desgraciado pollito cojo cuyos hermanos de aventura acosaban sin piedad. Entre tantas tristezas y fracasos, sintió una desproporcionada alegría al saber que su pollito (¿suyo?) había sobrevivido, convertido en un pollo adulto y de tan malas costumbres como los otros, imposible de distinguir entre el manojo de plumajes descuidados, agolpados en una celda demasiado estrecha para crecer con dignidad, aunque esta fuera tan solo ovípara.

Micaela se levantó del sillón con el pretexto de ir al baño y al regreso evitó volver a sentarse en la terraza. El momento en que los polluelos dejarían de ser naturaleza viva, inocente de su destino de caldo y fricasé, se estaba acercando. No podía dejar de pensar cómo las manos de Lola que habían alimentado, calentado, quizás acariciado con algo parecido a la ternura serían las mismas que... Micaela no se atrevía ni siquiera a escenificar la imagen en su pensamiento.

Al despedirla en la puerta, Lola le preguntó, con mal disimulada angustia, cuándo iba a volver.

YUYA

Dice Yuya que ella nació en el solar conocido como Los Muertos de la calle Ánimas. Y que eso no le bastó a los santos. Su madre, Georgina, de quien heredó su nombre y la piel amulatada, murió en el parto. Su padre, José, el gallego albañil, se cayó de un andamio el día antes de su bautizo. Dice Yuya que a ella la recogió su pobre abuela y la crió, mientras pudo, lavando para la calle. A los trece años se quedó sola en el mundo. Pero dice Yuya que todo ese comienzo de su vida siempre le pareció una buena señal. ¿Qué otra cosa mala podría ya pasarle?

En el velorio de su pobre abuela, las vecinas del solar le aconsejaron a Yuya que se hiciera de una carrera. Corría el año 1960 y Yuya cuenta que no le costó mucho decidirse entre la batea de ajena ropa sucia y los libros. Así que terminó la Escuela Pública Superior y unos meses más tarde, se inscribió en las Brigadas de Alfabetización, el sueño de su pobre abuela que nunca supo leer ni escribir.

Dice Yuya que entonces la mandaron de maestra a un caserío entre Las Tunas y Holguín, en las quimbambas de Oriente, conocido como Arroyo El Muerto. En casi todos lo pueblitos de Cuba se acostumbra hablar de un jinete o de un caballo sin cabeza que sale a trotar de madrugada, aterrorizando a los lugareños. Dice Yuya que ella vio una vez, en medio del cafetal a un negro, con cuerpo de lobo, comiéndose una jutía viva y alguien le explicó que se trataba del espíritu de un haitiano que, por no morirse de hambre, se colgó de una guásima, allá por los años cuarenta, y desde ese entonces se transformaba en distintos animales, según le pareciera, ya fuese lobo, gato salvaje, cangrejo, lo que fuera.

En Arroyo El Muerto, Yuya se enamoró de un guajirito de su misma edad y salió preñada. Cuando la panza se empezó a notar, ya terminaba la campaña. Se despidió, sin perder el ánimo, de sus alumnos, regresó a su cuchitril del solar y tuvo a su hija, Eulalia. Dice Yuya que durante las primeras semanas con la niña, sola y sin un centavo, se le unió el cielo con la tierra. Gracias a su buena estrella, la vecina del cuarto de al lado, Etelvina, la ayudó como si fueran familia. Cuando estaban en los preparativos para celebrar el primer cumpleaños de Lalita, la pobre Etelvina se ahogó de asma y le dio un infarto. Dice Yuya que esa misma noche se le apareció su fantasma para nombrar a Lalita como heredera universal y le orientó a Yuya que abriera una puerta en el tabique que separaba las dos piezas, la suya y la de Etelvina.

Junto con la habitación y los muebles de la pobre Etelvina, Yuya se hizo dueña de todos sus contactos y listados para el juego de la Bolita y la Charada,[23] y del altar de San Lázaro, venerado por su vecina. También encontró, guardado en un baúl de roble, entre paquetes de naftalina, y ramitas de romero, un ajuar intacto de novia, algo amarillento.

Al día siguiente puso en funcionamiento de nuevo el banco de Bolita y Charada y aireó el ajuar de novia para el futuro de Lalita. Ah, y dice Yuya que le puso una vela y un tabaco a San Lázaro, a su padre Babalú, agradecidísima.

MARÍA ESTHER

A la primera mujer de Martín no le gustaban nada los desbordes sentimentales y con los años fue aumentando aquella tendencia a repeler lo que llamaba "salidas fuera de tono". María Esther y Martín se habían hecho novios de casualidad, por así decirlo, en el segundo curso de la carrera durante la fiesta de fin de año. En la terraza, las parejas se fueron armando según avanzaba la noche. Alrededor de las once y media, solamente ellos permanecían sin bailar, cada uno en una esquina como boxeadores mal entrenados. Alguien atenuó las luces y eso hizo posible el tránsito del *twist* y el *rock* hacia los instrumentales o los cantantes dulzones al uso de Doris Day que permitían "apretar". Desde el tocadiscos se escuchaba un rayado y ya fuera de moda *Secret love*.

Martín sacó a bailar a María Esther y a las doce de la noche,

---

[23] *La Bola (o Bolita) y Charada,* es una referencia a varios juegos y prácticas culturales que son populares a pesar de su alto nivel de complejidad. Con elementos de Bingo, Tarot y Lotería, la interpretación de sueños y augurios pronostica futuros eventos y a veces se consideran pistas para apuestas en juegos de azar.

después del beso ritual de bienvenida a aquel nuevo año de 1967, le pidió que fuera su novia y ella aceptó. Lo que quedaba de la velada lo pasaron discutiendo sobre Antonioni y Godard, sobre *El desierto rojo* y *Pierrot le Fou*, sobre los últimos estrenos de la Nueva Ola francesa en la Cinemateca. A Martín no le gustaban esas películas, en su fuero tan interno como inconfesable no las entendía, aunque formaban parte del estilo de los estudiantes de la Escuela de Letras. Había que saber y hablar de todo aquello como un código entre iniciados. Martín prefería a Hitchcock y cuando lo declaró, María Esther lo cortó tajante: "No me agradan los enigmas policiacos. El gusto por ellos da muestra de poca espiritualidad. Ante la trascendencia de la muerte, ¿qué importancia tiene preguntarse quién fue el asesino?" Martín tuvo que convenir que sí, aunque le desilusionó esa aplastante lógica, esa racionalidad en una muchacha tan joven. No lo dejó ver por temor a ser acusado de troglodita. Además, la muerte nunca le pasaba a Martín por la cabeza.

A lo largo de su vida en común, durante aquellos neuróticos y aburridos años setenta, Martín le había escuchado muchas veces contar sobre la escuela de monjas donde María Esther había estudiado la primaria. Para un oyente poco habituado, las historias podían pasar como críticas, incluso burlonas. Sin embargo, bajo su tono irónico afloraba una rancia añoranza, un beneplácito. En algunas de las severidades morales de María Esther se reproducían los prejuicios religiosos, trasladados sin pudor a las reglas de la convivencia en la facultad donde ella daba clases de Literatura General. María Esther contaba que en aquella escuela de monjas, si las niñas andaban intranquilas, conversadoras o tan solo expansivas, las maestras religiosas las sentaban en penitencia por varias horas, los brazos cruzados a la espalda y la boca sellada con los labios apretados hacia adentro. Aquello siempre le había parecido a Martín un acto horroroso y María Esther lo decía como si nada, como si le hubiese gustado verlo implantado de nuevo en la disciplina escolar.

Ya en los estertores de la relación entre ambos, María Esther replicaba con silencios y el matrimonio terminó por naufragar en aguas tranquilas. Al cabo de un tiempo, ella volvió a casarse un par de veces más, divorciado otras dos, tenía un hijo, y vivía de forma intermitente con hombres casados. A Martín también le habían llegado rumores sobre su alcoholismo, aunque no los creyó del todo, dentro de sus normas estrictas de monja de clausura a María Esther jamás le había gustado empinar el codo, por el contrario.

A pesar de que María Esther nunca se había mudado de la casa de su infancia, en el barrio de la mamá de Martín, hacía un buen número de años que no se veían y ahora ella había enfermado de gravedad.

María Esther, demacrada y desfallecida sobre la cama del hospital, no se sorprendió de la visita de Martín y le hizo una seña para que se sentara, con un rescoldo de la autoridad de antaño. Su pedantería se mantenía igual y sus primeras palabras fueron para citar a los clásicos.

—No me digas tontas mentiras, Martín, ¿cuánto tiempo me queda? Al igual que Edipo, uno no puede dejar de buscar la verdad que ha de destruirlo.

MUJER QUE HABLA SOLA EN EL PARQUE

Abrieron un túnel y despertaron a las serpientes gigantes que dormían tranquilas bajo el Vedado. Y entonces las serpientes se escaparon, abrieron la bocazas y se lo tragaron todo de un bocado. Y La Habana se muere...

WILLIE

Me dicen Willie y sobre mí pesa una condena.

—¡Abre la puerta, Micaela! ¡Ábreme te digo!

La mujer que golpeaba la puerta se llama Daontaon. Tiene fama de buscapleitos y lenguaraz. Micaela, la persona que resistía el asedio, es la única vecina del edificio con buena educación, aparte de Miguelón y de mí. Y su puerta es también la única pintada y limpia de este vecindario.

—¿Habrá alguien ahí? —Daontaon arrimó la oreja. Me gustaría saber si arrimaría con igual confianza esa oreja a su propia entrada, manchada de asquerosidades imposibles de clasificar.

—¡Hay alguien! —se contestó Daontaon. Ella pertenece a esa categoría de personas que se preguntan y se responden a sí mismas.

Daontaon forcejeó con las persianas hasta que logró abrir un resquicio y mirar adentro.

—Veo una luz encendida. Ja. Estás ahí, lo sabía. Es más, huelo café. ¡Estás colando café!

Desde adentro, silencio total.

—Está bien, *oquei*, no me abras, desde aquí te lo cuento. Tuve un sueño contigo. Viajábamos las dos en un barco, así de grande como el *Titanic* de la película. Para dónde íbamos, no sé. Me imagino que rumbo norte... ¿tú no crees? ¡A dónde se va la gente sino para ALLÁ!

El "allá" con mayúsculas retumbó en la escalera. Y hablando de escaleras... se desconoce si otras tendrán la fortuna de esta que a lo largo de su recorrido de cuatro pisos alcanza alcurnias versallescas. Durante las recepciones palaciegas en el dicho Versalles, lo sé de buena tinta, cada cual se hacía pipi donde le viniese en ganas y por las escalinatas reales descendía el ambarino néctar de príncipes y princesas. Pues aquí lo mismo. Los vecinos no pueden contener sus urgencias y proceden al acto donde les plazca. Dicho sea de paso, más democráticos que la corte francesa, unen sus emisiones a las de perros y gatos, y hasta cerdos y caprinos que suben o descienden a su antojo por la nombrada escalera. "Nunca se había visto eso en La Habana", comenta, agraviado, Miguelón.

Miguelón ya cumplió ochenta y dos años. Según cuenta, lo ha vivido todo, aunque todavía se ofusca con el ruido de animales campestres en medio de la urbe: rebuznos, relinchos, balidos, aullidos de los inmolados en el transcurso de su sacrificio por matarifes. Por si cupiera alguna duda, los carniceros suelen ser los propios vecinos, ataviados durante el día como oficinistas o maleantes del común y transmutados en verdugos en cuanto les pica la hambruna. Y, para redondear el bullicio, no podía faltar un coro de ejecutantes del corral, a cualquier hora de la madrugada, gallos despistados por las luces de los apartamentos que los avechuchos confunden con su ancestral sol de la campiña.

Miguelón tiene su propia guerra con los criadores de pollos, carneros y cerdos del edificio. Hasta ahora ha perdido todas las batallas y se tiene que resignar a inhalar el tufo a bestias bien alimentadas que proviene del patio del piso superior y a ver transitar delante de su puerta a Tilingo con su manada de chivos que lleva a pastar en el jardín frente a su balcón.

—¿Viste la película del *Titanic* el sábado? Seguro que sí —ya es sabido que Daontaon se pregunta y se contesta—. En mi sueño, el barco se parecía a uno de esos cruceros gigantes que llevan hasta piscina dentro. ¿Te imaginas? Un yate con piscina, mi amiga, y tú y yo allá arriba con un par de tipos voladísimos. Millonarios, jóvenes, carilindos, con cantidad de pelos en el pecho. ¡Ay, Virgencita! ¡Micaela! ¿Tú me estás oyendo? Sí, me estás oyendo perfectamente. Y te estás bebiendo sola el café, egoísta que eres... y yo tomándome el trabajo de venir a contarte el sueño.

Llegado este punto, Daontaon cambió el tono. Atisbó de nuevo entre las persianas y se convenció de que Micaela no iba a ceder.

—¿No me vas a brindar café? No. Chica, ojalá que después que yo desembarque sola en los *Niuyores* y tú te quedes arriba del barco, ese *Titanic* choque con un pedazo de hielo y te atragantes con el café.

MARÍA ESTHER

Un rato antes de la llegada de Martín, María Esther simulaba dormir. Los médicos acababan de terminar el cambio de guardia y no se habían coartado a la hora de interpretar sin miramientos, en voz alta, su enfermedad. Por muy pocas nociones que tuviera de tecnicismos clínicos, las odiosas palabras, inequívocas, se empotraban en el espíritu de María Esther sin dejar resquicio alguno al engaño. Le había llegado el momento de dolerse por todas las probables vidas que no eligió o no le había sido dado vivir. Como tantas cosas que no debieran dejarse para después, y se dejan... Las derrotas, las penas, los fracasos, las posposiciones, hubiesen podido parecer remontables hasta que un tonto dolor de estómago daba la alarma de lo que ya no iba a ser posible. "Todo, todo se está muriendo", se dijo María Esther con apagado dramatismo.

"Y siempre falta tiempo".

Un gesto de impaciencia le hizo girar la cabeza desde la sombra acogedora de la habitación al resplandor. Bajo los párpados todavía cerrados, los ojos se le llenaron de luciérnagas que siguieron danzando aún después de abrirlos y mirar a la claridad que entraba por la ventana. Cuando las lucecitas se apaciguaron, quedó una sola moviéndose cerca del techo blanco y María Esther descubrió que se trataba de una mosquita real.

La mosquita revoloteaba inquieta, prisionera, como si tuviera mucho apuro por terminar algo. Y de repente, sin que nada pudiera hacerlo prever, cayó fulminada sobre las losas. María Esther, ella misma, no sabía que iba a morir antes de que terminara el año, cómo iba a conocerlo con tanta exactitud, pero la pequeña muerte de la mosquita le hizo darse cuenta de que, a partir de ese instante, todo lo que le pasara se ensamblaría, de una manera u otra, con el engranaje de su propia muerte.

En ese momento entró Martín, este Martín tan fisgón como siempre. No podía soportar la idea de dejarla morir sin un reencuentro. Muy característico de él. Tampoco tomaba las desgracias en serio, tiraba a coña lo malo, todo aquello obviamente malo.

Martín le sonrió, pero seguía tieso, sin contestarle, apocado ante la enormidad de lo que veía. María Esther, de largas trenzas rubias, delgada, con un aire permanente de niña con uniforme escolar, se había transformado en aquella mujer hinchada, con unas bolsas moradas bajo los ojos, con una piel ajada y amarillenta asomando por los pliegues del pijama. Y lo más turbador, sin pelo, calva.

Adivinando sus pensamientos, María Esther cambió el tono.

—Si te dejas ver, después de tanto tiempo, ya sé que me queda poco. Quita esa cara. Todavía no me voy a morir —habló con exagerada desenvoltura, con una jovialidad que venía a ser en realidad una súplica para que Martín tomase el control de la situación. Se pasó la mano por la cabeza y rió con una sombra de su antigua risa.

—Me pescaste sin peinar… Esto es por los sueros. En todo caso, no se puede temer mayor mal. Ya me ha pasado todo lo peor que podía ocurrir. Alcánzame ese pañuelo y busca un espejo de la gaveta.

Martín sostuvo el espejo delante de su rostro y María Esther se ovilló el pañolón con un toque de coquetería, esquivando encontrar su mirada.

—¿Cómo está tu mamá? —preguntó María Esther, con tono neutro.

Martín desvió la vista hacia los ventanales de cristal. Allá, a lo lejos, bajo un sol resplandeciente y sano, se veía el Malecón, el mar, unas nubecitas lechosas.

—Bien —contestó y le pareció que había dicho "mal, se está muriendo y no lo sabe"—. Bien —repitió Martín.

YUYA

Dice Yuya que no tiene por qué quejarse de la vida. Que siempre algo la ayudó a seguir echando para adelante. De su paso por la Escuela Superior le quedó la manía de leer cuanto papel le caía en sus manos, ya fuera un libro de historia o una revista de modas. Gracias a sus múltiples lecturas pudo penetrar con conocimiento en los juegos de azar. La Bolita, aunque al poco tiempo pasó al prohibido, se seguía tirando clandestina por la lotería de Miami. Gracias al radio de onda corta de la pobre Etelvina, Yuya se mantenía al día.

En cuanto a la Charada, su abuela le había enseñado en especial los entresijos de la charada de Matanzas, provincia en donde, la pobre, recién llegada de España, había trabajado como una mula en el ingenio Santa Rita, antes de mudarse para el solar en La Habana, al llegar la época de las vacas flacas.

Por iniciativa propia y típico de su curiosidad insaciable, dice Yuya que también se aprendió los números de la charada llamada Cubana, los de la charada India, muy imaginativa, y los de la charada Americana, ni fu ni fa. Yuya dice que lo hacía para cotejar la suerte. En la charada de Matanzas, "Muerto" es el número 3, en la India lo único parecido era "Entierro" con el 9, sin embargo, en la Americana se encontraba un "Muerto Grande" con el 64 y en la Cubana no aparecía un fallecido por ninguna parte. ¡Jesús mil veces! Dice Yuya que ella, a todos los efectos, se regía por la charada China, la más popular en La Habana. Para el cubano, el número 8 es, y será siempre, un "Muerto".

En una de sus visitas ingrávidas, la pobre Etelvina le indicó la gaveta secreta con la imagen del Chinito de la Charada. Dice Yuya que se veía que Etelvina lo tenía en alta estima porque el papel con el dibujo se notaba muy carcomido y Etelvina lo había pegado con esmero a un cartón que se cubría con otro, cosido con hilo negro en los bordes izquierdos, y que hacía las veces de una carpeta. En el cajón oculto, Yuya también se encontró con un fajo de billetes que dice que le vinieron muy bien.

El Chinito de la Charada impresionó mucho a Yuya. Lo colocó, con permiso del santo, en el altar de San Lázaro, una repisa por debajo, claro. Como no sabía qué debía ofrendarle, cuál alimento podía gustarle al Chinito, le ponía frituras de calabaza, mientras estuvieron a su alcance.

Para entender mejor su nueva profesión, Yuya se sentó noches enteras a analizar el dibujo: se trataba de un chino calvo y de largos bigotes caídos por las comisuras de la boca. Vestía un kimono y unas pantuflas ornamentados con los símbolos de la charada. De la mano derecha le colgaba un pez, el 10, "Pescado grande" y entre los dedos de la izquierda sostenía una pipa humeante, el 36, "Cachimba"; la pantorrilla derecha se ilustraba con la "Anguila" y la izquierda con el "Ratón"; en la oreja derecha, se reconocía la "Mariposa" y en la izquierda el "Marinero"; sobre el hombro derecho se apreciaba la "Monja" con sus manos cruzadas y en el izquierdo el "Venado", en espera de salir huyendo. Encima de la calva, punteando la cabeza, el "Caballo" en movimiento, el Uno, como debe ser.

El kimono del Chinito estaba repleto de estas figuras. Dice Yuya que la manga izquierda con la "Araña" le daba miedo, aprensión, mala espina. Yuya se quedaba con el brazo derecho: "Jicotea", "Caracol", "Elefante" y "Muerto", ese número 8 que, según Yuya, siempre le traía buena suerte.

GERTRUDIS

Llámenme Gertrudis. Aunque tampoco mi nombre es Gertrudis.

Hay varias *Gertrudis* famosas. La nuestra es la Gómez de Avellaneda, la grandísima, la que puso de cabeza a todos los poetuchos de su época, hizo con su vida lo que le dio la gana y se dejó llevar donde *el hado en su furor la* arrastrase. Es verdad, tuvo que pagar su precio. Fue calumniada, despreciada por sus amantes, nadie asistió a su entierro y una sarta de envidiosos le impidió entrar en la *Academia*. Por lo demás, ya dejó de importar todo eso. Ella, la grandísima, está allá arriba en el panteón de los dioses, de tú a tú.

La otra "Gertrudis", la Stein, fue aquella a quien el ingrato de Hemingway intentó sonsacarle todo cuanto pudo en París y luego se hizo el gracioso contando chismes malévolos en una novela. De que los hay, los hay.

A lo que vamos. Ahora la han cogido con eso de "¡qué lindos fueron los años sesenta!". Díganmelo a mí. Como si todo aquel tiempo hubiera sido pura diversión, la gente se pone a cantar *Imagine* y aquí no ha pasado nada. Se están haciendo los bobos, los chivos locos, los suecos, ¿o qué?

Óiganme, ¿nadie se acuerda o *no se quieren acordar?*

¿Resentimientos? Cómo no. Los muertos son los únicos que no pueden tenerlos. Y cada cual va a contar su historia según la quiera ver, igual que en *Rashomon*, o mejor decir, *Rashomona*.

Yo recuerdo muy bien cómo era la Escuela de Letras, cómo era la Colina, cómo era la "Beca de F y Tercera", cómo era la Universidad de los susodichos "años sesenta", lo malo y lo bueno. ¡Y cómo era La Habana entonces, caballeros! Un hervidero, un remolino, un barullo a toda hora. Lo mismo se estaba en una trinchera esperando que nos cayera un misil nuclear en la cabeza que en una banqueta del bar del hotel Flamingo oyendo tocar el piano a Meme Solís. Se empataba el día con la noche: las clases, el helado en Coppelia, la Cinemateca, el club Coctel, estudiar hasta el amanecer, exámenes, círculos políticos, conciertos, Chez Bola, el Cine Club Varona, bailes, la biblioteca, almorzar chícharos en el Comedor Universitario o una pizza en Vita Nuova, la playa Santa María del Mar, reuniones de la FEU, la piscina del hotel Riviera, lecturas de poesía en el "Parque de los Cabezones", trabajos voluntarios, el bar de La Torre, concentraciones en la Plaza, educación física, teatro en la salita Tespis, recital en la Talía, fiestas de sábado por la noche, la guardia, trabajo con el equipo de estudio, exposición en el Museo de Bellas Artes, prácticas de tiro, asambleas de la Escuela, conferencias, peñas, tertulias, cháchuras, Rampa arriba y Rampa abajo, lo de nunca acabar, ¿se acuerdan?

De noche, sobre todo, no pasaba el tiempo. Como si no se nos fuera a acabar nunca el tiempo.

MUJER QUE HABLA SOLA EN EL PARQUE

El puente se cayó y no se volvió a levantar, se derrumbó la esquina del torreón y así quedó. Y entonces tanto se lastimó el mar con los escombros que vino una ola grandísima, entró por Cojímar y tapó toda la ciudad. Y La Habana se muere...

MARTÍN

Por muchas veces, durante las últimas semanas, Martín soñó con la novela que nunca había podido escribir. En las primeras ocasiones, se despertó con una desazón que interpretó como la secuela de su rutinario estado de frustración. Llevaba más de diez años sin publicar algo que valiese la pena.

En sus sueños, Martín se encontraba en un recinto kafkiano, rodeado de anaqueles llenos de libros y más libros, todos idénticos. Hasta ahí nada original, aburrido, la estúpida pesadilla en blanco y negro que pudiera divagar en la duermevela de cualquier escritor neurótico, incluso de aquellos principiantes. Después el subconsciente afinaba la puntería y Martín veía *su novela:* en el centro de uno de aquellos estantes iguales, repetitivos en sucesivas hileras espejeantes, se destacaba la presencia de un volumen, un tomo grueso de portada roja y caracteres negros. No había necesidad de haber leído a Freud para adivinar, cualquier tonto podía haberlo hecho, que su propio nombre, el de Martín, ocupaba la portada.

Al principio, Martín quiso convencerse de que aquellos delirios nocturnos solo serían pasajeros. Con la insistencia de las apariciones, terminó por aceptar su procedencia del fondo de aquel maligno pozo de culpas que lo agobiaban por sus horas extraviadas de crapuloso tarambana, detrás del ron y de ejemplares como la tal Daontaon que pululaban en el ámbito farandulesco de la literatura, por sus períodos de pereza, por su remolonería, por su renuencia a admitir que hacía bastantes años que había dejado de ser una promesa. Carajo, nada más le faltaba orinarse en la cama.

—¿Qué te tiene tan preocupado? —la mamá de Martín lo observaba con suspicacia. La espera en la antesala del doctor se dilataba y ambos habían agotado los temas de conversación habituales.

—Nada —Martín pensó, sin embargo, en los desfavorables resultados de los análisis de su mamá, camuflajeados debajo de la solapa de un libro y cuyas cifras debería disimular ante ella a toda costa, mantener bajo secreto, incluso adulterar, si llegara el caso; en la expresión amañadamente jovial del rostro moribundo de María Esther; en los alarmantes rumores que circulaban por su vecindario sobre un asesino descuartizador. Ni se acordaba en ese momento preciso de la puñetera pesadilla sobre *su novela*.

—Una pesadilla que estoy teniendo —dijo Martín por salir del engorro.

—Cuéntamela, mi hijito —pidió la mamá de Martín y se acomodó en la silla. Martín la miró. Quizás todas las madres fueran así. Martín no conocía a nadie, aparte de los psiquiatras y su propia madre, que se interesara por enterarse de los sueños o las pesadillas de otros.

Después de escuchar, la mamá de Martín lo observó con aquella expresión suya que mostraba su sorpresa ante la sencillez del problema que atormentaba al hijo. Su razonamiento tan simple y natural lo dejó mudo.

—¿Y de qué trata tu novela?

Martín cayó en cuenta de que durante aquellas pesadillas no se había atrevido a hojear la dichosa novela.

La noche siguiente, Martín volvió a soñar que entraba al recinto. Esta vez se llenó de valor, alargó una mano que avanzaba, por supuesto, en cámara lenta, y sacó del anaquel el grueso volumen de portada roja y caracteres negros con su nombre. Lo abrió y alcanzó a leer una primera línea enigmática, "oro parece, plata no es", la vieja adivinanza del tío Félix.

MICAELA

Micaela esperó un rato sin moverse hasta que Daontaon se alejara. No andaba de humor para hablar de sueños con millonarios pilosos. De todas maneras, se quedó pensando en barcos hundidos y catástrofes. Mientras fregaba los enseres del desayuno, se le había caído al piso la última taza sobreviviente de la vajilla de porcelana china de su tía Candita.

La ley de las cosas, los objetos terminaban por envejecer de golpe, las sábanas se rompían todas a la vez, una mañana el gato dejaba de comer, los cristales se quebraban sin causa aparente, las begonias de la maceta se secaban a pesar del riego, las toallas lucían colores ajados, tan ajados como su propio rostro ante el espejo. ¿Cómo resistirse a la decadencia?

Hasta esa mañana, Micaela soportaba el ostracismo, la vulgaridad, los trajines inútiles. Pero, mientras recogía los añicos de loza, descubrió que el recuerdo de su tía se conservaba más joven que ella misma, y algo se descompuso en el mecanismo. Había llegado el momento. La evidencia de tal revelación le hizo tomar la decisión de deshacerse de las fruslerías coleccionadas a lo largo de los años. No tenía a quién dejarle sus recuerdos y la parte que le tocaba del pasado moriría con ella. ¿Qué duda cabía? Debía prescindir ya de los amuletos que había arrastrado durante la vida.

Micaela se vio muerta e imaginó a Daontaon tumbando abajo la puerta, registrando en sus gavetas, curioseándolo todo. Los intrusos, los desconocidos invadiendo el refugio de su habitación, el baño donde preservaba como tesoros astillitas de jabón para asearse como fuera, la cocina con su orden maniático en medio de tanta escasez. Y quién sabe qué. Se aterró de solo pensar que alguien descubriera el sobre amarillento con las cartas de Pavel y las colillas a medio fumar que tanto significaron una vez, y ahora ni siquiera lamentaba separarse de ellas. Pese a ello, no pudo evitar un temblor de la mano cuando lo vació en el cesto de la basura junto con los mil trocitos de pliegos rotos, los caracoles recogidos en una luminosa tarde de Guanabo, el reloj oxidado de su padre, la taza de porcelana cascada en mil pedazos, y tantas minucias que solo alcanzaban valor en el reino solitario de su memoria. Cualquier persona que no fuese ella misma los calificaría de desechos. Por eso, de nada valía seguir guardándolos. Ella, Micaela, no iba en el *Titanic,* así que nadie se iba a interesar por sus ridículas propiedades.

Candita, su tía, cuando algo no marchaba bien, se consolaba con aquello de "mañana será otro día". Micaela no estaba ya tan segura de eso.

ESTELA

Como de costumbre, Estela fue a pie hasta la oficina y llegó primero que los demás. La muchacha que limpiaba los pisos, una inmigrante de Jamaica, le abrió la puerta con una sonrisa de oreja a oreja, siempre se mostraba radiante, aunque Estela no se imaginaba ni remotamente cuáles razones podría tener, la infeliz. Por el camino, Estela compró un dulce en la pastelería francesa, un *chou chantilly,* su favorito, desbordante de crema. Se podía dar el gusto, a pesar de sus años se mantenía en la línea, igual que Oscar. Con un pañuelo de papel se limpió con cuidado los bordes de la boca y las puntas de los dedos, y se dispuso a leer los mensajes del fax, nada de interés. Uno, muy breve, de Oscar, anunciando la posposición de su regreso. Algunas voces altas y un portazo le indicaron que ya había hecho su entrada la secretaria. Olguita llevaba más de un año en Londres y seguía llegando tarde. Argumentaba que se perdía en los culebreos del metro, pero Estela no le creía ni una palabra. Al principio trataba de encontrarle una lógica a las tardanzas, alguna negligencia intencional, algún secreto recorrido o mañaneros percances imposibles de confiar a terceros, mas con los meses se resignó a interpretarlo como pura incapacidad. En esta ocasión, Estela ni siquiera levantó la vista de los papeles mientras le escuchaba decir que las escaleras eléctricas del metro estaban tan atestadas que había tenido que subir corriendo por la otra, la "escalera que no se movía", como le decía Olguita, "ughhh", suspiraba, todavía ahogada por el esfuerzo de subir "una pila de escalones". Olguita tiró su abrigo de plástico, imitación de piel de tigre, y se sacudió la melena teñida de rojo como si estuviera en plena jungla. De uno de sus muchos bolsos sacó un termo con café y le brindó a Estela. Lo hacía cada mañana sin darse por aludida del rechazo, tan campante iba por la vida, desbordada de aquella energía ramplona. Un rato más tarde, Olguita comenzó a tararear una canción en español mientras se cepillaba la cabeza, sin mostrar ningún apuro por emprender las tareas del día. Estela la miró de reojo y pensó que Olguita se comportaba como si siguiera estando en La Habana. Pronunciaba la palabra "metro" igual que hubiera dicho "guagua", se limaba las uñas mientras atendía a uno de los clientes o chachareaba durante horas y horas en el teléfono, Estela no podía dilucidar con quién. La oficina había pasado ya por varias secretarias. La anterior a Olguita no aguantó y quiso regresar a Cuba a los pocos meses. Decía que extrañaba el sol. Le dio por hablar del sol desde que llegó, el sol cubano para allá y el sol cubano para acá, y el sol londinense veraniego le había parecido un asco, así mismo dijo. En invierno le entró esa rara melancolía parlanchina y los incautos ingleses que se pusieran a su alcance se quedaban pasmados ante aquella demente que les revelaba todas las variantes del sol cubano. Finalmente empaquetó sus maletas y dejó plantado a su marido, un anciano, curador del British Museum. Estela no dejó de saborear el palmo de narices, bien merecido se lo tenía el vejete, una momia como las que él mismo cuidaba, por andar tonteando detrás de un trasero tropical, guantanamero por más señas. Una de las tantas secretarias que tuvo la oficina no sabía hablar inglés y todo lo resolvía citando fragmentos de las canciones de los Beatles. A los clientes, los despedía con un absurdo *Let it be*. Santo cielo. Y aquella otra que se las pasaba almacenando bolígrafos, sobres, carpetas, goma de pegar, hasta presillas, para mandarlos a Cuba. Sin duda alguna, por la oficina de Estela, la agencia de viajes a la Isla y al Caribe, desfilaba de todo y cuanto hay.

MARÍA ESTHER

Martín se sentó y echó una ojeada a su alrededor. No estaba mal, sobre todo si se comparaba con la dantesca sala de aquel hospital donde su padre había padecido los últimos días de su vida, sin agua en el baño, las persianas clausuradas, enfermeras gritonas y una comida repulsiva. Sin embargo, la habitación de María Esther, habilitada para dos pacientes, disfrutaba de sillones cómodos, teléfono, unas mesas auxiliares limpias, olía bien, la luz entraba por los anchos ventanales desde donde se veía el Malecón.

—¿Estás pasando inspección?

—Sí, claro —repuso Martín y María Esther notó que se sentía aliviado ante el giro que tomaba la conversación—. Al menos estás mejor que en la beca.

—La beca de F y Tercera. Mira de lo que te vienes a acordar. ¡Cuánto tiempo ha pasado! —sus respuestas se obligaban a ser sobreactuadas.

—El problema con el tiempo es la manera en que se va. Teníamos veinte años y de repente ya pasamos los cincuenta. Tuve una pesadilla anoche... —María Esther permaneció en silencio—. En el sueño yo estaba mirando la televisión —continuó Martín— y aparecía en pantalla mi propia cara con una máscara mortuoria.

Martín titubeó por su poco tacto. María Esther lo animó a seguir con un gesto de la mano.

—Tú no ves televisión nunca, ya sé. Te cuento entonces: se conmemoraba mi centenario y daban la pista "famoso escritor cubano..." y ahí seguía yo, con una orla negra alrededor —María Esther sonrió y Martín prosiguió—. Un panel de tres académicos debía adivinar de quién se trataba y los puñeteros no se acordaron de mi nombre. ¿Te imaginas?

María Esther dejó escapar una risita seca y después tosió. Se dobló con una mueca de dolor y se deslizó hacia atrás en la cama.

Martín siguió hablando, pretendiendo simular no percatarse de lo que ocurría. Por parlotear de cualquier cosa, le mintió que había comenzado por fin a escribir un manuscrito y en su próxima visita le iba a leer algunos capítulos. María Esther asintió con la mirada, en tanto se esforzaba para recuperarse. Luego se hizo un silencio y Martín sintió que no tenían más nada que decirse. No quería rebajarse, ni someterla a ella, con banales comentarios sobre la familia o la situación del país.

María Esther le agradeció que no le preguntara por la familia. ¿Cómo contarle que su único hijo, el médico, renegó de su juramento y solo pensaba en abrir un hospital privado en Buenos Aires para sacarle dinero a la gente y vivir bien? ¿Cómo hablar de tantas derrotas, una detrás de otra, difíciles de soportar?

—*De veras quisiera estar muerta.*

—¿Cómo?

—No te asustes, Martín, estoy citando a Safo. ¿No era ese el verso que repetíamos en las clases de Latín cuando nos moríamos de aburrimiento?

Qué caprichosa la memoria. Se le deja abierta una espita y saca a flote lo menos pensado. Después que Martín se fue, María Esther soñó con las bandejas abolladas y grasientas donde servían la comida en el comedor de la beca, precariamente avituualladas de un manojo de berro mal lavado y un caldo amarillo donde flotaban varios chícharos duros. Al despertar para el almuerzo del hospital, un mejunje sin sal ni consistencia, María Esther se sonrió ante el recuerdo, diciéndose a sí misma que podría haber sobrevenido a consecuencia de su tediosa alimentación de enferma. Después le vino a la mente otro detalle de su sueño: detrás de esa imagen de la bandeja, como en la cámara lenta de un documental, avanzaban en su pesadilla las manos, el cuerpo, el rostro convulso de La Difunta, la última vez que la vio.

LOLA

Con el televisor roto se moría, sencilla y llanamente no podía vivir.

Lola decidió entregar una vieja pulsera de platino, recuerdo de su madre, y los tres mejores pollos del gallinero a cambio del arreglo del televisor.

Micaela no había vuelto a aparecer. Tampoco llegaban cartas de Sara. Ni siquiera alguien, cualquiera, llamaba por teléfono. Día por día, Lola se afanaba en las tareas de la casa y dejaba avanzar la jornada bajo un aura de desazón y tedio. Al comienzo de la programación de la televisión, encendía el equipo y lo dejaba en cualquier canal, daba igual, como un ronroneo que llenaba la casa vacía. Después rendía la mente ante la pantalla iluminada para no tener que pensar. Le llegaba por fin el sueño, se quedaba dormida y ni se enteraba de cómo acababan las películas.

Un apagón inesperado sustrajo a Lola de una película de asesinatos y policías corruptos. Otra contrariedad de la vida. De la vidita, más bien.

Encendió una vela y abrió las ventanas para que la brisa apaciguara la piel de los calores y los mosquitos. Lola se quedó mirando por un rato la oscilación de la candelilla en el pabilo, mientras trataba de hacer oídos sordos a las obscenidades que llegaban desde el parquecito frente a su casa. Al cabo de una hora, la luz sucumbió y Lola se quedó a oscuras, con la temida avalancha de recuerdos, todos malos.

De manera burda, como suele ocurrir en las pésimas telenovelas, Lola se enteró de que su marido la engañaba. Eso había sucedido hacía muchos años y, sin poder evitarlo, los malos recuerdos se ordenaban encabezados por la traición de Evaristo. Evaristo ya llevaba muerto y enterrado más de veinte años, y su rostro seguía prisionero de aquella expresión cobarde, de carnero degollado, la vez que Lola lo había enfrentado a su sospecha.

Aunque las tristezas no se reparten por igual o de modo justo, Lola pensó, las gordas, las principales, suelen sobrevenirles a la casi totalidad de los seres humanos: muerte, enfermedad, vejez, pérdida. Hay otras que tocan a unos y a otros no. El hambre, por ejemplo. O la locura, la traición, el desengaño, el fracaso, el abandono. O la soledad. Al principio de su vida adulta no le temía a nada. Loca no era. La vejez y la muerte quedaban lejos. Le gustaba su trabajo y tenía además una salud de hierro. No había sentido ni siquiera el mal de ausencia, aquella penita que veía en los ojos de su padre si se hablaba de Asturias.

Entre las desgracias, primero le llegó la traición de Evaristo.

Después el abandono. Cuando Sara se quedó, en uno de los viajes a España, Lola se dijo que había separaciones equivalentes a la muerte. Ese segundo recuerdo se le imponía a pesar suyo: la cara de Sara detrás del vidrio del automóvil que la llevaba al aeropuerto, dejando revelar sus secretos planes en una mirada cargada de intenciones y dirigida únicamente a los ojos de su madre. El auto arrancó y Lola supo que se estaba despidiendo de Sara, quizás para siempre.

Por suerte, mientras transitaba hacia el tercer mal recuerdo, llegó la luz, comenzó otra de las tantas películas iguales, estúpidas, intrascendentes, y Lola se quedó dormida frente al televisor.

MUJER QUE HABLA SOLA EN EL PARQUE

Los gallos del campo avanzaron hacia la ciudad. Por la autopista, por la carretera central y desde todos lados. Y entonces vinieron las gallinas, pusieron huevos, los pollitos crecieron y, a picotazos, lo fueron destruyendo todo. Y La Habana se muere...

YUYA

Dice Yuya que su don natural para manejarse bien con los aparecidos también le favoreció el adelanto en la vida. Cuando iba al cementerio a ponerle flores a su pobre abuela, le pedía algún consejo que seguía a pie juntillas. Su abuela siempre tuvo a bien no hacerse presente en el solar, como manteniendo una distancia respetuosa con el territorio de Etelvina. Según Yuya, Etelvina no venía a menudo, solo en trances de emergencia.

Dice Yuya que, desde entonces, la carpeta con la imagen del

Chinito de la Charada no la ha abandonado nunca. Siempre le siguió intrigando por qué aparecían las figuras de unos números y de otros no. ¿Cómo desentrañar el código para determinar su posición en el cuerpo del Chinito? Algunas colocaciones de los símbolos resultaban claras de interpretar, como aquel "Caballo" primando los pensamientos o la "Mujer Santa", el 12, encima del corazón. Aunque otras, como la "Paloma" sobre la rodilla derecha y el "Sapo" sobre la izquierda, seguían desconcertando a Yuya.

Y así, gracias a sus rogaciones y las indulgencias del Chinito de la Charada, Yuya conoció a un hijo del celeste imperio que vivía en la calle Rayo. Cerró sus dos cuartos del solar hasta más ver y se mudó con Lalita, el altar de San Lázaro y el arcón con el ajuar de novia para la cuartería donde vivían hacinados los paisanos de Shu Shuang.

Shu, más avispado que los demás, se había apropiado de la azotea donde levantó varios cuartuchos con cocina y aposento de aseo para su exclusivo uso. Respirar el libre aire de la noche y poseer su propia tina para bañarse, con taza privada, fue para Yuya más de lo que esperaba de su buenaventura.

Dice Yuya que al principio trató de que Shu le explicara los significados de las posiciones de las figuras en la indumentaria del Chinito de la Charada, pero no le logró arrancar ni una palabra al respecto. Shu trabajaba como linotipista en caracteres chinos de uno de aquellos periódicos en lengua oriental que se vendían entre la congregación. Como casi todos los chinos auténticos que ella conocía, Shu era delicado, taciturno y desconfiado. Tenía sus propias creencias, ya algo adulteradas con la influencia de sus años por este lado del planeta. Junto a los impenetrables tributos a Sanfancón, los palitos de incienso, unos elefantes de jade verde veteado, un pote de madera labrada con un polvito gris en su interior, Yuya colocó respetuosamente la carpeta con el Chinito ilustrado de la Charada y el altar de San Lázaro, de su padre Babalú, protector de tullidos, perros sin dueño y desgraciados.

El mutismo de Shu desesperaba a Yuya. No obstante, dice Yuya, en el barrio chino se sintió como en su casa.

Eso sí, la cercanía le impidió probar de por vida la comida china. Dice Yuya que, desde su azotea, ella veía a los dueños de la fonda de la esquina poner a salar los pescados y a secar los vegetales, al descubierto sobre el terrado. Allí se quedaban las futuras pitanzas del menú con entero abandono en la madrugada y más de una vez Yuya vio el tránsito de gatos y ratones por encima del condumio.

Otra consecuencia de su traslado a la calle de relámpagos y truenos, fue evitar las maldiciones, siempre que fuera posible, y jamás invocar la fulminación de "Mal rayo te parta". ¡Jesús mil veces!

WILLIE

¡Mátalo! ¡Mátalo! ¡Mátalo!

Al compás de esa frase con un solo verbo conjugado como imperativo, me acabo de despertar. ¿A quién o a qué se proponen "matar"? Ni me levanto a averiguar. Puede tratarse de un pollo, un ciudadano o una jugada del dominó. Da igual.

Aunque quisiera no puedo cerrar las orejas o las narices con unos párpados que impidan la entrada de los ruidos y los hedores que los pobladores de este edificio generan durante las veinticuatro horas, sin ningún esfuerzo en particular.

Pero si lograse perder el olfato o adquirir sordera por un rato, y me pusiera a mirar el mar, el mar habanero, distinto y diferente a cualquier otro, valdría la pena vivir en este vecindario. ¿Ya había mencionado su nombre? *"Alamar"*, con comillas y cursivas, como diría Daontaon. Y sus habitantes… ¿alamarenses?, ¿alamareños?, ¿alamaruchos?, ¿alamarejos?

Alamar se caracteriza fundamentalmente por su ambiente sonoro: en cualquier momento del día o la noche, el sonido más persistente es el aullido de las madamas clamando por sus retoños. No se trata de tiernos clamores, no, al lado de estas madres se quedarían chiquiticas las gorilas de la jungla. Las criaturas, por su parte, cuando juegan frente al edificio, pierden buena parte de las características humanas. Aunque *jugar* no sería el término apropiado…

Otro componente acústico consiste en una barahúnda reconocida entre los miembros de la horda como "música" y que puede ser percibida hasta diez kilómetros a la redonda. Los aborígenes del edificio gozan con el hábito de intensificar al tope el audio de sus equipos estereofónicos para compartirlo con todos los moradores. En la mayoría de los casos, como mi vecina Daontaon, este estrépito se compone de la repetición de los mismos repiques, tamtanes y rugidos durante un período indeterminado que puede variar entre una semana y dos meses, hasta pasar a otros de parecida naturaleza.

Junto a los fragores propios de las bestezuelas que conviven con los vecinos —a quienes, sin temor a ofensa, puede catalogárseles también como selváticos—, otros bullicios habituales son los golpetazos propios de derribo y destrozo; la jerga de los muchachones, los "aseres", que emplean con preferencia las horas nocturnas para intercambiar alaridos; las riñas matrimoniales con acompañamiento de vidrios rotos; el feroz entrechocado de las fichas de dominó; las vociferaciones que acompañan las borracheras, el "bisneo" y las vendutas; el parloteo de la chismografía urbana y local; los golpes del bate con la pelota o de la pelota contra los cristales y las paredes del edificio, sumados a las expresiones típicas de las emociones de un juego de béisbol, casi siempre resumidas en dos vocablos del habla popular, o dígase mejor, carcelaria, que no pienso repetir.

El tema de los olores sería, así mismo, motivo de más disquisiciones. De todas formas, no lo pudiera desarrollar en este instante, porque veo abalanzarse hacia mi puerta a Daontaon con una cara lo bastante rara como para que me decida a dejarla entrar y brindarle café.

—Oye, niño, ¿me vas a abrir? Seguro que sí. Mira que lo que te voy a contar es mucho.

En realidad, no dio tiempo a operar el cerrojo y desde el pasillo ya me estaba informando de la aparición de un "torso" en el latón de basura de la Casa de Cultura, así lo describía ella, un "torso", sin piernas, ni brazos, ni cabeza, un "torso femenino", por más señas.

HERMI

Herminia y Tristán, vecinos desde niños, se parecían como dos gotas de agua, homónimos, ibeyis. Compartían detalles idénticos y otros, tenues, evanescentes, que los desigualaban. Desde la infancia, sin saber que repetían el juego de los mellizos de confundir identidades, se hacían pasar el uno por el otro para repetir golosinas, burlar tareas escolares e intercambiar novios y novias.

Sus semejanzas en el aspecto físico les propiciaba, ya de adolescentes, seguir trasmudando papeles. Una enamorada de Tristán fue novia, sin saberlo y en simultánea, de Herminia, Hermi. Y un dirigente de los *Jóvenes Comunistas,* muy de pelo en pecho y perseguidor de mariquitas, se besuqueó con Tristán en las butacas del cine Payret, sin sospechar que exultaban bajo los ropajes femeninos atributos tan contundentes como los suyos.

Poseían iguales gestos, sentido del humor y una secreta comunicación, sin palabras. Algo parecido al enamoramiento, si no hubiesen rechazado la idea por cursi.

Congeniaban también en ideas esenciales. "Detesto las ambigüedades, adoro las ambivalencias", afirmaba Hermi (¿o sería Tristán?) en aquel estilo de frases lapidarias, ampulosas, crípticas, sobre todo para la mayor parte de los interlocutores que se quedaban sumergidos en un limbo por buen rato.

En relación con lo demás, fueron cumpliendo diferencias y hasta se oponían. Por ejemplo, Tristán se inclinaba por lo antiguo, Hermi por lo nuevo.

Uno de los primeros televisores Philco que llegó a La Habana lo compró el padre de Hermi. Desde el instante en que la caja negra se iluminó en la sala, Hermi se inició en la fascinación por la imagen, a lo único que valdría entregarse, apenas con interrupciones para otros menesteres o percances de la historia. Al crecer, se apasionó por las noticias de cualquier sitio del universo y por la realidad concreta de la vida común como un gacetillero, por los anuncios comerciales, por las películas, por las telenovelas, por los programas de cocina o amanuenses del hogar, por los debates sociales, y hasta por los muñequitos.

Tristán, sin embargo, se sentía atraído por la magia negra, el esoterismo y las adivinanzas. Consideraba plebeya la televisión y prefería enfrascarse en la lectura de ciencias ocultas y en estudios sobre el más allá.

A mediados de los sesenta comenzaron a estudiar carreras distintas. Tristán matriculó Letras de donde fue expulsado a finales del tercer año. Hermi escogió Arquitectura y allí hubieran deseado contratarla como profesora, sin embargo, decidió abandonar la universidad por sus propios pies. No quería renegar de un concepto suyo, muy afianzado, de la estética y rendirle pleitesía a componedores de batea, pegadores de ladrillos, costureritos del cemento que se hacían pasar por arquitectos. Tampoco estaba dispuesta a dedicarse a encajar prefabricados, vigilar a pie de obra la construcción de edificios todos iguales y chapuceros, ni chocar con lo que Tristán llamaba, sin paliativos, estupidez y mediocridad.

Gracias a las relaciones de su padre con un antiguo productor de la CMQ, el canal de emisión televisiva con más *rating* en los cincuenta, Hermi pasó unos cursos sobre comunicación y publicidad, y entró a trabajar jovencita en los predios de Radiocentro, con ilusión de hacer algo nuevo, *cambiar la vida,* como pedía Rimbaud.

Tristán empezó la universidad decidido a chocar. Cuando un condiscípulo le pidió su ayuda en la confección de un "arbolito de Navidad" que resultara espectacular, Tristán se acordó de aquel reportaje de la crónica roja sobre una mujer descuartizada durante los años treinta, publicado en una vieja revista *Bohemia* que su madre conservaba.

El arbolito de Navidad se armó en el vestíbulo de la Escuela de Letras. De sus ramas, además de un preservativo, un condón inocente y limpio, colgaba una muñeca desnuda, cortada en pedazos. El escándalo fue mayúsculo.

LA INDIA

Se llamaba María Antonieta y, después de los acontecimientos, muchos pensaron que resultaría difícil encontrar nombre mejor puesto. A la hora del bautizo, ante la piel aindiada, los ojos rasgados, el pelo encrespado y rojizo, la parentela criticó a la madre por escoger apelativo tan afectado para la niña. Sea como sea, en el barrio de San Leopoldo, donde pasara la infancia y los años de adolescencia, nunca llegaron a usar el nombre completo. Quizás porque este les parecía muy aparatoso, por sus rasgos o por la arraigada tradición vernácula de identificarse con epítetos, alias, sobrenombres, apodos, motes, nombretes y seudónimos, los vecinos dieron en adjudicarle remoquetes. La niña respondía a ellos con más presteza que a su nombre de pila, aquel que su madre todavía insistía en utilizar.

La madre, Clara Luz, de apelativo La Catedrática (usado a sus espaldas), tenía sus ínfulas y no se codeaba con cualquiera, excepto para ejercer la profesión emergente de revendedora de productos transportados con alevosía desde Caimito. La sacrificada Clara Luz, cuánto había luchado para sacar a la hija adelante, por mucho que estudiase idiomas y técnico medio en artes gráficas en su ya lejana juventud, cuando el zapato (metafórico) empezó a apretar, lo dejó todo para tocar de puerta en puerta con fracciones de queso blanco, barras de dulce de guayaba y bolsitas de café mezclado con chícharos (y otros granos disponibles, la verdad sea dicha) para darle una vida ventajosa a la hija. María Antonieta, por su parte, de padre desconocido u olvidado a intención, se hizo notar desde chiquita, sonando duro las chancletas de palo por el patio del solar.

Cuando el "extranjero" (como suelen ser identificados) se tropezó con ella en el *lobby* del hotel Presidente, a María Antonieta se le conocía como La India. Patrick Rivière fue la segunda persona que la llamó "María Antonieta". Mal pronunciado, con una *erre* que se arrastraba a modo de ronroneo y con la última "a" que se perdía en un murmullo ahogado, podía ser tomado, sin embargo, como el cántico de los arcángeles.

Hombrecillo carniseco y desmañado, de rostro torvo y ademanes untuosos, "El Francés" (reconocido prontamente bajo ese epíteto por los vecinos de Clara Luz), amarraba su cabellera grasienta en una rala colita de caballo, compensando con su largura la calvicie. Un tipo anodino (la verdad sea dicha) e ignorante de reglas de higiene. Mas, ¡ojo!, francés, llegado de la vieja Europa.

El día que María Antonieta exhibió su trofeo en el solar, los vecinos lo recibieron con efusiones no exentas de curiosidad. De hecho, Patrick se convertía en el primer extranjero real, de carne y hueso, que les había tocado. A los pocos días, El Francés se había instalado en el cuarto junto con María Antonieta y su madre. Durante las semanas siguientes, a La India se le vio prosperar sin opulencias.

Pero... ¿qué hacía ese en Cuba? ¿A dónde iba cada mañana con aquel maletincito negro? ¿A qué se debía que se mostrara tan reservado? ¿Coleccionista de armas antiguas? ¿Por qué demonios cocinaba los espaguetis con albahaca? ¿No le gustaba la música alta? ¿Le molestaba la mesa de dominó en el pasillo? Un tipo extraño, muy fuera de lugar, según el modo de ver de los vecinos. Y por si fuera poco, en el solar no se conocían a ciencia cierta las razones que lo habían traído desde tan lejos.

En consecuencia, dieron en circular algunas fábulas acerca de duelos y muertes misteriosas que habrían provocado la escapada de su país. ¡Ah, esa Francia de mosqueteros y criminales como aquel Alain Delon de *A pleno sol,* usando mocasines blancos sin medias! De esos no se podía esperar nada bueno. Mas el aspecto pacífico del extranjero, y sus ocasionales (aunque discretas en gastos, la verdad sea dicha) atenciones con los vecinos, hicieron olvidar, por el momento, los comentarios fantasiosos. Los vecinos de María Antonieta se empezaron a mostrar, incluso, obsequiosos con Clara Luz.

LOLA

Desde la terraza de Lola se alcanzaba a mirar el sol hundiéndose en el poniente como una bola de fuego. La superficie del mar ardía y las nubes en el horizonte reverberaban con pigmentos naranjas y violetas. Aunque no estaba en un piso muy alto, se podían escrutar también las azoteas del Vedado, fragmentadas en colores como un rompecabezas, con sus tanques de agua, tendederas, casuchas improvisadas, respiraderos o tubos de chimeneas, antenas de variados tipos y formas, techos de planchas de zinc que cubrían habitáculos de animales. Algunos de esos terrados se veían limpios y otros como las ruinas después de un bombardeo. De tanto en tanto se dejaban contemplar unas manchas verdes de arboladas y el penacho de una palma extraviada en el asfalto. A la derecha se adivinaba el cordón del Malecón oculto por edificios. De noche, unas ráfagas intermitentes de luz indicaban el sitio del faro del Morro. De día, Lola observaba, ya sin asombrarse, el nuevo espectáculo de varias bandadas de auras tiñosas sobrevolando el rascacielos del Focsa.

En un muro de la acera de enfrente, se apostaba todas las tardes la Doctora Carvajal. Lola la observaba a hurtadillas. Se conocían de hola cómo está y Lola sabía que había enseñado Gramática por muchos años en la Universidad. Al igual que ella misma, la Doctora Carvajal había dedicado la vida a su trabajo. En tiempos pasados, se le veía salir temprano con una carpeta de libros y papeles, y regresar tarde en la noche, arrastrando las piernas hinchadas después de caminar a pie el trayecto entre la Facultad y su casa. Jubilada y solterona, la Doctora Carvajal se sentaba ahora todas las mañanas en el cruce de las esquinas y se colocaba una cajetilla de cigarros abierta sobre las rodillas. No decía palabra ni ofrecía nada, solo permanecía allí, sin moverse, petrificada de vergüenza, hasta que se acercaba un transeúnte y le compraba un cigarrillo suelto que la Doctora Carvajal vendía a peso para poder reforzar el magro retiro que ni le alcanzaba para comer.

Lola tenía mejor suerte. Tenía un comprador fijo en el edificio quien de un solo golpe adquiría a sobreprecio toda la cuota de cigarros asignada en la libreta de abastecimientos. Con esa ganancia, Lola aumentaba los suministros de café y, de tanto en tanto, se daba el lujo de conseguir leche en polvo en bolsa negra. Por culpa de su salud de hierro no le tocaba leche de dieta. Aunque ya se había acostumbrado a no comer por las noches, los días sin desayuno le minaban las fuerzas.

Sara había sido alumna de la Doctora Carvajal. Si la viera ahora revendiendo cigarritos... Lola sacudió la cabeza para espantar los malos pensamientos. En cierta ocasión, estando de visita, Micaela salió a la terraza y la descubrió. Atónita, le había preguntado, "¿Esa que se ve allí no será, madre mía, la Doctora Carvajal?". Lola no supo qué responder. Micaela insistía con desesperación y furia. "Cómo es posible, a dónde vamos a parar, es que no hay nadie que haga algo, esa mujer le entregó su alma a la Universidad, y ahora mira para eso...". Micaela, habitualmente tan comedida, soltaba lava como un volcán y Lola no sabía qué responderle, siempre había preferido callar, no opinar, mantenerse al margen, no comprometerse. Y una vez más lo hizo. Micaela, al entrar de la terraza, miró los pollos encerrados en su jaula, lanzó una mirada hacia la Doctora Carvajal en su improvisado puesto de venta, giró la cabeza y observó la bandada de auras tiñosas. "El mundo se tiene que acabar", dijo.

Lola prefirió simular que no había escuchado.

MUJER QUE HABLA SOLA EN EL PARQUE

Una algarabía tremenda, música a todo meter, bailongos, tambores, broncas, motores, sirenas, bullicio, tumultos. Y entonces se reventaron todos los edificios como si fueran tímpanos. Y La Habana se muere...

MARTÍN

Sabía que escribir sobre la propia biografía funcionaba más o menos con éxito entre algunos novelistas; pero, aparte de sus aventuras con guaricandillas como Daontaon, no se le ocurría nada. Mientras se metía en la boca un puñado de semillas de maní garapiñado para matar la gula de la madrugada, Martín abrió un libro de Borges. La frase que saltó ante sus ojos tenía una insólita inflexión sentimental, *sentí lo que sentimos cuando alguien muere: la congoja, ya inútil, de que nada nos hubiera costado haber sido más buenos. El hombre olvida que es un muerto que conversa con muertos.*

"Un muerto que conversa con muertos", masticaba pensativo la sentencia, al tiempo que seguía mordisqueando con parsimonia los dulzones granos. Martín se sentía medio muerto y su tío Félix sería de los pocos con quien le habría gustado echar un conversadito.

Recordó la vez que el tío Félix lo llevó a conocer la televisión, tan ilusoria como pudiera serlo un trozo de hielo. La fórmula de la memoria, redactada así, crujía carcomida, y Martín la desechó.

Cuando entraron los primeros televisores a La Habana, quedaron exhibidos como fenómeno de circo en una vidriera frente a la casa de la abuela Antonia, "Amistad casi esquina a Barcelona". Al tío Félix solo le fue necesario cambiar de acera con Martín de la mano, para iniciarlo en la fascinación de lo que parece y no es.

Oro parece, plata no es, sonaba bien como título, una alegoría de la realidad, las puñeteras apariencias.

Martín conservaba otros recuerdos perturbadores de la calle de su niñez. En el mismo cruce de las esquinas se confrontaban el almacén de bicicletas, una bodega con venta de bebidas, la fabrica de cigarros H. Upmann y una casa de citas. Esa metáfora de llamar "casa de citas" a una hostería para amores ilegales o de tránsito se registraba entre los clásicos eufemismos cubanos, anotó mentalmente Martín, como una observación para su manuscrito. Citas con putas, con adúlteros o tan solo entre amantes sin techo, orígenes eventuales de tumultos, cuchilladas y pronunciamientos alcohólicos. Algunas veces aparcaba la "perseguidora", otra metáfora, el carro policial con cuatro gendarmes de uniforme azul. Las ventanas de persianas y cristales esmerilados del llamado Hotel Amistad permanecían cerradas y por más que Martín intentaba descifrar las incógnitas de aquel sitio, al cual su abuela Antonia fruncía el ceño como a una caldera del infierno, nunca percibió nada excitante detrás de los visillos. La emoción se inflamaba al lado del hotel, en la vidriera de la tienda, en aquellos cajones con una pantalla como el hielo y unas figuritas apresadas en su interior.

Cada mañana, Martín se iba con el tío Félix de expedición. Al pasar por el restaurante El Vegetariano realizaban una primera parada para saludar a los parroquianos consuetudinarios; luego seguían su ruta hacia la esquina de San José donde se encontraba la farmacia de turno permanente, siempre urgidos de adquirir sales estomacales para la abuela Antonia o abstrusos envoltorios. Enfrente se ubicaba un club nocturno, también de carácter enigmático, sobre todo cuando se abría su hermética escotilla de entrada y Martín vislumbraba una oscuridad helada que expelía un vaho de olor agradable y desconcertante. En los dos ángulos restantes del cuadrivio, se ubicaban la carnicería de clientela asidua como la propia abuela Antonia y la cafetería predilecta para el cotidiano café con leche espumoso y las lonjas de pan untadas de mantequilla. Si doblaban hacia la derecha, en dirección al Capitolio, se transitaba frente al cine Campoamor y, cruzando el Parque Central, se alcanzaba el edificio del Centro Asturiano. En cambio, siguiendo recto por Amistad se llegaba a San Rafael, la vía preferida de Martín por los cines, los deslumbrantes escaparates de los comercios y los quioscos de golosinas. Aunque, casi siempre, el tío Félix enrumbaba la travesía hacia la izquierda, hacia la calzada de Galiano, hasta vararse ya llegado el mediodía, en el bar Casa Granda de la calle Águila, con su timbiriche para comer ostiones y sus fascinantes barras de madera que terminaban en una canal hacia la que rodaban, sin romperse, las botellas vacías de cerveza.

Frente a la casa de la abuela Antonia se estacionaban dos vendedores ambulantes con su carretilla rebosante de platanitos manzanos y plátanos verdes, lechugas americanas, naranjas, cebollas, mameyes y aquellos mangos bizcochuelos que tanto le gustaban a la mamá de Martín. "¡Caserita!", clamaban. A media tarde llegaba el heladero con su carro, sonando unas campanitas y, al rato, "manicero, maní", avisaba después una anónima voz que Martín hubiera reconocido entre miles.

La casa ocupaba todo el primer piso. En la azotea, el abuelo Severino tenía su taller de carpintería; en los bajos, la vecina Dolores alquilaba la parte delantera a un sastre y en el hueco de la escalera se había instalado un menguado negocio de joyería. Finalmente, al lado izquierdo, se ubicaban la redacción y los rotativos de *La tarde*. Cada día, a un horario preciso, llegaban los vendedores callejeros de periódicos a recoger su carga, en tanto unos peones acumulaban los paquetes de diarios recién impresos para ser montados luego en un camión cerrado.

Intensa mezcla de oficios, herramientas, sonidos y fragancias que Martín asimilaba mientras esperaba la llegada de su hora preferida. Por fin, antes de que empezaran a aparecer las parejas más vistosas a encerrarse tras las persianas del Hotel Amistad, Martín, sujeto por la mano cómplice del tío Félix, se quedaba pasmado ante la pantalla de hielo con los muñequitos de Super Ratón, los episodios de Boston Blackie y los fascinantes anuncios *Taca taca taca camisetas Taca; Chi que crece Chi que desgrana Chi que le va a gustar; Con Texaco saco más; Pedacito de Domingo con Hatuey, mi compay; Camay embellece desde la primera pastilla; Esto es Cuba, Chaguito.*

En los caprichos de la memoria se fundía el tecleo de los linotipos y el ronroneo de las máquinas de coser, el olor a tinta fresca y a papel crudo, el chirrido de la sierra del taller del abuelo, los pregones de legumbres y frutas frescas, el estampido de los fardos de tabaco, junto con las putas que entraban y salían de la casa de citas, y el descubrimiento del televisor. El mundo era muy ancho y nada ajeno, opinó Martín, y lo anotó en un papelito, aunque también le sonaba familiar.

ESTELA

Estela miró por la ventana de cristales. Apenas las cinco de la tarde y ya anochecía. Los árboles del parque se iluminaban desde hacía rato con las luces amarillas de los faroles. Observó el hormiguear de la gente y a dos abrigados ancianos que se habían acomodado con displicencia en los bancos del Cartwright Gardens. Trató de rebuscar alguna emoción sin obtener ningún resultado. De algún modo se alegraba de carecer de efusiones, cualquier forma de exaltación la llenaba de repugnancia y desaprobación. Por suerte ya se había marchado Lucía. Estela y Lucía se conocían desde niñas. Habían estudiado en la escuelita pública de Güines y luego pasaron la beca juntas. Lucía logró convertirse en una notable científica, especialista en caracoles o algo por el estilo, aunque, según el modo de ver de Estela, seguía comportándose como una campesina. Cuando entraron los faxes avisándole su llegada a Londres camino de Manchester y que, por una noche, necesitaba del apoyo de Estela, dormir solamente, Estela aceptó a regañadientes. Ya sabía que vendrían algunos malos ratos, pero resultaba imposible negarse. Para empezar, cuando Lucía la abrazó en el aeropuerto, Estela sintió un cosquilleo de vergüenza por el aspecto de las maletas de Lucía. Se veían maltrechas y anticuadas. La facha de Lucía no se mostraba mucho mejor. Quizás la infeliz pensaba que andaba elegantísima. A la legua se notaban los zapatos baratos y el traje sastre mal cortado por una modista casera, quizás la propia mamá de Lucía. ¿Cómo se llamaba? No podía ya recordarlo, aunque fueron muchas las veces que Estela pasó los fines de semana en casa de la familia de Lucía, cuando ya ellos estaban en La Habana y todavía los padres de Estela insistían en seguir viviendo en aquel pueblucho. Estela sentía cierta intolerancia ante la intrusión de los recuerdos. Durante los primeros meses de su vida en Londres, el pasado parecía estar cerca y de repente, con brusquedad, se alejaba, como en un corte cinematográfico se ennegrecía la pantalla y desaparecía la imagen para volver al presente, sin música de fondo. Lucía se le había colgado al cuello y la apretujaba con aquel sentimentalismo que siempre había sido su lado flaco. Lucía olía a agua de violetas, el mismo olor de niña, y esa constatación irrumpió en el corazón de Estela con un deleite metamorfoseado al instante en molestia. Estela escrutó a su alrededor para detectar si algún conocido andaba recreándose con la escena, solo vio a turistas, apresurados hombres de negocios y viajeros despreocupados. Lucía la zarandeaba y mostraba alegría y nerviosismo de encontrarse en Londres. Por cortesía, Estela le ofreció tomarse un café. Afortunadamente, Lucía prefería ir directo a la casa y darse un baño. Mientras Lucía se duchaba, Estela registró con curiosidad la maleta abierta sobre la cama del cuarto de huéspedes. Descubrió una foto de familia enmarcada en una cartulina. "¿Cuántos hijos tienes?", preguntó. Lucía, desde el baño, respondió que dos y se enzarzó en un monólogo sobre qué buenos muchachos le habían salido, uno practicaba balompié y el otro se mostraba como un lince para los idiomas, y *bla bla bla* que Estela dejó de oír y fue a prepararse un trago. Cuando Lucía salió del baño parecía rejuvenecida, llevaba el pelo húmedo envuelto en una toalla y se había arrebujado en una bata de felpa como si se tratara de un abrigo de pieles. "Si quieres llévate esa bata para Manchester", le ofreció Estela. Lucía la aceptó con tanta naturalidad que Estela tuvo otro repunte incomprensible de irritación. Entonces Lucía dio un grito y salió corriendo al balcón. "No puedo creerlo, no puedo creerlo", y se pellizcaba con teatralidad, "no puedo creer que yo esté en Bloomsbury, ay, mi madre". Estela sonrió a pesar suyo, siempre Lucía tan infantil, tan exagerada. Estela se paró junto a ella y miró también hacia el parque. "¿Te imaginas, Estela, quién nos hubiera dicho que íbamos a estar juntas en Bloomsbury? ¿Te acuerdas cuando querías ser escritora? Nos leímos más de diez veces *La señora Dalloway*. ¿Has escrito algo después que…?". Estela percibió el enmudecimiento prudente, aunque no descifró bien a "después" de "qué" se refería Lucía, a cuál de todos los "después que" de su vida. Ya sabía Estela que iba a pasar algunos malos ratos. "Cartas", contestó en broma, "muchas cartas, muchos documentos, muchos informes". Mas ya Lucía había pasado, como era su maldita costumbre, a otro tema. "En La Habana de entonces no se dormía. ¿Te acuerdas, Estela?". Estela no quería acordarse de nada. "No", le contestó con sequedad, "no me acuerdo, ni tampoco me quiero acordar". Lucía la miró con un asomo de agravio que reprimió, tal vez al descubrir su condición de apenas un huésped, y se esforzó por seguir hablando, impedir a toda costa un silencio irremediable entre las dos, aunque no pudo evitar que se le trastornase la voz hacia un tono melancólico. Impersonal, le pareció a Estela. "Muy bonito tu barrio", comentó Lucía, ya sin ningún entusiasmo.

HERMI

Cuando los padres de Hermi tomaron la decisión de emigrar, ella eligió quedarse, probar suerte con los "pobres de la tierra", resistir en la fe de lo nuevo. Se quedó sola en la casona, llena de antigüedades y trastos familiares que quedaron bajo su custodia, junto con una apreciable cuenta de banco a su nombre. Tristán, harto de las incomprensiones paternas, se mudó con ella y se adueñó de uno de los cuartos desocupados, sacó los aparatosos muebles y dejó una camita, una mesa de mármol y dos sillas, las paredes desnudas, con intención conventual. Allí, tranquilo, se aficionó a acumular libros raros, estudiaba por su cuenta varios idiomas, incluidos los muertos, y traía a sus amantes ocasionales. Se levantaba tarde y se acostaba a las cinco de la mañana, leyendo y estudiando la mayor parte de las veces.

Hermi, por su parte, transformó su habitación en un estudio psicodélico con afiches de cine pegados en las paredes. Pintó los muebles de magenta y puso el colchón de dormir en el piso. Cambió la lámpara de lágrimas de cristal por un globo de papel y cubrió las ventanas con esteras asiáticas. Por último, trasladó el televisor y lo colocó frente a la cama. En ese entorno, pintaba manchas abstractas en telas de lienzo, garabateaba diseños de escenografías, escribía guiones y veía televisión. También se agenció una novedosa grabadora de casetes.

Los vecinos no vieron con buenos ojos los cambios, la extrañísima música, el trasiego de "peludos", de "enfermitos" como solía llamarlos el vulgo, los horarios y las incomprensibles actividades de Hermi y Tristán. Ellos dos, enfrascados en sus mundos, no percibían cómo se iban convirtiendo en sospechosos.

Para colmo, Hermi solía venir acompañada de un hombre mayor que abandonaba la casa a altas horas de la noche en un auto "VW". Cuando una comisión de vecinos presentó de forma confidencial una denuncia por inmoralidad en el trabajo de Hermi, se llevaron un chasco. En efecto, el tipo era casado, pero militante del partido y jefe de un departamento en la CMQ. Volvieron con el rabo entre las piernas, aunque decididos a sanear la cuadra de indeseables y de "lacra", otra palabra que se iba imponiendo en la prensa.

Una señal grave de que las cosas no andaban bien fue cuando desapareció un amigo de Tristán que estudiaba Matemáticas. En la universidad nadie sabía qué le había pasado, ni tampoco la familia. Desesperada, la madre recorrió hospitales, estaciones de policía e incluso la morgue. Nada, a Tomás se lo había tragado la tierra.

Unas semanas más tarde, Tomás hizo una llamada desde el Hospital Militar. Apareció allí, flaco, pelado al cero, acribillado de picadas de mosquitos, ensimismado, con una tos perruna y una herida larga, profunda, en la pierna. Se negó a contar nada, ni a dar explicaciones a nadie. Excepto a Tristán, quien logró sacarle que lo habían llevado a una finca de trabajo obligatorio en Ciego de Ávila, cercada de púas, donde laboraba de sol a sol en el corte de caña, bajo la vigilancia de soldados armados. La brigada de Tomás se componía de unos cien reclusos, casi todos jóvenes melenudos, algunos entre ellos Testigos de Jehová o miembros del Bando de Gedeón. Se lo contó a Tristán porque cuando lo recogieron en la esquina de L y 23, y lo metieron en una camioneta enjaulada, Tomás lo estaba esperando para encontrarse con él. ¿Qué estaba pasando?

"¡Alertas!", había advertido Tristán (¿o sería Hermi?) con una de sus frases ampulosas, rebuscadas, "el empeño resultaría en vano si por descuido o debilidad, se dejase de ser uno mismo".

MUJER QUE HABLA SOLA EN EL PARQUE

Las calles se llenaron de quistes y de fístulas. Y entonces los huecos se hicieron tan profundos que las guaguas se caían por ellos al fuego del centro de la tierra. Y La Habana se muere...

WILLIE

Daontaon tomó uno de los taburetes de la sala y lo arrastró hasta el balcón. Se sentó y echó una ojeada al vecindario como si desde los otros balcones pudiera atraparla una pandilla de asesinos destripadores. Ahora se tomaba su tiempo. Se había ido la luz y nos envolvía el silencio.

El apagón provocaba que los indígenas y sus equipos de audio cayesen fulminados por algunas horas. El ambiente gótico se completó con una vela y un mechón de querosén.

—¿Tú sabes qué clase de día yo he tenido? Qué vas a saber —afirma Daontaon, con una expresión terrorífica provocada por la iluminación del cirio.

—Cuéntame en detalle lo del torso. En **detalle** —cuando el caso lo requiere, también suelo hablar con negritas y cursivas.

—Niño, mira que tú eres morboso. Un *torso*, un *torso* descuartizado de mujer, metido en un saco. Me estoy tratando de acordar de alguna película relacionada con los hechos.

Daontaon se dispuso a revisar su catálogo de filmes. Por mi parte, en cuanto a mutilaciones, solo tenía a la mano la escena de la cabeza del caballo en la cama del mafioso, *El Padrino,* primera parte. No pegaba, me parece.

—Tchhh, no me logro acordar de ninguna —contrariada Daontaon, después de unos segundos retomó la narración—. Como te decía… Un *torso* envuelto con trapos, metido en un saco amarrado con alambre, y colocado, como si tal cosa, al lado del latón de basura, en la Casa de Cultura. ¡*Una barbaridad*! Imagínate… ahora soy la **principal** sospechosa.

—Claro que sí… y yo también.

—¿Cómo que TÚ también? Niño, no chives, que esto es serio. —Daontaon parecía ofendida.

Me encogí de hombros. No le estaba quitando protagonismo a Daontaon. A fin de cuentas, como los mayordomos de las novelas policíacas, pase lo que pase estoy bajo sospecha. Eso pensé, pero le di un giro a la conversación:

—¿Y cómo se dieron cuenta de que adentro había un muerto?

—*Una muerta* —rectificó puntillosa—. Tres zangaletones, fugados del Tecnológico, de esos que se pasan el día sin hacer nada, abrieron el bulto y se encontraron con el numerito. ¡Y ahí mismo la que se armó…! En menos de cinco minutos llegó la patrulla y cercaron el área. Niño, a mí por poco me da un soponcio. Pusieron al *torso*, tapado con una manta en el parqueo. ¿Alguna vez tú has visto ALGO SEMEJANTE?

Esta vez no le di chance para responderse a sí misma, porque el recuerdo se revolvió como un gato furioso y me arañó un pliegue del cerebro donde debe de haber estado guarecido mucho tiempo. Hace como treinta años iba camino de la universidad en la ruta 27. Era mediodía y el sol relumbraba como si nada perverso pudiese ocurrir. Por la calle Línea, a la altura de E, la guagua se detuvo por un tranque y luego empezó a avanzar despacito hasta que, desde las ventanillas fue posible distinguir, en medio de la avenida, un pequeño cuerpo cubierto por una sábana. La gente se agitó para averiguar de qué se trataba. Resulta casi imposible no meter las narices en la desgracia ajena, se siente un conjuro, algo parecido a "si le ocurrió a otro, no me pasará a mí". La guagua seguía transitando remisamente y lo que estaba sucediendo en la calle se percibía como en cámara lenta. Los peatones en la acera, los vecinos en los balcones, los policías, todos miraban. Yo también miré. Me llamó la atención lo esmirriado, lo menudito, lo desvalido que parecía aquel bulto ante los curiosos. ¿Qué había ocurrido allí? ¿Un accidente? ¿Un crimen? ¿Un suicidio?

—Sí, hace mucho, mucho tiempo.

—No me digas...—se sorprendió Daontaon y en realidad estaba queriendo decir: "dímelo todo, cuéntamelo en **detalle**".

—¿Ya se sabe quién es la descuartizada? —respondí a mi vez, desviando su estupor chismoso hacia el muerto que le competía.

Daontaon se quedó pensando en esta última pregunta. Resultaba obvio que no se le había ocurrido. La impresión causada por la aparición del cadáver junto al latón de desperdicios donde ella misma tiraba su propia basura, el acto en sí del cuerpo troceado y el interrogatorio policial, habían ocupado de manera tan potente su mente que había pasado por alto el hecho esencial de la identidad de la víctima.

Esta es la primera vez, al menos delante de mí, que Daontaon se queda callada.

GERTRUDIS

¡Cómo era La Habana! A nuestros pies, desde el piso 23 de la beca de F y Tercera o desde las alturas del bar de La Torre, iluminada con miles de fulgores, en todo su esplendor. Era como para morirse, ¿se acuerdan? Y ese Malecón resplandeciente, la travesía que comienza en el torreón de Miramar hasta la entrada del puerto, con el faro del Morro lanzando las ráfagas de luz, a intervalos como si respirara viva la ciudad.

Si en aquel entonces alguien me hubiera preguntado qué habría querido hacer en la vida, hubiera contestado sin titubeos que cuidar un faro. Una isla desierta, la naturaleza salvaje rodeada de mar, silencio, nadie a la vista, ni teléfono, ni reuniones, ni guaguas llenas, ni colas, ni apagones y que el trabajo fuera ese, encender la lámpara por la noche, apagarla por la mañana, todo el tiempo para contemplar el panorama, leer, pensar, mientras las luces daban su vuelta en redondo. Como *Robinsona Crusoe*. Esa idea me surgió cuando leí *Al faro* de Virginia Woolf y, sin pensarlo dos veces, comenté en medio del aula que me gustaría vivir en un faro. Cómo no. Se lo guardaron bien guardadito y en cuanto tuvieron una oportunidad me llamaron a capítulo: "ese no es oficio para mujeres". Y encima, me acusaron de individualismo y me pusieron una sanción con nota al expediente.

Pues ellos ganaron, nunca más volví a soñar con vivir en un faro.

Volviendo al tema, *pica y pasa*, como se dice bien dicho en *El coloquio de las perras, que sea tu intención limpia, aunque la lengua no lo parezca,* allá arriba, en el último piso del Focsa, en el bar de La Torre, se podía alcanzar la ilusión de estar en un faro, tranquilo, oscuro, con filin, vista al mar y bebiendo un "cubanito", ron con jugo de tomate, versión criolla del *Bloody Mary*. Sospecho que a los fareros no se les permita "ingerir bebidas alcohólicas". Cada circunstancia tiene sus propias leyes. Cómo no. Aunque algunas terminan por resultar muy absurdas.

En la beca de F y Tercera les estaba prohibido a "las hembras" entrar o salir del edificio vestidas con pantalones, excepto durante el permiso que se otorgaba con el fin de asistir a los trabajos voluntarios en el campo.

¿Se acuerdan? Óiganme, se cuenta y no se cree. Ante ordenanza tan estúpida, no quedaba más remedio que jugarle cabeza a las autoridades: para ir a la playa la artimaña consistía en colocarse una saya encima del pantalón, remangarse los bajos hasta las rodillas, las "calzas", dicho sea en propiedad, hasta alejarse apenas media cuadra y quitarse, en plena avenida G, el disfraz. Y al regreso de la playa, la misma operación a la inversa: la falda ocultando los pantalones para poder penetrar de nuevo a los predios de la beca. Como en *El extraño caso de la Dra. Jekill y Mrs. Hyde*. Por tonto que pareciera, no se podía discutir, era El Reglamento. Y como aquello, muchas tantas cosas, y peores, que obligaban al disimulo, a una doblez, a la astucia para subsistir. *Las dos mitades de la vizcondesa.*

¿Nadie se acuerda de nada de lo que pasó? Al menos, en aquel entonces, podíamos ver La Habana desde el bar del Focsa.

DAONTAON

A media mañana, Daontaon se levantó de la cama tratando de calcular las cosas que haría si le quedase una semana de vida. Qué va, tenía que empezar a tomar medidas, tantos muertos y tantas situaciones lúgubres le estaban aniquilando el sistema nervioso. Para empezar, decidió cogerse el día libre y no ir a trabajar. Mientras se preparaba el café, sintió un estruendo HORRIPILANTE que bajaba por la tubería de desagüe. A Daontaon no le extrañaría nada que un *torso* humano estuviera descendiendo por la cañería. Como para volverse loca. De una cosa sí estaba segura: antes de morirse le prendería candela al edificio.

Se sentó en su balcón mientras bebía el brebaje y recorrió de una mirada la parcela de hierba silvestre donde varios círculos de tierra pisoteada evidenciaban a las claras los movimientos de los primitivos jugando a la pelota. Desde varios de los apartamentos emergían tempraneros aullidos, martillazos y estruendos de pelea. Durante la madrugada, unos energúmenos habían acumulado una considerable cantidad de botellas de ron vacías, algunas en pedazos, sobre el banco ubicado debajo del único farol todavía con su bombillo. En la ruta que daba acceso a la escalera, sujetos desconocidos habían olvidado a propósito unos cartuchos de algo que parecía, y olía, como pescado podrido. Entre los latones de basura desbordados pululaban unos perros reconocibles a simple vista, aunque las otras figuras que escarbaban entre las inmundicias podían ser sus propios vecinos o criaturas de cualquier linaje.

Por el medio del *center field* avanzaba Tilingo con sus chivos a pastar. A Daontaon no le constaba, pero... Ja. Lo más probable fuese que Tilingo comiera hierba también.

Según Willie, el índice por metro cuadrado de anormales, deficientes, fronterizos, tarados, oligofrénicos, deformes, mongos, ñongos, morones, retrasados mentales e imbéciles de este edificio podía ser aceptado, sin objeciones, como *record*. Tilingo, catalogado entre uno de los más connotados, no trabajaba al igual que la mayoría, andaba sin camisa y con un ripio de pantalón que mostraba sus "partes", el *culo,* para decirlo rápido y se entienda. Tilingo, con el trasero al aire y su recua de animales, se decía *enviado de Dios*. Dígame usted.

En efecto, mientras no se hablara de religión, Tilingo se comportaba como loco pacífico, mas si le daba por oler la chamusquina del infierno o escuchaba el aleteo de los ángeles, vociferaba anunciando el castigo de los pecadores, provocando la hilaridad general y la desbandada aterrada de su chivos.

A la derecha, se asomaba a su balcón "La Mataperros", conocida bajo distintos apelativos según la variedad de su comportamiento. Daontaon daba por sentado que "esa compañerita" no se bañaba desde el paritorio del menor de su progenie, uno de los vándalos que vagabundeaban por los alrededores. De su apartamento se desprendían *fluidos,* estancados durante semanas en el pasillo de la escalera hasta que las leyes de la física los hacían descender por gravedad hasta la planta baja.

¿Se acababa ahí el desfile? Seguro que no. Baja trotando por la escalera el nieto de Palacios. ¿Qué andará tramando? Nada bueno. A pesar de su corta edad reunía cualidades suficientes para la obtención de un tercer lugar o encabezar el equipo de Mongos cadetes, solía secundar a "La Mataperros", aunque empleaba con preferencia sus ocios en golpear a la abuela.

Para completar la comparsa, el "Flaco cachicambiao" de la segunda escalera ha entrado con sigilo en su casa, con un paquete disimulado bajo la camisa. Daontaon se sentía incapaz de memorizar todos los nombres... pero *sabía* que el "Flaco cachicambiao" se libró por un pelito de una condena por sustraer botellas de alcohol de 90 grados del policlínico y, por el momento, se dedicaba a reparaciones menores en el barrio y a robar chirimbolos como destornilladores y seguetas en casas de incautos que permitían su acceso. Aunque si se fuera hablar de ladrones..., ¡apaga y vámonos!, en este edificio se robaban hasta las piedras.

Daontaon sintió un escalofrío. Le acababa de "bajar un muerto". Con toda seguridad, algunos de sus vecinos dormían en ataúdes y salían a chupar sangre por la noche. No le extrañaría para nada que conviviera entre ellos un asesino en serie o el mismísimo DESCUARTIZADOR. Convino consigo misma en que, sin abusar del uso de las mayúsculas, estas venían muy a propósito.

Daontaon terminó de tomarse el café y cerró el balcón con un portazo. Allá salían de sus cubiles otros especímenes y no quería ni verlos. Prefería los tarados, los ladrones y hasta los asesinos, a los **farsantes**. Y de esos sí que había un montón en el edificio. Ja ¡Pregúntenselo a ella!

MUJER QUE HABLA SOLA EN EL PARQUE

Con el alquitrán desprendido de los baches y la grasa de los motores se engendró una nata que sobrenadaba en las calles. Y entonces se trepó a las aceras y remontó las casas hasta cubrir las azoteas. Y La Habana se muere...

LA INDIA

Al poco tiempo se anunció el compromiso entre El Francés y La India. Por mejor decir, la boda, pues de novios no duraron nada. Formalizadas las relaciones, hasta el día de las nupcias apenas pasaron cinco semanas. Ante tan apresurado matrimonio, siempre hubo, claro está, el comentario malicioso acerca de un embarazo, búsqueda de ciudadanía europea u otro desvío de la virtud.

Ocurrido el acto civil sin muchos protocolos, se instalaron en un apartamento alquilado (ilegalmente, la verdad sea dicha) que hizo las delicias de los flamantes esposos.

Si el pasado de Patrick Rivière no se conocía en el solar, aquel de María Antonieta era harto sabido: prostitución, hurto y escándalo público. Sin embargo, a sus veinte y tantos años, conservaba unos residuos de inocencia. Se maravillaba con las fruslerías que le regalaba El Francés, soñaba con acunar un bebé de ojos claros y se esperanzaba con sacar de la cuartería para siempre a su madre Clara Luz, ponerla a vivir en una "casita independiente", el sueño de todo cubano desde los tiempos del jabón Candado: "Tu casa, mamá, tu casa".

El Francés y La India, por lo que podía apreciarse desde afuera, se llevaban en armonía. Ni una voz más alta que la otra, ni acaramelamientos excesivos. Parecía que andaban en camino de convertirse en una de esas parejas que remontaban la madurez rodeada de nietos y con los rescoldos de un pasado azaroso ya sometido a la rutina. Clara Luz, llamada La Catedrática, abandonó sus trasiegos de productos agropecuarios y abrió un centro (mínimo, dada la estrechez de su habitáculo, valga la aclaración) de consultas espirituales.

Sin aviso, había comenzado ya a tejerse la desgracia.

Unos días antes del macabro hallazgo del torso, un antebrazo de mujer cuidadosamente afeitado (envuelto en papel de estraza y amarrado con alambres, empatados unos a otros por nudos un poco raros), fue desenterrado por un perro en un terreno baldío de Guanabo y arrastrado hasta el patio de una casa habitada. Informadas las fuerzas policiales, decidieron guardar discreción para no levantar terrores en la población. De hecho, la crónica roja había sido erradicada de la prensa hacía más de treinta años.

Por esas mismas fechas, El Francés, con el poco pelo revuelto y la cara desencajada, se personó en el cuarto de la madre de María

Antonieta para denunciar la desaparición de su esposa. La única pista consistía en una nota manuscrita, con faltas de ortografía (faltaba más) donde ella anunciaba su partida con un amante. Cabe añadir: en un bote con rumbo desconocido, presumiblemente norte. Ante tamaña historia, Clara Luz procuró localizar a los fugitivos a través de varias apelaciones telefónicas a la prima Cusita, residente en Hialeah.

Como de las tales llamadas no se alcanzó a obtener información alguna, cabía conjeturar (si el testimonio de El Francés fuese fidedigno) que La India y su supuesto amante habrían sido pasto de los tiburones de las aguas del Golfo, ya habituados a semejantes presas gastronómicas.

Por su lado, las investigaciones pertinentes en torno al antebrazo femenino hicieron pensar a las autoridades que tendrían que vérselas con un asunto peliagudo. En el análisis forense parcial a la extremidad cercenada se encontraron muestras de violencia que permitía inferir feroz lucha entre el asesino y su víctima, antes de que aquel pudiese consumar el crimen. Logró constatarse, asimismo, que el fragmento del cadáver había sido separado del cuerpo con un objeto puntiagudo y de borde ancho, tal como un espadón antiguo.

Entonces se descubrió el torso envuelto en papeles de estraza, atado con los conocidos alambres y dentro de un saco, en un montón de basura (acumulada durante años, la verdad sea dicha) junto a la Casa de Cultura de Alamar. Los agentes del orden se desplegaron en emergencia, aun cuando la difícil identificación de los restos dificultaba la captura del asesino. Como de costumbre, la prensa silenció los sucesos. *Radio Bemba,* no obstante, entró en funcionamiento y a las pocas horas todos los habaneros sabían sobre el caso de "una mujer cortada en trocitos".

Mientras iban surgiendo los despojos, resultaba duro de aceptar que aquellos pedazos malolientes pudieran haber sido alguna vez la hermosa India.

Por otra parte, en el solar nadie se había tragado el cuento de la fuga de La India con su supuesto cómplice. No se trataba de que ella fuese incapaz de pegar cuernos, tarros o cualquier protuberante asta (la verdad sea dicha), sino que se le veía demasiado ilusionada con su botín europeo como para abandonarlo y largarse al albur de las mareas. Además, María Antonieta, insistía su madre, tenía fobia al agua, no sabía nadar y ni siquiera, por su pánico a los océanos, le había interesado nunca solearse en Varadero.

Muchos años atrás, Clara Luz había acompañado a una vecina a identificar el cuerpo de su hija, muerta en circunstancias imprecisas. Sobre la camilla y tapada con una frazada, en una sombría sala del hospital Calixto García, yacía el cuerpo de la muchacha. La vecina reconoció su rostro y se desmayó. Clara Luz estuvo varias horas acompañándola en el Cuerpo de Guardia hasta que la pobre vecina se repuso un poco. Luego, como acto de piedad, la ayudó a vestir a su difunta. Clara Luz se acordaba como si fuera ayer de sus pies sanos, sin una magulladura, con las uñitas bien recortadas, mientras le ponía unas medias escolares antes de encerrarla en el ataúd. Desde aquel entonces no había vuelto a ocurrir otra desgracia semejante en el solar.

Cuando llegó el rumor de la aparición de un torso femenino, los vecinos del solar dieron por sentado que pertenecía a la desaparecida India y, todo lo demás, meras patrañas del sanguinario extranjero, a estas alturas casi seguro un espía de la CIA o un oficial nazi, cuando menos.

YUYA

Dice Yuya que se encontró por segunda vez con el espíritu en pena del haitiano, muy lejos de su área de aparición primigenia, nada menos que en el parquecito de Dragones, frente a la Estación de Policía.

Todas las tardes, a Yuya le gustaba emprender junto a Lalita un paseo que empezaba en el *Ten Cent* de la avenida Galiano. En la cafetería merendaban un club sándwich con leche malteada, después curioseaban entre los mostradores y cumplían con una visita obligada al segundo piso, al final, donde se vendían las lámparas. Allí las esperaba Luisa, antigua vecina del solar y la única amiga de Yuya, vestida de impecable blanco y con un pañuelo colocado en el bolsillo de la blusa, abierto como una flor de muchos colores, adorno de las empleadas de rango. Luisa se las arreglaba para recibir la visita diaria de Yuya sin dejar de atender a los clientes con una sonrisa de dientes perfectos. Cuando se quedaban solas las tres, Luisa simulaba un pase mágico y sacaba un caramelo del pañuelo para su ahijada Lalita.

Lalita, deslumbrada por las luminarias, se deslizaba entre ellas, convencida que provenían de un palacio de hadas, mientras Yuya y Luisa chachareaban un rato sobre la vida y sus milagros.

Dice Yuya que luego caminaba con la Lalita de la mano, mirando un rato las vidrieras, hasta llegar a la calle Zanja, muy cerca de la azotea de Shu. No obstante, Yuya alargaba la caminata, disfrutaba deambular por la movida vía del barrio, con sus olores a pastica china y especias agridulces; con los puestos de chicharrones, helados de fruta en barquillo y naranjas peladas en la maquina que les sacaba entera la cáscara en una serpentina; los soportales furtivos de los pasajes donde antaño al atardecer se dejaban ver las damiselas en espera de un marchante; los faroles de papel transparente iluminados como solecitos nocturnos en días de fiesta, sobre todo durante la celebración del Año Lunar; el respeto de los transeúntes asiáticos que siempre las dejaban pasar con una reverencia.

Al cruzar la calle Manrique, dice Yuya que no podía dejar de observar con curiosidad, desde la acera de enfrente, el intrigante edificio del Teatro Shangai. Hubiera dado lo imposible con tal de entrar, aunque fuera una sola vez, a ver el espectáculo "solo para hombres". Incluso llegó a cruzarle la idea de disfrazarse con ropa de Shu. La dificultad mayor consistía en su rubicundo busto, pues su pelo largo se solucionaba fácil con una trenza, común entre los señores, y que no llamaba la atención.

De buenas a primeras, el Teatro Shangai, el inescrutable, fue clausurado.

En sus recorridos, a veces Yuya tomaba por la calle Dragones, más estrecha y abigarrada. De tanto en tanto se tropezaba con personajes curiosos como "Bigote de Gato" o con un anciano que hablaba solo y se parecía a su Chinito de la Charada, o realizaban una parada frente al portalón por donde entraban y salían los estudiantes de pintura de la Escuela San Alejandro. Dice Yuya que a ella le hubiera gustado estudiar allí, disfrutaba con el olor del óleo, de los barnices y el papel nuevo. Y aunque nunca compraban nada, Lalita y ella visitaban la tienda El Arte, como si fuesen duchas en tales utensilios y sustancias.

Tres o cuatro veces a la semana, Yuya adquiría una libra de picadillo de res de primera, la comida favorita de Shu, en la carnicería de Campanario y Dragones. Dice Yuya que Lalita sentía una incomprensible fascinación en ver salir la carne cruda por los hoyitos de la picadora convertida en largos tubitos rojos como blandos fideos. En la bodega de esa esquina, Yuya compraba alcaparras y un real de aceitunas en un cucurucho de papel destinadas al picadillo, y un "peter" de chocolate para Lalita. En el bar de enfrente, había una de aquellas vitrolas y, esta, en particular, siempre estaba sonando y repitiendo una canción del Benny, "mi son, Maracaibo, para que tú lo bailes". En un recoveco de la bodega, un viejo molía maíz con una manigueta que chirriaba sin cesar. Desde los altos de una casa, llegaban los acordes de un piano, a veces una pieza completa bien tocada, otras las escalas machacadas una y otra vez por una mano inexperta. Dice Yuya que el recuerdo de esa combinación de diseño sonoro siempre le sigue sacando las lágrimas.

En esa misma ruta, cruzaban frente a la Escuela Superior donde su progenitora había estudiado inglés en la escuela pública nocturna. Aunque no conoció a su madre, dice Yuya que a veces tenía la impresión de que se asomaba por la puerta del edificio y se les quedaba mirando, a ella y a Lalita.

Al llegar al parquecito, se tomaban un granizado de fresa y descansaban en un banco a la sombra de los árboles, antes de retomar el camino de regreso. Según Yuya, esa vez vio al haitiano en la transfiguración de un perro moribundo con la cabeza del negro.

Yuya lo interpretó como un aviso y supo que había llegado el momento de dejar la apuntación de la Bolita y la Charada. Decidió cambiar para una ocupación sin tantos riesgos y dirigió sus habilidades a la interpretación de los sueños y otras cábalas.

DAONTAON

—¿Daontaon es un nombre chino? —le había preguntado Braulio, el nuevo jefe, haciéndose el bárbaro, el culto, el interesante.

—Hum hum —negó con la cabeza y se quedó callada, para darle más cuerda.

—Oye, es muy extraño. ¿De dónde lo sacaron tus padres? —insistió Braulio.

—De una canción —y Daontaon esperó a que el nuevo jefe cayera en el jamo, él solito. Ja. Así mismo fue.

—Ah, no me digas. Mira, te invito a comer y me lo cuentas —Braulio se acercó a la silla donde se había acomodado Daontaon—. Oye, mira que aquí podemos hacer un buen trabajo. Más actividades culturales para la gente... Yo te quiero a ti cerca de mí, ¿me copias?, en la captación de artistas, y eso.

Daontaon lo miró con una ceja levantada. Nada. Otro **farsante.** Ese impulso lo traían siempre al principio y después todo se iba a la *mierda,* perdonando la grosería.

—¿Esta tarde? —insistió el nuevo jefe.

—Esta tarde tengo una reunión en el municipio.

—Que vaya otro en tu lugar —el nuevo jefe volvió a sentarse detrás de su buró—. Tómate el día libre y a eso de las tres paso a recogerte por tu casa... anótame aquí la dirección.

Daontaon dudó. Observó de reojo al nuevo jefe y pronto lo catalogó como inofensivo, manejable. Lampiño, seguro, y *casado,* faltaba más, no crearía dificultades. Ja. Otro idiota como el tal Martín, su vecino. A este, Braulio, al menos le iba a tumbar una comida cara en un restaurante. De modo que apuntó en la agenda el número de su edificio y del apartamento.

—Es en "La Siberia", allí todo el mundo me conoce —explicó Daontaon.

Una algarabía en la escalera de la Casa de Cultura interrumpió la conversación. Tres tipejos, mugrientos y ripiados, se zarandeaban unos a otros por una discusión nebulosa, al menos para Daontaon.

—¡Música de "blanquitos"! —vociferaba un negro alto y de pelambre decolorada, con las venas del cuello infladas como cordones morados. "¡Racista!", le replicaba furioso un pelirrojo que ocultaba su piel, tal vez clara, bajo numerosas capas de polvo, grasa y churre. Un tercero, irreconocible su filiación étnica bajo los ropajes, aullaba improperios indecorosos, capaces de ruborizar a un estibador de los muelles. Unos párvulos del taller de pintura azuzaban risueñamente a los contrincantes. El nuevo jefe no pareció inmutarse. Salió de la oficina contoneándose y, por arte de magia, la trifulca se transformó en una plática afable entre los cuatro sobre el juego de pelota de la noche anterior.

Daontaon se despidió con una sonrisa y Braulio le correspondió con otra, satisfecho.

Uh, al menos alcanzaría a dormir un poco al mediodía. La madrugada completa se la pasó en vela por culpa de una pesadilla ESPANTOSA con los asteroides asesinos. Una lluvia de aerolitos, bólidos de roca, caía del cielo sobre su edificio y allí no se salvaba ni el gato.

Qué va, si no escapaba pronto de Alamar, iba a terminar loca o *descuartizada*. Tenía que "maniobrar" inteligentemente con el nuevo jefe. Prosperar. Hilar fino. Nunca se sabe... ¿sí o no? Ja.

MUJER QUE HABLA SOLA EN EL PARQUE

Truenos y centellas. En el gran apagón se iluminó toda la bóveda celeste, bramaron los horrísonos aquilones y cayeron tres mil rayos a la vez. Y entonces explotó la ciudad como un siquitraqui. Y La Habana se muere...

LOLA

Lola escuchaba, a su pesar, el repulsivo programa radial sobre los orgasmos femeninos. No se trataba del tema, sino de la forma jocosa del guión y, sobre todo, los comentarios del sujeto que animaba el programa. Movió el dial e irrumpió una tonada que inundaba el espectro sonoro de la ciudad sobre alguien que decía estar "arriba de la bola". Ridículo e incomprensible para Lola. Apagó el radio y cerró las vidrieras de la terraza para atenuar la vocinglería de la calle. Se estaba poniendo vieja.

Solo le quedaba un pollo y Micaela seguía sin aparecer. La semana pasada, al menos, había llegado correspondencia de Sara. Una tarjeta de Navidad muy bonita. Al abrirla, soltaba una musiquita metálica con los acordes de *Jingle Bell*. Lola la abría una y otra vez a pesar de estar retrasada en fechas, el correo se demoraba tanto que la postal había llegado a principios de septiembre. No le informaba mucho sobre Sara, mas allí estaba su letra apretada deseándole un buen año. Lola hubiera preferido una verdadera carta, una foto, no obstante se conformaba con la postal.

La Doctora Carvajal había muerto de un infarto la semana anterior. Cuando Lola dejó de verla, vendiendo los cigarritos en su puesto, conjeturó que algo le podría haber pasado. Ayer la habían encontrado muerta. Estuvo agonizando, sola en su apartamento, por más de tres días. La policía tuvo que romper la puerta para entrar, después que los vecinos dieron la alarma por el mal olor.

Lola pensó que, a las diez de últimas, fue mejor así, peor hubiese sido que se quedara incapacitada. ¿Quién la iba a cuidar? Lola deseó lo mismo para ella, que cayera un rayo del cielo y la partiera en dos de una sola vez, porque no quería pasar por lo que estaba sufriendo su vecina de los bajos. Llevaba inválida dos años y la familia apenas se ocupaba. El hedor a orines subía desde el cuarto piso y a veces en medio de la noche se escuchaban gritos e insultos.

Además, no podría soportar, eso no, por Dios, que alguien pasara malos ratos por su culpa. Inevitablemente, los malos ratos de Lola estaban identificados con un rostro. El tercero de la lista tenía el rostro de la madre, la madrugada de su muerte. Llevaba tantos días en coma que su partida significó un alivio, se daba por terminado un dilatado calvario para las dos. Lola quedó atontada junto a la cama sin saber qué hacer. Después de pensarlo por un tiempo interminable, se decidió a pedirle ayuda a un vecino. Lola ni sabe de dónde sacó fuerzas para la simulación, fingió que creía a su madre viva todavía. Había escuchado tantas horrorosas historias acerca de los engorrosos trámites de varias horas para declarar una defunción en el domicilio que se decidió por el fraude, la treta, la siniestra pantomima. El vecino acomodó el cuerpo inerte, todavía cálido, como una marioneta descoyuntada, en el asiento trasero del auto junto a Lola y las llevó a las dos a toda velocidad hasta el hospital. Durante el trayecto, Lola pasó su brazo sobre sus hombros, como había hecho tantas veces en otras ocasiones y, mientras la sostenía, reclinó sobre su pecho, por última vez, la cabeza sin vida de su madre.

El médico de guardia, después de auscultarla, le anunció que su madre ya estaba muerta. Ante la mirada conmiserativa del joven, Lola sintió una llamarada de bochorno y turbación. Aunque no se trataba de esa mentira lo que ahora la seguía torturando.

El rostro de su madre, lívido y sin tapar, en una oxidada camilla de un pasillo de la sala de urgencia del hospital, mientras se esperaba por la autopsia, le venía a la mente a Lola cada vez que pensaba en la muerte. Lola miraba desde un banco a su madre en la camilla y ni por un momento le pasó por la cabeza cubrirle la cara. Las enfermeras, médicos, asistentes de limpieza, pacientes de urgencia, transitaban continuamente por su lado. Y a Lola, ahora se lo reprochaba, no se le ocurrió ni siquiera ponerle un pañuelito sobre la cara, como su madre, tan pudorosa, hubiera esperado de ella.

Sí, una época dura. Con cada desastre parecía que se iba a acabar el mundo y nada podría ser peor. Lola fue aprendiendo que el mundo no se acababa o por lo menos no se terminaba en aquella forma, distante a este discurrir en un lento y tortuoso acabose.

MICAELA

La noche anterior, Micaela había tenido otro sueño muy obvio con la tía Candita. Candita, vestida en bata de casa de seda amarilla con floripondios morados, rebuscaba en la basura del latón de la esquina hasta encontrar los fragmentos de su taza de porcelana china. Sin mediar otra escena, se aparecía en su propia habitación con aquella absurda bata de casa, la vasija rota en el cuenco de las manos y le exigía a Micaela que la recompusiera, que pegara los pedazos. "Es el pasado, Micaela", le decía, "arréglalo como sea".

Micaela se despertó melancólica. Las elecciones de su vida terminaron por convertirla en un fracaso. Cuando los ojos de la memoria miraban hacia atrás, solo percibían una historia arrasada. Todo, todo había sido pisoteado, sus sueños, sus esperanzas, su familia, sus creencias. Su pasado yacía sepultado por un presente degradado y aburrido.

Antes de salir del país, Candita, su tía, le había dejado a Micaela parte de su patrimonio, retratos irreconocibles de la familia, un cuchillo de cocina todavía en buen estado; un juego de copas de bacará, polvorientas en la vitrina del comedor; algunas ropas que fueron rebajándose hasta convertirse en trapos de cocina hacía siglos; un cuadro de *La última cena* con los Apóstoles y Jesús en relieve plateado, un espanto de fealdad arrinconado en el closet; una cadena de oro con una medalla de la Virgen de la Caridad del Cobre y unos aretes de brillantes, canjeados en su momento por aquellos certificados para comprar en las tiendas de divisas y que a Micaela le alcanzaron apenas para un ventilador y una cafetera; también aquella taza de porcelana china que, hecha añicos, había terminado en el basurero.

¿La tía Candita? Sin noticias, fuera como fuera, se seguía entre los vivos. O muriendo poquito a poquito en la distancia, se dijo Micaela. Ya terminaría por morir del todo cuando llegase la "novedad", como solía nombrarse con ese anómalo vocablo que absorbía anuncio de lo nuevo y muerte. La eternidad de los famosos, consideró para sí Micaela, se pregona enseguida. La gente común, como ella misma, duraban vivos una temporada extra. La familia se enteró del fallecimiento de la bisabuela en Galicia veinte años más tarde. En todo ese tiempo, el abuelo de Micaela le había seguido escribiendo trabajosas cartas, contándole de Cuba, de su prole, de sus rutinas. Micaela, una niña a la sazón, se alegró de que el abuelito hubiera continuado teniendo a su madre durante aquellos muchos años y el desconsuelo de huérfano le llegara en sordina, parecido a leerse un periódico viejo con noticias que han sido sobrepasadas por otras, frescas y acuciantes. Pero Micaela no se quedó muy clara de si esa falsa prórroga constituía buena o mala suerte. La Doctora Carvajal continuó viva hasta tres semanas después de su entierro. Micaela la había seguido imaginando en su reventa clandestina de cigarritos en la esquina, humillada y vencida. La terminó de matar una llamada telefónica de Lola anunciando lo sucedido.

Por mediación de Lola, Micaela se había enterado también de que los vecinos tiraron al vertedero los papeles de la Doctora Carvajal, sus álbumes de fotografías, y hasta la biblioteca. Micaela estuvo toda esa noche sin poder dormir. A pesar suyo se le mantenía clavada la imagen de los bárbaros irrumpiendo en la intimidad desvalida de la muerta, los destrozos, la pérdida de libros valiosos. Total, preferible que ella misma haya botado en una pocilga sus recuerdos antes que lo hiciesen los extraños. Una punzada se le alojó en el pecho junto al dolor de la impotencia y la soledad.

Cuando por fin logró conciliar el sueño, casi al amanecer, había entrado en escena la tía Candita con la bata de flores, la taza rota y pidiéndole imposibles.

HERMI

Burlona, imprevisible, torturada y brillante, Hermi cayó como una patada en la CMQ. Se reía de todo y no había aprendido a avistar el peligro. Apenas se percataba de las suspicacias que levantaba y creía confiadamente en la simpatía de sus colegas. Le gustaba lo que hacía y aunque encontraba obstáculos aquí y allá, lograba escapársele al diablo.

Metiendo las narices donde nadie la llamaba, Hermi propuso innovaciones en las escenografías y reescribió unos guiones que, modificados por ella, dieron un aire renovador a un rutinario programa dramático. Fascinó a la teleaudiencia con la producción de un musical. Llegaba primero que nadie y se iba la última, transitaba de oficina en oficina dando ideas, opinando y, según los comentarios, hacía lo que le parecía, "andaba por la libre" dijo alguien en vago tono de crítica que Hermi no percibió. Tenía las horas contadas, pero no podía saberlo. Nadie se acercó a prevenirla, ni siquiera el tipo del "VW".

Mientras se urdía con embozo su perdición, Hermi matriculó inglés y francés, al mismo tiempo, en la Escuela de Idiomas; se inscribió en el departamento circulante de la Biblioteca Nacional y se hizo socia de la Cinemateca. Semana tras semana acompañaba a Tristán a los debates del Cine-Club Universitario en el Teatro Varona y a los ensayos de teatro en la Sala Tespis. Todavía le alcanzaba el tiempo para cumplir a pie juntillas y jovialidad con las obligaciones políticas, los trabajos voluntarios y las guardias nocturnas en el barrio.

Sus padres le hicieron llegar varios pliegos de cartulinas y una caja llena de tubos de óleos y pinceles. Con una magnífica cámara fotográfica rusa, Hermi se acostumbró a tomar estampas de la vida cotidiana en La Habana. Abusando de la cuenta bancaria, abarrotó sus libreros con toda la colección de ejemplares de la editorial Aguilar que se vendieron en La Moderna Poesía y añadió un par de volúmenes de un catálogo de arte universal.

Entre las facilidades que otorgaba la biblioteca se incluía el préstamo por un tiempo de una reproducción de pintura. Hermi carreteaba todos los meses un cuadro distinto de piezas clásicas o contemporáneas. Una de sus favoritas, *Desayuno sobre la hierba* de Manet, le intrigaba sobremanera. Representaba un paisaje campestre con dos mujeres desnudas, escamoteadas sus pudibundeces por el pintor, y dos hombres vestidos de cuello y corbata que mantenían, sin embargo un aspecto bohemio. Hermi se sentía perturbada por la laxitud de los cuerpos, la cesta volcada con las frutas y, en particular, por la mirada intensa de una de las damas hacia el ojo de la cámara, o del artista, o de cualquiera que se detuviera a mirar la escena... ¿Qué significaba esa mirada?

En un cuaderno rayado y forrado con papel naranja, Hermi anotaba los planes para el futuro: estudiar ruso, hacer una exposición de pintura, dirigir una película, visitar el Louvre, aprender guitarra, escribir un libro sobre arte cubano. ¡Comerse el mundo colorado!

MUJER QUE HABLA SOLA EN EL PARQUE

Por todas partes aparecieron fueguitos y fueguitas que ardían, quemaban, y achicharraban lo que encontraban a su paso. Y entonces la ciudad entera se convirtió en una loma de cenizas. Y La Habana se muere...

MARTÍN

Seguía de un humor endemoniado. Se había tomado todo el día para escribir y se mantenía obtuso, trabado. Encerrado en su habitación, con las ventanas cerradas a pesar del calor, no dejaba de escuchar el continuo piar de la cría de pollos de Tilingo. El *cri cri cri* y unos aullidos lastimeros de tanto en tanto, le impedían concentrarse. Por mucho que Martín intentara trazar la atmósfera nostálgica de una infancia gloriosa, no lograba pensar más que en enfermedades, desgracias y muertes inopinadas.

La memoria, la suya, estaba haciendo lo que le daba la puñetera gana. Los personajes lo mangoneaban y empujaban hacia rumbos inquietantes, por decir lo menos. Entre tantos vagabundeos con el tío abuelo Félix cómo era posible que solo irrumpiera en sus cavilaciones aquel paseo. Para ser exactos, no podía catalogarse como "paseo".

Caía el atardecer de la Nochebuena. Martín se había antojado de un juguete, un capricho a esa hora, el coche de bomberos que vendían en la juguetería de la calle Galiano. En las divagaciones de Martín se interponía ahora con una insufrible precisión, sobre todo tomando en cuenta el esfuerzo que le costaba ahondar en detalles acerca de tópicos de inobjetable envergadura, la fútil visión de un carrito de plástico rojo, con un depósito para agua y una manguera que expulsaba el líquido a remedo de los auténticos artilugios contra incendios. Una llave le daba cuerda y caminaba un tramo, sonando una sirena y encendiendo una luz encarnada que giraba con un centelleo. Estos manejos los ejecutaba detrás de la vidriera un sonriente Santa Claus que conversaba a través de un teléfono con los niños, apostados como él en la calle, mirando aquellas maravillas y elaborando mentalmente su listado de peticiones a los Tres Reyes Magos. Martín temía que aquel extraordinario artefacto fuera entregado por los Reyes Magos a otro de mejor comportamiento.

A la casa de la abuela Antonia ya había ido llegando la parentela. El árbol de Navidad refulgía con sus bolas de colorines y las guirnaldas de luminarias que se encendían y se apagaban, cubiertas por una delicada capa blanca, fingimiento de nieve que la mamá de Martín llamaba "cabello de ángel". A sus pies se extendía el minucioso Nacimiento con las figuritas que reconstruían el Belén, las montañas de cartón donde pastaban las ovejas, los sembrados de verde papel crepé, el lago de espejo redondo y el simulacro de río elaborado con tela satín azul de brillo. A Martín le fascinaba un puente sobre el que se sentaba un pescador, cada año en la misma posición, atrapando el pez que coleaba inmóvil en el aire. Más que los camellos o el pesebre, le gustaba a Martín aquel muñequito del pescador con un pie hacia delante, la espalda reclinada en el acto de sacar el pececillo del agua, en mínima perfección de porcelana.

El olor a jamón asado y a frijoles negros se sumaba al ronroneo de festividad. Sobre un aparador de la sala, la mamá de Martín había colocado dos fuentes con turrones de alicante y de jijona, un pote de aceitunas, varios quesos en una bandeja de plata, una cesta con nueces, avellanas, higos y dátiles. Abuela Antonia velaba por el pavo relleno. Los hombres de la familia bebían vino sin alborotos. Las tías cantaban, acompañando un disco de Pedrito Rico, "mi perrita pequinesa"...

A pesar de que casi llegaba el momento tan esperado de sentarse a la mesa, Martín insistió en salir a comprar el carro de bomberos, quizás por tratarse de otra miniatura perfecta, tan fascinante como el pescador sobre el puente. El tío Félix terminó, como siempre, por acceder y fueron caminando desde la casa de la abuela Antonia, bajando por la calle Amistad hasta doblar por la esquina de San Miguel que daba acceso a la juguetería por un costado.

En este punto se producía un salto, un hueco en la memoria y ya Martín se veía de regreso con la caja del juguete, tomado de la mano del tío Félix, por la calle Galiano, aparatosamente iluminada con fulgurantes orlas navideñas que cruzaban sobre la avenida. En Galiano estaban también las oficinas del *City Bank* donde trabajaba el papá de Martín. Cuando cruzaron frente a sus verjas, Martín los volvió a ver. Era un grupo de mendigos que se sentaban en los portales junto a la entrada del banco, la mamá, tres niños y un bebé en brazos de una muchachita. Siempre estaban allí, flacuchos y sucios, los niños agazapados en trapos y la mamá, con la cabeza gacha y la mano extendida. Martín se había acostumbrado a su presencia, darles unos centavos de limosna y continuar. Aunque esta vez lo sorprendieron. ¿También en Nochebuena había mendigos? ¿No tenían dónde pasar esa noche, para Martín tan portentosa? Martín iba hasta ese momento tan contento, con el coche de bomberos en los brazos, la mano segura del tío Félix indicando el camino, la familia que aguardaba para cenar, el Nacimiento con sus figurillas, plagio de la vida.

Cuando llegaron a la casa, Martín tiró el juguete en un rincón y corrió a contar aquello que había visto. Su abuela Antonia lo abrazó en silencio y se quedó rebuscando un consuelo. "¿Qué les pasa a ellos, abuela, quiénes son?", insistió Martín. "Unos pobres hijos del Señor", respondió la abuela Antonia, a modo de evasiva. "¿Cuál Señor?", preguntó casi gritando Martín, "¿Cómo puede haber un señor que abandone así a sus hijos en Nochebuena?". Ahí se cortaba el recuerdo.

El domingo pasado, Martín fue invitado por un matrimonio de colegas alemanes a la playa Santa María. Al fin había logrado deshacerse de las amarguras de días anteriores, el mar estaba delicioso, la compañía buena y, para completar, saboreaba una cerveza helada. Entonces se acercó la mujer. Contrastaba con los otros bañistas por la forma rara en que iba vestida, la cara se le torcía en una mueca y caminaba con un brazo encogido. Con un sonido gutural pidió "un peso" y añadió, con una entonación avergonzada, que padeció una enfermedad y se había quedado "así". Y ahora necesitaba un peso. ¿Un peso o un dólar?, fue la pregunta silenciosa que se hicieron los alemanes con la mirada. Martín sacó un billete de cinco pesos, pero la mujer no lo aceptó. "Un peso", insistía casi llorando, "un peso". Martín no tenía un puñetero peso suelto, ni mucho menos un dólar, en el caso que se hubiera decidido a dar esa mayúscula limosna. La mujer se alejó cabeceando sin aceptar los cinco pesos y el misterio quedó flotando con melancolía en la playa.

Un niño que simulaba pescar en la arena hizo el mismo gesto de aquel pescadorcito de porcelana en el Nacimiento navideño de la casa de la abuela Antonia y Martín se acordó del puñetero carro de bomberos y aquella pregunta de qué clase de señor podía ser aquel que abandonaba a sus hijos. Desde ese día no se le iba de la cabeza.

ESTELA

Cuando Estela dejó a Lucía en la estación para que tomara el tren para Manchester sabía que no se volverían a encontrar. El día anterior la había complacido en sus niñerías. Lucía, con tono de disculpa, confesó que traía dos anhelos. Uno, cruzar la calle Abbey Road como en la portada del disco y tomarse una foto frente al muro de *Apple* donde los Beatles dieron su último concierto en la azotea. Lucía sonrió a la cámara y levantó dos dedos en ángulo, como una "V" de victoria. Los mismos lugares en que se retrataban todos los turistas idiotas, se dijo Estela, con resignación. Dos, ir a Highgate Cemetery para visitar la tumba de Karl Marx. Santo cielo. Estela pensó que los cubanos de Cuba salían con cada majadería. Ellos, Estela y Oscar, aunque llevaban más de diez años en Londres, no se les había ocurrido jamás ir allí. Mientras caminaban por el cementerio, una ardilla corrió y se subió a un árbol. Lucía empuñó su añeja camarita Kodak y trató de capturar la imagen de la ardilla con su par de ojos brillantes. Según dijo, para asombro de Estela, "esta era la primera ardilla de su vida". Excepto estos comentarios, en todo el trayecto no hablaron mucho, casi todos los temas parecían escabrosos o podrían desatar la verborrea de Lucía, su ingenuo apasionamiento por cada detalle. Menos mal que no pidió ir de compras, esa situación hubiera obligado a Estela a inventar un pretexto. Cuando Lucía la abrazó, antes de subirse a su vagón, Estela le dijo desvaídamente que no dejara de llamarla a su regreso de Manchester. Lucía respondió "seguro", sin mucha convicción. Estela esperó a que el tren arrancara y eso fue todo. Misión cumplida.

Al regreso a la oficina se encontró con un recado de un tal Emilio que le traía noticias del padre. Estela se sintió desfallecer, otro cubano, otro antojado, qué querría hacer este, ¿visitar la casa de Sherlock Holmes en Baker Street?, ¿hacer el recorrido de Jack el Destripador por Whitechapel?, ¿visitar el museo de cera de Madame Tussaud?, ¿comprar pacotilla? No, no, no. Esto era demasiado. Estela no estaba para seguir perdiendo el tiempo con semejantes tonterías. De ningún modo iba a permitir que se le complicara la existencia si a todos los cubanos les daba ahora por pasar por Londres y llamarla. Ring ring, sonó el timbre y Estela salió ella misma al teléfono. Allí estaba el cubano, "sí, soy yo", aceptó Estela, "ah, gracias, en realidad tengo muy poco tiempo, puedo dedicarle solo unos minutos, trabajo cerca de la universidad, nos encontraríamos… sí, llegar aquí es muy sencillo, ¿tiene un mapa del metro a la mano? Bien. ¿Dónde está parando usted? Bien. Hasta aquí lo trae la línea Piccadilly, la azulita, esa misma, en dirección norte, hacia arriba, sí. Primero debe tomar la línea Central, la roja, sí, y cambiar en Holborn. No, cómo se va a perder, para nada, es muy sencillo, aunque sea la primera vez que lo haga, ya verá, y la parada, después de cambiar, es Russell Square. Ahí se baja y allí lo espero, sí, en la propia estación del metro. Bien. A las doce del día, no hay perdida posible, chao". Cuando Estela colgó se dio cuenta de que no habían amarrado cómo reconocerse, pero al cubano lo distinguiría ella sin necesidad de indicación alguna. A las doce lloviznaba con fuerza y de inmediato lo fichó, el único hombre sin paraguas ni sobretodo, apenas una chaqueta de aquellas rusas, empapada en aguanieve. El tal Emilio temblaba de frío y se veía asustado por su primer trayecto en metro. Había algunos cafetines abiertos, con calefacción, bebidas calientes y pasteles, mas Estela supuso que el cubano estaría muy corto de fondos y ella no podía seguir gastando de su propio bolsillo en cada personaje que pasara por ahí, así que lo abordó y sin permitirle dar muchas explicaciones, allí mismo y de pie, le aclaró que estaba muy apurada, que lamentaba no poder atenderlo, que quizás en otra ocasión. "No se preocupe, no quiero molestarla", se excusaba, apenado, el cubano, "estoy solo por unos días para un congreso y regreso otra vez a La Habana, le traje esta carta de su papá, no sé si usted querrá mandarle algo..." Estela parpadeó y no dijo nada, un tanto desconcertada. El cubano depositó un sobre en sus manos y se despidió. Estela lo vio desaparecer en dirección a los vagones y guardó el paquetico de Cuba en la cartera.

WILLIE

Miguelón es el recalcitrante del barrio. A la más mínima oportunidad, suelta la descarga completa de los tiempos del machadato y "las vacas flacas": por mucha hambre que se haya pasado, nunca, declara sin que nadie se lo pregunte, pero nunca, se había visto tanta guajirada, tanto latrocinio, ni tanta mala educación en La Habana, y que ser pobre no se convertía en pretexto para apropiarse de lo que a uno no le pertenece. Su madre que en paz descanse, la de Miguelón, se ganaba la vida como encargada de un solar en la calle Ánimas y allí no permitía ningún relajo, ni palabrotas, ni animales de granja, ni porquerías, todo brillaba de tan limpio que se podía comer en el piso; si se quedaba olvidada una herramienta o se dejaba caer una peseta en el patio común, ahí se quedaba hasta que aparecía el dueño.

Como Tilingo no tiene nada en qué ocuparse aparte de sacar sus chivos a pastar, se sienta a escucharlo y Miguelón aprovecha para que los vecinos se enteren y se vayan poniendo el sayo que les venga mejor. Aunque nadie le hace el más mínimo caso. "Viejo chocho, que se acabe de morir de una vez". "¿Quién se piensa que es?" "¿Acaso se cree el dueño del edificio?".

Y cuando Miguelón salía de su casa con rumbo a la panadería le tiraban piedras a sus ventanas y regaban con gasolina sus macetas. ¡Un modelo de comunidad!

Daontaon opina que Miguelón habla demasiado, el *único* que protesta por todo. Eso sí, muchos piensan igual que Miguelón y se muerden la lengua por temor a las represalias.

—¿Sí o no? Seguro que sí. Niño, todos esos **farsantes** tienen el tejado de vidrio y no hay techo que aguante esas pedradas.

Mi teoría es algo más compleja y trata sobre la plasmación y asentamiento de La Nata. La Nata se compone en su núcleo duro por vagos, maleantes y borrachos, aunque puede aceptar adhesiones ocasionales y pasajeras. La Nata tiene movimiento propio, independiente de las partes que la forman. A veces se traslada sin rumbo fijo hasta encontrar un área apta para su estacionamiento. Al tomar posesión de un territorio, este enclave puede durar horas, semanas o meses, según las condiciones ambientales y la lógica interna de La Nata. Si el lugar resulta adverso, La Nata se desplaza; aunque en caso de que logre establecer sus reales sin impedimentos notables, se instala de forma fija. Pueden existir varios tipos de Nata: de embriagamiento, de peña beisbolera, de depredación, de elaboración y ejecución de timos, de mesa de dominó, de fornicio, así como de otras variantes según la libérrima imaginación de sus dispositivos. Alguna Nata, incluso, puede absorber todos y cada uno de los módulos mencionados. La Nata adquiere un lenguaje propio y además se acompaña de sonido artificial.

La Nata de mi edificio ha decidido hacerle la vida imposible a Miguelón.

¿Qué suele pasar cuando un pollo cae en desgracia dentro del gallinero?

YUYA

Dice Yuya que el secreto de los platanitos maduros fritos consiste en que hay que sacarlos a tiempo. En el aceite hirviendo se dejan freír las tajadas solo hasta que comiencen a dorarse. Ya colocadas en el plato se oscurecen por sí solas. Dice Yuya que si se les deja adquirir un color algo oscuro mientras se fríen, al cabo de un rato al aire los platanitos maduros se ponen tan prietos, feos y duros que son incomibles.

Según Yuya, con la vida pasa lo mismo, hay que saber salirse a tiempo.

Luisa, la madrina de Lalita, dejó atrás las lámparas del Ten Cent, los pañuelos de colores en el pecho y su sonrisa dirigida a la clientela, para casarse con un militar de alta graduación. Se mudó para una casona de Miramar y nunca más la vieron por el solar de Los Muertos. Ni siquiera Yuya volvió a saber de Luisa ni Lalita de su madrina.

La Escuela San Alejandro también se perdió de allí. La trasladaron para Marianao y con ella se fueron los estudiantes que alegraban la calle Dragones. Los chinitos se quedaron sin papel de China para construir los papalotes. Tampoco se encontraba la pólvora necesaria en sus pirotecnias y dejaron de fabricar los minúsculos cohetes rojos que estallaban en cadena. El viejo que molía maíz se fue a un asilo. Se esfumaron los farolitos y las damiselas de ojos tristes. Cerró el bar y se apagó para siempre la vitrola. Tampoco se escuchaba más el piano. Ya el barrio chino no era ni la sombra de lo que fue, y dice Yuya que tomó la determinación de mudarse.

Shu estaba renuente; pero veía por los ojos de Lalita, que en unos pocos años cumpliría sus "quince". De ninguna manera podía celebrarse el arribo a tan señalada fecha en la azotea de la calle Rayo.

Según Yuya, los magos de la tierra de Shu escribían sus hechizos en color amarillo. Yuya se encomendó a Babalú, al Chinito de la Charada y a todos los santos del panteón cristiano. Después, para asegurar, envolvió la lista de sus deseos en una bata amarilla de Lalita. A los pocos días se desplomó la casa. Por fortuna, no hubo que lamentar a ningún paisano con heridas graves y además Yuya logró rescatar intactos los muebles y otros objetos. De inmediato, los beneficiaron con un apartamento de estreno, para ellos tres, en Alamar, por ese entonces, un reparto florido al este de La Habana, frente al mar, de edificios recién pintados, todos iguales.

Una vez más fue trasladado el altar y el arcón de roble con el ajuar de novia, herencia de la pobre Etelvina.

Como un islote de rareza, en unas casitas individuales construidas en los tiempos de antes, se había instalado una colonia de soviéticos y europeos del este. A las pocas semanas, Yuya se hizo amiga de Liudmila, la búlgara, adivinadora como ella.

DAONTAON

¡Apaga y vámonos! Vivir donde Daontaon vive, en "La Siberia", es lo último de los muñequitos. Donde el diablo dio las tres voces, el **culo**

del universo, puntualizaba en letras "negritas" Daontaon, sin ánimo de desdorar a las otras zonas del municipio.

El fin del mundo se acercaba y si ella seguía por ese camino la iba a pescar en compañía de los anormales de su edificio. De eso nada. Tenía que arreglárselas para mejorar su vida. Basta ya de viciosos, escritores, raperos y aberrados. Braulio, el nuevo jefe, su esperanza para ascender en la crónica social, no solo se mostró lampiño como un cerdito recién nacido. A la hora del cuajo le rogó lloriqueando a Daontaon que le pegara con un machete en el trasero, unas nalgas gordas y blancusas que daban terror pánico a mariasántisima.

¡Dar plan de machete!, dígame usted.

Plan de machete les daría Daontaon, sin que nadie tuviera que pedírselo, a los **farsantes** de su edificio. Ja. Había que verlos. Tan seriecitos allá por sus trabajos, tan formales, tan protocolares en la reuniones de vecinos y a las espaldas se pegaban los cuernos unos a otros: la rubia de la primera escalera apenas esperaba que se fuera el marido para hacer subir a su apartamento al mulato de la segunda; el flaco de la segunda se encerraba con la mulata de la tercera en el garaje; el calvo del último piso se entendía con la fulana de al lado; la fulana de al lado, en sus ratos libres, dejaba entrar al ingeniero; el negrón de la tercera hacía desfilar por su casa, en ausencia de su esposa, a cuanta chiquita de secundaria se le pusiera a tiro. Y luego, si te he visto no me acuerdo, ojos que te vieron ir, paloma torcaza, a lavar y guardar la ropa.

Por ni mencionar la chismografía, los chanchullos, reventas de cosas robadas, tráfico de marihuana, juegos al prohibido, brujerías, chantajes, sobornos y conspiraciones.

¿Quién iba a hacerle un cuento a ella, a Daontaon? *Nadie.*

Bien merecido se tenían que les cayese encima una lluvia de aerolitos asesinos, un pedazo del *Skylab* o que los exterminara la cola de un cometa.

Daontaon no estaba para *eso*. Qué va. De un tiempo a esta parte, se le ponían los nervios de punta. En la pesadilla de anoche, tenía que contársela a Micaela, Daontaon abría la gaveta de la cómoda y encontraba un brazo humano, ese brazo le parecía *muy pero muy* conocido; luego, en otro compartimiento, aparecía una pierna, ese pie se le figuraba tan *familiar;* finalmente, en el último cajón, reposaba el *torso* desnudo, arrugado, paliducho, y ese *torso,* ya lo reconocía, solo podía pertenecer a su vecina, a la propia Micaela.

¡Los fósforos! Tenía que inventar cómo salir de allí urgente. Ya quedaba poco para el fin del milenio y nada bueno podía esperar si seguía rodeada de aprovechados, descuartizadores y **farsantes.**

MUJER QUE HABLA SOLA EN EL PARQUE

De la tierra empezaron a salir unas garrapatas gigantes que se multiplicaron por todas partes, y saltaban de perro en perro, de gato en gato, de chivo en chivo. Cuando ya no hubo más perros, ni gatos, ni chivos, saltaron para arriba de la gente. Chuparon tanta sangre que flotaban en el cielo como globos y explotaban. Y entonces caía una lluvia de líquido rojo sobre la ciudad. Y La Habana se muere...

HERMI

Por seguir la broma de la infancia, Hermi se había cortado el pelo del mismo tamaño restringido que debía usar Tristán para entrar en las aulas, al estilo del actor en la película *Accatone* de Passolini. Rebuscó en las gavetas y encontró unos lentes montados al aire del bisabuelo. Luego se las ingenió para adaptar los cristales graduados de su miopía a aquella armadura de oro con tanto "swing", con tanta onda. También cometió el hallazgo de otros tesoros como una boquilla y un anillo de masonería.

¡Era una época gloriosa! Hermi vivía convencida de que formaba parte de aquella gloria y también de los sacrificios. Sentía lejanos los conflictos de la universidad contados por Tristán y ni por asomo calculaba que sus propios correligionarios pudiesen expulsarla del nido donde se fraguaba el grandilocuente futuro por ella elegido.

Pero sí: la consideraban ya una apestada. A sus espaldas, se iba cocinando el caldo para comerse viva a Hermi: "¿por qué no se pone maquillaje?", "¿vive con un hombre casado?", "¿y con quién más?", "¿para qué estudia inglés?", "¿y esa falda tan desvergonzada que usa?", "¿y esos espejuelitos raros y el pelo tan corto?", "¿fumar con una decadente boquilla?" "¿Extranjerizante?" "¿Desviada?".

La primera advertencia formal de atención ocurrió cuando mencionó al signo de Aries en uno de los guiones y salió al aire. El horóscopo, ¡qué es eso!, no se podía tolerar ese rezago del pasado, semejante superchería, peligrosísima.

La llamaron de inmediato a constar. Hermi seguía sin comprender tanto alboroto por tal nimiedad. Para embrollar más la situación, citó un pasaje de la Biblia en su alegato. No captó las miradas de inteligencia y las expresiones de contubernio en los rostros que expresaban a las claras: "esto no tiene arreglo". Intervino el tipo del "VW" invocando, a modo de defensa, festinación e ignorancia en Hermi. Ella lo miraba con los ojos agrandados, incapaz de entender que aquellos calificativos se emitieran como atenuantes de su conducta. Cuando fue a rebatirle, el tipo del "VW" la silenció con un severo "no interrumpa cuando yo esté hablando". Ofendida, Hermi se mordió la lengua. En consideración al tipo del "VW", la dirección fue tolerante y dejaron pasar esta vez solo con una amonestación pública, aunque le comunicaron que debía mejorar su apariencia personal.

Por ese entonces, último mes del año 1966, en la Cinemateca de 23 y 12 fue programado un ciclo sobre diez clásicos de la historia del cine, como para no perderse ni una película, dos horarios, a las seis de la tarde y a las nueve de la noche, por cuatro semanas. Tristán y Hermi hacían ambas colas. Entre una y otra, se comían un helado con un perro caliente en el Tropicream de la calle 21.

El día que tocaba en primera tanda el *Acorazado Potemkim,* cuando terminó la proyección salieron impresionados y debatiendo las imágenes. En la esquina, mientras mataban el tiempo, se encontraron con Guillermo, el amigo inseparable de Tomás, casi a punto de entrar en la pizzería Cinecittá. Guillermo sonreía de oreja a oreja y los ojos le brillaban.

Se saludaron como siempre y Guillermo los invitó a colarse con él y comerse una pizza antes de entrar a ver juntos *La quimera del oro*. Parecía una noche perfecta, de suerte…

Mientras comían, Guillermo intercalaba frases graciosas y comentarios agudos sobre el cine silente. De pronto se quedó mirando fijo la pizza como si fuera un hoyo insondable en medio de la mesa. "¿Saben de dónde vengo?". Nadie respondió la pregunta retórica. Guillermo insistió sin despegar los ojos de aquel hoyo que parecía abrirse como un boquete oscuro en la mesa. "¿Saben de dónde vengo?" Y sonrió. Luego añadió: "Del cementerio".

Hermi y Tristán sonrieron a su vez, en espera de una historia jocosa o atrevida. "Tomás se pegó un tiro". Y la horrible sonrisa apareció de nuevo.

Luego, entraron los tres a ver *La quimera del oro*. ¡Era una época gloriosa!

GERTRUDIS

En el bar de La Torre se reunía el grupo de vez en cuando, incluida La Difunta. Con una o dos libaciones, repasábamos los cuentos de cómo le iba a cada cual por su lado. La dispersión, después de terminar el preuniversitario, envió a algunos hacia la CUJAE a estudiar las ingenierías, otros para las becas de 12 y Malecón o F y Tercera, unos pocos para las universidades de otras provincias, dos o tres no se becaron.

Desde el edificio de F y Tercera, ¿se acuerdan?, si tocaba la suerte de vivir en un piso alto se veía toda la ciudad, las azoteas del Vedado, los rascacielos y la entrada de la bahía de La Habana. Al bar de La Torre no se podía ir todos los días, el bolsillo de estudiante apenas alcanzaba para helados de Coppelia en verano y chocolate caliente en invierno. Aedas griegos, ¡inspiren una oda dedicada a aquellos chocolates con churros del Carmelo! Cuando comenzaba el viento norte, nos apostábamos en una mesa de la terraza del Carmelo de Calzada, frente al Teatro Auditórium, con una taza de brebaje hirviente que solía durar hasta que cerrara la cafetería, mientras algunos de nosotros se preparaban para los exámenes de Literatura de "La Doctora", averiguar por qué calla Paolo, descifrar el escudo de Aquiles y preguntarse el significado del conjuro de las tres brujas que aparecían al comienzo de *Lady Macbeth*, *¿Cuándo volveremos a reunirnos las tres? ¿En el trueno, los relámpagos o en la lluvia? Cuando finalice el estruendo, cuando la batalla esté perdida y ganada.*

Mi sundae de chocolate en Coppelia y mi chocolate caliente con churros en El Carmelo, dos vicios de los años sesenta, consagrados a la altura venerable de "mi mojito en La Bodeguita y mi daiquiri en El Floridita".

Casi todo el tiempo restante a pan con croquetas, si acaso. Por mucho ahorro que se hiciese del "estipendio" universitario, doce pesos incrementados cada año hasta terminar la carrera con veinte, no alcanzaba para costear restaurantes como El Polinesio, El Emperador, Monseñor, El Conejito o La Roca, el circuito gastronómico vedadense por antonomasia. Por lo demás, podía resultar más fácil contactar con un extraterrestre que ligar un turno por teléfono. Cuando la rueda de la fortuna lo concedía, una anónima voz en la madrugada, tal Zeus Tonante en persona, otorgaba la merced de una reservación, una divina mesa para seis comensales. Allá nos íbamos locos de felicidad a saciar el apetito acumulado durante semanas.

¿Se acuerdan?, en plenos años sesenta, aquellos tan "lindos", los capitanes, *maitres,* se sentían con poderes celestiales y cuando olfateaban la pinta de estudiantes desarrapados y hambrientos procedían con menosprecio de dioses ante simples mortales que pretendiesen almorzar un bistec de palomilla con congrí y tostones en el Olimpo. Nos trataban como *Las de abajo*. Sin embargo, cuando hacía su aparición algún señorón de guayabera, doblaban el espinazo y se arrastraban serviles. Había sus excepciones, aunque en aquel entonces daba la impresión de que ningún mesero ni ningún capitán se había dado por enterado de la consigna de "igualdad", ni nada de eso. Y hablando de equidades, tampoco se permitía entrar a un restaurante a ninguna mujer vestida con pantalones, por muy elegante que estuviera.

En la beca de F y Tercera éramos iguales, iguales para El Reglamento,

iguales en subir por la escalera cuando se descomponía el elevador, iguales para la hora de entraAy6aaaaaaaaaaaaaaaaaaaaasYTI9O `
da, iguales para hacer la guardia de madrugada, iguales para comer los chícharos duros y el berro con lombrices, iguales para limpiar el área común ¿Se acuerdan? Como el agua no llegaba por las cañerías, y la mayor parte del tiempo el elevador estaba roto, el líquido para el baño y la limpieza tenía que ser carreteado en cubos a lo largo de veintitrés pisos. Pero nada de eso cansaba. Éramos jóvenes y con ganas de comernos el mundo, al estilo heroico de *Sandokana,* fuertes y puros. Y aunque por aquellas épocas se suscitaba mucha confusión y sobresalto con los deslindes entre la pureza y la impureza, *soy sucia, Milena, irremediablemente sucia, por eso armo tanto alboroto con la pureza,* ¿se acuerdan?, nuestra cita predilecta de esa tipa arisca y medio extraña que inventó una historia sobre una sabandija llamada *Gregoria Samsa,* a pesar de todo, nos sentíamos puros. Cómo no.

MARTÍN

Martín hojeó una de sus novelas programáticas, de las inspiradoras cuando se empantanaba. Recordó un truco de los escritores, una treta repetida que siempre surtía efecto. Se levantó y fue hasta la cocina, abrió el pote de polvo de café y calculó que alcanzaba para un brebaje pasable. Lavó la cafetera maquinalmente y la puso al fuego, meditando en ese final del *Gatopardo,* con el perro de la familia, en las últimas páginas disecado y convertido en felpudo, el pormenor banal de los inicios, sin justificación aparente que apenas podría tomarse como una digresión de relleno y mucho después, en el desenlace incluso, se desenmarañaba su significado, el revelado de símbolos, tal vez la médula misma de la cuestión. O la exasperación de un acto irracional, al modo existencialista. Por ejemplo, si él, Martín, escritor con pánico a la página en blanco, arrojase la cafetera hirviente contra la vecina Daontaon que movía su trasero por el trillo en dirección probable a la Casa de Cultura, podría interpretarse como una acción gratuita. Solo luego, cuando se fuesen develando los motivos, estas puñeteras semanas llenas de confusión, el episodio hubiera encontrado el acomodo, su razón de ser.

En lugar de lanzar el proyectil, Martín llamó a la oficina y advirtió sobre una gripe que lo tendría tumbado toda el día; luego se sirvió una taza de café, le añadió una cucharada de azúcar, otra de ron y, mientras lo bebía sorbo a sorbo, trasladándose de un lado a otro por el apartamento, se sintió menos embrollado. Un detalle significativo, eso necesitaba. Martín se acordó de cuando el tío abuelo Félix lo traía de regreso del colegio, jugando a no pisar la raya, el que cruza la raya pierde.

Como todas las tardes, el tío Félix había ido a buscar a Martín a la escuela, haciendo el recorrido de vuelta por la calle San Rafael, caminando desde el Parque Central hasta Amistad, mirando las tiendas, la cartelera del Cinecito, comprando cucuruchitos de maní, "luego llega a la casa y no come nada por los atracones que se da por ahí", peleaba la mamá de Martín, granizados de fresa, durofríos, agua mineral La Cotorra, barquillos de vainilla, batidos de chocolate, frituritas de malanga, churros, chicles bomba, bombones, pirulís, melcochas, avanzando los exploradores por la acera, sobre las losas de cenefas paralelas, serpientes de granito negro aplastadas contra el granito café con leche, flujo claro, peligroso, que se tragaba a los que no obedecen a sus tíos, donde pululaban tiburones, pirañas y cocodrilos. Por la zona oscura avanzaban los expedicionarios, sin mirar a los lados ni salirse de la franja, hasta llegar a salvo a las taquillas del Duplex y del Rex, sin pisar ni una sola vez el coto donde se emboscaban los monstruos de las profundidades. Si se pasaba de la raya era hombre muerto.

Último viernes de junio, fin de curso, el tío Félix pisó la raya. Para distraerlo, acaso suponía tan tonto a Martín, de buenas a primeras anunció que iba a escribir la historia de la familia. "Todo lo acontecido", dijo, "desde que llegaron de España".

¿La raya como lindero entre realidades y sueños? Obvio, puñeteramente obvio.

LOLA

Cuando Lola se despertó aquella mañana no reconoció su propia habitación. La luz apenas se filtraba entre los cortinajes. Las colgaduras de damasco rosado cubrían las ventanas desde los años cuarenta y, pasado tanto tiempo, habían ido cobrando un tinte grisáceo que opacaba aún más la escasa luminosidad. La cama matrimonial de cedro, herencia de sus padres, ancha y sólida, ocupaba todo el espacio, escoltada por el escaparate de tres puertas y la cómoda con el espejo arrasado con cicatrices del azogue. Sobre la pared despintada permanecían algunos cuadros que Lola se resistía a descolgar: la foto de boda con Evaristo, el bautizo de Sara, un retrato iluminado a mano de los tiempos en que la joven Lola se mostraba como una mujer desafiante y bella. Sobre la cómoda, colocados en orden, los objetos cotidianos: el frasco de colonia, el cepillo de pelo con mango de nácar, la vacía polvera de cristal de murano, los pomos con los medicamentos, la tijera, el cofre con los anillos, monedas, llaves en desuso y chucherías; una figurilla representando un fauno con una flautita en los mínimos labios de loza coloreada en tonos pastel y una Torre Eiffel en miniatura. ¿Quién le había regalado esa torrecita? Y aquellas medicinas... ¿a quién pertenecían? El cepillo de pelo con mango de nácar pertenecía a su madre. "¿Mamá?", llamó Lola en voz alta.

Antes de levantarse de la cama, Lola se dispuso a identificar los sonidos interiores de la casa, el tic tac del reloj de pared en el comedor, el goteo de la canilla en la cocina, el ronroneo apagado del refrigerador, el tableteo de las oxidadas bisagras de la ventanuca del baño y el susurro del aire por el pozo de ventilación.

Como hacía varios días que no había entrado agua al edificio, Lola decidió conservar las abluciones matinales en una palangana y con el agua espumosa regó la planta de manzanilla que atesoraba en una maceta en la terraza. Después cortó con la tijera unas ramitas y se preparó un té de desayuno.

Todavía no había terminado de tomarse la infusión cuando le

pareció escuchar unos toques en la puerta. Al mirar por la mirilla le costó reconocer a su prima Esperancita. Esa mañana, a Lola todo le resultaba extraño y ajeno.

—Entra, Esperancita, cuánto tiempo sin verte.

Esperancita se acomodó con timidez en el sofá y miró de reojo la taza de té que Lola sujetaba en la mano.

—¿Quieres un té? —le ofreció Lola.

Esperancita aceptó con un gesto de la cabeza y mientras se lo tomaba a sorbos pequeños y educados, Lola sufrió una bofetada en el rostro ante la contemplación de la estridente pobreza de su prima.

—¿Y eso tú por aquí tan temprano?

Esperancita levantó aquellos ojos ajados de solterona y la miró con mansedumbre.

—Vengo del cementerio —explicó—. Hoy es el Día de los Fieles Difuntos...

Lola convino en silencio, aunque en honor a la verdad, ni se acordaba. Sin embargo, en su fuero interno se sorprendió de que ya hubiera llegado noviembre.

—Fui al panteón de la familia. No tenía ninguna flor para llevar, Dios me perdone —Esperancita se excusó como si se tratara de un delito—, corté algunas ramas de un flamboyán y las puse allí. ¿Hace mucho tiempo que no vas?

Lola se encogió de hombros. Cómo contar los años que no ponía un pie en el cementerio. Sin poderlo evitar, le vino a la mente el sepelio del tío Sebastián, el padre de Esperancita, un asturiano cuyo rostro humillado daba alma a aquel mal recuerdo, archivado en lo profundo de su memoria.

El tío Sebastián se había infiltrado en su lista de malos recuerdos por la visita inesperada de Esperancita. Durante muchos años había sido el coime, el mozo de los billares del Centro Asturiano donde, gracias a su rectitud, regía la decencia, y las señoras acompañaban a sus maridos mientras se celebraban los partidos de billar o de dominó. A principios de los sesenta, cuando cerraron los billares, al tío Sebastián le faltaban unos meses para jubilarse y algún cretino lo mandó a barrer las calles de la Quinta Covadonga. Lola se lo encontró una vez y prefirió escabullirse sin dejar notar su presencia que, tal vez, hubiese atribulado más al anciano que barría con manos temblorosas. Luego, el tío Sebastián tuvo un derrame cerebral y quedó postrado en una cama. Esperancita lo cuidó devotamente durante diez años.

—¿Por qué no te quedas a almorzar conmigo? —Lola pensó en la última gallina que le quedaba—. Y hago un arroz con pollo.

A Esperancita se le iluminaron los ojos y asintió con aire avergonzado. En la cabeza gacha de su prima, Lola reconoció el mismo gesto abatido del tío Sebastián mientras pasaba la escoba con humildad y resignación por las callejuelas del hospital, recogiendo hojas secas y desechos.

MUJER QUE HABLA SOLA EN EL PARQUE

Palmas reales, palmeras y matas de coco nacieron y crecieron por todos lados, en las aceras, en los parterres. Y entonces la ciudad se volvió un bosque tan tupido de penachos que parecía de noche siempre. Y La Habana se muere…

LA INDIA

Los vecinos del barrio no olvidarían nunca aquella tarde de canícula pegajosa cuando llegaron, en acción fulminante, tres vehículos de la fuerza pública y se llevó a cabo la detención de Patrick Rivière, más conocido como "El Francés" o también como "El marindango de La India", acusado del homicidio de su esposa.

En el patio del solar se escucharon frases como "nada bueno se podía esperar de un extranjero", "La India se lo buscó" (e incluso un bando se inclinaba por el aquello de "se lo tenía bien merecido por puta", la verdad sea dicha). Clara Luz, llamada La Catedrática, cerró, por precaución, el centro espiritual y retornó a su puesto laboral, una imprenta del Instituto del Libro.

De los trámites policíacos se fueron filtrando pocas novedades. Aunque se hicieron numerosos interrogatorios, a El Francés no se le sacó nada más de lo ya sabido. Insistía en que había llegado a Cuba como profesor de lenguas gracias a unos convenios con una universidad francesa, su maletincito negro solo contenía prospectos turísticos e inocuos ejemplares de *Le Monde Diplomatique* y repetía la misma historia una y otra vez, si bien, con el transcurrir de los días, su actitud empezó a resultar desconcertante. No intentaba defenderse y su mirada, en principio desdeñosa, se fue apagando hasta convertirse en un rescoldo gris, apenas encendido a ratos, sobre todo al escuchar el nombre de María Antonieta. El Francés no salió de su apatía, como si hubiese perdido noción de la grave inculpación recaída sobre su persona.

Entretanto, como un rompecabezas, habían ido apareciendo por distintos sitios del litoral norte de La Habana, los miembros cercenados de un cuerpo de mujer, limpios en lo que cabe, empacados en el mismo papel de estraza y anudado con los inevitables alambres. Mas, excepto los propios del pubis, no se encontró ningún vello, objeto ni seña exterior.

Sin nuevas pistas, a los investigadores encargados del caso se les presentó otro contratiempo severo cuando fueron halladas, en un recoveco de rocas costero del llamado "Reparto de Pastorita", las dos manos carbonizadas, sin rastro de huellas digitales y en el clásico atildado envoltorio. No dejaba de llamar la atención la inclinación perversa del criminal hacia al área del este habanero, donde se apareaban zonas turísticas como Bacuranao, sitios históricos como Cojímar y barrios excrementales como Alamar.

Pero ni la cabeza ni el muslo derecho aparecían.

Patrick Rivière, por falta de evidencias probatorias, fue liberado bajo fianza, aunque le retuvieron su pasaporte y limitaron sus movimientos al perímetro de la panadería, bodega, puesto de vegetales y las "shoppings" de Centro Habana.

A cada rato, se presentaba un niño tembloroso, una mujer espantada, un hombre lívido, con un paquete de papel estraza entre los brazos. Ya todos sabían lo que aquello podría significar, sin embargo, fueron pasando las semanas y la cabeza cortada de María Antonieta (nunca mejor dicho) seguía sin aparecer.

Ante tal inconveniente, los investigadores forenses acudieron a un estudio exhaustivo del cadáver de la víctima, acoplando fragmentos, haciendo mediciones, enjugando líquidos, hasta llegar a la conclusión de que, en efecto, el cadáver pertenecía sin duda una mujer entre los veinte y treinta años, mestiza, de estatura mediana y complexión fornida, además de otras particularidades más específicas que correspondían todas con las señas de la escamoteada India.

El muslo derecho apareció en las ruinas de unas taquillas abandonadas de la playa Boca Ciega. Una furtiva pareja de adolescentes del sexo masculino, buscando un sitio para protegerse de un aguacero inclemente, según declaración jurada en la Estación de Policía de Guanabo, se pegaron un susto al toparse con el anca maloliente de "La Descuartizada del Municipio Habana del Este", como ya se le conocía.

Y aunque algunos todavía se resistían a creerlo e imaginaban a La India con todos sus pedazos en su lugar, soleándose en otras arenas (de "Miami Beach", valga la aclaración) tuvieron que rendirse a lo aparente cuando la madre, entre alaridos y gimoteos, reconoció un pálido rastro, cicatriz en el muslo que su hija se había procurado con una lata a medio abrir de carne rusa, marca que el minucioso asesino, tan empeñado en desaparecer cualquier vestigio de identificación, parecía haber pasado por alto.

No quedaba sino esperar la cabeza.

YUYA

Dice Yuya que, al principio, le gustaba Alamar. Sobre todo a media tarde. Con un termo de té polaco y galleticas de sabor a cartón que se conseguían de estraperlo gracias a unos vecinos hebreos de su edificio, se iba con Liudmila y Lalita a la costa, a tomar un baño de mar en la "playita de los rusos". El agua se mantenía cristalina y, si lo pretendían con convicción, hubieran podido ilusionarse que habitaban en una isla desierta.

Mientras caía el sol a la izquierda, Lalita buscaba caracoles, erizos y fósiles marinos, Yuya miraba la línea del horizonte que cambiaba de tonalidad según avanzaba el crepúsculo y Liudmila contaba de su infancia después de la guerra en su natal Sofía y hacía vaticinios para el futuro de la isla.

Según Yuya, Liudmila aclaraba que para esas profecías no necesitaba de bolas de cristal, de pirámides mágicas ni de naipes, viniendo, como ella venía, de "allá", y alargaba la mano blanquísima en dirección opuesta al sol que se sumergía en las aguas del Golfo.

Liudmila llegó a Cuba, como tantas, detrás de un joven mulato que conoció cuando este pasaba un curso de ingeniería hidráulica. A los pocos años se aburrió de ella, sin embargo Liudmila eligió quedarse bajo el sol caribeño. Además, como le confesó a Yuya, tenía problemas en su lejana casa: un apartamento minúsculo, muchos hermanos, cuñadas, sobrinos y hábitos severos de conducta. Aquí vivía con su estilo, a su aire, en una coqueta casita decorada con carteles turísticos sobre La Habana, con jardín y a tres pasos del mar; disfrutaba de bonos para comprar en la tienda del Focsa productos ya exóticos como carne y queso; y, mediante un comedido trasiego de latas de alimentos y las adivinaciones con las barajas españolas, ampliaba su sueldo actual como traductora. Bulgaria quedaba remota y ella vivía enamorada de todos los cubanos. Allí era una más del montón y aquí se había transformado en "La Búlgara que echaba las cartas", "la extranjera", la única, o casi.

Dice Yuya que le hacía gracia el aplatanamiento de Liudmila, su argot barriotero con acento europeo, su gusto por el chachachá, su "entra y sale" de novios y su afán de recolectar todo el oro posible, incluso el de las dentaduras.

Unos años después, Lalita entró en la universidad para estudiar Biología y sus compañeros del aula comenzaron a venir a estudiar a casa de Yuya y Shu.

Dice Yuya que la crisis tuvo lugar en el segundo año de la carrera. Alguno de sus amigos se fue con el chivatazo, hubo una delación a las autoridades competentes y en una tumultuosa reunión amenazaron a Lalita con la expulsión de la universidad por culpa de las creencias familiares, el oscurantismo en que había sido educada y que, como cargo agravante, sus padres, ellos, Yuya y Shu, actuaban como practicantes, instigadores, adoradores, no de uno, sino de todos los cultos imaginables, en eso consistió la denuncia que desquició a Lalita.

Ya Yuya lo había visto venir. La visión de un pez boqueando, con la cabeza del haitiano, le indicó que algo estaba por pasar.

Lalita llegó como loca a la casa. Entre las imputaciones que le hicieron de "desviacionismo ideológico" y "blandenguería", lo que más le dolió fue que acusaran de antisociales ¡a su familia completa! Y le exigieron que, como primer paso para una demostración de su interés por participar en la formación del estudiante *nuevo* que exigían los tiempos, una prueba del principio de su redención, su regeneración, como vía de reintegración al universo de los virtuosos, debía renegar, destruir, desaparecer el altar, foco de contaminación y corrupción de los ideales más puros.

Lalita no quería ni oír hablar de semejante cosa. Que se metieran la universidad por donde les cupiese.

Dice Yuya que las circunstancias ameritaron reconcentrar todos los poderes posibles. Pidió ayuda a Liudmila y a sus antepasados gitanos. Hizo una visita en el cementerio a su pobre abuela para que incorporara en la operación a los dioses del panteón celta. Pidió una asistencia al espíritu solidario de Etelvina. Rogó a Sanfancón, a Babalú, a San Lázaro y le hizo una promesa a la Virgen de la Caridacita de llevar a Lalita al Cobre. Convocó al haitiano errante y le suplicó que colaborara. Y, por último, de común acuerdo con Shu, mudó una vez más el altar, esta vez para el closet del último cuarto y allí se quedó escondido, hasta más ver.

Lalita, a regañadientes, obedeció a Yuya y simuló su conversión. Tres años después se graduó de bióloga marina. ¡Jesús mil veces!

HERMI

Por mucho tiempo, Hermi había sentido fascinación por un extraño cuadro que colgaba detrás del mostrador para préstamo de libros, en la sala de consulta de la Biblioteca Nacional. No sabía el nombre del autor, ni tenía idea de cuál sería la iglesia pintada en el lienzo, aquella iglesita colorida que parecía flotar en una nube, bordada de palmas, campanas, faroles, rejas, unas incongruentes botellas, cruces fantasmagóricas que se sobreponían a la fachada, y una paloma que ascendía. Una iglesia volátil como un ave, en su transparencia y gracilidad. ¿Quién sería capaz de captar con tanta sutileza la espiritualidad? Hermi amaba aquel cuadro y hubiese sido capaz de secuestrarlo con tal de alcanzar la posesión, frente a su mirada para siempre.

Tristán le había advertido que no fuera a perderse la muestra que se exhibía en el Museo de Bellas Artes. Hermi conocía ese tonillo suyo, exultante y presumido. Y también la inutilidad de pretender que adelantara las razones. A Tristán le encantaba sorprenderla. No obstante, le previno que se trataba de un pintor desaparecido misteriosamente durante un viaje trasatlántico en su regreso de París a La Habana. Acosta León, con un poco más de treinta años, abandonó por mar el viejo continente en diciembre de 1964 y nunca llegó a tierra firme. Tristán no se conformaba con la teoría de accidente o suicidio y elaboraba una complicada trama de celos, envidias y pasiones nefandas que culminarían con un empujón criminal hacia las aguas del océano. ¡Borrado del mapa!

El tipo del "VW" insistió en acompañar a Hermi a visitar el museo, tenía esas "horitas" a su disposición, la esposa no lo esperaba temprano ese sábado. A regañadientes, aceptó ir con él, no tenía deseos de complacerlo después de su actitud en la reunión de vilipendios, arrogante hacia ella y lacayuna con los superiores, cuidando su posición y sacrificando a Hermi en aras de... ¿qué?

Había entrado un norte de febrero y lloviznaba agua helada. El tipo del "VW" parqueó el auto en una distante callejuela para que nadie lo viera bajarse en su compañía y dispuso que Hermi caminara sola hasta al museo y luego se encontrarían en el vestíbulo, como "de casualidad". Tantos subterfugios para no ser descubierto como adúltero ya no la divertían, resultaban más bien patéticos. Empezaba a reconocerlo como realmente era, buen amante, pero necio y fanfarrón.

Apenas Hermi había recorrido unos pasos en la galería, se topó con ¡el cuadro de la iglesita! Allí, en la exposición de Acosta León, estaba la pintura, tan cerca de sus ojos que Hermi se sintió flotando también por aquel salón. ¡La Iglesia de Paula! Ese era el templo representado en el cuadro. Emocionada y presintiendo una jornada de revelaciones avanzó entre carricoches, guaraperas, barcos zoomorfos, rostros de ojos tristes, colombinas, tranvías, carruseles, tiñosas, carretillas monstruosas, semáforos, juguetes, ruedas, tornillos, hélices, palmas; y cafeteras y coladores, las únicas *catedrales de los cubanos*.

Ahí estaba en su plenitud, encerrado en un recinto de La Habana, el concepto del arte con mayúscula para Hermi. El drama de la vida estallando en una carcajada altisonante, irónica; la humildad de los objetos rearmados en una dimensión aterradora y risueña a la vez; amor y odio, creación y destrucción, agua y fuego, goce y sufrimiento, soledad y humanidad.

Sin percatarse de lo que sucedía, el tipo del "VW" aspiraba a adelantar la visita con rapidez para apurar el mal trago de la vista de aquellos artefactos incomprensibles y fuera de toda realidad racional, pura basura. De tanto en tanto, intentaba acelerar el paso de ella, sin resultado alguno. Su irritación fue aumentando en la medida que transcurría el tiempo y se alejaba la posibilidad de disfrutar un rato a solas. Se preguntaba por qué tenía que perder el tiempo con aquella mocosa decadente. La miró de lejos y la vio mal vestida y medio turulata, sintió bochorno y, a la par, aumentó su deseo de dominarla. Unas cuantas "veces" más y se deshacía de esa chiflada. No podía poner en riesgo su matrimonio por semejante rollo.

A la salida del museo, caminaron separados hacia el auto tal si se tratara de dos desconocidos. Él se sentó primero y desde el timón le hizo una seña de que subiera. Hermi lo miró, negó con la cabeza y, sin palabras, le hizo un gesto de ruptura, la palma de la mano derecha deslizándose con brusquedad sobre el dorso de la izquierda, de "esto se acabó", luego le dio la espalda y empezó a alejarse. El tipo del "VW", estupefacto, arrancó el auto con rabia. ¿Quién se creía ella que era para dejarlo así como así?

Mientras caminaba bajo el goteo helado, Hermi sintió como si se estuviera hundiendo, desvaneciéndose en las aguas de un mar hostil.

MUJER QUE HABLA SOLA EN EL PARQUE

Un edificio se puso bravo y empujó al de al lado, y el de al lado empujó al otro, y el otro empujó al de más allá. Y entonces se armó un dale que dale hasta que todos, uno por uno, se fueron cayendo. Y La Habana se muere...

ESTELA

A tramos, la avenida Brompton Road se encontraba cubierta de parchones de nieve sucia y áspera. Estela decidió ir de compras sabatinas. La nevada caída el día anterior se había convertido en fastidiosas plastas grises. Las botas se le hundían hasta el tobillo en una escarcha, a veces compacta como granito, a veces licuosa. Estela entró a los almacenes Harrods como lo estaban haciendo buena parte de los transeúntes, algunos a comprar, otros a entibiarse y a protegerse por un rato de la humedad, otros a disfrutar de los decorados navideños. Los tránsitos techados de la enorme tienda, permitían recorrer toda la mole sin pasar frío alguno. Cada cierto trecho, las guirnaldas rojas y los árboles artificiales engalanados con bolitas color perla provocaban una impresión de castillo de fantasía. La muchedumbre cumplía con entusiasmo sus adquisiciones con el pretexto de la epifanía, a pesar de que los precios se colocaban a alturas estratosféricas. Estela buscó un agua de colonia para después de afeitar y pidió que se la envolvieran en papel de regalo, Oscar estaría a punto de llegar en fecha para las fiestas y quería ponerle su obsequio junto a la chimenea. Debía comprarle también algo al padre, pero después de darle muchas vueltas al asunto supuso que sería tirar el dinero, qué iba a ponerse él de vestir en aquel sitio, Estela prefería ni siquiera darle un nombre, donde se encontraba ahora. Ni pensar en un pijama de seda como los que se ofrecían en el departamento de hombres, eso no sería más que desperdiciar una considerable cantidad de dinero. Mejor le llevaba, cuando fuera de visita a La Habana, algunos retazos de tela para que alguna modista del barrio le hiciera cualquier vestimenta útil. Estela sintió la necesidad urgente de regalarse a sí misma un presente arrebatador. Vagabundeó en la planta baja entre los perfumes de marca y los relojes, luego se paseó, solo para admirar, por las modernidades de la computación, subió y curioseó entre los enseres domésticos, convenía en que poseía de todo lo anterior más de lo puramente imprescindible, así que, por último, en la sección de ropa de invierno eligió una chaqueta de cuero curtido color beige. Al mero tacto se sentía una maravilla, delicada, tersa, cremosa, con apenas unas rugosidades sutiles. A la verdad, costaba un ojo de la cara, pero la quería poseer. De inmediato. Después de salir del probador y pagarla con la tarjeta de crédito, guardó su abrigo de uso en la bolsa y se estrenó la prenda. Mientras buscaba una de las salidas de Harrods, se sintió segura y elegante. De tanto en tanto se deslizaba la manga por la nariz para apreciar el inconfundible aroma a piel nueva, a flamante objeto todavía no contaminado por sudores o emanaciones de la vida urbana. Camino de regreso, empezó otra vez a nevar. Estela bordeó con premura el parque y entró en el edificio caldeado. Había planeado pasarse el fin de semana en París, e incluso llegó a hacer la reservación en el Eurotúnel, aunque el mal tiempo le hizo desistir. Se anunciaban temporales y ventiscas en la "meteó" y la gracia de París consistía en caminarlo. Para permanecer encerrada en un hotel mejor se quedaba en su cálido apartamento de Bloomsbury. Ya en su habitación, Estela se cambió la chaqueta por un grueso albornoz y se sirvió una copa de cognac para entrar en calor. Afuera había arreciado la caída de los copos de la nevisca sobre la cancha de juego pavimentada y protegida de intrusos por una cerca metálica. En unos minutos se revistió de una virginal capa que parecía una parcela de algodón escoltada por arbolones desnudos como un regimiento de puyas erizadas. Inesperadamente, de seguro por culpa de la visita de Lucía, le vino a la memoria el malhadado recuerdo de La Difunta. La Difunta siempre hablaba de conocer la nieve y de ir a París, aquellas eran una de sus tantas impertinencias ideológicas, de las que más le chocaban a Estela. Esa forma de ser la había llevado a la ruina.

DAONTAON

Daontaon tenía esa mañana la cabeza malísima. Apenas salía de la casa, se topó con la cara de idiota del tal Martín, vigilándola desde el balcón. Nada más que eso le faltaba, que la supervisaran. ¿Será chivatón? Ja. Capaz que sí.

Aquel sueño de la noche antepasada... Daontaon matando caracoles de tierra en la azotea del edificio. **Crash,** sonaban los carapachos aplastados bajo la suela de sus zapatos. **Crash y crash, crash** y más **crash,** hasta el amanecer. ¡Ave María Santísima!

Luego, no la tranquilizaron para nada las interpretaciones que le dio Yuya, la vidente. La tal lechuzona le mostró a Daontaon una cartulina con el dibujo de un chino viejo y feo.

—El caracol reside en su manga derecha, ¿lo ves? —le explicó, relamiéndose de devoción.

Nada. Daontaon no veía nada en aquel papelucho roído por polillas, pero dijo que sí para salir de *eso.*

—Soñar con caracol avisa la llegada del Rey de Copas —precisó la vidente—. "Hombre rubio, modelo de probidad, cercanía de las artes".

Ja. Para "las artes" estaba Daontaon. ¿Y el supuesto "modelo de probidad"? ¿Dónde estaba ese marciano, a ver? Ni en Marte. Como para morirse de la risa si estuviera de ánimo.

Según su propia interpretación de los sueños, en caso de que llegara un Rey de Copas se trataría de un artista borracho. Seguro, seguro. Y los caracoles, atraso y encierro.

Así mismo fue. Daontaon estuvo toda la noche de ayer en la Estación de Policía por culpa de un pintor de manchones y garabatos (ahí estaba el "hombre rubio, modelo de probidad"). Lo tenían encerrado con otro que lo ayudó a transportar los huesos del padre. Hágame usted el favor. El esqueleto del difunto padre del *artista,* que radicaba originalmente en un panteón prestado desde hacía cuatro años, tuvo que ser removido de su reposo por vencimiento del plazo en el hospedaje mortuorio. Después de la exhumación y sin tener sitio donde ubicar los restos paternos, el *artista* y su compinche en los hechos se tomaron unos cuantos tragos para sobrellevar la tristeza (¡ahí estaban las Copas!) y cayéndose de la borrachera, viajaron de noche en bicicleta por toda la ciudad con la intención de llegar a Regla donde el acólito poseía un patio con tierra, pedaleando el socio, el artista en la parrilla y el padre en una mochila. Interceptados por la autoridad y conminados a declarar qué portaban dentro del bulto, el pintor confesó que se trataba de **un muerto.** "¡UN MUERTO!", se sorprendió el vigilante. "Sí, mire, mire, es la osamenta de mi señor padre, que en gloria esté", y el artista, ni corto ni perezoso, desempaquetó la calavera ante los ojos severos del policía, "Muéstreme el conduce", solicitó el uniformado. "¿El conduce?", se asombraron en su turno los susodichos. "El conduce", continuó imperturbable el patrullero, "el permiso para trasladar un objeto de cualquier naturaleza desde un sitio a otro". No, no tenían ningún "conduce" para su padre. Pues todos, incluido el esqueleto, presos.

¡Atraso y encierro!

Daontaon estuvo hasta la medianoche en la estación convenciendo al oficial para que los dejaran libres, fíjese, compañero, que se trata de una *personalidad* del municipio. La "personalidad del municipio" dormía la mona y roncaba, abrazado a la mochila con los huesos de su difunto.

Si cuando ella lo decía: La Habana está llena de gente trastornada. Y se reconcentran en Alamar.

MARTÍN

—¿Una transfusión de sangre? ¿A mí? ¿Para qué? —preguntó la mamá de Martín.

—*Para verte mejor* —respondió Martín con tono grandilocuente, reproduciendo la frase del Lobo ante Caperucita. Aunque pretendía ser ligero, inocente, su voz sonaba artificial, tan fraudulenta como el manuscrito que intentaba escribir. "Voy a hacer el almuerzo" fue la respuesta de ella y salió de la habitación, el cuarto de los padres de Martín, con los rostros amarillentos de los abuelos colgados en la pared, un cuadro con una ninfa reclinada en un triclinio, revoloteada por angelitos encuerusos y una foto suya, de Martín, disfrazado de pirata. Por algún sitio del armario todavía quedaban retazos del disfraz pergeñado por la mamá de Martín, de satín negro y rojo, tapaojos, pañuelo en la cabeza, una capa con la calavera y los huesos cruzados, una camisa de seda blanca y una simulación de botas en hule negro.

Abrió el escaparate y se puso a registrar las gavetas, llenas de documentos ya inútiles, sus calificaciones de la escuela primaria en el Plantel Jovellanos, las condecoraciones en "Letras" y en "Ciencias", las invitaciones a las fiestas de fin de curso, conservadas con esmero por la mamá de Martín, todo caduco e inservible. Entre tantos papeles viejos, Martín encontró una foto antiquísima, impresa sobre cartón y con rostros fantasmales que se allegaban de un pasado muy lejano. ¿Quiénes fueron estos? ¿Qué habrá sido de ellos?

La mamá de Martín regresó de la cocina y se sentó a su lado. Martín tenía muchas preguntas que hacerle y no se atrevía, atenazado por una nueva variante de pánico: la palabra hablada consumaba los hechos, descubría la angustia por el poco tiempo que les quedaba juntos, aceleraba su partida, su ausencia. Daba esa impresión. De qué manera rellenar, sin embargo, los espacios en blanco de su historia. Ella, su madre moribunda, la última que podía contarle de su pasado. Como un puñetero vampiro se sentía.

La abuela Antonia y el tío Félix viajaron a América durante los primeros meses de la Guerra del Catorce. Venían de un caserío, San Juan de Parres, situado a la vera de un polvoroso camino de tierra que desviaba el rumbo a la derecha, unos pasos antes de cruzar el puentecillo medieval a la entrada del poblado Cangas de Onís, dominado por el monte Auseva, la ermita de la Virgen y la real tumba astur. A la aldea regresaban, forrados de dinero, los llamados "indianos", se hacían construir unas mansiones extravagantes con jardines de palmas y artilugios del trópico, y se sentaban en el café de la plaza a contar fascinaciones de aquellas Indias donde las pepitas de oro se cogían bajitas como las frutas. Así brillaba en la distancia "la Perla del Caribe", aquella isla Juana hollada por los ancestros, conquistadores, armeros, navegantes, labriegos, segundones, clérigos, donjuanes y prófugos de la justicia, esa "Cubita la Bella" de donde arribaban hablillas de enriquecimientos relampagueantes, mulatas musicales y un clima de paraíso, allende el mar, esa tierra soñada de pectorales de oro que nunca aparecieron por ninguna parte y sí bodegas, tintorerías, sastrerías, la "Mayor de Las Antillas" con sus cotorras y sus palmeras, la "Llave del Golfo", simbolizada en el enhiesto Morro de los daguerrotipos que acarreaban los indianos hasta las faldas del Santuario de la Covadonga, los bisabuelos descendientes del orgulloso rey Pelayo, de aquellos astures que nunca se rindieron a los moros. Y en medio de tanta hambre y tantas guerras, en la tierra lejana de Cuba tal parecía que el oro caía como el maná.

Puro pasado. Martín anotó la idea como probable título. O quizás *Quimérico ayer.*

YUYA

Dice Yuya que el ambiente se puso malo. Más malo que en el solar de Los Muertos, que ya era mucho decir. Alamar perdió su imagen florida y se llenó de basurales, facinerosos, plagas, animales hambrientos y personas cuyas vidas aparentaban haberse estancado.

Poco a poco se fueron despidiendo los rusos con sus samovares y pepinillos encurtidos. También los chilenos y la familia hebrea del edificio. Los vecinos de puerta con puerta construyeron una balsa y en ella llegaron hasta los cayos de la Florida, del mismo modo que muchos conocidos de Yuya, incluido su dentista. Liudmila le tenía pánico a los aviones; no obstante, según Yuya, de una isla nadie puede irse caminando y Liudmila terminó también por decir adiós.

Dice Yuya que la algarabía de matanzas de cerdos y chivos, fragores no propios de la urbe, se volvió cosa de todos los días y estaba obligada a cerrar las ventanas a cal y canto para escapar de los aullidos que le rajaban el corazón. ¡Jesús mil veces! En la impunidad de la noche, las botellas de cerveza salían volando desde los apartamentos altos y se estrellaban contra la acera. Los edificios se destiñeron y las barandas de las escaleras, oxidadas, se cayeron a pedazos. Las áreas verdes fueron pisoteadas y trasmutadas en páramos de tierra e inmundicias. Los estropicios, fechorías, trifulcas y groserías convirtieron a Alamar en un gigantesco conventillo patibulario. En una favela residencial, en un "llega y pon" de mampostería, según Yuya. Ya ni era seguro ir a la antigua "playita".

Dice Yuya que Lalita regresó de una de sus tantas excursiones científicas con una amiga que no tenía donde vivir. Lalita convenció a Yuya y a Shu de que podía alojarse con ella en su propio cuarto. Yuya no estaba muy conforme con esos arreglos, pero si a Lalita se le metía algo en la cabeza no había manera de hacerle comprender las conveniencias.

Según Yuya, cuando le habló a Lalita del arcón de cedro, herencia de la pobre Etelvina, con el ajuar de novia, listo y preparado para su boda, Lalita la miró con una expresión extraña y le respondió que ese ajuar tendrá que sentarse a esperar. La respuesta sorprendió a Yuya por lo tajante, y por cierta sombra de ironía, desconocida en el trato con su hija. Shu levantó una ceja y, como de costumbre, no opinó ni se sorprendió de nada.

Un domingo, Lalita y su amiga fueron a la costa a tomar el sol. Al cabo de un rato regresaron lesionadas. Unos tipejos desconocidos les cayeron a golpes. La amiga de Lalita tenía un ojo morado y el labio partido que sangraba profusamente. No paraba de llorar y se encerró en la habitación. Lalita sufrió arañazos, puntapiés y una herida en la frente, pero dice Yuya que lo que más la asustó fue la mirada en los ojos de Lalita. Por más que Yuya le preguntó, se trancó en un silencio hosco.

Dice Yuya que, después de mucho pensar y darle vueltas al asunto, unos días más tarde aprovechó que había entrado un norte, se abrigó bien y se fue a recorrer la costa. La orilla en invierno estaba desierta, las olas batían contra los arrecifes y el salitre iba cubriendo la piel de su rostro que le picaba a causa del fuerte sol. Sin embargo, el viento helado enfriaba los pensamientos. Yuya caminó sobre los dientes de perro observando los caracoles, las gorgonias, las algas secas, las latas vacías y la infinidad de maderos. El mar expulsaba sin piedad lo que no consideraba aceptable.

Dice Yuya que decidió sacudirse de encima toda esa tristeza y tomó la decisión de irse. Dejar atrás Alamar. Ni en balsa ni en avión, sino en un camión de mudanza. Permutar para el Vedado.

GERTRUDIS

Puros y distintos, cómo no. *Canto a mí misma, El retrato de la artista adolescente, La gran Meaulnes, La idiota, Tonia Kruger, Demiana, Prometea encadenada, Juana Cristobalina.*

A lo que vamos. La comparsa, cuando se mueve en bloque, no suele tolerar a los solistas, a las excepciones de las reglas, *la estrella que alumbra y mata*, ni que se les restriegue en la cara su uniformidad. Primero fueron las *iluminaciones* y después, a pagar el precio de la ingenuidad, no tardaría en llegar una *temporada en el infierno... ¡Condenados, si yo me vengase!*, invocábamos como conjuro los versitos de aquella niña francesa, *yo soy otra*, que encubriera su genialidad bajo el nombre de un primo pedante y aventurero. Para ser franca, nunca me convenció aquella traducción, sonaba demasiado arcaica, bruñida. Hubiera preferido ¡Malditos, si yo...!. O mejor, todavía más claro, *¡hijos de puta, si yo me vengara!*

¿Alguien escuchó alguna vez la historia de los gorriones chinos? Pues bien, como la superpoblación de gorriones afectaba las cosechas, se les ocurrió la solución de poner a todos los chinos, durante horas y horas, a golpear una lata con un palo. Mantenían así a los gorriones volando, espantados, sin posarse en ningún sitio, hasta que caían desfallecidos de cansancio, y morían apaleados, miles de millones de gorriones. ¿Habrá sido auténtico este cuento? No sé, pero cada vez que recuerdo los años sesenta me salta a la mente.

Durante esa década florecieron las prohibiciones. ¿Se acuerdan o no se acuerdan? Desde aquella época, por poner un ejemplo, ninguna mujer ha podido entrar sola o acompañada por una amiga a un bar. ¡Ni aunque se tratara siquiera de su propia madre! Penélope y Telémaca escribían la *Odisea* mientras Ulises se iba de parranda con los amigotes.

Por ese entonces se dedicaba mucho esfuerzo social para mantener a las estudiantes universitarias con el virgo intacto. No solo el pelo largo masculino era motivo de discusión en asambleas y comités de base de los *Jóvenes Comunistas,* también la virginidad de "las hembras", ¿se acuerdan? Cuando alguna la perdía, y gracias a un chivatazo se hacía público su extravío, lo más seguro fuese que le costara la beca y, según los agravantes, incluso hasta los estudios. Si los hechos ocurrían en el extranjero, a la pecadora la enviaban de regreso castigada deshonrosamente, expulsada. Con el peor de los sumarios, cómo no, si en el amorío estaba implicada alguna exótica alma eslava.

A los varones, por su parte, también se les prohibía andar con atributos considerados "feminoides" como sandalias, zapatos sin medias o aretes. Tampoco se les permitía vestirse con pantalones estrechos, ni pelarse al rape o tener un "spet drum", y mucho menos dejarse el bigote o la barba.

Acuérdense, no se podía usar minifalda ni espejuelos negros, ni practicar yoga, ni colgarse crucifijos, ni gorras de peloteros del "Habana" o del "Almendares", ni tampoco jugar a las barajas, ni leer muñequitos como los de Superman o novelas de Corín Tellado.

En este último caso no nos afectaba esa prohibición. Óiganme. Nosotras no leíamos a Corín Tellado. No, qué va. Queríamos estar en la vanguardia, en "la última", el amor libre, el pop art, la antipoesía, el free cinema, el rock. Aunque el mundo quedaba lejos, de tanto en tanto se filtraban novedades. Gracias a Yuri Gagarin nos enteramos que el planeta Tierra lucía completamente azul y en un noticiero del ICAIC pudimos ver con nuestros propios ojos, por primera vez en movimiento, una imagen furtiva de los Beatles.

Todo aquello, tan provocador que parecía entonces, suena ahora tan cándido.

Como un espejo ladino, la música dulcifica el reflejo cruel de la memoria. Esos eran los buenos ratos. Todos los días de la semana, noche por noche, once menos cuarto, *A solas contigo*, en Radio Progreso, cantaba Elena "una melodía nace de lo hondo de mi corazón"; seguía Meme, "hecha con mi música que es un poco triste como yo", y continuaba "pero déjame decirte que si me ves llorar..."; hasta terminar confesando a dúo, Meme y Elena, junto al cuarteto, "no es de infelicidad, es que me emocionas tú". Después llegaba la hora de *Nocturno*.

Los sábados, diferentes costumbres, con solo cuatro pesos en el bolsillo, la Cinemateca, la pizza en Vita Nuova y el helado en Coppelia. Con lo que quedaba, nos pasábamos las horas oyendo cantar a Teresita en El Coctel, el clubcito nocturno de la candorosa bohemia. Teresita se sentaba en la esquina del sofá, "no puede haber soledad para ti mientras yo exista", cada uno pensaba que la canción le venía bien, ya llegaría alguien que prometiese ahuyentar la soledad. *Un amor de Madame Swann*. Sin haber aprendido todavía, con *Segismunda*, que la vida es pesadilla, y las pesadillas pesadillas son, nos apretujábamos en los cojines dispersos por el piso o desde los taburetes de la barra, estirando un único jaibol, coreábamos "me has dicho que me quieres, y estoy llorando..."

La Difunta se sabía todas las canciones.

La noche de las becadas se acababa con las campanadas de las doce, como la madrugada de Cenicienta en el baile que conoció a *La Princesa*. El Reglamento ordenaba entrar a la beca antes de la una de la mañana. Después de esa hora dependía de quién estuviera de guardia, si se hacía de la vista gorda o ponía un reporte.

Alrededor iba cambiando la atmósfera, sin darnos cuenta. *La conjura de las necias.* Estábamos tan campantes y de repente empezaron a golpear las latas.

Así hasta que un día saltó del diccionario la palabra "depuración".

Año 1967, Giggiola Cinquetti decía que no tenía edad, pero nosotros sí la teníamos. Todos teníamos veinte años. Marta Strada pedía que la abrazaran fuerte y la olvidaran, Ela O'Farrill le decía adiós a la felicidad.

MUJER QUE HABLA SOLA EN EL PARQUE

El cielo se cubrió de auras tiñosas. Volaban en bandadas e hicieron sus nidos en las azoteas de los rascacielos. Y entonces millones de auras tiñositas salieron de los huevos y se lanzaron a buscar carroña por la ciudad. Y La Habana se muere…

MICAELA

A través de las persianas entornadas, Micaela vio aflorar la bola de fuego sobre la raya del horizonte del mar. Le dolía la cabeza como si se le fuera a rajar en dos y no se sentía con fuerzas para enfrentar la rutina del día. Un fuerte olor a desinfectante provenía de la escalera del edificio y el perrito desconocido acababa de comenzar con sus llantos tempraneros. Encima de todo, su gato seguía sin querer comer, aunque Micaela le sirvió en su plato la última reserva de leche que quedaba en la casa. Para ella misma se preparó un vaso de agua con azúcar prieta, luego se tomó una aspirina y se untó un poco de pastica china en las sienes. La noche de insomnio la había dejado maltrecha y con hambre. Rebuscó en los calderos y alcanzó a rescatar unas cuantas cucharadas de la raspa del arroz. Desayunó de pie, vigilando al sol que subía y subía por delante de un cielo rojo encendido. Desde que el ciclón Flora se había llevado volando el techo del bohío donde dormía la brigada de Micaela durante la cosecha del café, desconfiaba de esos cielos acandelados.

En la pasada madrugada, para alejar los mosquitos que zumbaban a su alrededor y espantar el desvelo mientras se alargaba el apagón, Micaela construyó un mechero artesanal con unos trapos a manera de mecha, metidos en una botellita rellena con un poco de querosén, de la misma forma que aprendió a hacerlo con los guajiros para alumbrarse en aquellas largas oscuridades del campo. El tufillo de la chamusquina y el humo negro que tiznaba el techo, el rostro y hasta las paredes interiores de su nariz, evocaban otras noches semejantes, allá en su juventud, a la luz de un quinqué, en medio de las montañas de la sierra, con la brigada de recogedores de café, con La Difunta, su amiga desde la secundaria.

De la muerte de La Difunta se enteró por casualidad, a través de una llamada a casa de Sara, cuando habían pasado ya tres días. Micaela recordaba que se le cayó de la mano el auricular del teléfono público y salió corriendo, corriendo, calles y más calles, hasta llegar a la barriada donde había vivido La Difunta. Recorrió hasta el final del pasillo de la cuartería, como había hecho mil veces en su vida, golpeó con los nudillos en la puerta y volvió a tocar. Al cabo de un rato escuchó levantarse la cancela, entreabrirse un resquicio y vio asomado el perfil de un hombre con expresión extenuada. Micaela balbuceó unas frases de pésame que el hombre escuchaba, asintiendo con la cabeza, sin abrir la boca. Desde el interior se dejaban oír unos sollozos continuados. Por último, el hombre murmuró unas "gracias" y cerró la entrada. Micaela se dio cuenta de que ni siquiera le había dicho quién era ella.

Al buscar la salida del lugar, Micaela descubrió las medias de La Difunta colgadas en el patio. No les hubiera hecho antes ningún caso, mas, en tales circunstancias, las reconoció con un sobresalto. Ahí se habían quedado aquel par de medias sobrevivientes. En sus buenos tiempos fueron rojas, con dos rayas blancas, un grueso par de medias que denunciaban ahora, con sus agobiados colores, una larga permanencia al resol y a la lluvia. Y allí seguían aún, colgadas de la tendedera del solar, olvidadas, exhibiéndose sin rubor, gritando su "¡aquí estamos todavía!". Un oscuro silencio se adensaba detrás de las puertas cerradas de los otros cuartos del solar. Micaela no volvió nunca más por allí.

Un rato antes del amanecer, Micaela buscó otras ocupaciones para distraer la mente. No quería retomar la novela rusa que le provocaba tanta pesadumbre y decidió renovar la gastada libreta de teléfonos, plagada de tantas personas que ya no estaban. Al llegar al nombre de La Difunta se acordó de aquellas medias rojas en la tendedera. Estuvo un rato, paralizada, mirando los apellidos que ya nadie mencionaba, la dirección de una calle extraviada, los numeritos que había marcado tantas veces, vestigios, pistas perdidas, rastrojos del pasado... Después de darle unas cuantas vueltas al asunto, no se decidió a tacharlo y copió las señas de La Difunta, con aquel teléfono que había dejado de existir hacía mucho, a la nueva libreta. Desistir de hacerlo le hubiera parecido como darle el tiro de gracia.

Micaela volvió a mirar la bola de fuego ya instalada en el cielo. El horizonte seguía estando rojo y Micaela se dijo que venía mal tiempo seguro.

HERMI

Como los rayos en tiempos de seca que matan sin prevenir, Hermi nunca sabría qué le pasó.

Empezaron por acusarla de inmadura, luego descubrieron que se carteaba con sus padres establecidos en New Jersey y, para coronar el sumario, el tipo del "VW", antiguo amante despechado, corrió el rumor por los pasillos de que daba abrigo en su casa a Tristán y a sus amores contranatura. Sin proponérselo, Hermi causaba mucha desconfianza y la pusieron bajo vigilancia.

Tiempos rudos, el bombardeo a Hanoi cubría por entero las noticias, cualquier conducta podría tacharse de descarriada o producto del "veneno de una ideología decadente". Y se fue cerrando el panorama: ya no podía ser usada ninguna escenografía que se tomara como "surrealista" o "psicodélica"; ni tampoco mencionar a la Marquesa o al Caballero de París, ¿qué pintaban allí, en esta sana televisión, esos locos vagabundos?; ni hablar de nada que se acerque remotamente a la publicidad, a los "surveys", al análisis freudiano o a la crónica roja; ni mentar el existencialismo ni a Dios, ni palabras de confusionismo religioso como "inclemencia" o "fanático", mucho menos divulgar historias sobrenaturales o presentar los individualistas programas con nombre propio que exaltaran una sola figura. Mucho más, y, por supuesto, satanizados para siempre los personajes de Pototo y Filomeno, y hasta el de Mamacusa Alambrito.

Hermi compuso entonces un libreto sobre el cine verdad y el *free cinema*. Acababa de ver *La oveja negra* de Milos Forman. Hermi escribió con pasión sobre el cine checo, los conflictos generacionales, los adolescentes y sus problemas de enfrentar un espacio de adultos, la oposición a los esquemas tradicionales. Por esos días hacía furor otra película, *El amor se cosecha en verano,* que fue retirada de cartelera y excomulgada.

También el guion de Hermi fue censurado y le pidieron que en lugar de la película prohibida comentara una idiota versión eslava de cowboys, *Limonada Joe*. En respuesta, Hermi escribió un análisis sobre el estructuralismo. Y esto ya fue el colmo de los colmos.

A partir de un impreciso momento, todos sus proyectos fueron rechazados sin explicación, o con alguna posposición absurda; le mutilaban fragmentos de los guiones sin tomarse la molestia de consultarle; dejaron de avisarle de las reuniones y bajo cualquier pretexto la dejaban fuera de los emisiones; le daban tareas áridas y aburridas; le ponían los horarios de mayor sacrificio y en compañía de los colegas más tontos. Una marea negra había caído sobre Hermi.

De tanto en tanto le dejaban caer frases como "manzana podrida" o "problemática". El tipo del "VW" le retiró el saludo y, junto con él, buena parte de los jefes y sus secretarias. Algunos colegas eludían su encuentro, miraban hacia el cielo raso o tomaban por otro pasillo cuando la veían aparecer.

La trasladaron para la programación infantil de la radio donde "podía ser más útil". Tristán se percataba de que la estaban apartando sin compasión del camino de las grandes posibilidades, con aquella forma tangencial de confinamiento a un sitio insignificante, donde se supone que no estén en juego las ideas. Hermi confiaba que con su dedicación al trabajo bastaría para salir del bache.

La tapa al pomo fue cuando, interfiriendo en la reunión de programas dramatizados para televisión a la cual no había sido citada, propuso la adaptación del libro *A sangre fría* para una telenovela, y lo defendió con argumentos irrebatibles y acaloramiento. Hermi fue removida del puesto, quedó en la calle y le colgaron el cartelito de "conflictiva" que cargaría, probablemente, hasta su oración fúnebre.

DAONTAON

La pasada noche hubo luna llena, y ella, Daontaon, por si las moscas, se trancó temprano a cal y canto en su casa, no fuera a ser que le saltase arriba un hombre lobo (o mujer loba que es lo mismo o **peor**) porque en este barrio suyo podía pasar CUALQUIER cosa, ¿Sí o no? Seguro que sí. Encima de la descuartizada sin cabeza (y de que a su vecina Micaela le estaba dando por hablar sola, válgame Dios), en el intercambio de regalos de la asamblea de balance le tocó una *cortina de baño,* ¡dígame usted! Si desde que ella vio esa película, *Psicosis,* no ha podido volver a bañarse más nunca con cortina de baño, ni aunque la hubiera tenido, para que usted lo sepa. ¡Los fósforos! A fin de vigilar la llegada del loco asesino y encontrarse en condiciones de repeler la agresión, en el proceso de sus abluciones diarias, Daontaon jamás le daba la espalda a la puerta, por lo demás abierta de par en par, y se ha seguido echando el agua a jarritos como hacía allá en Banes, ni loca iba a usar la ducha, en caso de que hubiera líquido corriente en las cañerías. Que tampoco lo hay, vamos a estar aquí.

Hasta anteayer, el jefe Braulio la había llevado suave durante tres semanas, en una pincha cómoda, censando niños sordomudos para un coro. Pero después se armó el correcorre por el chequeo de tareas y la inspección que venía "de arriba".

Que si conseguir un dentista para reparar la prótesis de Francisquito el roquero; que si un radiador aunque fuese "de uso" para el Moskovich del compañero traductor de húngaro y otros idiomas; que si resolver un corsé para la vieja viuda del profesor de canto lírico que se fracturó una vértebra en una trifulca con los nietos; que si reclamar en la aduana el video incautado a la novia del primo del Aguilucho Tusao, el rapero de la zona 7. ¡Si cuando ella lo dice! Este trabajo era un doble nueve tras otro. ¡Apaga y vámonos!

Lo peorcito de ayer fue la encomienda de recoger una donación de un anciano que conservaba en custodia las pertenencias de su sobrina. Un caso *tristísimo,* dado que su parienta se había *quitado la vida.* De eso hacía ya un millón de años, mucho antes que Daontaon soñara ni con venir a La Habana, aunque el pobre señor "volvía a pasar" (así mismo dijo) "por *aquel infierno* día por día, hora por hora, minuto por minuto". "¿POR QUÉ lo hizo?" "¿Cómo fue que NADIE le tendió una mano?" "¿Dónde estaba yo que no hice NADA por ella?". Daontaon percibía las mayúsculas vibrando como cencerros en cada una de las interrogantes. No se me ponga así, abuelo, que le va a dar un patatún. Tómese un tilo. ¿O un meprobamato, no tiene? Sí, pues mejor. ¿Me pueda dar uno a mí también? Gracias. Que Dios se lo pague.

Cuando por fin sacaron del closet la maleta de madera con los bienes que el anciano iba a legarle a Cultura, se desmoronó como si fuera galleta mojada. Adentro, en lugar de los tesoros que el tío esperaba haber guardado con celo por tanto tiempo, habitaba una colonia de comejenes. Todo el contenido de la caja se había transformado en papilla, en un mazacote oscuro por donde reverberaban los bicharracos prósperos y felices. Daontaon no se atrevía ni muerta a meter una mano allí. El viejo, llorando a moco tendido, empezó a rescatar lo que restaba de una medalla escolar, el abanico de marfil de la primera comunión, una alcancía metálica con monedas, las piezas de un ajedrez en miniatura, la cabeza de una muñeca mutilada. Todo lo demás, lo que fuese que hubiera habido dentro (Daontaon no lo supo nunca) había sido devorado, no quedaba algo que valiera la pena. Mire, abuelo, estoy un poco apurada, meta todo eso en una bolsa y yo me encargo. Es más, dijo Daontaon con la solemnidad propia del momento, en nombre de Cultura del Municipio Habana del Este y por agradecimiento de su noble gesto, le hago entrega de esta cortina de baño nuevecita, ¿le viene bien? Claro que sí, cómo no le va a venir bien.

Antes de encerrarse en su casa con todas las persianas cerradas y pasados todos los pestillos, no la fuera a atrapar un hombre lobo, Daontaon tiró la bolsa (con comejenes incluidos) al basurero de la esquina, nada servía para nada. Bueno, ella se quedó con el abanico de recuerdo.

LOLA

Lola abrió uno de los cajones de la cómoda. Se sentó en la cama y desde allí se detuvo a tratar de recordar qué iba a buscar, entre decenas de fotografías y documentos de todo tipo que había ido almacenando a lo largo de los años, sobres de manila en los que, por un tiempo, se propuso una tentativa de clasificación, recortes de recetas de cocina sacados de revistas desaparecidas hacía décadas, manuales de equipos que ya no existían, entre ellos el del televisor que compró su padre a principios de los cincuenta, la propiedad de la bicicleta de Sara, el expediente médico de Evaristo, centenares de cartas en cajas de zapatos o anudadas con cintas marchitas, una estuche enorme con los diplomas y los reportes de calificaciones de la propia Lola, moldes de vestimentas infantiles, agendas viejas, libretas de teléfonos, programas de teatro, periódicos amarillentos. No logró acordarse qué buscaba. Revolviendo y revolviendo, encontró una carpeta con el nombre de su hija. Lola pasó con lentitud las páginas de aquel cuaderno mecanografiado con los poemas que Sara había dejado atrás. También encontró su única obra de teatro, llena de añadidos y tachaduras con la caligrafía infantil de Sara en tinta roja. Lola recordó que unos estudiantes de su curso acusaron a Sara de "desviaciones ideológicas" por culpa de la obra de teatro y la expulsaron de los *Jóvenes Comunistas*. Lola no supo cómo ayudar a su hija en aquel entonces y Sara comenzó a apartarse de ella sin remedio.

Lola se dijo que debía pedirle ayuda a Micaela para auxiliarla a tomar decisiones sobre la papelería de Sara. Desde aquellos incidentes en la universidad, no quiso volver a escribir ni una línea. Y Micaela…

¿desde cuándo no llamaba?

Lola permaneció un rato sin moverse del borde de la cama con los escritos de Sara en el regazo, aplastado el corazón por una sensación de tristeza e inutilidad. Los toquecitos en la puerta interrumpieron el tránsito de sus pensamientos. Apenas unos días atrás alguien la había visitado, aunque Lola no recordaba quién. Se acordaba de que había cocinado arroz con pollo y la persona lo agradeció mucho, pero por más empeño que hiciera, Lola la había olvidado.

Cuando abrió la puerta, sin quitar la cadena de seguridad, vislumbró en el rellano de la escalera a una mujer mulata, algo desbordante en carnes, de la misma edad de Sara, vestida con un atuendo estrambótico. O eso le pareció a Lola. Tenía un pañuelo de colorinches en la cabeza cubriendo parte de la cabellera pintada de un amarillo fosforescente, un vestido ancho de estilo hindú y una cantidad de cadenas, gangarrias, pulsos, anillos, aretes que rodeaban todos los espacios visibles de la piel. El intento de parecer juvenil fracasaba, no así el aspecto de exotismo que podía confundirse con un personaje de los bajos fondos de una película. La saya, larga y holgada, se fruncía en la cintura y caía luego alrededor de las rollizas caderas. Usaba unas medias negras de seda, extravagantes sobre todo porque sus pies iban calzados con unas sandalias de cuero por donde sobresalían los deditos enfundados en la delicada prenda. Sin embargo, su semblante cordial decidió a Lola a abrir la puerta.

El extraño personaje se presentó como Yuya, su nueva vecina.

MUJER QUE HABLA SOLA EN EL PARQUE

Millones y millones de comejenes salieron volando por la ciudad, ocuparon sus posiciones, establecieron reinados y colonias. Y entonces se dieron a comer cuanta madera encontraron. Y La Habana se muere...

MARTÍN

El balcón enfrentaba la línea de la costa y la extensión del mar del golfo. Esa mañana, sin pizca de viento y bajo un cielo color granate, límpido de nubes, el agua como un plato reverberaba bajo el sol. En la lejanía, unos pescadores flotaban sobre unas gomas de camión con los sedales en espera de la presa. Un par de perros negros correteaban alegremente por los arrecifes, junto a un segmento de vergel silvestre entrelazado a uvas caletas. Con unas orejeras de las usadas por los caballos de tiro y enfocando la mirada solo hacia el fragmento marino, Martín hubiera podido alcanzar la ilusión de encontrarse en una isla desierta. Si desviaba la cabeza apenas unos centímetros a la derecha o a la izquierda, la vista podía caer sobre un solar yermo y las construcciones ruinosas de no se sabía cuál proyecto sin terminar. Los escombros se cubrían de inmundicias y mostraban al aire su esqueleto oxidado de hierro. Apenas unos metros más allá, se repetían las moles despintadas, decenas de edificios todos iguales, sin gracia ninguna, como hipopótamos de piedra cubiertos de barro.

La burbuja de silencio se quebró e irrumpió la algarabía cotidiana. Martín anotó en una de sus tarjetas mentales que la sala no era la sala, ni el mar era el mar.

¿Por qué diablos le resultaba tan difícil escribir un puñetero párrafo gentil? Uno solo, uno solito con "amor y escualidez", sin hipopótamos. Una historia donde oro pareciera y plata fuese, no tenía necesidad alguna de embellecer su infancia, todo lo contrario, tan perfecta era que se sentía obligado a atenuar aquel paraíso perdido.

La abuela Antonia añoraba el terruño, las montañas de Asturias, los labrantíos en las faldas del santuario de la Virgen de la Covadonga, los hórreos. Para la otra abuela, la madre de la mamá de Martín, el terruño se colocaba un poco más al oeste, por el camino de Santiago, los gallegos predios de San Xil que ella nunca había vuelto a visitar. El pasado era, pues, todo un terruño inalcanzable. Sencillo y detenido en el tiempo.

¡Qué distinto a la hora de ponerlo por escrito! Una sola página se podría comer cuarenta años de un tirón y al revés, quinientos folios para que no pasara nada.

Martín, una y otra vez había vuelto a rehacer la primera línea, según se dice, la más difícil. "El colibrí ciego se posó, tornadizo, en la ventana". Va y esta puñetera primera línea corría el mismo destino de las anteriores, pliego arrugado en el fondo del latón de basura.

"Ahí está el problema, mi hijito", había dicho la mamá de Martín, "es muy enredado". Y Martín no sabía a qué se estaba refiriendo ¿a la novela, a la vida...?

Encima... ¿dónde colocar la perspectiva, el puñetero "punto de vista"? ¿Primera persona o tercera?, ¿un niño, un adulto o mezclando las dos? ¿O acaso convertirlo en "una niña" para confundir a los jurados feministas? En el tono se jugaba la suerte, como le gustaba repetir a él mismo en los talleres literarios con la partida de borrachos, imberbes y jovenzuelas pretensiosas que se creían escritores. Pero ese tono se le escapaba, se le encartonaba.

¿Y qué nombre usar? ¿Dejarlo genérico, algo así como "El niño"? Nada de eso, el anónimo infectaba como una plaga la mala literatura.

El tío Félix se llamaba tío Félix casi siempre. Según el lugar donde estuvieran ocurriendo las aventuras, aire, mar, islote, el desierto, las montañas Apalaches, la selva amazónica, otro planeta, el Polo Norte, podía ser conocido como Davy Croquett, Capitán Nemo, El Halcón Negro, Flash Gordon o cualquier patronímico por el estilo. Si la mamá de Martín estaba molesta, le decía "el dichoso tío"; y el señor Hemingway, con quien conversaba de cuando en cuando en la barra del Floridita, le llamaba "amigou". El tío Félix se pasó cuarenta años tratando de escribir una novela, aunque solo componía la primera línea. Escribió muchas "primeras líneas" y de ahí no salió. En una ocasión, el tío Félix hizo el intento de leerle al escritor una de sus famosas primeras líneas y se vio interrumpido por un "vete a la puñeta con la literatura de mierda". El tío Félix no se lo tomó a mal, porque eso mismo decía el señor Hemingway de sus propios libros, a pesar de ser un escritor célebre. De lo que uno está escribiendo no se puede hablar ni media palabra o se corre el riesgo de joderlo todo, esa es su teoría. Además, si el tío Félix quería continuar tomándose un trago con él, tenían que conversar sobre los empinados culos de las cubanas, de perros callejeros, de la receta de bacalao a la vizcaína, de la buena época de pesca en Cojímar, de lo único que valía la pena hablar en esta vida.

YUYA

Dice Yuya que su buena ventura la ayudó una vez más a salir del apuro. Lalita se mostraba remolona en pagar la promesa de viajar hasta Oriente para ofrendarle sus agradecimientos a la Virgencita de la Caridad. Ponía los más variados pretextos y Yuya no tenía forma de hacerle entender que un voto incumplido iba a atraerle desgracias y malquerencias. Cada vez que se acercaba un ocho de septiembre, Yuya le recordaba a su hija el compromiso con la santa y siempre Lalita le respondía que cómo iban a subir hasta el Cobre.

No dejaba de ser cierto la casi inexistencia del transporte hacia las provincias, que los horarios y tareas de Lalita ocupaban todo su tiempo y andaban cortos de dinero, que Shu estaba negado a quedarse solo ni siquiera por un fin de semana y Yuya empezaba a padecer de dolores en la columna.

Dice Yuya que, aunque se piense que siempre va a sobrar tiempo para hacer algo en la vida, rectificar, pedir perdón, respetar la palabra empeñada, no, el tiempo es de las cosas que nunca alcanzan.

Las soluciones a sus problemas llegaron inesperadamente. Yuya se enteró que la Virgen del Cobre, la auténtica de la ermita, iba a realizar una especie de gira por las iglesias habaneras, con misas en su honra. Yuya vio los cielos abiertos y con mucha circunspección le preguntó a Lalita si estaría dispuesta a acompañarla a cumplir lo prometido en una de las estaciones de la Virgen durante su recorrido por La Habana. Lalita respondió que si ello servía para condonar su deuda, entonces de acuerdo.

Según Yuya, si uno no puede ir a la loma del Cobre, con seguridad la loma viene a uno.

Después de algunas averiguaciones sobre el trayecto de la sacra imagen de la Patrona de Cuba, se supo que al siguiente domingo, la Virgen de la Caridad del Cobre, la que viste y calza, regiría el altar de la iglesia parroquial de El Salvador del Mundo, en Santo Tomás y Peñón, en El Cerro, lejísimo.

Dice Yuya que pasaron tantas dificultades y realizaron tantos esfuerzos como si hubieran ido al genuino santuario. La adquisición de un ramo de flores resultaba impensable, así que el día antes recorrieron algunos jardines sobrevivientes a la desidia y recolectaron marpacíficos y vicarias, además hirvieron unos huevos duros, tostaron pan viejo y llenaron varias botellas con agua de tomar para el trayecto. Partieron hacia su destino mucho antes del amanecer. Después de esperar horas por la guagua, cambiaron tres veces de ruta y, por último, pagaron un dineral a un destartalado carromato que las acercó por la avenida de Agua Dulce hasta el entronque con la Calzada de Palatino, y desde allí una caminata de más de seis cuadras. Yuya se sentó con falta de aire en uno de los bancos del parque frente a la añosa iglesita y agradeció para sus adentros a todos, a Etelvina, a su pobre abuela, a su padre San Lázaro y al Chinito de la Charada, por no haberse tropezado ni una sola vez con el alma en pena del haitiano y llegar antes de que diera comienzo la misa.

La amiga de Lalita, declarada atea e incrédula, las acompañó en el peregrinaje y a fin de cuentas, después costó convencerla para abandonar el templo, fascinada por su antigüedad y el aura de quietud.

Al salir de la ceremonia, se sentaron a aguardar una guagua de regreso. Durante casi cuatro horas que duró el plantón y conversaciones entre un grupo de fieles congregados en la parada, Yuya consiguió la permuta desde Alamar para el Vedado.

En buena hora. El mismo día que por fin se mudaron de allí, Yuya se enteró de la aparición en su zona de una mujer descuartizada. Según Yuya, lo tomó como una buena señal.

HERMI

Entretanto, Tristán se había embullado a colaborar en un grupo de teatro, ayudar en lo que apareciera, como tarugo cargando tramoya si fuese necesario.

Después de la apoteosis de *La noche de los asesinos,* se fueron poniendo en boga las versiones de sagas clásicas, y pululaban las medeas, edipos y electras paseando sus peplos por los escenarios. A Tristán se le ocurrió presentar a consideración una obra de Sara donde un Caronte joven y bello trasladaba con gentileza en su barca, hacia la Otra Orilla, a cualquier alma muerta que se lo pedía, sin reclamar óbolo ni rito previo. "No hay por qué añadir mezquindad al ya infligido dolor de las víctimas", comentaba Tristán con una de sus frases crípticas. "La morada de Hades no discrimina", añadía. (¿O sería Hermi?).

El proyecto de decorado apenas consistía en un paisaje marino intencionalmente artificioso de telón de fondo, una cortina raída y una ambigua efigie de adolescente con una mancha de sangre encima de la sien que cubría un retazo del ojo derecho, versión libérrima de *La mémorie,* en homenaje al recién fallecido Magritte. Sobre el tablado, arena en un costado, hojas secas en el otro y en el centro una alfombra gris tapizada por astillas de espejos que configuraban esquemas Op-Art. Lo demás, a imaginación del público. Al añadir la mezcla de canciones de Bola de Nieve junto a la música de una banda llamada *The Doors* y un "baby, you can light my fire" interminable, el libreto resultaba inquietante.

Durante los ensayos, Hermi y Tristán pudieron asistir a una puesta en escena única, el "Happening" de Teatro Estudio. "Ni se te ocurra cometer la imprudencia de mirar, detrás de ti está sentada Marguerite Duras", advirtió Tristán. Cuando dio comienzo el desconcertante espectáculo, oyeron al traductor haciendo lo imposible por volver comprensibles los textos, "¿Cómo debe ser la forma de un cigarro, redondo, cuadrado, de pico, cómo? ¿Cómo debe ser la forma de un carnet?", aunque creyeron escuchar risitas secas de asentimiento que provenían desde el asiento trasero. En los minutos finales, los actores empezaron a desplazarse entre el lunetario arrojando pintura y los espectadores se vieron obligados a escapar a gatas por los pasillos. En el tumulto, Hermi perdió de vista a Marguerite Duras y se frustró la gran oportunidad de citarle de memoria líneas completas del guión de *Hiroshima mon amour*.

Nunca más volverían a representar humoradas como aquella. También la obra de Sara fue rechazada.

Por su parte, Hermi presentó en el Instituto de Cine una solicitud para emplearse allí en lo que fuera, comenzar por abajo. Al cabo de algunos meses de espera, se enteró por una infidencia que un capitoste le había tirado bola negra, a cuenta de las malas lenguas. "Dudosa moralidad" fue el dictamen que la alejó para siempre del sueño de hacer cine. Nadie nunca le explicó nada, ni le permitieron defenderse.

Hermi introdujo un bluyín, dos camisas, una lata de leche condensada, una cuchara, un plato de metal y un jarro de cocina, junto a una bolsita con artilugios de higiene personal y el libro de Marcuse forrado con papel de cartucho, todo revuelto, en una mochila de "Alfabetizador" que había pertenecido a Tristán, y luego se fue a cosechar viandas, sin que nadie la mandara, al Cordón de La Habana, la tarea de choque de los jóvenes. Los fines de semana regresaba muerta de cansancio y cubierta de tierra roja, lavaba la ropa, elaboraba en baño de maría otra lata de dulce para la siguiente semana y, vestida solo con un pulóver, se ponía a dibujar en las paredes nubes pastosas y unas delgaduchas lunas Miró.

Al poco tiempo, el jefe de brigada del Cordón le pidió que abandonara su trabajo en la agricultura, aunque para esta decisión tampoco le dieron razón alguna.

En eso andaban, cuando llegaron noticias retrasadas de la era de Acuario, del "Flower Power" y de los hippies en San Francisco. Y casi al mismo tiempo, sin transición, la caída del Che en la guerrilla, la matanza de Tlatelolco, los asesinados en Kent y los tanques sobre las calles de Praga. La euforia de la época en que todos tuvieron veinte años había llegado a su fin y el mundo cambió.

DAONTAON

Si algo odiaba Daontaon más que a los escritores era a los "niños escritores". En la pantalla de la televisión, aferrada a un micrófono, se presentaba uno de esos ejemplares con un peinado arlequín petrificado en dos oleadas que descendían hasta sus hombros, aullando unos versos que rimaban musaraña, con lasaña, con lagaña... ¡Apaga y vámonos!

—Se merece que la corten en pedacitos —comentó Daontaon, mordiendo con saña una galleta dulce—. Ja. A ella, a su mamá y a sus abuelitas.

—¿Hay alguna noticia nueva de la descuartizada?

—Ay, Willie, no me vuelvas a hablar más de eso que estoy con mucho "estrés" —Daontaon se observó con inquietud las manos—. Préstame una lima de uñas. Los rollos de Cultura me tienen la vida acabada. No hago más que pensar en comejenes y hormigas bravas. Me he pasado toda la noche con una pesadilla de lo más extraña. ¿Te la cuento? Sí. El edificio... ¿Cuál va a ser, niño? *Este edificio*. No me interrumpas con tus muecas que pierdo el hilo. Este edificio se había quedado completamente desierto, cuando te digo desierto es que desapareció de golpe el montón de tarados y delincuentes vecinos, no quedaba por todo esto ni uno solo de los hijos de puta que viven aquí. Nada más que yo y un *escritor*.

Las cursivas centellearon en la habitación como una colmena revuelta.

—Lo mejor del caso es que el susodicho *escritor* tenía la misma cara del zángano ese que vive aquí cerca, en el edificio de al lado, el tal Martín que se cree cosas. Ja. Pues resulta ser que al darse cuenta de que era un completo cretino, un **farsante,** que no lograba escribir su puñetera novela, el *escritor* la emprendía a machetazos con todo y cuanto hay. ¿Por qué me miras así, niño?

—Sigue, sigue contándome tu pesadilla...

—¿Vas a colar café? Menos mal. Pero ese es el final. Antes de eso, yo trataba de pedir auxilio por teléfono y ninguno funcionaba. Te dije que no me hicieras muecas... En eso, empezaban a aparecer fantasmas por todos lados... unas niños degollados jugando pelota, la descuartizada con la cabeza bajo el brazo, la sobrina difunta del viejo reclamándome un abanico, la coja que se prendió candela, ¿tú te acuerdas?, porque el marido le pegaba los cuernos. ¡Hasta el alma en pena de la tía de Micaela que se fue para el Norte! Dígame usted. Y por una escalera...

Daontaon apuntó con la lima de uñas, empuñándola como si blandiera un hacha, al supuesto sitio detrás de las paredes que debía estar ocupando la escalera del edificio.

—Por una escalera igualitica que esta... ¿qué tú crees que caía de piso en piso? ¿Oleadas de caca? ¿Marejadas de pipí? No, qué va, niño. ¡Caía sangre! Cataratas de sangre. Y el zángano de Martín hecho un loco, machete en mano, acabando con la quinta y con los mangos. A ver... ¿Qué culpa tiene uno de que no pueda escribir ni un mierdero cuento? ¡Hay cada chiflado suelto por ahí! Pero el responsable de todo esto es mi jefe, el cerdo de Braulio, desde que le estoy dando de lado me asigna cada tareíta que le zumba la matraca, perdonando la expresión. ¿Tú sabes cuál fue la del lunes? No, niño, tú no te la puedes ni imaginar. La cotorra del historiador que vive en Bahía se escapó de la jaula y a la idiota no se le ocurrió salir volando como es debido. No. Tuvo que prenderse a unos cables pelados de alta tensión y allí mismo se quedó achicharrada, con las plumas del cocorioco echando humo. Al historiador le dio un soponcio y hubo que llevarlo corriendo para el Hospital Naval a que le pusieran diazepán en vena. Lo más complicado de todo fue convencer a los tipos de la Empresa Eléctrica para que se treparan a bajar al avechucho. Porque al historiador se le metió en la cabeza conservar disecada a la cotorra frita. ¿Tú te acuerdas de aquella película donde un montón de bicharracos voladores no dejaban títere con cabeza?

—*Los pájaros.*

—Esa misma, lo único que me falta es que venga toda la parentela de la cotorra electrocutada a cogerla conmigo. ¡Los fósforos!

MUJER QUE HABLA SOLA EN EL PARQUE

Los leones del Prado tenían tanta hambre que se cansaron de estar tiesos como estatuas y bajaron de los pedestales. Y entonces se comieron todo lo que se les puso por delante. Y La Habana se muere...

GERTRUDIS

Los recuerdos están de tal manera furtivos que hay que sacarlos de sus escondrijos. A la fuerza si es necesario. Cómo no. Óiganme, hubiera hecho falta tatuárselos en la piel, *La mujer ilustrada,* para no extraviarlos y reescribir con ellos nuestra versión de *La historia* como hiciera Herodota. O contar en trescientas páginas aquel único y mínimo suceso, la *Vida y opiniones de Tristana Shandy. Funes la memoriosa. El libro de las muertas.*

Las noches aburridas de la beca cambiaron cuando La Difunta hizo dos aportes fundamentales: unos binoculares de teatro y un receptor de radio más viejo que Matusalén.

Gracias a aquel aparato se garantizó la puntualidad a clases con el tictac de Radio Reloj y, además, mantener constante una música de fondo. La banda sonora de la nostalgia puede ayudar a refrescar la memoria mejor que cualquier panqué remojado en té, digan lo que digan.

¿Se acuerdan? Del sonado Festival de la Canción en Varadero se quedó la Massiel como himno al disparate con aquel "cartel de no funciona", su "aleluuuuuuya" y sus "rosas en el mar". De *La dolce vita,* el instrumental *Patricia* que evocaba invariablemente el *striptease* de la escena que levantó tantas ronchas entre los puritanos. De *Cleo de cinco a siete,* un desgarrador *Sans toi,* más relajado en la versión del cuarteto de Meme. ¡Y aquella memorable *Mrs. Robinson!,* aunque solo pudimos llegar a verle la cara cuando estrenaron la película veinte años más tarde.

Al concierto de Jean Ferrat en el Amadeo Roldán no pudimos entrar, pero fuimos más de diez veces a ver *La vieja dama indigna* y nos aprendimos de memoria su tema *On ne voit pas le temps passer.*

Eran los tiempos en que The Mamas and The Papas cantaban *Monday Monday* y una rubia inglesa, Petula Clark, aquel *Downtown*... Y "María Caracoles baila mozambique", y de todos y cada uno de los clandestinos discos de placa de los Beatles, no habría ni que decirlo.

Los domingos por la mañana, en la playita de 16, coreábamos *Cuando calienta el sol*, la "Venecia" sin nosotros y *Blowing in the wind*. Y, naturalmente, "muchas veces te dije que para hacerlo había que pensarlo muy bien..." y "si yo tuviera un martillo..." En la noche, el punto de encuentro era siempre en la cafetería de la antigua funeraria Caballero en la esquina de 23 y M, transformada en una Casa de Cultura de colores sicodélicos hasta que la clausuraron, para luego salir a rampear, Rampa arriba y Rampa abajo, al ritmo de la caminadora, "caminando va, guarachando va..."

Aunque nos querían hacer sentir culpables y lavar el pecado de estudiar Letras con un esfuerzo físico, ensuciarse las manos con la sagrada tierra y sudar el sano líquido del trabajo manual, para quitarnos la "blandenguería" de cachorros de intelectualoides a costa de labores rudas, ¿se acuerdan o no se acuerdan?, a nosotros nos encantaba ir a los campos agrícolas aquellos fines de semana de los llamados "tres por uno". Tres semanas no y una sí. O los meses completos de las vacaciones a recoger cítricos en Isla de Pinos o fresas en Banao, roturar surcos para hortalizas o limpiar campos de caña en cualquier parte.

De autor anónimo, allí cantábamos hasta el cansancio "Yo quisiera recordar las ansias que al pasar..., cenizas de ilusión..." Y también del viejo cancionero de los partisanos y de la guerra civil española, inspirado por la voz desafinada de alguna profesora, "y si yo muero en el combate toma en tus manos mi fusil..."

La Difunta, por su parte, entonaba aquello de "yo me subí a un pino verde por ver si la divisaba y solo divisé el polvo del coche que la llevaba... Anda jaleo jaleo, ya se acabó el alboroto y ahora empieza el tiroteo..."

Íbamos cantando en los vagones de los trenes, en los camiones sin techar, en las guaguas destartaladas, en la cubierta del ferry, en las carretas tiradas por un tractor, cantábamos en la Plaza Cadenas, en la escalinata de la universidad, en la beca, bajo los árboles de la entrada de la Escuela de Letras, en el albergue, alrededor de una fogata, en el surco, cantábamos y cantábamos. No parábamos de cantar.

El día a día no tiene banda sonora, pero el pasado sí.

LA INDIA

¡Cómo se desploma la suerte del caído en desgracia! ¡Qué volubles son las muchedumbres!, sobre todo las aglutinadas en solares, conventillos y edificios múltiples.

Cuando fueron llegando las noticias al vecindario y se supieron cuáles habían sido los violentos actos del asesino sobre el cuerpo (ahora trucidado, antaño motivo de codicia) de La India, los conocidos de El Francés (incluso beneficiarios de prebendas y donaciones, la verdad sea dicha), se confabularon en una partida vengativa. Allanado el apartamento de la malhadada pareja, arrasaron con todo lo que pudiera tener algún valor y ello explicaría, meses más tarde, la absurda presencia de arcabuces, dagas y floretes en distintas casas habaneras.

Ese fin de semana, mediante la ingestión de unas cuantas botellas de vino rojo sustraídas en la incursión justiciera, los ánimos se caldearon en el solar y se llegó hasta a planear una golpiza al "blanquito sucio ese". Sobre todo se exasperaron más las pasiones después de la transmisión, en la noche del sábado, de una película sobre negros buenos y blancos malvados del Mississippi. Patrick Rivière no entendía nada, ni mucho menos que le gritaran "Abajo el Ku Klux Klan". Tampoco alcanzaba a comprender que los insultos y bramidos de furia fuesen adquiriendo ritmo y cadencia, hasta irrumpir la rumba atronando los cajones, "no la llores, no la llores, que fue la gran bandolera, enterrador, no la llores". Pero, por si las moscas, El Francés se puso a buen recaudo en un hotel de dos estrellas, incluido en el perímetro de su arresto.

Mientras tanto, Clara Luz, llamada La Catedrática y madre de La India, se mantenía a base de brebajes de tilo y pastillas de meprobamato, en la expectativa de alcanzar el completamiento del cadáver y proceder a un enterramiento como Dios y otras paganías mandan. Lo que quedaba de María Antonieta (nombre de tan mal destino) después de su inquieta vida y aturullada muerte, y posterior aún a haber pasado por las manos del descuartizador, de los perros callejeros, de la policía y de los forenses, se seguía enfriando en uno de los compartimentos de la morgue, en espera de la malandante cabeza.

Por ese entonces comenzaron a circular habladurías horripilantes acerca de las incursiones de la extranjería entre la grey mujeril de la trágica Habana de los noventa. Se comentaba de germanos sádicos que colocaban a sus esposas como sirvientas con grilletes del medioevo en los tobillos, de italianos secuestradores de mulatas para negocios de la mafia siciliana, de vejetes españoles ávidos de reinstaurar la tradición de los harenes, de ingleses traficantes en busca de mano de obra para la pornografía, se habló mucho de un millonario árabe quien, bajo engaño, sustrajo las córneas de su prometida.

A esta altura de los sucesos, El Francés se negó a prestar ninguna otra declaración. Hasta ese momento había seguido insistiendo en su versión del amante y la náutica escapatoria. Aparte de esa historia, no se le pudo sacar palabra. Seguían pasando las semanas y la cabeza de María Antonieta no había hecho aún su aparición.

Por otra parte, con la intrusión de la horda enfurecida en el apartamento de marras quedaron destruidas todas las posibles pruebas de cargo. Los vengativos vecinos irrumpieron y no solo cargaron con los objetos de mayor calibre y los alimentos preservados en el refrigerador, sino incluso con los palitos de tendedera. Y si hubo papel de estraza, alambres, escalpelos, lancetas u otros objetos perforocortantes que hubieran podido ser utilizados en el tasajeo de un cuerpo humano, ahora se encontraban dispersos por todo el barrio de San Leopoldo.

Otros detalles hicieron vacilar a la justicia. Los expertos notaron que las ataduras de los fúnebres paquetes solo podían provenir de alguien muy ducho en el ejercicio de nudos marinos, lo cual venía a reafirmar, en algún sentido, el relato del marido y la existencia de un amante cercano a las artes náuticas. Patrick Rivière no tenía una coartada, aunque tampoco un móvil, como no fuese el inferido de los celos, así fue haciéndose fuerte la posibilidad de más sospechosos, quizás el propio amante. Por demás, la decapitada podría pertenecer a cualquier otra identidad desconocida. Sin la aparición de la cabeza, no cabría dar curso a una acusación, basada hasta ese punto en las afirmaciones de una madre sobre una rajadura de la piel, tal vez la mencionada cicatriz o una imperfección de nacimiento.

Algunas preguntas seguían sin respuesta: ¿de dónde procedía el papel de estraza? (¿o de dónde había sido desviado el recurso del papel de estraza, la verdad sea dicha?), ¿qué tipo de arma había sido utilizada en el degüello y posterior trinchado del cuerpo?, ¿por qué esa predilección malsana por la zona del levante capitalino?

La cabeza de "La Descuartizada del Municipio Habana del Este" sería lo único que podía completar el expediente para un juicio tan complejo.

Entretanto, los rumores del crimen corrían de boca en boca e inspiraron a varios escritores de los talleres literarios algunos cuentos y hasta una décima.

MARTÍN

Al llegar al Nuevo Mundo, la abuela Antonia se quedó a vivir en casa de un pariente, dueño de una panadería. El tío Félix fue a parar al corte de caña en Matanzas. Durante las peripecias del viaje atlántico, a la abuela Antonia le sobró tiempo para enseñarle a leer y escribir. Gracias a ello, se mantuvieron unidos por el correo.

"De la manía de la epístola, saltó al vicio de la literatura", se lamentaba la abuela Antonia, los cestos siempre llenos de papeles, la aglomeración de libros por los rincones, la costumbre de teclear en la máquina de escribir hasta las tantas de la madrugada, los versitos, incluso de lenguaje erótico, la malísima reputación de tener un escritor en la familia, que es como decir un orate, un tonto de siete suelas, un depravado, un indigente, un vago, siempre en la Luna de Valencia, "maldita sea su estampa y la hora en que lo saqué de burro y lo contagié con el abecedario", concluía la abuela Antonia.

La mamá de Martín levantó la vista al cielo raso como hacía siempre que sus pensamientos tomaban un desvío por algún vericueto. Luego lo miró, un tanto perpleja por tantas falsedades mezcladas con recuerdos fidedignos, "mi hijito, tu tío, que en paz descanse, nunca vivió en Matanzas". La mamá de Martín siguió leyendo con atención, pero sus ojos incrédulos se alzaban con frecuencia hacia el techo.

El tío Félix, con un cargamento de cincuenta libretas empastadas donde había tomado costumbre de anotar cuanto veía a su alrededor, se apostó en el último cuarto del pasillo, compró una cama individual de hierro, un chiforrober y una mesita de madera y mármol. Sobre ella colocó una Remington de uso, su único lujo, carretada desde el ingenio azucarero dentro del fardo de las ropas.

Al mediodía, la familia se reunía a almorzar, el papá de Martín se daba una escapadita del banco, el abuelo Severino bajaba del taller, el tío Félix salía de su encierro poético. A Martín le gustaba observar el movimiento de la casa, escondido detrás del escaparate de la abuela Antonia, apostado como un indio, mirando por la rendija entre la pared y la mampara. La mamá de Martín atravesaba el pasillo rumbo al comedor con las manos ocupadas por un plato de sopa, imponente tazón rebosante de menudos de pollo, papas de color amarillo y fideos, recipiente de porcelana transportado tal si se tratara de una corona real. La abuela Antonia, tan intransigente en todo, en el tema de la sopa se mostraba indulgente. "Si al niño le disgusta, dale otra cosa". "Ay, Antonia", se atrevía a ripostar la mamá de Martín, sin mucha fuerza.

—No sé qué le encuentra este niño a estar encerrado atrás del escaparate tanto rato. Se va a volver loco de tanto leer.

—Nadie se vuelve loco por eso —terciaba el tío Félix.

—Tú no te metas —replicó la abuela Antonia desde la cocina—. Lleva como tres horas allá adentro y ya es la hora de almuerzo.

En medio de las praderas del Lejano Oeste a nadie le importa la hora del almuerzo.

La mamá de Martín avisó en voz alta que se enfriaba la sopa. El tío Félix, sentado a la mesa, se llevó la mano a la boca, tapándosela y destapándosela, con un ruidito intermitente, como los indios. Entonces, desde la cocina se escuchó un grito. "No es para tanto...", empezó a decir el tío Félix. Su frase quedó cortada por el golpe del cuerpo de la abuela Antonia contra las baldosas. La mamá de Martín salió corriendo, "aydiosmío, aydiosmío, aydiosmío".

La mamá de Martín escrutaba el manuscrito con desaprobación. "Nunca te obligué a tomar sopa. Qué mentiroso eres, mi hijito."

HERMI

"Para rendirle pleitesía a la Aniquiladora de Palacios, señora de nuestras mil y una noches habaneras", dijo Hermi (¿o sería Tristán?), mientras compraba un ramo de lirios en la esquina de Zapata y 12, a la entrada del Cementerio de Colón.

Guillermo necesitaba compañía y los había citado allí. Tocaba ya "sacar" a Tomás, la exhumación de su sepulcro provisional, como era la tradición de aquellos mausoleos colectivos, y mudar sus huesecitos para un nicho definitivo.

Tampoco Hermi ni Tristán estaban de muy buen ánimo. Las conclusiones de la comisión de purga, la llamada "parametración" en el sector teatral, habían acabado el mes pasado y, tal como temían, Tristán fue expulsado del grupo. Por último, conminado a trabajar como herrero en Cubana de Bronce, so pena de declararlo "vago" y sufrir encarcelamiento por ley.

Tristán, después de más de ocho horas en el taller, llegaba al anochecer con la ropa tiznada y grasienta, tomaba un baño y se dedicaba a quitarse el hollín de las uñas, antaño bien cuidadas y ahora maltrechas como sus manos, laceradas por cortaduras y ampollas. Luego comía lo que hubiera, de pie, sin hablar, y terminaba por caer como un muerto en la cama, noche por noche. A la jornada siguiente, Hermi lo sentía partir antes del amanecer, compadecida y asombrada por su determinación de no darse por vencido, de no rendirse. Una hora más tarde, ella misma se iba, sin desayunar, a clasificar los libros en el almacén de una biblioteca en Arroyo Naranjo. El empleo de Hermi era, al menos, más higiénico, aunque la humedad concentrada y la falta de luz le producía coriza persistente. Como beneficio, a la hora del almuerzo se le permitía leer algún ejemplar raro.

Guillermo llegó por fin, con un envoltorio de paños limpios y un pomo de perfume, según exigía la tradición, para guardar con propiedad los despojos de Tomás, en su descanso permanente. "Hubieran hecho falta también unas berenjenas de tributo a Oyá, la Furiosa Patrona".

Mientras caminaban por la alameda central, flanqueada por árboles que atenuaban la reverberación de las tres de la tarde, un taxi cruzó por delante de ellos, se detuvo dando un frenazo y la madre de Tomás descendió, mostrando un aire apurado. Venía vestida con excesiva elegancia y abrazaba contra el regazo un bolsón de tela. Le hizo señas a Guillermo para que se acercara y conversaron unos minutos. Al cabo, regresó Guillermo empapado en sudor frío. Movió los labios con un mohín que pretendía resultar tranquilizador y de su garganta salió un murmullo ronco. La madre de Tomás le había pedido, exigido casi, que se fuera, que aquel era un trance estrictamente familiar.

El taxi se adentró por el laberinto de callejuelas silenciosas y ellos lo siguieron a distancia, sin cruzar palabra. Cuando el auto se detuvo frente a cuatro sepultureros que conversaban con animación, Hermi, Tristán y Guillermo se mantuvieron alejados un trecho, escondidos detrás de una capilla como malhechores y allí se dispusieron a esperar. Al rato fueron apareciendo otras personas cargando sus respectivos paquetes de lienzos y fragancias, algunos en autos, otros a pie, atravesando los senderos resquebrajados, cubiertos de malas hierbas, entre los sepulcros. El cielo estaba completamente despejado, sin una sola nube. El resol de la hora derramaba fuego y los rostros se iban cubriendo de polvo mezclado con las secreciones corporales. Por fin, los empleados dieron comienzo a su trabajo y sin mucha ceremonia fueron colocando los ataúdes en hilera a lo ancho de la avenida. Cada allegado se acercaba a los despojos, escarbaba entre las ruinas humanas, y las guardaba en las telas perfumadas. La mezcla de las distintas emanaciones llegó en un vaho hasta donde se encontraban apostados. "Mi camisa naranja", murmuró Guillermo. Desde allí vieron cómo la madre de Tomás guardaba en el bolsón los restos de su hijo, entreverados con unos retazos podridos de la camisa naranja que tanto le gustaba a Tomás y que le había servido de mortaja.

—Se lleva los huesos de Tomás para México de donde era el abuelo. Ella dice que se va de aquí y no deja a su hijo atrás.

Cuando todo terminó, todavía Guillermo con el envoltorio en las manos y Hermi con los inútiles lirios, se sentaron a descansar bajo un florido flamboyán. Rodeados de tanta calma, Guillermo les contó de un libro que estaba leyendo, *El país de las sombras largas,* en uno de sus capítulos se describía cómo los esquimales abandonaban en la intemperie a los ancianos cuando dejaban de servir para algo. "Ya nosotros estamos a la intemperie", dijo Guillermo, con algo de sorna, "al menos, cuando nos toque, que nos entierren juntos y una sola lápida con el mismo epitafio *al fin en todas las listas negras*".

—Nuestra generación se muere primero que sus padres —cerró Tristán la conversación (¿o sería Hermi?) y colocaron los lirios sobre una tumba abandonada.

Era sábado y tenían la tarde libre. Caminaron en silencio, bajando por la calle 12, siguieron después por el Malecón hasta Paseo, sin nada qué hacer. Se acordaron de que en el bar del hotel Riviera a veces cantaba Marta Valdés y entraron a la deleitosa penumbra para tomarse una cerveza fría.

Los meses que siguieron, Hermi se dedicó a pintar con furor unos cuadros surrealistas con vacas pastando en La Rampa y balcones vacíos derritiéndose al sol, de cuyas barandillas colgaban en ristras las cabezas repetidas de una mujer decapitada a las que no se les veía el rostro. La cabeza siempre la misma, copia fiel de un cuadro terrenal de Dalí, "la culona de espaldas" que mira el mar a través de una ventana. La bahía proveyó el paisaje de fondo con un Cristo de La Habana arrodillado ante una mujer crucificada, la pecadora redimida por el sufrimiento.

WILLIE

—Ja. Ni *muerta* voy a permitir que me velen *aquí* —dijo Daontaon, derrochando su lógica natural.

El *aquí* a que se refiere con esas dramáticas cursivas es a La Funeraria de Alamar. A primera vista parece una nave de depósito, un taller mecánico sin equipos, un almacén vacío, una oficina de administración, cualquier lugar menos el sagrado recinto del MAGNO ADIÓS.

Cuando se le observa con detenimiento, permanece la misma impresión, un mero local para cumplir un trámite. Cabría decir, en vena poética, que le falta la pátina del tiempo, la acumulación de dolor que santifica y ennoblece.

No creo posible que escaseen los clientes, pero si llegara a ocurrir, la Funeraria de Alamar pudiera reconvertirse en un gimnasio o en un círculo infantil.

Miguelón se murió la semana pasada. El Consejo de Vecinos recogió dinero para la corona de flores, toca una solamente por mortuorio. Empadronar aquel matojo mustio como "ofrenda floral" sonaba pretensioso, pero imagino que al implicado le daría igual. En una tirita de tela morada con letras color oro rezaba "Querido Miguelón, no te olvidaremos nunca". Tampoco pienso que eso le vaya ni le venga ya.

Dentro de un endeble cajón gris, confeccionado con "cartón tabla", Miguelón permanecía ceñudo y recalcitrante como siempre, amortajado con su camisa de rayas mil veces zurcida en el cuello y el único pantalón de vestir. El sudario no incluía medias ni zapatos para no desperdiciar objetos tan deficitarios ni provocar la tentación del robo sacrílego. No sé por cuáles razones, los pies descalzos de los muertos me desataban un aluvión de reparos pudorosos.

A eso del atardecer, La Nata en pleno se asentó en la capilla ardiente, más que "ardiente", calurosa y sofocante. Con una inocencia que conmovía hasta el tuétano, comentaban "¡Cómo lo vamos a extrañar!", y era la más estricta verdad.

Mientras se iba acercando el horario de la telenovela, los asistentes al velatorio se fueron escurriendo de la nave de depósito, primero con discreción, y luego ya, al filo de las nueve de la noche, en franca estampida.

Después de las doce, aparecieron dos o tres borrachitos, una pareja desvelada, como siete desconocidos más y un chofer de ómnibus que arrimó el vehículo abarrotado de pasajeros frente a la funeraria, para tomar una tacita de café a la memoria de Miguelón a quien no habían visto nunca en su vida.

A las tres de la mañana, el celador dormía a pierna suelta y Daontaon se abanicaba a la luz de la única lámpara que funcionaba. Los mosquitos zumbaban y una fila de hormigas bibijaguas se dirigía en formación hacia el ataúd.

—Oye, niño, me voy a dormir para mi casa. ¡Qué va! ¡Esto no hay quién lo aguante!

Y volví a quedarme solo con un muerto. La vez anterior fue cuando Tomás se pegó el tiro. En la madrugada, la madre se desmayó y la llevaron para el hospital. Dados los sucesos, nadie, aparte de mí, la persona que más lo amaba en el mundo, acompañó a Tomás hasta el final en la "magna" despedida.

Al entierro de Miguelón tampoco asistió ninguno del edificio porque el transporte se ha puesto muy malo. Antes de hacer descender la caja en una fosa común, llegó apurada la nieta del occiso, una joven paliducha con cara ella misma de cadáver. Fue una ceremonia rápida, sin lágrimas ni panegíricos.

Por unos días se guardó compostura y un silencio se cernió sobre los equipos de audio y hasta las aves de corral limitaron sus píos píos. No puedo dejar de pensar cómo hubiera disfrutado esta tranquilidad el buen Miguelón, pero a veces hay que morirse...

A mí me toca morirme pronto. El plazo se hace cada vez más corto. Nadie lo sabe, ni siquiera Daontaon... Puntos suspensivos.

Con seguridad los vecinos harán otra ponina para encargar una corona de flores, la más grande que voy a tener, y la única. Murmurarán sobre mis pecados, "¿pero tú no sabías que Willie...?", con algo de picardía, un tin de desprecio y otro poco de compasión. Y luego se marcharán aliviados, satisfechos del deber cumplido, y apurados para no perderse un capítulo más de la telenovela. Desconocidos agradecerán tomarse un cafecito extra de la cuota a costa mía. Nadie asistirá a mi entierro porque a quién se le puede pedir que se mande hasta allá con los calores, las colas y lo malas que están las guaguas. En la fosa común, Miguelón me hará sitio y tendrá finalmente a alguien que le oiga sus peroratas por toda la eternidad.

Lo único que me sigue atormentando es la idea de mis pies desnudos.

Por algunos días, La Nata guardará una debida circunspección y Tilingo controlará lo mejor que pueda a sus chivitos.

Eso sí, para el fin de semana ya estará armado de nuevo el bailongo, no me llamo a engaño.

—*Niño, tú mismito te lo buscaste* —dirá Daontaon por toda elegía, con cursivas y punto final.

MUJER QUE HABLA SOLA EN EL PARQUE

Las bibijaguas construyeron grutas en las paredes. Las obreras socavaron los terrenos y fabricaron silos, abrieron fosos y covachuelas donde asentaron los nidos de sus reinas. Durante la noche, mientras los zánganos se esmeraban en la procreación, las guerreras salían en formación a avituallarse de comestibles y a extender sus posesiones. Y entonces las bibijaguas se apoderaron de la ciudad. Y La Habana se muere...

MARÍA ESTHER

Los romanos creían que el alma continuaba cerca de los hombres bajo la superficie del suelo. ¿De dónde había sacado ella eso? María Esther, con los ojos cerrados, trató de hacer memoria. Ah, de *La Eneida*, nada menos. Virgilio daba cuenta en detalle sobre la operación de encerrar el "ánima en la tumba". Durante la ceremonia se rogaba que al espíritu le fuera ligera la tierra, acompañado por todos los objetos que pudiese necesitar, caballos, perros, esclavos, armas, joyas, jarras, vestimentas, vino para la sed y leche para el hambre. Con esa parafernalia, se suponía que los sagrados manes permanecerían reposados al fin y satisfechos en su morada subterránea. Si se descuidaba el protocolo o no se cumplía el ritual con la debida solemnidad, el alma quedaba condenada a errar. ¿Estaría el alma de La Difunta vagando sin consuelo?

El encuentro con Martín incitaba a María Esther a desarmar el rompecabezas y volver a armarlo con las piezas dislocadas, separadas de su cuerpo como amputadas, fuera de su sitio tradicional, buscando una apariencia más exacta que la anterior.

Rompecabezas. ¿Por qué le había dado por pensar ahora en los rompecabezas? En la niñez, su técnica consistía en buscar los fragmentos de borde liso y las esquinas, de afuera para adentro, separando los pedazos de cartón por colores. De vez en cuando alguno se extraviaba, y un segmento del acertijo quedaba inconcluso.

La Difunta era una pieza perdida de los entresijos de su vida.

Las voces de los internos pasando la inspección médica de rigor sacaron a María Esther de los vericuetos en que la había inmerso Martín. La comitiva rodeó como un avispero a su nueva compañera de cuarto, una jovencita.

En las semanas que llevaba María Esther ingresada, por la cama vecina habían desfilado heterogéneos tipos de enfermas. Pacientes en fase terminal, anémicas, ancianas desahuciadas... Todas ellas con abundante parentela que se congregaban durante los horarios de visita a intercambiar comentarios sobre la familia, las enfermedades y la situación nacional. Venían con termos de café, cantinas con rebuscados alimentos, bocaditos de queso, pastelitos de guayaba, jugos, según los gustos y posibilidades económicas de cada cual. Invariablemente se compadecían del aislamiento de María Esther, sin acompañantes ni visitas, y la convidaban a participar en las comelatas o en las rondas de café. María Esther compartía con una o dos palabras de mera cortesía, aunque aceptaba agradecida la buena fe, y, sobre todo, aquellos buchitos de café, entre las cosas que más extrañaba de su antigua existencia.

Mientras el doctor Argüelles y los internos debatían con desenvoltura los padecimientos de la paciente en su propia presencia, escudriñaban a trasluz las placas y asentaban los datos en la historia clínica con conclusiones que desasosegaban a María Esther, la muchacha enferma se mantenía silenciosa y con sus ojos muy abiertos. Había llegado la tarde anterior y, a diferencia de las otras internadas, se mantuvo hosca y abstraída, casi hostil. A la hora de la visita nadie vino a verla, no probó bocado de la comida y, para asombro de María Esther, el televisor se mantuvo apagado. La muchacha se tapó la cabeza, se viró hacia la pared y aparentemente se quedó dormida. Al amanecer murmuró un enrevesado "buenos días" mientras consumía con desgano el desayuno. Tenía un semblante amarillento y los labios apretados en un rictus de dolor o desprecio. María Esther la observaba con curiosidad y algo de turbación: o se estaba volviendo loca o la muchacha se parecía como un fantasma a La Difunta.

María Esther se enteró, a pesar suyo, de que la muchacha desconocía el paradero de su padre, que la madre vivía en Londres y no tenía más familiares.

—Mi niña —la alusión cariñosa no lograba atenuar la noticia—, hay que operarte de urgencia.

La voz del doctor Argüelles dando por terminado el examen a la muchacha, le llegó a María Esther en sordina, extraviada como estaba en uno de los recovecos de su propia angustia.

ESTELA

Otro fin de semana sin noticias de Oscar. Estela empezó a romper los papeles ya caducados, entre ellos el viejo fax de Lucía anunciando su llegada. Mira que Lucía venir a acordarse de cuando querían ser escritoras. Futilidades de la adolescencia. Ya estaban todos demasiado viejos para andar recordando aquellas tonterías. ¿Dónde estarían guardados los poemas? La próxima vez que fuera a La Habana tendría que hacer una limpieza a fondo en su casa, es decir, en lo que fuera la casa de sus padres. Bajo los papeles, en la gaveta, encontró el encargo enviado por su padre con el cubano. Caramba, lo había olvidado. Estela lo palpó y sintió una sensación arenosa en los dedos a través del sobre. Abrió el pequeño bulto y se encontró con una nota escrita a lápiz que servía de funda a otro envoltorio. La letra era de su padre, casi irreconocible, "feliz hija" y, con una flecha señalizadora, se intercalaba la extraviada palabra "cumpleaños". ¡Ups! También Estela había dejado en el tintero su propio cumpleaños. El regalo de su padre consistía en un paquetico de café "de la bodega", la asignación mensual de la libreta de abastecimientos, unas pocas onzas del grano mezclado con chícharos quemados. Azorada, Estela colocó la exigua cuota de polvo sobre el buró como si se tratara de una granada sin espoleta. "Estela, necesito hablar un asuntico contigo", la voz contrariada de Olguita la tomó de sorpresa. Sin esperar respuesta, Olguita se sentó en la esquina del escritorio con muy poca consideración. Se miró las uñas pintadas de naranja, se ahuecó el pelo y se ajustó una de las argollas que llevaba en las orejas. "Tengo que tomar vacaciones", declaró después de ese preámbulo. Estela la observó primero extrañada y luego, "imposible", contestó tajante, "estamos en plena temporada alta, navidades, ¿cómo se te ocurre?". Olguita titubeó y la boca se le contrajo en una mueca que nunca antes Estela le había notado. "Me avisó un vecino, a mi hija la ingresaron de correcorre en el hospital. Está muy enferma parece". Estela no sabía si creerle o no. "¿Tienes una hija? Me acabo de enterar. ¿Cuántos años tiene?" "Dieciocho". Estela la observó, Olguita no aparentaba tener una hija de tal edad. "La dejé encargada al abuelo, pero mi suegro falleció. Ella no tiene a nadie a su lado. El padre vive afuera, hizo otra familia allá, dejó de escribirnos y no supimos más de él". Olguita soltó todas las frases como si estuviera rezando con cansancio una oración aprendida de memoria. Estela miró el paquete de café de la libreta. "Lo siento, Olga, pero si te vas ahora, tengo que sustituirte por otra persona, no puedo prescindir de nadie en la oficina. Yo misma perdí a mi madre y, mira, no pude…" Olguita la interrumpió con un ademán. "Pues, vete buscando otra, Estela, en el primer avión me voy para La Habana". "Como quieras". Olga se levantó de la esquina del buró y se sacudió la falda como si hubiera estado sentada sobre cenizas o pavesas volcánicas. Colocó una tarjeta sobre el buró. "Ah", dijo en tono opaco, "y trajeron esto para ti hace un momento". Se sacudió la melena rojiza, salió de la oficina de Estela y, prácata, le metió un tirón a la puerta. Estela tomó la tarjeta y vio con desagrado que se trataba de una invitación para una "fiesta latinoamericana" como se les solía llamar. Otra vez a pasar por el mismo suplicio: un montón de argentinos deprimidos que a las primeras de cambio pedían algo regalado, lo que fuera, un libro, un afiche, una invitación para viajar a operarse gratuitamente, todos "solidarios", pero bien lejos del atraso y la pobreza, faltaba más, tomando whisky y comiendo *paté de foie gras;* dos o tres colombianos nostálgicos, unos chilenos trasnochados que recitaban de memoria poemas de Guillén; luego, para redondear, el recorrido por las mismas cantaletas de siempre, los tangos, las cumbias, las rancheras y los bolerones. Por último, antes de caer todos ebrios y llorando sus añoranzas, claro, no podía faltar, los frijoles negros con arroz blanco, tostones y bistecs de filete con mucha cebolla frita, la cena a "lo cubano" preparada por Tussy, la compatriota que llevaba mil años allí. Se había quedado viuda a mediados de los ochenta y procuraba atraer a su lecho a cuanto paisano desfilaba por Londres. Algunos se quedaban una temporada en su casa bien avituallada y luego, si te he visto no me acuerdo. Otros duraban más, como el matemático que a la postre la había dejado plantada por una holandesa de mejor ver. Mientras el matemático se albergó en Londres, las fiestas tuvieron música cubana asegurada porque el zutano, para sobrevivir, había montado una especie de orquestica, con un piano electrónico, un casete de grabadora con música acompañante y un compinche escocés que había aprendido a tocar la tumbadora mal que bien. Estela no se acordaba del nombre del grupo que ahora "actuaba" en un cafetucho de Ámsterdam, engañando a los pobres europeos duros de oídos que confundían el galimatías del matemático con auténtica música caribeña. Santo cielo. Los cubanos la sacaban del paso. Estela rompió la tarjeta en varios pedacitos y, junto con el envoltorio del café, los tiró al cesto de basura.

GERTRUDIS

Con los prismáticos de La Difunta oteábamos el horizonte marino, los barquitos pesqueros, los cargueros y los buques petroleros que anclaban esperando por la lancha del práctico para entrar en la bahía, vigilábamos la cadencia de las olas y, cuando había mal tiempo, el oleaje que saltaba sobre el muro del Malecón e inundaba la plazoleta de la calle G; curioseábamos los interiores de las casas de los alrededores, las azoteas, la cola del Recodo; sobre todo, los sábados patrullábamos la entrada del club Turf cerca de la esquina de Calzada, famoso para las parejas debido a la oscuridad de su salón, y desde una ventana del piso 23 nos dedicábamos a espiar quién entraba y quién salía del Turf, y acompañado de quién, los amores clandestinos, los novios escapados de sus novias oficiales después de dejarlas a resguardo en la beca, los vecinos adúlteros con sus esposas durmiendo confiadas. Pero todo inocente, sin ninguna maldad.

En efecto, el Turf era ideal para enamorar, como el Pico Blanco para oír filin, el Salón Rojo al igual que El Parisién para bailar entre un show y otro, Las Cañitas del hotel Habana Libre para repasar antes de los exámenes y El Ruedo para conversar.

Quince mujeres van en el Cofre de la Muerta. ¡Ay, ay, ay, la botella de ron!

A la salida de la Escuela, en los días de mucho calor, cuando no teníamos nada mejor que hacer nos metíamos en El Ruedo, la taberna de G y 23 con penumbroso ambiente español, ¿se acuerdan? Al entrar, desde el resplandor del sol, nos quedábamos cegatos, tropezando entre las sillas. Por un solo vaso de sangría, los camareros servían gratis varias bandejas con alitas fritas de pollo y con eso se mataba el hambre, mientras alrededor de una mesona de madera discutíamos a gritos sobre política, cine, filosofía o literatura, acompañados al piano por pasodobles y con la aterradora testuz de un toro pendiente de nuestras cabezas.

El Ruedo era bueno para pasar el rato, hasta que se estropeó. Aquella tarde, nadie había invitado a ese tipo, uno del aula, a venir con nosotros, pero se nos pegó y estuvo dando la lata desde el principio, escarbándose las encías con un bolígrafo y haciendo preguntas capciosas. Sobre las siete, igual que todos los días, subió al estrado un guitarrista y arrancó a cantar algo parecido a un fado, luego la bailarina de flamenco, vestida con un traje blanco de lunares rojos lleno de vuelos, pliegues y fruncidos, comenzó su danza, coreada por palmadas de los parroquianos. Todo iba bien hasta que, por un inusitado despliegue de luz, nos percatamos de que aquella bailarina regordeta debía de tener como quinientos años, varias capas de pintura le tapaban las arrugas y sobre el colorete repuntaban los lunares artificiales como moscones. Si uno se fijaba, a pesar del taconeo alegre, tenía una mirada desastrosa, "igual a los payasos", comentó La Difunta. A la verdad, cantaba requetemal y bailaba peor, pero era lo que llevaba haciendo toda la vida, aquello era su vida, su vida de artista, el aplauso del público, el brindis de los borrachos con vino tinto, los aguardientosos "oles", y nosotros los dábamos siempre de buena gana. Poca cosa a cambio de las fuentes y fuentes de alitas de pollo... De improviso, aquella tarde de marras, el tipo del bolígrafo se subió al tablado para hacerle la competencia a la bailarina. Al principio, ella aguantó a pie firme y trató de sobrellevar la situación, de todas formas ese era su trabajo y por ello le pagaban, y hasta de vez en cuando le caía una propina. Pero cuando el imbécil, a risotadas, pidió un aplauso para su "abuela", la bailarina gordinflona empezó a llorar y salió corriendo. Entonces La Difunta también se trepó a la tarima, con lo pequeñita y enclenque que parecía, y sentó al tipo de un bofetón. El escándalo fue público. Como era de esperar, la reprimenda le cayó más fuerte a La Difunta por tratarse de una mujer envuelta en semejante reyerta. Y ahí mismo se fastidió El Ruedo y los buenos ratos que pasábamos allí.

Después de aquel incidente, yo no podía escapar a una sensación de inseguridad. Los acontecimientos parecían continuar el mismo recorrido conocido y en solo un segundo, con un traspié en la secuencia de los hechos, se ingresaba en otra dimensión ajena y amenazadora. Aunque no lo sabíamos, además de la cabeza de toro encima, ya teníamos una espada semejante a la que colgaba de un pelillo de crin sobre la cortesana de Siracusa, aquella señorita Damocles que reía y cantaba sin saber lo que le iba a caer arriba.

Chas, de un momento a otro se iba a encender la hoguera. Y tendríamos que volver a plantearnos la máxima pregunta del final de *Galilea Galilei*. ¿Salvar el pellejo o perseverar en la verdad como Giordana Bruna?

Acuérdense, iban a querer quitarnos hasta lo bailado.

YUYA

Dice Yuya que salir de un apartamento en Alamar para cualquier parte es casi imposible, pero para el Vedado... ¡un milagro! Bien es verdad que la carta guardada del cuarto en el solar de Los Muertos fue una jugada maestra.

Merced a las heredades del cuarto del solar, olvidado por todos, hasta por Lalita, y cerrado bajo dos candados todo aquel tiempo, Yuya pudo hacer el ofrecimiento mágico de las permutas: "dos por una", es decir, dos viviendas por una, la de Alamar y la de la calle Ánimas, nada menos que por un apartamento de tres cuartos, terraza con vista al mar y dos baños, de primera categoría, en el barrio más codiciado de La Habana.

El apartamento necesitaba pintura, reparación de ventanas y un mantenimiento de la plomería, mas Yuya se sentía triunfante. El primer cuarto, con baño y salida directa a la terraza, fue ocupado por Lalita y su amiga; Shu y Yuya se acomodaron en el segundo, con proporciones más grandes que la casa completa del matrimonio en aquella desaparecida azotea del barrio chino; el tercero, pequeño y sin ocupación aparente, se convirtió, por obra y gracia de los tiempos que corrían, en el cuarto sagrado del altar, con todos los santos y protectores en exhibición, como se lo tenían bien ganado.

A la semana de mudarse, ya Yuya se consideraba una vedadense de nacimiento. Lalita sonreía después de muchos meses, Shu estaba descansado y ella sentía que estaba cumplido su destino. ¡Jesús mil veces! ¡El trabajo que le había costado ir descifrando los innumerables laberintos en que se le iba enredando la vida entera! Según Yuya, ni ella supo a derechas el comienzo de su cuento, mucho menos el final, mas su buena estrella la había ayudado a desentrañar los misterios con que se fue topando en el camino.

Después de muchos años se volvió a encontrar con Luisa en el Correo de Línea. Casi no la reconoció. Yuya sabía de los estragos de la vejez en su propio cuerpo, pero le sorprendió el deterioro de la imagen de Luisa, tan bella y radiante cuando vendía lámparas en el Ten Cent de Galiano y ahora una mujer desarreglada, con la boca crispada por una mueca de amargura, parada en la cola para cobrar su pensión de jubilada, unos cuantos pesos que no alcanzaban para llegar a fin de mes.

Se sentaron en uno de los bancos de la calle Paseo. Amenazaba con empezar a llover de un momento a otro y la ventolera que llegaba del mar arremolinaba las hojas secas a sus pies. Luisa parecía no tener ningún apuro y, según Yuya, sin que ella preguntara nada, le contó todas sus desgracias: de la casona en Miramar, del galán militar y de la buena vida no quedaba nada. El militar la engañó, durante años, con su asistente, una pelandruja de la misma edad que su hija menor; Luisa descubrió que, encima, su marido tenía un hijo natural anterior a su casamiento; las dos hijas se pelearon con su padre y entre sí; se vieron obligados a dividir la casona en tres viviendas y al matrimonio le tocó la más pequeña, pasillo interior, aunque en el Vedado. Al militar lo retiraron del servicio en el mal año de 1989 y se enfermó de los nervios, luego le dio por la religión y no salía de la iglesia. El hijo natural, repudiado por su padre, vino a verlo de Miami y se reconciliaron. Ahora los "ayudaba" de tanto en tanto. ¡Gracias a eso! Una de sus hijas decidió instalarse en Europa, "consiguió una beca allá" según la interpretación de Luisa y hace mucho tiempo que no saben de ella. La otra no les habla, ni siquiera les ha dejado conocer a los nietos. Para rematar, se inundó el garaje cuando el último ciclón y el Lada había quedado inservible.

Según Yuya, la noche anterior había soñado con el temido brazo izquierdo del Chinito de la Charada y con el Dos de Espadas. Tiñosa por partida doble. Falsedad, infidelidad y superchería. Se levantó inquieta, tratando de interpretar aquel mensaje. Mientras Luisa le contaba su historia, respiró tranquila, la alegría no le competía de modo directo, se trataba de un aviso del encuentro, resumen, en una sola figura, de muchos años del destino de Luisa. A pesar de todo, Yuya sintió una oleada de compasión hacia su antigua amiga.

Ahora Luisa tenía que hacerlo todo: cuidar al inútil de su marido, comprar los mandados a pie, limpiar la casa; elaborar unos "cakes" de coco para vender y aumentar las entradas para ir tirando... ¿Acaso Yuya no le quisiera encargar uno? Se lo daba más barato por tratarse de su comadre.

¡Las vueltas que da la vida!, dice Yuya.

LOLA

Lola abrió la puerta de la terraza y expuso su cuerpo a la oscuridad del apagón y al viento frío que provenía del mar. Tanteó en las sombras y se sentó en el sillón, tan lleno de olores y rasguños en la madera que podía reconocer idénticos en su propia piel. Un silencio, el temido silencio que abría la compuerta de la memoria, le oprimió el alma como una garra. ¿Cuál? ¿Cuál de todos sus malos recuerdos vendría a atormentarla?

Para su sorpresa, un hueco negro, terrorífico, peor que todos los malos recuerdos, se abría como un pozo vacío en su cabeza. ¿A dónde habían ido a parar todos?

—¡Lola! ¿Está despierta? —una voz desconocida la hablaba con familiaridad desde la terraza vecina—. Lola, es Yuya, su vecina. Hice una natilla que me quedó buenísima. ¿Quiere probarla?

¿Yuya? Lola no se acordaba de nadie llamado así.

—¡Lola! —ahora la voz provenía del pasillo de entrada—. ¿Se encuentra bien?

Lola descubrió un tenue fulgor que se agitaba por los resquicios de las traviesas.

—Si —respondió—. Estoy...

—Ay, que susto me dio, Lola. Llevo una hora llamándola. Ábrame, que le traje un poquito de postre.

Lola caminó con precaución hacia la luminiscencia y abrió la puerta.

Con una sonrisa de oreja a oreja, un candil en una mano y un platico con dulce en la otra, estaba su extravagante vecina. Lola la dejó entrar.

—Los apagones son distintos en el Vedado que en Alamar —afirmó Yuya, con una lógica incomprensible para Lola—. Huelen distinto. Venga, Lola, cómase esta natilla. Le va a caer bien.

Mientras Yuya hablaba sin parar, Lola se sentó obediente y, despacio, goloseando como cuando era una niña, se empezó a comer la blanca crema, olorosa a limón y espolvoreada de canela en abundancia. ¡Qué tiempo hacía que no comía algo así!

—¡Ah! —exclamó Yuya, casi gritando—. ¡Ya llegó la luz, a tiempo para ver la novela! ¿Y esto?

Sobre la mesa del comedor, se encontraba desparramado un manojo de fotos: Sara con doce años vistiendo el uniforme de la Alfabetización, abrazada a un enorme lápiz; un grupo posando para la cámara, Lola con Sara en brazos el día de su bautizo, apiñados ante la puerta de la Iglesia del Cristo; Sara en la terraza, la víspera de la partida y con cara de circunstancias; Sara, muy abrigada, en la Plaza de San Marcos, con una paloma posada encima y mirando con ojos irónicos; Lola y Evaristo con Sara, joven y sonriente, inclinándose para asegurarse de entrar en el encuadre; Sara, con sus amigos de la carrera, en la Escalinata de la Universidad imitando, con los brazos abiertos de par en par, la estatua del Alma Mater; Sara, acostada boca arriba sobre la arena en la playa de Varadero, sin saber que el fotógrafo se encimaba sobre su rostro dormido; Sara, muy niña, abrazada a un gato.

Yuya señaló a Sara y le preguntó a Lola quién era.

—El gato de mi hija.

Yuya iba a insistir, pero se detuvo ante el rostro apenado de Lola.

—Se murió hace mil años. No me acuerdo cómo se llamaba.

Lola tomó la jocosa foto del Alma Mater y señaló a una muchacha de lentes, acuclillada a los pies de Sara.

—Y esta es La Difunta. Uno de mis peores recuerdos —dijo Lola.

MUJER QUE HABLA SOLA EN EL PARQUE

De uno de los baches en medio de la calle salió expelida una inmensa columna de humo, y luego otra, y otra más, se dispararon por todas partes. Y entonces brotaron surtidores de hollín y miles de fumaradas asfixiantes. Y La Habana se muere...

MARÍA ESTHER

María Esther perdió la fe. Se había convertido en una apóstata desde la adolescencia. Su tránsito de la religiosidad al ateísmo se produjo sin fricciones ni incertidumbres de conciencia. Nadie la obligó, ni fue motivo de conflicto. Un día Dios estaba todavía ahí y al siguiente no estuvo más, tan natural y reposado como una hoja seca que cae por su propio peso.

Cuando niña, había cumplido con un aprendizaje concienzudo del catecismo y la historia sagrada. A la edad requerida tomó con seriedad la primera comunión. Los viernes se abstenía de comer carne y profesó las doctrinas como lo indicaban sus maestras, las santas monjitas de la escuela católica María Auxiliadora.

A lo largo de los años sesenta, supo que algunas de sus condiscípulas sufrieron y se atormentaron por la perdida de los credos; otras, por el contrario, fueron víctimas de la intolerancia que enturbiaba el escenario. Ella ni siquiera sintió dudas o remordimientos.

En una ocasión, durante un congreso literario en Río de Janeiro, María Esther fue invitada por sus colegas a conocer el Cristo Redentor en la cumbre del Monte Corcovado, visita obligatoria. Durante el ascenso en automóvil por el parque de Tijuca, atravesando una lujuriosa vegetación, el ambiente se mantenía risueño y dentro de las habituales bromas entre académicos. Al llegar al estacionamiento, en el último tramo del ascenso, un inusual fenómeno atmosférico al decir de sus acompañantes, cubrió toda la cima con una niebla volátil que no dejaba ver más allá de las narices. María Esther avanzó a pie, desprevenida entre la bruma, hasta llegar a la plazoleta circular que rodeaba la base del monumento. De buenas a primeras, el viento despejó los celajes y la efigie, la mole de concreto de treinta y ocho metros, se reveló ante la espantada mirada de María Esther, convertida súbitamente en una partícula ínfima del universo. La fe le fue devuelta como un puñetazo que le quitó el aliento. Ante sí, no tenía una estatua, sino La Creación misma.

La sensación duró apenas unos segundos. La fe volvió a desaparecer como había venido, arrastrada por una ventolera, pero María Esther no pudo olvidar aquel momento de desfallecimiento, de vulnerabilidad, de insignificancia.

Nunca se lo contó a nadie. Los vivos suelen olvidar que aún pueden hablar con otros vivos.

La segunda vez que se sintió tocada por los misterios del evangelio ocurrió cuando su propia madre agonizaba. Según recordaba de su niñez, en semejantes casos lo único que quedaba era rezar, confiar en un futuro encuentro, donde fuese; pero María Esther estaba incapacitaba para creer. No obstante, en su fuero interno pidió en plegaria poco ortodoxa, si bien ella no fuese creyente, su madre sí, por favor, que muera con la paz merecida.

Durante aquellos meses de la enfermedad de su madre, el cielo se le juntó con la tierra. Como suele suceder siempre en los momentos de crisis, todas las desgracias ocurrieron al mismo tiempo, sin anestesia: el hijo se marchó definitivamente del país, murió el viejo perro de la familia, descubrió una conspiración en su trabajo para destituirla del cargo y se rompió el refrigerador.

María Esther hubiera necesitado el consuelo de la fe. Por aquellos tiempos, empezó a beber. Ahora, acostada en aquella cama de hospital, con los días contados, quisiera poder creer. Con cualquier religión o certidumbre todo sería más fácil, pero no podía, no podía y no podía.

La silenciosa muchacha que se parecía como un fantasma a La Difunta no regresó del salón de operaciones. La enfermera le dijo que fue trasladada para la sala de terapia intensiva. Allí se debatía por vivir, o eso quiso pensar María Esther.

Un viento ciego, como aquel del Corcovado, arrimaba a su recuerdo los años superfluos de su vida, los abandonos, las lejanías, las culpas, los muertos inútiles.

ESTELA

Olguita se fue sin despedirse. "Mejor así"., pensó Estela. La oficina de Estela se mantenía por el momento silenciosa, mientras no llegara otro de los tantos especímenes que solían recalar por allí. Estela revisó los faxes y luego intentó infructuosamente una comunicación con La Habana para hablar con Oscar. Las líneas congestionadas por el feriado justificaban, en parte, la incomunicación, aunque, cuando al filo del mediodía, hora de Cuba, logró por fin establecer la llamada, la operadora le anunció que daba timbre y timbre, y no salía nadie. "¿No tiene otro número?" "No", contestó Estela, "no tengo otro número". Cerró bajo llave los archivos y la puerta encristalada de su despacho y se despidió de sus colegas con el clásico "Hasta el año que viene", o igual a decir, hasta el miércoles, dentro de cinco días. La niebla londinense, un manto tupido que desaparecía los objetos al largo de su brazo, la estimuló a caminar un rato, como moviéndose en un hálito fantasmal que la convertía en invisible. De tanto en tanto, un cuerpo desconocido emergía de las sombras tejidas en lino blanco y cruzaba a su lado sin mirarla. Atravesando Leicester Square, con todos los teatros y la majestuosa Royal Opera House, se sorprendió pensando que a Lucía le hubiese gustado pasear por allí. Ella debía estar ya de regreso, a sus banales preocupaciones por "conseguir leche en polvo" y "poner el motor del agua... cuando entre", según le había contado en su aburrido monólogo. Por fortuna, Lucía no le había hecho ningún comentario sobre La Difunta. Al menos supo guardar compostura en ese sentido, entre todos era la única que hubiese podido endilgarle algún reproche. Lucía "sabía" y "sabía que Estela sabía que ella sabía", en esa retahíla de oscuras sabidurías que no estaba permitido compartir. Por lo demás, Estela no sentía ningún arrepentimiento, a pesar de aquello que pasó "después que", el "después que" de La Difunta antes de que aún no fuera La Difunta. Mejor no revolver aquel episodio, dejarlo así, sin menear. Lo pasado, pasado. Nunca se había vuelto a encontrar con aquel hombre que las citó a las dos con mucho misterio a una habitación vacía, en el sótano de la Escuela de Biología, junto al "Parque de los Cabezones". Solamente Lucía y Estela. Ni siquiera Oscar podía enterarse. En la extraña reunión, "hablen de lo que quieran" casi ordenó, mientras enrollaba uno de los extremos de una cinta de grabación en el otro carrete y apretaba una tecla que puso en funcionamiento el enorme equipo que ocupaba prácticamente todo el mueble. Sentadas en una esquina, Lucía y Estela intercambiaron miradas desconcertadas por la situación. Chirrín chirrín chirrín, rasgueaba la bobina, mientras el hombre las observaba, aguardando, con una sonrisa congelada en el rostro muy afeitado. De repente, Lucía, tan impropia, soltó una carcajada. El hombre apretó con autoridad el "stop" y acercó su silla, hasta colocarse frente a frente. Con aire paternal, les explicó lo que se esperaba de ellas dos. "Se necesitaba", usó todo el tiempo los verbos en forma impersonal, que ella y Lucía "se acercaran" a La Difunta que todavía no era La Difunta. Que le demostraran amistad, ganaran su confianza; en definitiva, hizo un gesto falso de contrariedad mostrando su disgusto por verse obligado a usar esa expresión, que "la sonsacasen". Averiguar todo lo que se pudiera, cómo piensa, con quién se reúne, qué quiere hacer con su vida, el hombre les hablaba en tono untuoso, amigable, "es por el bien de ella", casi parecía que con aquel engranaje puesto en marcha se le iba a hacer un favor a La Difunta que todavía no era La Difunta. "Y sin detalles, por supuesto", añadió, "pero sus relaciones amorosas son del máximo interés". Lucía se negó y abrió los ojos como dos platos cuando Estela aceptó. El hombre precisó que, dadas las circunstancias, aquella conversación quedaba entre los tres porque así "se le podía ayudar mejor" a La Difunta, cuando todavía faltaban unos meses para que llegara a convertirse en La Difunta. Justo al cruzar Estela la calle, cerca de Covent Garden, la neblina se disipó por completo y dio paso a un aguacero. Un pub a orillas del Támesis, limpio y bien alumbrado, la animó a entrar y pedir una cerveza. Hacía mucho tiempo que no entraba a un bar. Y sola, a decir verdad, nunca lo había hecho en la vida.

MICAELA

Esa foto de Candita, su tía, Micaela no la miraba nunca y ahora parecía como si la llamara, igual que en los sueños. "Micaela, ten compasión". Tenía el pelo recogido en un moño que le daba un aspecto autoritario y avanzaba inexorable el mentón de un rostro pálido, exigente. Micaela guardó la caja de fotografías en el armario, con cautela, como si la tía Candita pudiese saltar de la cartulina y sacudirla por los hombros.

La memoria era tan traicionera como el mar con resaca, se dijo Micaela. En los retazos de letargo que robaba a la vigilia, volvía a ver las medias rojas de rayas blancas de La Difunta colgando olvidadas en el patio del solar. Para colmo, las últimas apariciones de la tía Candita le hicieron soñar a cuentagotas, en las madrugadas de sus insomnios, con la casa donde había vivido en su juventud, aquellos tiempos en que todavía nadie se había muerto, ni nadie se había ido, y entraban y salían... Y volvían a entrar y volvían a salir el montón de amigos, vecinos y parientes de Micaela, una familia grandísima que no cabía en ninguna parte a la hora de celebrar algún acontecimiento, y terminaban siempre congregándose en la humilde azotea de la calle Ánimas, tocando el abuelo la armónica y la tía Candita bailando una jota.

En aquella azotea, convertida ahora en escombros, también acostumbraba a reunirse el grupo para preparar las asignaturas a examen cuando estudiaban en la universidad. Micaela volvió a ver en sueños el tapiz de descolorido brocado detrás del sofá donde se sentaban a tomarse una limonada, las meriendas que preparaba su mamá con galletas untadas de mayonesa y empanadas gallegas de la panadería de la esquina, el tocadiscos de aguja para las fiestas del sábado, el tapetico tejido por su abuela y colocado de adorno sobre el televisor, el padre dándole manotazos al radio para que echara a andar, el tío leyendo el periódico en el sillón de balance, los vasos boca abajo sobre la bandeja encima del refrigerador Westinghouse, la única silla Thonet al lado de la repisa del teléfono, en aquel pasillo por donde transitaban continuamente abuelos, tíos, primos, su papá y su mamá, la tía Candita, la mulata Etelvina que le cosía sus batas de niña, el grupo, La Difunta, la perra Lobita y sus crías. Detrás de cada pestañazo de sueño la estaban acechando sus muertos queridos. Con los reclamos de la tía Candita no podía seguir eludiendo, aunque quisiera, pasar revista a aquel pasado, un catálogo de pecios, de naves hundidas.

Micaela se encapuchó con su veterana parka rusa y caminó hasta la costa, solitaria a esa hora. El mar se veía tranquilo, pero de un color acerado como solía estarlo cuando amenazaba tormenta. Mientras caminaba por los dientes de perro, se levantó un viento rabioso, los granillos de arena se le metían por los ojos y la boca con tal fuerza que le cortaban la respiración. Sintió que la cabeza le iba a estallar.

Sobre la aparente calma, la ventolera golpeaba con sus aspas, segando las capas de olvido que, una tras otra, Micaela había dejado ir cayendo encima de aquellas historias, historias arrinconadas desde hacía ya tantos años, cuando Sara, los otros, La Difunta, ella misma, eran tan jóvenes que cada uno creía que estaba cambiando el mundo por su propia cuenta.

Miró esa orilla marina arrebatada por los golpes de viento y le pareció un remedo de todo lo que le estaba pasando: un temporal que arrasaría con cualquier intento suyo, una vez más en la vida, de ponerse al socaire, Micaela comprendió al fin.

Pero... cómo era posible que se hubiera olvidado de la silla Thonet. ¿Dónde habrá ido a parar?

LOLA

Lola bajó con dificultad la escalera para buscar su pan, aquel que "le tocaba", el panecito racionado de la libreta de abastecimientos, una sola pieza diaria por persona, aplastada, correosa y con gamas verdosas. Cuando llegó a la cola, la venta se seguía demorando y los que aguardaban desde horas tempranas, todos viejos y con aspecto enfermizo, comentaban con voces alteradas sobre la aparición de una mujer descuartizada en Alamar. ¿Alamar? Ese nombre le traía a Lola alguna resonancia vaga. ¿Quién vivía en Alamar?

Lola trató de no escuchar los detalles inquietantes. Mientras esperaba, sintió ganas de alejarse, escapar, caminar unas cuadras por el barrio. ¡Hacía tanto tiempo que no lo hacía! Las mañanas de domingo en el Vedado lucían distintas, Lola no podía definir exactamente en qué consistía. Tal vez el aire apacible cobraba una inusual luminosidad bajo los arbolones de los parterres, quizás la quietud confería un concierto de sonidos peculiares, hasta los olores daban la impresión de manifestarse con mayor nobleza.

Lola se acordó de cuando aún se compraba la flauta de pan crujiente, oloroso a harina y mantequilla, en la panadería de Calzada y 18. Su madre le contaba que la calle Calzada fue de las primeras en el barrio, quizás la más antigua. Por aquel entonces, Lola todavía una niña, Calzada era estrecha y los terrenos baldíos se ocupaban poco a poco con casonas de exuberantes jardines delanteros y portales umbríos. Al Vedado en construcción se llegaba desde La Habana de intramuros en un tranvía que cruzaba, paralelo al perfil de la costa, por la calle Línea, nombrada así, pensaba Lola, mientras cruzaba ahora la propia calle Línea, desierta en esta mañana de domingo, por el mismo tránsito del tranvía. Se asombró de recordar con nitidez los traqueteantes carros, la campana que avisaba su presencia, las barras y los asientos de madera, y los rieles todavía visibles hasta hacía algunos años.

Los padres de Lola la llevaban en tranvía a tomar aire de mar a los conocidos "reservados", dispuestos en los arrecifes al terminar la calle E, llamada Baños por aquellos balnearios en las rocas, en las pocetas acordonadas para que los bañistas no se salieran mar afuera a riesgo de tiburones. Los padres de Lola alquilaban una caseta en "El Progreso", con bancos para desvestirse y una pudorosa privacidad de aquella época, cada familia dueña de un charco marino tapiado por tabiques a las miradas de los otros veraneantes.

Lola caminó unas calles más hasta llegar a la esquina de Calzada y 4. A la cuadra siguiente se encontraba el hotel Trotcha donde Lola y Evaristo habían pasado su luna de miel, tres días en una habitación del segundo piso del edificio anexado al costado de la magnífica construcción original y que su dueño, el viejo catalán Buenaventura, amigo del tío Sebastián, con olfato para los negocios había bautizado como "Edén".

La puerta de la habitación, la última de la izquierda, se abría al pasillo que enfrentaba el jardín, la ventana del costado a un muro de verde vegetación y la trasera daba al océano, desde donde llegaba un viento del litoral. Lola recordaba como si hubiese ocurrido ayer el sabor salino depositado en sus labios y la vista de las esmeradas parcelas de césped entre senderos, las florestas y una plazoleta con mesas para sentarse a tomar el sol o conversar a la luz de las farolas. El jardín del hotel Trotcha y el mar al atardecer, los únicos recuerdos bondadosos que Lola se permitía de aquellos primeros días de su matrimonio con Evaristo, del "edén" había pasado a un prolongado limbo que culminó con el infierno de la traición.

Mientras Lola avanzaba trabajosamente, con sus adoloridas piernas casi a rastras, recordaba el elegante estilo neoclásico del hotel Trotcha, con sus cuatro columnas y el techo rojo a dos aguas sobre un impresionante segundo piso, cuyo acceso se consumaba por una regia escalinata escoltada por espejos e iluminada por fogosos cristales coloreados donde imperaba aquel rojo único, exclusivo de los vitrales habaneros.

La última vez que lo vio, unos meses antes de la partida de Sara, conservaba todavía parte de su jardín. Lo demás ya había sido convertido en un terreno de juegos con malezas y escombros a todo su alrededor. Desde las habitaciones, transformadas en cuartos de ciudadela, colgaban ropas íntimas sobre las barandas. En el cuerpo principal del edificio se seguía irguiendo el frontispicio sostenido por las cuatro pilastras, con los vitrales despedazados. Un espejo sobreviviente, manchado de azogue, devolvía la quebrada imagen de la basura acumulada en los rincones del antiguo vestíbulo. En aquel lejano día, Sara había recogido del piso un fragmento roto de vitral rojo.

Cuando Lola alcanzó por fin la esquina de Calzada y 2, y se detuvo frente a las ruinas de lo que antaño había sido el hotel Trotcha creyó que se había equivocado de sitio. En un solar yermo apenas quedaban los despojos de la fachada y el frontón sostenido por las cuatro columnas mordidas de salitre. En una esquina del techo roto crecía absurdamente un arbusto, irónico vestigio del vergel de antaño.

Enmarcado en uno de los huecos de entrada que no conducían a ninguna parte, Lola creyó distinguir, a plena luz del día, el fantasma de una mujer descuartizada con un pedazo de vitral en su regazo.

MUJER QUE HABLA SOLA EN EL PARQUE

Todos los calderos de las cocinas reventaron a la vez. Y entonces las calles se inundaron de potaje de chícharos, duros o desbaratados, de color amarillento y nauseabundo olor a aceite rancio. Y La Habana se muere...

YUYA

Dice Yuya que a causa del calor, los mosquitos y la impaciencia de la espera por la luz que no acababa de llegar, le agarró la madrugada de aquel sábado, desvelada y con malos presagios. Cuando se acabó el apagón, Yuya tenía endurecidos los párpados de tanto otear en la oscuridad. Salió de las sábanas pegajosas, se dio una ducha y encendió el televisor. Una persecución de carros por las calles de Manhattan en la pantalla y una sirena de ambulancia por el vecindario se confundieron en su cabeza. Ni siquiera el ventilador a todo meter paliaba el bochorno de la noche. Y algo, algo, algo, no andaba bien. Nada bien. Entonces vio al haitiano, dice Yuya que no se podía creer aquello, el haitiano de Arroyo El Muerto, vestido de *dandy* y rodeado de mafiosos, la miraba con intensidad desde la escena en unos muelles nioyorquinos; su cabeza apenas se mantuvo visible unos instantes antes que la balacera que se armó allí lo derribara entre los primeros.

Terminó la película, sonaron las notas del Himno Nacional, y todavía Yuya no podía pegar ojo. Los fatales augurios se habían multiplicado, plagados de galimatías, como esa araña que se paseaba desfachatada por el borde de la baranda del balcón. Disgusto, dolor, aflicción forzosa. *New York,* por su parte, en la charada china se jugaba con el 87, anuncio de algo repentino. A todo eso se le sumaba que, apenas ayer, había llegado por correo una desoladora carta de Liudmila la Búlgara desde su tierra natal, donde su amiga le contaba con amargura, en su jerga barriobajera de La Habana, que por allá "la cosa se había puesto durísima" y le advertía no dejara de tomar precauciones con la centena 160 *sol oscuro* y el Tres de Espadas, *extravío, alienación mental...* ¡Jesús mil veces!

En el interior de la casa de Lola titilaba un bombillo de luz fría y Yuya se percató de que las puertas de su terraza permanecían abiertas de par en par, cosa rara a esa hora tan tarde. Quizás Lola también se había dejado arrastrar por el insomnio. Yuya no dudó en llamarla para ofrecerle una taza de té. Pensándolo bien, no había visto a Lola en varios días. Según Yuya, la última vez que la visitó, hacía ya casi una semana, Lola había tenido una conducta anormal, más que chocante, extrañísima. Ella, tan reservada, de tan pocas palabras, le confesó una difusa historia sobre una tal Difunta. Dice Yuya que mientras la escuchaba, su propio corazón se llenaba de compasión, sobre todo porque no había nada que se pudiera hacer.

Dice Yuya que cuando el arroz se pasa de sal no hay forma de enderezarlo, mejor botar el caldero completo y volverlo a hacer. Pero el destino no es como cocinar arroz, si uno se equivoca no se puede echar para atrás. Según Yuya, hay que comérselo salado.

—Ya han muerto todos sus dolientes y puede contarse sin herir a nadie —fue lo último que Yuya le oyó decir a Lola.

—¡Lola! —dice Yuya que la primera llamada la hizo en voz baja. Y la segunda también. Pero, cuando no recibió respuesta ni siquiera tumbándole la puerta a porrazos, despertó a gritos al edificio completo y a las once mil vírgenes del Vedado.

Dice Yuya que ya casi ni se acordaba del rostro de Etelvina, mas su presencia insistente en el espejo de la sala le indicó que tenía que mandarse a correr, se trataba de una auténtica emergencia.

MARÍA ESTHER

Por fin ya había terminado el horario de visita en el hospital y los bulliciosos familiares de su actual compañera de cuarto abandonaron la habitación. El televisor seguía encendido, aunque a María Esther había terminado por resultarle indiferente. No demandaba de ella ningún movimiento ni decisión, tan solo brillaba y gorgoteaba como un decorado de fondo. Hubiese querido echarle mano a la canequita de ron que durante años transportó escondida en su cartera, para aturdirse y caer dormida, con una ausencia completa de recuerdos, de aquellas presencias que no la dejaban evadirse de los roles que ella misma se fue asignando en la vida. El insomnio, mezclado con una turbulencia confusa, la había martirizado por mucho tiempo antes de caer enferma. Ahora, la laxitud provocada por los medicamentos la inclinaba a la memoria, aunque fuese dolorosa, al repaso de los escenarios, al conjuro de fantasmas.

¡Los espectros que Martín había despertado! No pensaba que su "ex" repetiría la visita. Desde que lo conoció en los atolondrados años sesenta, tuvo tendencia a la frivolidad, a desmontar la realidad en función de restarle compromiso. ¡Y así quería llegar a ser un gran escritor! En lugar de irritarse como solía, María Esther accedió a sentir compasión. En cada persona había muchas personas. Ella no fue capaz de reconocerlo a tiempo y ya parecía demasiado tarde, sobre todo con su hijo.

La compañera de cuarto comentaba en voz alta las incidencias del noticiero. María Esther asentía sin prestar atención, llevaba casi cuatro meses ingresada, lo que sucediera afuera no tenía comparación con la destrucción de su cuerpo. Se miró las manos cubiertas de manchitas pardas y al levantar la cabeza para repasar otra vez la cicatriz del abdomen, sintió un desvanecimiento. Cuando volvió a abrir los ojos, el *run run* del televisor continuaba, la enferma de la cama vecina mantenía el mismo monólogo y la habitación del hospital parecía clavada en el tiempo.

Un rato después, entró la enfermera a pasarle el suero y María Esther volvió a preguntarle por la muchacha que, tal vez, se afanaba por seguir viva en otro frío salón del edificio.

—¿Quién? —la enfermera parecía auténtica en su desconcierto.

María Esther no insistió. La muchacha se había borrado, había desaparecido como las mosquitas de luz que entraban por la ventana. Los fantasmas del pasado parecían más vivientes y tangibles que todo lo que la rodeaba.

Martín, La Difunta… ¿y los otros? ¿Dónde habrán ido a parar?

¿Qué fue lo último que le había dicho La Difunta cuando se la tropezó en la calle aquel maldito día? No lograba acordarse. ¡Madre mía! ¿Cómo era posible que lo hubiera olvidado? "Primero queremos escapar al recuerdo y después es el recuerdo el que se nos escapa". ¿Quién rayos escribió eso? ¿O lo acababa de inventar? En su memoria, la boca de La Difunta se abría y se cerraba, mas no emitía sonido alguno.

ESTELA

Los ruidosos parroquianos del pub, acodados en grupo junto a la barra, estaban presenciando un juego de fútbol entre el Manchester United y su archienemigo Milan. Se trataba de una grabación en video y aunque todos allí conocían de memoria el final, celebraban los goles con entusiasmo y fiereza. Estela se sentó apartada en una mesa *pullman* con vista al río Támesis, gris y salpicado de troncos que navegaban río abajo. Alejó hacia una esquina el cenicero y se entretuvo, mientras esperaba para dar su orden, en observar el pabilo de la vela que oscilaba cada vez que la puerta de entrada se abría o cerraba. Una joven vestida de negro y con una minifalda más corta que su delantalito de encajes, se inclinó para preguntarle qué iba a tomar. Estela se sintió sacudida por la voz tan cercana a su oreja y trastabilló como la llama de la lamparilla, cuando su inquietante perfume la envolvió. "Una cerveza Guiness", dijo, imitando a Oscar cuando solían salir juntos una que otra noche. La joven se alejó, camino de la cantina y sus efluvios quedaron instalados en el *pullman*. Estela miró por la ventana, el río en ese tramo no era tan ancho y, como la neblina se había disipado por completo, podía divisar un batel blanco con la quilla roja que caboteaba alejándose de los postes del embarcadero. Talán talán, sonó su campana, vibró un silbido y las ruedas de paleta empezaron perezosamente a girar. El barco se separaba del muelle y comenzaba a bogar río arriba, alejado de la corriente rápida del centro, de la que huían también los patos. "El embrujo de la vía fluvial", había dicho aquella vez La Difunta cuando ya casi era La Difunta, mientras se montaba en un bote que alquilaban en los muelles recreativos del río Almendares. No había sido nada difícil para Estela ganarse su amistad. Durante unos meses, Estela se pegó al grupo como una garrapata, iba a sus aburridas fiestas de twist y rock and roll, a los conciertos de la Sinfónica del domingo, en los trabajos productivos de fin de semana procuraba que su hamaca cayera lo más cerca posible, compartían el surco de la labranza, la acompañaba a los interminables cine debates y a la decadente bohemia de los sábados, con el helado en Coppelia y las canciones infantiles de Teresita. Cuando La Difunta la invitó a ir a jugar golfito al parque, Estela aceptó aunque consideraba un sacrificio pasarse una mañana de domingo tratando de meter bolitas por una canal dándoles con un falso palo de golf. Estela no le veía la gracia, pero los del grupo se reían como tontos. Así estuvieron como un par de horas, hasta que La Difunta propuso un paseo en bote. Estela se negó, pero fue testigo presencial de la travesía de La Difunta por el río con varios muchachos amanerados y de pelo largo. Uno de ellos, expulsado no hacía tanto de la Escuela, abrazaba dando chillidos simulados de susto a una muchacha que se le parecía mucho y que Estela era la primera vez que veía. Otro del grupo cargaba con los cuatro tomos de *Juan Cristóbal*. "Ven, Estela, ven a divertirte con nosotros", gritaban desde el bote. Esa misma noche, Estela escribió un detallado informe sobre el "embrujo de la vía fluvial", la presencia de manzanas podridas entre el estudiantado universitario, las malas influencias de lecturas que promovían el homosexualismo. Días antes, Estela había sustraído algunas páginas del diario de La Difunta y las sumó al informe. La muchacha del pub colocó delante de Estela una copa fría sobre el portavasos del eterno perro Guiness, luego abrió con gesto seguro la botella y la puso al lado de la copa. "*Thanks*", murmuró Estela y no pudo dejar de observar las piernas firmes y la piel lustrosa de sus muslos. Pestañeó varias veces mientras procuraba alejar unos tortuosos pensamientos que le cruzaron por la cabeza. Se obligó a pensar en Oscar. El día anterior llegó un fax explicando la causa de su demora, un ascenso en el trabajo, en la Isla, tenía que permanecer allá por lo menos dos años. Estela debía regresar de inmediato. Ella recordó la última vez que estuvieron de vacaciones, todo en La Habana le había parecido ajeno, despintado, mugroso, oscuro. Cada gestión, la más mínima, tomaba un tiempo incalculable. Le dolía ver su barrio en ruinas. Pero sobre todo se irritaba. Cuando llegó el fax, Estela pensó tomarse un tiempo para contestar. Aunque allí, sentada en el pub, con la copa fría y la vela que daba un ambiente acogedor, se dijo que no, no iba a regresar. Estaba harta de oír hablar de problemas. Cuba se había quedado atrás para siempre. Además, allá en La Habana no hubiera podido usar nunca su bella chaqueta de cuero. Le hizo una seña a la muchacha y pidió otra cerveza, faltaba un día y medio para que se terminara el año, y no dudó en sonreírle a la muchacha, desearle felicidades y mirarle a los ojos como solían hacer todos en Cuba, mirarse a los ojos, costumbre que resultaba desfachatada en otros lares. La muchacha se acercó de nuevo y a Estela le pareció que rozaba su mano al servir la segunda cerveza. O quizás fuera solo una imaginación suya. En la cubierta del segundo piso del barco, unos tripulantes observaban la orilla con displicencia, acodados junto a los salvavidas. Estela sintió la imperiosa necesidad de saludarlos y levantó la mano, agitándola de derecha a izquierda. Seguramente nadie se fijó en ella porque no recibió respuesta. Como si acabara de suceder, en el pub los parroquianos celebraban ruidosamente la vieja victoria.

DAONTAON

Nada. ¡El mundo se tenía que acabar! ¿Esto es *vida*, compañeros? No. De una en otra. Pero ella sí que no. Basta ya. De una vez y por todas, Daontaon tenía que librarse del tal Braulio. Ja. **Un *hijo de puta*,** así, dicho con todas las letras, en negritas y cursivas.

—Óyeme, Micaela, te has quedado con la boca abierta, no me vengas a decir que la tía abuela Candita nos está escuchando. ¿Tú te crees que yo exagero? Me quedo corta. ¿Quieres que te cuente? Seguro que sí.

El tal Braulio, el lampiño, el del plan de machete, ese mismo, no hacía más que atosigarla con tareas y más tareas. Seguro le estaba pasando la cuenta a Daontaon por sus desaires. ¿Qué se habrá creído el empachado ese? ¿Se creerá que es el "bárbaro"? Ja.

La semana pasada le había encomendado a Daontaon una misión **clasificada**, secreta, "en silencio", tú sabes cómo es.

—Me hace falta quitarme de encima a una Fulana que me está complicando la existencia —le había dicho a Daontaon, con la mirada disimulada detrás de unos espejuelos oscuros que no se quitaba ni para ir al baño (dicho de una manera elegante), y usando aquel tono de "Oficial Corrupto" del FBI, de *películas de los sábados*—. Y necesito una ayudita tuya, Daontaon. Hazme el favor, preséntate hoy mismo en estas oficinas —anotó una dirección en una tarjeta—. Voy a hacerle la vida un yogurt a esta Fulana hasta que se vaya para el carajo...

Daontaon dejó revolotear a su alrededor un montón de puntos suspensivos, mientras el "Oficial Corrupto" anotaba también el nombre de la Fulana. "La acusas de todo y cuanto hay..." El "Oficial Corrupto" golpeaba la tarjeta con su dedo como si estuviera machucando la cabeza de un infractor de la ley contra la carrocería de un carro patrullero en un oscuro callejón de Brooklyn. "Inventa, que tú tienes para eso y más. No tienes que denunciar nada en concreto, insinuaciones, con eso es suficiente para empezar. Lo que me hace falta ahora es que siembres la sospecha..."

Volvieron a revolotear los ponzoñosos puntos suspensivos de una forma que a Daontaon le pareció malévola. El "Oficial Corrupto" levantó la cabeza y aunque ella no podía apreciar sus ojos detrás de los cristales nevados, *sabía* que la observaba con lascivia.

—Y esta noche no te olvides de venir a la inauguración —le ordenó con prepotencia.

Para completar el apocalipsis, ay, la tapa al pomo la puso la inauguración de la exposición "Vegetales y cuerpos crudos", de esa escultora que fabrica unos guindalejos espantosos. Daontaon tuvo que cargar de un lado a otro unos yerbajos y unas coles malolientes, y ayudar a colocar los espantajos *artísticamente.* A la hora de la apertura, todos los matorrales y legumbres ya se habían puesto mustios. El *cuerpo crudo* lo aportó la propia escultora que salió desde detrás de unos rábanos de cartón gigantes completamente en pelotas, como Dios la trajo al mundo. Dígame usted. ¡Y allí, en primera fila, junto a un ramo de albahacas tiesas que brotaban como un "alien" de una lavadora Aurika, estaba el compañero Ministro con toda su comitiva! ¿Qué te voy a contar, Micaela? La hecatombe. Braulio, la nueva secretaria, el tal Martín, disimulaban como si ahí no pasara NADA. La cara del compañero Ministro era un poema. Ja.

Luego, cuando se acabó todo, vino el "Oficial Corrupto" a echarle la culpa a Daontaon, que si no podía confiar en nadie, que si todos eran una partida de incapaces, que si tenía que estar en todo, que si el deber de ella era haber revisado antes el programa de la actividad. Dígame usted. Como si alguien, en específico Daontaon, pudiera impedirle a esos *artistas* que se encueraran en público. Ella le contestó que seguro las croqueticas del brindis estaban confeccionadas con picadillo de *vacas locas* porque si no en qué cabeza cabía, con dos dedos de frente, que semejante mamotreto con celulitis muestre "sus partes" al Ministro. ¡Vacas locas han comido todos esos "artistas" en este país!

El jefe Braulio, con su peor cara de "Oficial Corrupto", le dijo a Daontaon que la iba a sancionar por los sucesos. Alguien tenía que pagar los platos rotos, y quién mejor que ella, el totí. Pues, Daontaon, para que usted lo sepa, ha pedido su baja de Cultura.

Menos mal que al regreso de aquella **misión secreta** destinada a sacar del juego a la Fulana, en una guagua llena hasta los topes de zarrapastrosos y forajidos, se encontró con un extranjero finísimo llamado Patrick que dice que le gusta mucho Alamar. Daontaon lo invitó a visitarla un día de estos. "¿Tú no te habrás comido una hamburguesa de vaca loca? ¿Verdad que no, mi amor?"

—Va y sí, porque hay que estar quemado, Micaela, con guayabitos en la azotea, para querer venir a vivir a Alamar. ¿Tú me entiendes? Sí. Pero cada loco con su tema. Patrick es lampiño, pero como dijo no sé cuál filosofo... "¿Nadie es perfecto?" *Nadie*.

MUJER QUE HABLA SOLA EN EL PARQUE

El sol se quedó quietecito en el cielo a las doce del día y no se movió de ahí. Y entonces el pavimento se derritió, las aguas empezaron a hervir y a evaporarse, los puentes se fundieron y los edificios se calcinaron en cenizas. Y La Habana se muere...

GERTRUDIS

Si perdiera el sentido de la visión, con tan solo una dádiva de la memoria recorrería sin perderme por el trayecto que hicimos juntos millones de veces. Cómo no. Pero algunos de esos recuerdos pueden llegar a ser casi insoportables.

De camino desde la Escuela de Letras, por el costado del hospital Calixto García y subiendo la loma, para empezar estaba la ruta del café. Todas las tardes, en un mostrador del Comedor Universitario lloviera, tronara o relampagueara, en el horario del receso largo de la tarde se hacía la cola del café. Una tacita del brebaje por cinco centavos y continuar la conversación que ya había tenido sus comienzos en el aula o en el benemérito Banco del vestíbulo.

Por ese mismo derrotero, se bordeaban las gradas del Stadium

Universitario hasta llegar frente a la entrada del hospital y la parada de la ruta 20, entonces se cruzaba la corta calle Labra y se entraba al recinto propiamente dicho de la Universidad de La Habana, con la guarnición de la milicia en los bajos de la Escuela de Física, el Auditorio Varona a la derecha y el Aula Magna al lado de la Biblioteca Central a la izquierda. Luego se desembocaba en la Plaza Cadenas con sus bancos de mármol, las palmeras, la tanqueta y los peldaños de piedra que daban acceso al llamado "Hueco" de Ciencias Políticas con el sempiterno busto de Humboldt rodeado de una tupida vegetación y sus asientos umbríos y frescos donde estaba emplazada la cafetería, según las épocas, fiel proveedora de croquetas, spaghetti o "pan con nada". Para terminar, la peregrinación en orden invertido a la tradición, se llegaba al Rectorado, a la estatua del Alma Mater, y, por último, a la Escalinata.

En aquel entonces la Escalinata de la Universidad estaba siempre llena de palomas que habían hecho sus nidos en los entreveros de los frontones. Día por día, a cualquier hora, llegaba la anciana. Desde lejos, por la calle Neptuno, emergía tarde o temprano, su figurita perfectamente reconocible, caminando rápido, algo encorvada, como si tuviera mucho apremio. Llevaba sus canas atadas en un par de trenzas, no se ponía ningún tipo de zapatos y usaba el mismo vestido descolorido y limpio. No sabíamos su nombre, la veíamos llegar, siempre descalza, arrastrando bolsas repletas de pan viejo, con el ansia de cumplir su destino diario de alimentar las palomas. Apenas la veían aparecer, cientos de palomas la rodeaban, acostumbradas a su presencia. La señora de las palomas, como la solíamos llamar, las saludaba con un gorjeo que imitaba a la perfección los sonidos de arrullo de las aves y todas venían a comer de su mano. Mientras esparcía los cientos de miguitas, ella sonreía y canturreaba de felicidad.

El recorrido sigue siendo ahora el mismo, aunque las palomas de la escalinata solo permanecen revoloteando en el recuerdo. Alguien contó alguna vez que los jagüeyes de la Escuela de Letras crecían sobre un camposanto, el olvidado Cementerio de los Molinos en la falda de la Loma del Príncipe, instalado allí para albergar los cuerpos infectos por la epidemia de cólera que azotó bárbaramente a la población habanera a comienzos de los ochocientos. Nadie volvió a acordarse de ese detalle hasta que también nos convertimos en apestados.

La señora de las moscas. La noche de las asesinas, Las niñas terribles, La marquesa de Sade, Emilia o la educación, Las cuitas de la joven Werther, La profeta. ¿Visión de las vencidas?

¿Alguien ha presenciado alguna vez cuando un pollito es acorralado por los suyos dentro de su propio gallinero?

A lo que vamos.

Un suceso ha quedado colgado en la memoria, más nítido que otros. En una asamblea multitudinaria de los *Jóvenes Comunistas* en el teatro Chaplin, el coliseo completo exigía a gritos destemplados la punición de "la gente de Humanidades". ¿Se acuerdan o no se acuerdan? Azorados, tratábamos de entender qué estaba sucediendo, cuando de repente distinguí a La Difunta del otro lado del pasillo. No me separaban de ella ni siquiera tres metros, sin embargo no podía ayudarla. Al sentarse, había quedado aislada en una masa de airados muchachos que estudiaban Medicina, abucheada y estigmatizada solo por el hecho de estudiar Letras. Durante minutos que parecieron eternos se vio obligada a permanecer allí, escuchando indefensa todos los agravios imaginables coreados por un circo de implacables leones. Por primera vez reconocí una extraña forma de fragilidad y de impotencia.

Después llegó el año de gracia de 1968 y con él y por mucho tiempo, delaciones, falsos testimonios, interrogatorios y ensañamientos... Ya nada volvió a ser igual.

En el parlamento final de *Una enemiga del pueblo,* la *Dra. Stockmann,* repudiada por la turba, llegaba a una atroz conclusión: *Escuchad. La mujer más poderosa del mundo es la que está más sola.* Todavía al cabo de treinta años me sigo preguntando cuál fue el sentido de todo aquello. Pensándolo bien...aún sigo esperando por las respuestas.

MARÍA ESTHER

María Esther identificó los clics metálicos de las bandejas con las jeringuillas. Alguien manipuló su brazo derecho y frotó sobre la piel un algodón que impregnó la atmósfera refrigerada de un olor nauseabundo. Luego sintió un pinchazo. Quien quiera que haya sido, olvidó colocar de nuevo su mano bajo las mantas y María Esther sintió frío, mucho frío. Sin embargo, un ardor febril le calcinaba los labios. Trató de pedir agua y de que la abrigaran bien con una frazada, mas las palabras no le salían, ni lograba abrir los ojos. Tenía tanto frío y tanta sed como en aquella borrascosa mañana de lluvia y viento mientras recorría el cementerio de Montparnasse para cumplir con la vieja encomienda de visitar la tumba de Vallejo.

La escala de unas horas y los escasos francos en el bolsillo alcanzaban lo justo para los tickets del metro y el pago de la entrada a la necrópolis. María Esther no podía permitirse el lujo de comprar ningún bebestible, aunque añoraba como nunca una taza de cualquier brebaje caliente. Entreveía a los parisinos tras las vidrieras de los cafés, protegidos del temporal, sorbiendo con parsimonia, como un ritual, líquidos humeantes, mientras ella franqueaba las calles aprisa, con la cabeza descubierta y un inútil abriguito de otoño. La gélida llovizna de enero le calaba los huesos, todos, los húmeros incluidos; pero así y todo quería cumplir la promesa de su juventud, aquel romántico juramento dado a sus amigos, a La Difunta en primer lugar, el primero que alcanzase la fortuna de llegar a París pondría un ramo de flores en la tumba del poeta, yaciente en aquella lejana ciudad como luego tantos de sus seres queridos quedarían desparramados por el planeta.

Un vigilante guarnecido de la intemperie en una garita, se acercó cojeando a la ventanilla, con expresión lúgubre y desconfiada. ¿A qué loco turista podría ocurrírsele transitar entre los sepulcros con un tiempo como este? Displicente, y auxiliado por una uña empercudida, le indicó a María Esther un cuadrante de la calzada Nord.

El cementerio completamente solitario metía su miedo. María

Esther avanzó por las callejuelas, escoltada por bustos de bronce que verdeaban de moho, nichos descuidados, mausoleos relucientes, cruces cubiertas de hiedras secas, tiestos de plantas calcinadas por la última nevada, arbustos marchitos, chapoteando en charcos de aguanieve, bajo ramajes pelados de donde provenían ruidos hostiles como el graznido de cuervos o algún otro pajarraco. Medio arrepentida de la aventura, helada, sedienta, con coriza, María Esther trataba de identificar la ruta de su destino. Pero, ¡increíble!, cada vez que creía acercarse al pasaje donde debía encontrarse el túmulo vallejiano arreciaba aquel pérfido chaparrón; cuando se alejaba, unos ridículos entreveros de sol parecían indicarle que equivocaba el camino. Un gato amarillo saltó desde una rama, se atravesó en el pasadizo y se le quedó mirando con desaprobación. María Esther se dijo que bastaba ya de bromas.

—No —exclamó en voz alta, como dirigiéndose al gato que la escuchaba imperturbable—. No me voy a morir aquí con aguacero, nada de eso.

Extraviada por completo, en la bocacalle de la vía Ouest, al bajar unos escalones, María Esther se topó con un panteón modesto de la segunda fila, sin rimbombancias de diseño, aunque abarrotado de flores naturales, rosas de papel y hasta unos cursis gladiolos plásticos, humildes artilugios de todo tipo, un lápiz sin punta, una copa de cobre oxidada, caracoles, ramas secas y piedras de todas las formas y colores, un croquis a plumilla del familiar rostro del ocupante sobre una servilleta de tela, empapada, con la tinta corrida por lo estragos de la lluvia y un letrero escrito a mano "Gracias a ti, Charles". Ese tono confianzudo, familiar, le sorprendió. Como si entre el dibujante y el escritor homenajeado continuara un diálogo, apenas interrumpido por una minucia tal como podría serlo la muerte. De repente reparó que iba con las manos vacías, ni una flor para Vallejo había podido comprar con su estrecho peculio, por lo cual María Esther decidió tomarle prestado un ramillete a Baudelaire, entre tantas no notaría la ausencia de unas pocas, unas flores del mal, nunca mejor dicho. El más maldecido, censurado y pateado de los poetas que en el mundo han sido, el demonio execrado y cultivador de todos los huertos malignos imaginables, no se lo iba a tomar a pecho.

—Supe que estuvo preguntando por mí —la frase sacudió un poco a María Esther de la modorra. No logró discernir, en principio, a quién correspondía la voz ni la mano que le daba palmaditas afectuosas en la suya—. El bien que me hizo cuando estaba allá abajo, muerta de miedo.

"Allá abajo", "muerta de miedo", se repitió para sí María Esther. Frío, dolor, soledad, las palabras le llegaban entrecortadas, en un eco. María Esther dudaba si las escuchaba en realidad o provenían de alguno de sus propios abismos. Podía tratarse también de algunos de esos espíritus que la merodeaban.

—Pues sí, me salvé —insistió la voz—. Soy la paciente grave, la compañera suya de cuarto… ¿se acuerda de mí?

¡Claro que sí! María Esther quiso asentir con la cabeza, aunque nunca supo si lo llegó a lograr.

—Está muy agitada, ¿será que quiere algo? —la voz se había alejado y parecía dirigirse a alguien más. María Esther sintió que alguien la cubría con una manta y le mojaba con delicadeza los labios.

—Vine a despedirme y a darle las gracias —insistió la voz.

—Gracias a ti, Baudelaire —logró articular María Esther con un esfuerzo supremo.

—¿Cómo? —la voz parecía asustada.

Como hubiera dicho el viejo Baudelaire, en aquella muchacha la muerte no logró plantar, pensó María Esther sonriendo para sus adentros, sus cipreses.

Cada vez más lejanamente, María Esther escuchaba frases sueltas: "parece que está preguntando por algún pariente", "está delirando", "ya falta poco…"

Después se instaló de nuevo el silencio.

¡Oh, Muerte, Capitana, es tiempo ya! ¡Levemos anclas!

MARTÍN

La mamá de Martín estaba pasándole un paño húmedo a las hornillas. Lo hacía siempre después de preparar el desayuno. La cocina olía a pan tostado y a café recién colado. Martín tomó un sorbo de la taza, levantó la vista y reconoció aquella mirada, mezcla de reproche y pena.

—¿Y el hijo logró venir al entierro? —preguntó la mamá de Martín.
—No, no. Y nadie de la universidad. Yo me vine a enterar tarde. Tampoco pude ir.

La mamá de Martín abrió aún más los ojos y azotó el aire con el trapo como espantando un bicho. Eso hacía cada vez que le venía un mal pensamiento a la cabeza.

La casa se había quedado medio vacía cuando se llevaron a la abuela Antonia en una ambulancia para la Quinta Covadonga, con un silencio pastoso que casi se podía tocar con los dedos. Los vecinos de los bajos cerraron la sastrería temprano como si a la abuela la estuvieran operando en la cocina. El abuelo Severino se encerró en su taller. Si Martín prometía no tocar nada se podía sentar en aquel rincón, tranquilito. Los sonidos y olores de la carpintería no se podían olvidar nunca: la sierra eléctrica cortando los tablones como lascas de queso, la madera cruda, los potes con clavos de todos los tamaños, la cola hirviendo en una lata, los envases de barniz, el mágico imán de dos patas, la escuadra y, lo mejor de todo, el inquietante nivel, regla de madera con un tubo de cristal y una burbujita verde que viajaba de derecha a izquierda, según los movimientos de la mano. Aquella mañana, Martín observaba al abuelo reclinado sobre el banco, dando cepillo y cepillo, desgajando las virutas de mil formas distintas, y, sobre las virutas, caían las goticas de agua que se desprendían de la cara del abuelo. Parecía muy cansado, aunque seguía cepillando la madera. En la casa sonó el teléfono y el abuelo Severino se paralizó con el cepillo de lijar en una mano y la otra sosteniéndose la frente como si la cabeza se le fuera a caer. Cuando entró la mamá de Martín, el abuelo la observó con los ojos rojos como dos tomates.

—No me ocultes nada —le dijo.

La mamá de Martín no habló, pero se abrazaron llorando. Luego, el abuelo Severino salió corriendo del taller.

Entonces, la mamá de Martín lo descubrió, sentado en el rincón y tuvo una de aquellas salidas suyas, "mi hijito, no has comido nada desde por la mañana". Al rato regresó con un pomo azul de leche de magnesia Phillips y una cuchara. Borra de café en la planta de los pies para bajar la fiebre, un vaso de jugo de naranja todas las mañanas para evitar infecciones, leche con Quaker para el calcio de los huesos en crecimiento, bacilos búlgaros para el catarro, toques de azul de metileno para la garganta mala, lavados de estómago en cualquier circunstancia, cocimiento de orégano para las flemas, té de tilo para dormir y cucharadas de magnesia siempre que se presentaban acontecimientos importantes, fueran buenos o malos.

En las láminas de los libros, cuando alguien se muere se ve un humito transparente que sale del cuerpo. Cuando se murió el gato Raskolnikov del tío Félix, no se divisó ningún humito. De todos modos debe haber ido a parar al cielo de los gatos. Lo malo fue que no lo vieron más, y eso le pareció a Martín lo peor de morirse.

La mamá de Martín empezó a menear la cabeza. Nunca hubo un gato en la casa de los abuelos y con ese nombre tan raro menos. Para la mamá de Martín, la Muerte viene vestida de negro y carga una guadaña, unas veces tiene cara de señora y en otras una calavera, pero la mayor parte no se distingue el rostro detrás de una caperuza, no se le ve el pelo. ¿Será por eso que la llaman "la Pelona"?

Recién llegada, la abuela Antonia elaboraba luengas cartas contando los trabajos, las mudadas, los nacimientos, las costumbres sorprendentes de los cubanos, las enfermedades de los muchachos, sin esperar respuesta. Allá en la lejanía, el patriarca de la familia no sabía leer ni escribir. También viajaban tarjetas de navidad, esquelas mortuorias, telegramas de felicitaciones por cumpleaños, giros postales, recordatorios de bautizos, pliegos y pliegos que cruzaban el océano a un destinatario mudo, hasta que un buen día el párroco del pueblo, abrumado de tanta correspondencia sin destino, se decidió a enviar un oficio avisando de una muerte remota que ya no resultaba estremecedora para nadie. Salvo para la abuela Antonia y el tío Félix, quienes de golpe veían desaparecer la venia que les había librado de ese dolor por muchos años, todos los que llevaba de muerto el padre. En la intensidad del luto no mediaba para ellos el tiempo pasado. Pálido consuelo, en todo ese tiempo el patriarca de la familia había sido pensado como vivo, y de hecho había seguido viviendo así unos años de gracia.

—Lo malo no es morirse —concluyó la mamá de Martín—, sino morirse completamente cuando nadie se acuerde de uno. Tienes una cara... ¿Por qué no te tomas una cucharada de magnesia?

MICAELA

La última noche, Micaela se despertó agobiada, con los ojos abiertos de par en par, por otro de aquellos ridículos sueños. Las manecillas del reloj indicaban que eran las cuatro de la madrugada, esa fase previa a la amanecida en que el universo completo daba la impresión de haberse detenido. Le seguía doliendo el pecho como en la tarde anterior, a pesar de que se había tomado dos pastillas de meprobamato, después que Daontaon la dejara en paz por fin, con todas aquellas historias acerca de mujeres sin cabeza, denuncias, comejenes, aerolitos, hormigas funerarias, ministros, descuartizadores y niños infectados con las artes literarias.

Pero en una cosa sí tenía razón:

—Micaela, ese gato ya ni come. ¿Qué tipo de vida es esa? *Una vida de mierda*, perdonando la expresión. Acaba de llevarlo a sacrificar...

Micaela comprendió que, en efecto, ya no podía seguir dando largas. Lo estaba manteniendo vivo a la fuerza y no era capaz de distinguir con claridad si lo estaba haciendo por el bien del gato o por ella. Tenía que tomar la decisión de ponerlo a dormir. "Ponerlo a dormir", horrible eufemismo, se dijo Micaela. A propósito... ¿cómo estarán los pollitos de Lola? ¿Y Lola? Micaela no había tenido ánimo de volver a llamar.

Se levantó dando tropezones y se tragó otras dos pastillas. Le esperaban horas de desvelo. Micaela decidió emprender varias tareas aplazadas y que quería dar por terminadas esa misma trasnoche: con una cuchilla de afeitar se cortó el pelo bajito; luego se sacó las cejas y se limó las uñas; después escribió una detallada carta, contando de su supervivencia en La Habana de fines de siglo a su amiga Sara que vivía, probablemente, una existencia que podría ser una réplica lujosa y bien alimentada de la suya; más tarde terminó también la dichosa novela rusa y, por último, se dispuso a escoger el arroz.

Micaela extendió sobre la mesa un pedazo de tela limpia y le lanzó encima dos tazas de arroz. Sabiendo a conciencia que imitaba los gestos de su madre, fue separando con paciencia los granos hábiles de los vanos, de las piedras y las pajillas que venían con el arroz de la cuota. De súbito, Micaela reconoció ese paño, era el tapetico tejido que solía estar encima del televisor, azar o fatalidad a que la enfrentaba el destino para recordarle que las jugarretas de la vida podían ser tan elocuentes como los sueños.

Micaela terminó aquella última tarea y volvió a acostarse. Ya casi estaba amaneciendo y sabía que le esperaba un día duro. Otro más. Como si adivinara, el gato saltó a la cama y, confiado, se acurrucó en su regazo. Micaela lo acarició y supo que ya no habría otras ocasiones como esa.

Dentro de un rato se dormiría. Dormirse y no despertar, olvidarse de todas las catástrofes. Pero en cuanto cerrara los ojos y le entrara el sueño, lo sabía, iban a estar allí, esperándola, las medias rojas y blancas de La Difunta. Y retornaría Candita, su tía, pidiéndole que tuviera compasión, no la abandonara allá lejos y la ayudara a traer sus cenizas para Cuba.

De nuevo, en la quietud, se reanudó el llanto de aquel perro...

Volvió a sentir la punzada en medio del pecho y Micaela abrió la boca varias veces como un pez moribundo. Luego cerró los ojos hasta que las lágrimas se apiñaron detrás de sus párpados. Al cabo de un rato sus gemidos se fueron acompasando a los del perrito.

MUJER QUE HABLA SOLA EN EL PARQUE

Las casonas se pusieron a gemir y a quejarse, lloraron y lloraron de abandono hasta que se cansaron. Y entonces comenzaron a crujir y a quebrarse, y terminaron por quedar convertidas en polvo y ceniza. Y La Habana se muere...

LA INDIA

El extraño caso de "La Descuartizada del Municipio Habana del Este" debió ser engavetado sin resolver.

Después de registros, excavaciones, dragados, podas y limpiezas excepcionales (esfuerzo extra fuera de la temporada ciclónica) en las áreas del susodicho municipio, no se encontró objeto alguno que pudiera tomarse, entre las muchas inmundicias acumuladas durante años, por una cabeza humana.

Se repasaron otra vez los interrogatorios a antiguos conocidos de La India y vecinos del solar. Se verificaron llamadas con escuchas a Cusita en Hialeah. Se presionó al encausado, el llamado "Francés", para que revelara el escondite de la pieza ausente en el rompecabezas criminal. Se tanteó en la existencia de un posible cómplice, quizás alguna madama, quien tendría a buen recaudo el faltante capital. Y nada de nada.

Patrick Rivière se mantenía prácticamente recluido en su habitación de hotel donde, según informes, se dedicaba con frenesí a escribir en unas libretas rayadas de escolar.

Como resultaba impropio continuar retrasando el enterramiento de los restos mortales de La India (o de quien fuesen), se entregaron todas las fracciones a su supuesta madre, Clara Luz, de apelativo La Catedrática, para el cumplimiento de los funerales. De esta manera, se efectuó el sepelio del tronco y las extremidades en una bóveda prestada por un vecino (beneficiario de tal privilegio por cotizar en la sociedad gallega Naturales de Ortigueira) y bajo la promesa de las autoridades competentes de proceder a una exhumación de los restos para su completamiento, en fecha y hora en que se cometiera el hallazgo de la extraviada cabeza.

La acusación se derrumbó por falta de pruebas incriminatorias y su único sospechoso, el ciudadano de nacionalidad francesa Patrick Rivière, más conocido como "El Francés" o "El Descuartizador del Municipio Habana del Este", exonerado sin cargos. Aunque, por precaución, sometido a vigilancia permanente.

La madre de La India, Clara Luz, viendo restablecidos los contactos con su prima Cusita de Hialeah (gracias a los horripilantes hechos, la verdad sea dicha), se embulló, presentó su solicitud en el sorteo de visas para Estados Unidos, se sacó el "bombo", cursó la entrevista sin contratiempos, obtuvo las documentaciones pertinentes, se despidió para siempre del cuarto en el solar de San Leopoldo y viajó en avión (¡nunca por vía marítima!) en busca del sueño cubano de una casita.

Pasados los penosos trámites, Patrick Rivière decidió instalarse como traductor de idioma francés para una editorial que requería los conocimientos de su lengua natal. Se ha filtrado el barrunto de que ha acometido la empresa de escribir una novela policíaca, plagada de obscenidades, atiborrada de prostitutas, balseros y marginales, ubicada su acción en la zona este de La Habana.

Por su parte, la cabeza de María Antonieta, La India, "La Descuartizada del Municipio Habana del Este", sigue dando guerra en algún sitio. Pudiera continuar empacada en papel de estraza dentro de la maleta de alguna dama de moralidad dudosa o andar rodando bajo las losetas de un apartamento de Alamar.

LOLA

Como si un huracán hubiese arrasado su pasado, Lola cruzó tambaleante la avenida Paseo. "Mire por donde camina, vieja comemierda", aulló el conductor de una bicicleta que estuvo a punto de atropellarla. Al parecer, ella no le escuchó y siguió avanzando a trompicones por la calle Calzada, tantas veces había hecho aquel recorrido, los pies se le iban solos, siguiendo la mágica ruta de las matinés dominicales de la Orquesta Sinfónica y los almuerzos en El Carmelo, de eso hacía ya muchísimo tiempo. ¿Por qué año andábamos?

Lola se detuvo para tratar de hacer memoria. Acordarse... ¿pero de qué?

A su izquierda, un depósito de basura daba la impresión de flotar a la deriva sobre las aguadas fétidas empozadas en la vereda. A su derecha, tras unos barrotes improvisados, sobre los antiguos jardines, lujuriosos cármenes de su infancia, ahora de hierba calcinada, revoloteaban nubecillas de moscones y guasasas. Un cartelón ruinoso frente a la entrada del salón de belleza, otrora famoso entre las damas de la farándula, lo declaraba *cerrado por reparación*. Una cuadra más allá, en el umbral de Teatro Estudio, una pandilla de adolescentes, con una botella de ron viajera de mano en mano, vociferaba frases brutales, jactándose, ante una muchacha. Cuando Lola pasaba, uno de ellos se levantó y le pegó una bofetada a la joven que se quedó paralizada por unos segundos y luego cacareó una risita.

Por fin, Lola alcanzó la esquina del Teatro Auditórium, devastado por un incendio. ¿Qué estaba pasando?

Lola se dejó caer, consternada, en una de aquellas butacas de pedernal que conformaban la parte trasera del hemiciclo donde tocaba antaño la banda de música, en el parque de Calzada y D, el parque de su barrio, como había sido siempre desde que su abuela la llevaba los domingos a escuchar la retreta. Nunca se preocupó por averiguar a quién pertenecía el busto que daba la espalda al podio en semicírculo.

Comenzando por delante del Carmelo, a Lola le gustaba recorrer el corredor de columnatas, con la celosía de madera cubierta por una frondosa trepadora que protegía de la canícula, pasearse alrededor del estanque de agua clara, hasta sentarse en la glorieta de enfrente, escoltada por arbustos y farolas, cuyo propio semicírculo y efigie sobre otro pedestal reflejaban, como un espejo de mármol, el escenario al aire libre.

Lola miró a su alrededor. Hubiera jurado que allí había estado, desde fechas inmemoriales, una estatua de Neptuno con su tridente y las guedejas de pelo petrificadas. ¿Dónde habrá ido a parar?

Bajo un banco dormitaban dos perros famélicos, acurrucados uno al otro. A pocos pasos, una mujer hablaba sola. La mujer la miró y, en sus ojos, Lola vio el reflejo de su propia mirada.

De repente, Lola sintió una urgencia, un apuro. Tenía que regresar. ¿A dónde? Se habían ido yendo las horas y la deberían estar esperando. ¿Quién, quién la estaría esperando? Se había hecho ya demasiado tarde... ¿tarde para qué?

Las casas marchitas, los arbustos podridos, las miradas rancias de los transeúntes, se le figuraban un acto de expiación por no sabía cuál de todos sus pecados. La Difunta. ¿Acaso La Difunta le estaba imponiendo, con aquella debacle, el significado extraviado de los recuerdos? Perdón, perdón, pidió desde el fondo de su alma.

Como si adivinara sus propios pensamientos, la mujer que hablaba sola le dijo: "Y La Habana se muere…"

YUYA

Según Yuya, Lola le había dicho que de tanto huir de los recuerdos, luego ya no tenía manera de que la obedecieran.

Con ayuda de algunos vecinos, Yuya forzó la cerradura y entró a casa de Lola con el corazón en la boca temiendo qué se iba a encontrar. El apartamento desierto la llenó aún más de zozobras. No parecía faltar nada ni se notaban huellas de violencia. Sobre la mesa del comedor, una taza cubierta de hormigas y un plato con restos de natilla maloliente indicaban que la ausencia de Lola databa de varios días.

Al lado de la vajilla sucia seguía la foto de La Difunta, colocada en el mismo sitio, tal como se la había mostrado en aquella conversación. Dice Yuya que empezó por contarle que toda su vida, ella, Lola, había trabajado como jefa de despacho en una oficina de esas importantes de la cultura. Yuya no se acordaba de cuál, a estas alturas daba lo mismo. Lola había visto llegar e irse a más de un jefecillo, pero su Patrón, el dueño y señor, temido y adulado, se suponía eterno. A pesar de sus caprichos y lo histérico que se mostraba la mayoría de las veces, Lola le obedecía a pie juntillas, sabía cuál era su lugar y cuánto se exigía de ella. Se tenía muy bien aprendidos los códigos, filtraba las llamadas, diferenciaba lo placentero de lo fastidioso, servía de barrera protectora y espantaba a los visitantes cargosos. En eso consistían sus deberes y los cumplía con eficiencia y hermética discreción.

Según Yuya, La Difunta se le presentó de repente a Lola, sin avisar, allí mismo en la dirección a pedirle ayuda, y en tono descompuesto se quejó acerca de una injusticia que se estaba cometiendo contra ella. La acusaban de no entendió Yuya qué cosa, y a la verdad es que no quería ni saberlo. Lola conocía bien a La Difunta, una muchacha como su propia hija, educada y estudiosa, mas no podía hacer lo que suplicaba La Difunta, tan encarecidamente, de concederle unos minutos con el Jefe. Colarla, nada menos, sin cita previa, y para semejante problema. No podía ser de ningún modo, las demandas de ese tipo catalogaban entre las más desagradables que se viniesen a plantear, y, para colmos, de alguien desconocido, de una doña nadie. No correspondía a esa instancia, ni su reclamo podía tener cabida. Lola se mantuvo intransigente ante las lágrimas, su puesto mismo estaba en juego, no podría comprometerse de tal manera. Eran tiempos difíciles.

¿Cuándo no?, dice Yuya que pensó, ¿cuándo no ha habido tiempos difíciles?

Dice Yuya que Lola no podía olvidar el estado de desesperación de La Difunta al abandonar la oficina, soy inocente, repetía, no he hecho nada.

Unas horas más tarde, Lola se enteró que La Difunta se había tirado de un piso dieciocho desde un edificio de la calle Línea. Según Yuya, lo que más le horrorizó al escuchar aquella historia fue darse cuenta de que los verdugos no venían de otro lado, eran los mismos nuestros.

Dice Yuya que entonces descubrió la ausencia de la libreta de abastecimientos, no estaba en su lugar habitual. Lola debía haber salido a buscar el pan y algo le pasaría. Hasta el amanecer estuvieron Shu y Yuya dando vueltas por los hospitales y por las estaciones de policía, sin encontrarla.

Dice Yuya que, por fin, dieron con Lola en el parque de Calzada y D, completamente ida y deshidratada. Habría que avisarle a alguien, dice Yuya, pero avisarle a quién. ¡Jesús mil veces!

MARTÍN

Al entierro de La Difunta tampoco fue nadie. En aquella ocasión, Martín esperaba a la entrada del cementerio, bajo el pomposo pórtico de la necrópolis de Colón, camposanto de La Habana con sus sacramentales estelas de piedra y su falsaria, engañosa inscripción latina, *ianua sum pacis*. ¿Paz? En el aniquilado corazón de La Difunta no hubo ni habría ya posibilidad de paz alguna.

El carruaje funerario, despintado y con una abolladura en el capó, sin coronas ni ornamentos, seguido por un taxi, tan cacharroso como el coche mortuorio y con solo dos personas en su interior, se detuvo apenas unos segundos. Martín vio al chofer bajarse y dirigirse a las oficinas de la administración, firmar un papel y luego retornar a su puesto con apresuramiento. Dentro del taxi, sentado en el otro asiento delantero, un hombre de mediana edad, con el rostro contraído y vestido con un overol lleno de grasa, daba la impresión de haber tenido que salir de urgencia de un taller, sin siquiera cambiarse de atuendo para el sepelio. En el sitio de atrás, como en una balsa, flotaba la madre de La Difunta, mirando fijamente hacia delante. Martín no se atrevió a acercarse. El chofer encendió con dificultad el motor que torpedeó un ruido desagradable, se apagó y por fin volvió a arrancar. El esmirriado desfile, sin flores y sin dolientes, prescindió del trámite religioso en la capilla, tomó velocidad y no se detuvo hasta llegar a la zona de las fosas comunes.

Martín se apuró, cortando entre las callejuelas, en vano. El cortejo fúnebre había avanzado con demasiada prisa y, mientras Martín trotaba, con la lengua afuera por el calor y la ansiedad, vio cómo dos enterradores hacían descender, ayudados por unas correas mugrientas, el barato cajón de pinotea. El chofer se mantenía al timón con el encendido funcionando y el estrépito mecánico se escuchaba a decenas de metros a la redonda. Cuando Martín ya se venía acercando, la madre de La Difunta y el hombre de overol que la sostenía por los hombros, sin reparar en su llegada montaron otra vez en el taxi y se alejaron hacia la salida del cementerio. El entierro había durado menos de cinco minutos. La Difunta se había acurrucado por última vez en un hoyo de tierra universal, junto a otros desgraciados. Pero ninguno más desgraciado que ella.

Por su parte, a Martín no le había sido posible conseguir siquiera un miserable ramito de flores silvestres. Era una época dura.

Martín llegó a creer por mucho tiempo que las palabras podían quizás cambiar la realidad. Cambiar el mundo no, pero la percepción de la vida sí, tal vez. ¿Contar algo de buena manera lo convertía en bueno? No había forma de hacer bueno aquel entierro. Las palabras servían entonces, al menos, para hacer doler.

La última persona que había conversado con La Difunta antes de los sucesos fue María Esther. Martín reparó que nunca le dio interés por saber qué le había dicho, cuáles habían sido sus extremas palabras, pero ya también se había vuelto demasiado tarde para preguntarle a María Esther. Aunque no estaba seguro de querer enterarse. Y en caso de que hubiese pretendido buscarlas, ya jamás aparecerían las piezas que faltaban del rompecabezas. Por aquellos años, Martín se vio obligado a callarse opiniones para no meterse en problemas. Los mares se agitaban procelosos y en esas aguas tenían que navegar, o sucumbir como La Difunta. Los cobardes como él, los puñeteros cobardes como él, seguían navegando.

Sus memorias de infancia y todas las fatuas pretensiones de "amor y escualidez" se le antojaron baladíes, indecorosas.

La mamá de Martín doblaba los calcetines, metía uno dentro de su par y los convertía en una bolita, bolitas blancas de algodón que acumulaba en un puñado en la cama a su costado. Ya apenas podía levantarse y se había mudado para el apartamento de su hijo. Martín la cuidaba día y noche, aunque dejaba que realizara pequeñas tareas para que no se aburriera. También necesitaba verla igual que siempre, la ilusión de que estaba ahí para guardar sus medias en orden.

Tan solo con mirarle las manos, Martín supo que *ella sabía*. ¿Un mes, una semana, unos días? Ambos conocían que quedaba muy poco tiempo, pero ya tampoco importaba. A pesar de todo, la vida les había concedido aquella mínima prórroga juntos.

—Vuelvo enseguida—dijo Martín.

Caminó hasta la orilla, los arrecifes costeros de Alamar, y se sentó junto a un perro sin dueño. Martín le acarició la cabeza mientras con la mano libre tiraba las hojas mecanografiadas a las olas que golpeteaban la roca. Los manuscritos no arden, mejor ahogarlos, que se pierdan en esas aguas. El mar no es el mar, el mar es el traspatio de la casa. Quizás una buena primera línea. Una puñetera primera línea.

HERMI

Todas las historias se reducían a una sola, a la anécdota que puede durar apenas unos segundos, y que se repetía y cambiaba sin dejar de ser lo mismo.

Y esa raya que se cruzaba o no...

Aquella ya lejana mañana de sus vidas, Hermi y Tristán vieron precipitarse el cuerpo, con los brazos desarticulados como alitas rotas. Vieron caer a La Difunta.

Durante los sucesos del Mariel, en una camioneta vinieron en busca de Tristán y Herminia. Los sujetos portaban un listado y sus nombres aparecían allí. Hermi y Tristán habían envejecido tan parecidos como ibeyis, homónimos, que cabía la pregunta de "¿cuál era cuál?". Daba igual uno u otro, los dos sobraban.

Por varios días, una turba de vecinos cubrió la fachada de huevos, papas podridas, piedras e injurias. "Que se vayan que se vayan que se vayan que se vayan que se vayan".

Hermi, desde entonces, limitó el infinito a las paredes de su casa. Qué horrible podría llegar a ser que, al paso del tiempo, se viese fraternizando con los mismos que acercaron el precipicio. Eso nunca. La calle, el barrio donde habían nacido, quedó del lado de afuera de una muralla, una pared de ladrillos y una raya invisible. Tenían permiso de entrada las luces, los gatos callejeros, los gorriones, las lagartijas, los sonidos de la ciudad y los olores de La Habana, pero la gente no. Hermi se encasquilló, atrancó las ventanas, llenó la sala de carretadas de tierra, sembró matas, semillas, verduras, y regaba todas las tardes. Desde los altos vitrales, el sol cubría la habitación y brotaban, crecían, daban flores y frutos las plantas que cultivaba. La sala no es la sala, la sala es el huerto, un jardín reducido, pero rabiosamente libre.

Tristán se instaló en Puerto Rico. Estaban a unas tres horas de vuelo.

Para el caso era como estar en galaxias distintas, a años luz uno de otro. "Solo cuando pase el tiempo se encontrará sentido a la terquedad de ser uno mismo", decía Tristán con una de sus frases sentenciosas (¿o habrá sido Hermi?).

Un acto de renuncia. ¿Qué otra cosa quedaba ya por intentar?

Años más tarde, en algún envío de Tristán, le llegó a Hermi la reproducción de una de las tablas pintadas por el Bosco, su apocalíptico *Caída de los condenados,* una obvia burla por los tan diversos destinos de los bienaventurados y los réprobos. En la confusión y oscuridad de los colores ocres, los torsos fragmentados en posición descendente y fuegos sibilinos que parecían arder en las alturas, unos brazos intentaban sujetar un cuerpo que se hundía, ¿o precipitaban su desgracia? En el silencio ominoso de la pintura, donde solo se podía imaginar el ruido y el torbellino de las ánimas que se despeñaban del empíreo, una luz plateada añadía horror y belleza a la escena.

Hermi había dejado de pintar, aunque colgó, en una de las paredes de su lujurioso jardín, el exorcismo socarrón del Bosco.

Cuando La Difunta caía para siempre, ellos también caían. Todos caían.

MUJER QUE HABLA SOLA EN EL PARQUE

Y entonces el cloro se desbordó y todos los documentos, manuscritos, legajos, contratos, cartas, informes, bulas, títulos, pergaminos, plaquetes, certificados, inventarios, cédulas, oficios, actas, memoriales, expedientes, registros, programas, revistas, periódicos, folletos, libros, escritos y por escribir, se fueron borrando hasta quedarse con las páginas en blanco. Y La Habana se muere…

GERTRUDIS

Llámenme Gertrudis. Aquella cacería llegó a su fin.

De cuando en cuando, los hombres necesitan procrear héroes

retozones y transformar las miserias en proezas. Todo falso y banal. Como vieja víctima de humillaciones y maltratos, la anciana pescadora de Cojímar conocía muy bien la real verdad: *una mujer puede ser destruida y además derrotada.*

Unos días antes de los sucesos, La Difunta me envió una carta de su puño y letra que nunca, nunca, me he atrevido a leer. La conservo cerrada como llegó, entre papeles inofensivos y cada cierto tiempo vuelve a aparecer a la vista, como si una dinamita oculta entre las palabras esperase su turno por explotar. También me hizo algunas llamadas telefónicas que no respondí y, después que todo pasó, cuando yo me reclamaba a mí misma por qué, solo encontraba silencio y culpa. Al principio deseaba creer que mi alejamiento había sido lo conveniente, mi vida andaba entonces por caminos escabrosos y no quería quebrar con más dilemas la fragilidad de La Difunta, perjudicarla o empañar su inocencia. ¡Finalmente lograron hacernos sentir tan sucios!

Se suele soñar con reencuentros, pero los suicidas son personas que no quieren volver a encontrarse con nadie.

Alguien me contó que se quitó los zapaticos, también el reloj y lo guardó dentro de la bolsa que dejó al pie de una ventana. Aparentemente, no hubo misterio alguno. No pidió perdón, no echó su sufrimiento en cara de nadie, solo decidió que no más. Como podía haber dicho no escribo más, no pinto más, no toco más el piano... En el fondo solo se trataba de eso.

¿Se acuerdan o no se acuerdan?

¿Quién mató a la Comendadora? Fuenteovejuna, señora... Todos a una.

Nosotros pudimos seguir quejándonos de que nos sentíamos casi muertos, pero La Difunta siguió permaneciendo como la más muerta de todos.

Algún día quizás me arme de valor y lea aquella carta.

Las mujeres amantes del impío Omar Khayyam, ocultas tras la máscara del marido, escribieron blasfemas cuartetas llenas de dudas y dolores que ellas no tenían ningún derecho a expresar, so pena de ser lapidadas:

¿Dices que el vino es el único bálsamo?
¡Traedme todo el vino del universo!
Mi corazón tiene tantas heridas… ¡Todo el vino del universo
Y que mi corazón conserve sus heridas!

SOBRE LA AUTORA

Después de graduarse como bachiller en el Instituto Pre-Universitario Especial "Raúl Cepero Bonilla", para estudiantes talentosos, Mirta Yáñez (Cuba, 1947) entró en la Universidad de La Habana en 1965. Cinco años después se graduó con el título en Licenciada en Lengua y Literaturas Hispánicas. Continuó con los estudios de pos-grado en la misma institución y obtuvo el Doctorado en Filología en el año 1992. Su área de especialización es la literatura latinoamericana, y en particular la de Cuba, con un enfoque secundario en el discurso femenino. Profesora y académica durante muchos años en la Universidad de La Habana, desde hace ya algunos años se ha concentrado en la producción literaria y en la promoción de las escritoras cubanas.

El premio de poesía en el Concurso 13 de Marzo (1970), por la colección *Las visitas,* fue el primero de los muchos que ha recibido Mirta Yáñez a lo largo de su trayectoria multidimensional de escritora. Considerada relevante entre las intelectuales de su generación, ha sobresalido en casi todos los géneros literarios que ha trabajado: poesía, cuento, novela, testimonio y ensayo. Guionista para cine y televisión, además tiene una extensa bibliografía de ensayo periodístico y crítico.

En el año 2004 Mirta Yáñez fue seleccionada para el programa MEET de Escritores en Residencia de la Maison des Écrivans et des Traducteurs en Saint-Nazaire, Francia, donde terminó la breve colección de cuentos cortos *Falsos documentos,* libro publicado bilingüe en francés y español. Varios de los cuentos de este volumen se tradujeron al inglés y están incluidos, junto con otros cuentos de la autora—la mayoría traducidos también al alemán y a otras lenguas—, en *Havana Is a Really Big City* (Cubanabooks 2010). Yáñez ha recibido cada vez más atención crítica en los Estados Unidos, hecho constatado por las sesiones de discusión de su obra en conferencias importantes como la de la Asociación de Lenguas Modernas (MLA) y la Asociación de Estudios Latinoamericanos (LASA).

Mirta Yáñez ha sido invitada y docente en instituciones académicas de prestigio en diversos países, tales como Italia, República Dominicana, Puerto Rico, México, Chile, España, Estados Unidos, Inglaterra, Alemania y Francia, entre otros.

En 2011 su novela más reciente, *Sangra por la herida*, fue galardonada con el Premio de la Crítica en Cuba—la cuarta vez que ha recibido este prestigioso reconocimiento—. El año siguiente, a esta novela le fue otorgado el Premio de la Academia Cubana de la Lengua. Ha sido traducida y publicada en Francia e Italia.

Actualmente reside en Cojímar en La Habana del Este, poblado conocido como un lugar predilecto de Ernest Hemingway.

SOBRE LA TRADUCTORA

Originalmente de Texas, Sara E. Cooper (PhD Universidad de Texas, Austin, 1999) es Profesora de Español en la Universidad Estatal de California en Chico. Dicta cursos en español; producción cultural latinoamericana, latina, y chicana; y estudios de género y sexualidad. Es la editora de *The Ties That Bind: Questioning Family Dynamics and Family Discourse in Hispanic Literature and Film* y además *Lesbian Images in International Popular Culture* (un número especial de la *Journal of Lesbian Studies*). Cooper tradujo *Miel quemada/Burnt Honey*, del escritor chicano Antonio Arreguín Bermúdez, además de varios cuentos de *Havana is a Really Big City*, de Mirta Yáñez. Sus ensayos críticos aparecen en numerosas revistas, como por ejemplo: *Letras femeninas, Chasqui, Confluencia, Cuban Studies, Kunapipi, A Changing Cuba in a Changing World, Cultura y letras cubanas en el siglo XXI, Tortilleras: Hispanic and Latina Lesbian Expression, Journal of Lesbian Studies, Interdisciplinary Literary Studies,* y *Challenging Lesbian Norms.*

En 1998 Cooper empezó a enfocarse cada vez más en la literatura y cultura cubanas. Es la fundadora del Grupo de Discusión de la Expresión Cultural de Cuba y la Diáspora Cubana de la Asociación de Lenguas Modernas (MLA) y socia de la Sección Cuba de la Asociación de Estudios Latinoamericanos (LASA). A través de una larga y grata amistad con la autora Mirta Yáñez, Cooper ha podido conocer a las escritoras más brillantes y creativas de los círculos literarios en Cuba. La mayoría de estas mujeres talentosas y prolíficas prácticamente se desconocen en los Estados Unidos, o por los lectores de habla inglesa. Por eso, en 2010 estableció la Editorial Cubanabooks, dedicada a publicar a las escritoras cubanas en traducción al inglés.